Trasna na Dtonnta:

A Tale of Three Cities

"The sparse little cathedral ..." page 240

Trasna na Dtonnta:

A Tale of Three Cities

Christina Eastwood

First Printing: 2017

Mothers' Companion Publications

Hen Benygroes

Penrhyndeudraeth, Gwynedd LL48 6BT

www.motherscompanion.net

Ordering Information:

Special discounts are available on quantity purchases by corporations, associations, educators, and others. For details, contact the publisher at the above listed address.

Dedication

S.D.G.

Table of Contents

Acknowledgements

I would like to thank Wendy Swan for an unforgettable guided tour of Kilmore Cathedral, the staff of Penrhyndeudraeth library for so cheerfully finding all the obscure books I needed, Trudy Kinlock for editing the manuscript and my husband, whose never wavering enthusiasm for the story meant I could not give up.

Preface

This is a fictionalised biography of William Bedell which means I have woven into the events of history the imaginary story of Samuele and his friends.

The interactions between England, Ireland and Venice in the seventeenth century are a byway in history but perhaps this is because non-Christian historians have decided which events form the highway. When I read about this topic and some of the characters involved— Sarpi, Diodati, Bedell, De Domini, Wotton ... —I was fascinated by what I discovered. I hope you will enjoy the history too as well as the story itself.

The list of characters below will tell you at a glance who is made up and who is real: the names of the fictional characters are in italics in the list. Although many of Samuele's own adventures are not real and (as far as anyone knows) no Irish Old Testament manuscript ever made its way to Geneva, most of the events described really happened —including the very unlikely ones. William Bedell really did try to explain the difference between Catholic and Protestant in a stationer's shop in Venice, Antonio and his friend did conspire to kill Sarpi and did get found out because they dropped some letters and Dr Diodati did bump into his old friend in the street after coming to London accidentally after bad weather at sea. The prison tower where Bedell was imprisoned as an old man still stands in the waters of Lough Oughter, the sycamore tree he planted still grows in Kilmore (the ancestor—as far as anyone knows—of all the sycamore trees in Ireland) and if you go to Horringer (the modern name for Horningsheath) you will see the church where Bedell preached and held his catechism classes. The Irish tinkers really did mend pots and kettles with the copper sheets engraved with the pages of Wit-Spell. I have often used the actual words of the historical characters which have come down to us in diaries and letters and only once or twice have I taken a very slight liberty with the timescales or order of events. Where there are records of the details of things that happened I have followed them carefully, the ill-mixed wax, for instance, in chapter 12 or the escape of the ape in chapter 4. I hope you will enjoy the story and at the same time learn about this fascinating time in history.

List of Characters

George Abbot, (1562-1633) Archbishop of Canterbury

Dr Acquapendente, famous medical expert (1537-1619)

Brother Antonio, Servite

Nathaniel Barnardiston, puritan gentleman and Member of Parliament (1588-1653)

Leah Bedell, wife of William Bedell (c.1580-1638)

William Bedell (1571-1642)

Grace Bedell, daughter of William Bedell (c.1614-c.1624)

William Bedell, son of William Bedell (1612-1670)

John Bedell, son of William Bedell (1616-1635)

Ambrose Bedell, son of William Bedell (1618-1683)

Mrs Blagge, member of an old Horningsheath family

The Hon. Robert Boyle, (1627-1691) Great man of Science

Brady, Irish squatter

Philip Burlamachi, (1575-1644) Lucchese financier in London, brother of Signora Madeleine Diodati

Johannes Buxtorf, Hebrew expert (1564-1629)

Philippe Calandrini,(1587-1649) Lucchese merchant banker

Louis Cappel, (1585-1658) French Bible scholar

Carlo, nephew of Giovanni Diodati

Sir Dudley Carlton, (1573-1654) English ambassador to Venice

Richard Castledine, carpenter

Signor Cicchinelli, linen warehouse owner

Alexander Clogie, (1614-1698) chaplain to William Bedell in Ireland, married Leah Maw

Conall, post boy and guide, brother of Teagan and Lorcan

Archbishop De Domini, of Split, Marc Antonio de Spalatensis, (1560-1624)

Adrienne De Lange

Dr Jaspar Despotine, (fl.1632) Italian doctor who settled in England

Susan Despotine, wife of Dr Jaspar Despotine

Catherine Despotine, daughter of Dr Jaspar and Susan Despotine

Isabell Despotine, daughter of Dr Jaspar and Susan Despotine

Anne Despotine, daughter of Dr Jaspar and Susan Despotine

Charles Diodati, (1609-1638) son of Dr Theodore Diodati

Charles Diodati, (1602-1651) Son of Signora Madeleine Diodati and Giovanni Diodati

Dorothée Diodati, (b.1601) Daughter of Signora Madeleine Diodati and Giovanni Diodati

Elizabeth Diodati, (1609-1637) Daughter of Signora Madeleine Diodati and Giovanni Diodati

Eliza Diodati, wife of Dr Theodore Diodati (he did have a wife but there is no record of her name)

Giovanni Diodati, (1576-1649) Italian theologian and Bible translator

John Diodati, (d.1688) son of Theodore Diodati

Signora Madeleine Diodati, (1579-1633) wife of Giovanni Diodati

Marc Diodati, (1614-1641) Son of Signora Madeleine Diodati and Giovanni Diodati

Marie Diodati, (1605-1676) Daughter of Signora Madeleine Diodati and Giovanni Diodati

Philippe Diodati, (1620-1659) Son of Signora Madeleine Diodati and Giovanni Diodati

Pompeo Diodati, (1542-1602)

Renée Diodati, (1616-1697) Daughter of Signora Madeleine Diodati and Giovanni Diodati

Samuel Diodati, (1607-1676) Son of Signora Madeleine Diodati and Giovanni Diodati

Theodore Diodati, (1612-1680) Son of Signora Madeleine Diodati and Giovanni Diodati

Dr Theodore Diodati, (1573-1651) Lucchese doctor in London brother of Giovanni Diodati

Leonardo Donato, (1536-1612), Doge of Venice

Captain Doomer, Dutch sea captain

Hans Doomer, son of Captain Doomer

Francesco of Padua, conspirator to murder Paul Sarpi

Friar Manfredi Fulgenzio (fl.1606)

Micanzio Fulgentio, Servite, close friend of Paul Sarpi (1570-1654)

Galileo Galilei, (1564-1642) astronomer, mathematician and engineer

Geronimo, cousin to Giovanni Diodati

Mr James Glendinning, preacher

Guiseppe, stationer (there really was a stationer but we do not know his name)

Henrico, servant to Sir Henry Wotton

Dr Joshua Hoyle, (d.1654) Fellow of Trinity College, Dublin

Sir Thomas Jermyn, William Bedell's patron (1573-1645)

Mr Thomas Johnson, fellow of Trinity college Dublin, architect, engineer and author of *Witspell*

Cardinal Joyeuse (1562-1615)

Murtagh King, fellow of Trinity College Dublin

Arnaud Lamarche

William Laud (1573-1645)

Rabbi Leo of Modena, (1571-1648)

Lorcan, brother of Teagan and Conall

Lorenzo, shop boy

Richard Lovelady, sailor

Luigi, son of Philippo, fruit-seller

Signor Alessandro Malpietro, old friend of Paul Sarpi

Marino, Servite lay brother

Narcissus Marsh, Archbishop of Dublin (1638-1713)

Peter Martyr (1499-1562)

Edward Maw, (1607-1641) stepson of William Bedell

Leah Maw, (1604 – 1637) stepdaughter of William Bedell

Nicholas Maw, (1601- c.1635) stepson of William Bedell

Paul Mclure, (b.1641)

John Milton, poet, (1609-1674)

James Nangle, Irish translator

Land's Advocate Johna van Oldenbanenveldt (1547-1619)

M. Papillion, a Huguenot

Samuele Paul (b.1600)

William Perkins, (1558-14-602), puritan divine and author

Phillipo, bravo to Sir Henry Wotton

Piet, sailor from the Hague

Matteo Ricci (1552-1610)

John Ridge, English minister in Ireland

Henricus Rosaeus, (d.1637) counter-remonstrant preacher

Brother Santorio, Servite convent physician in Venice

Brother Paul Sarpi, (1552-1623) historian and theologian of the Order of the Servites in Venice

Signor Scaramelli, the secretary of the Venetian Council

Denis Sheridan (b.1612)

Léon Simoneau

Mr Smale, minister of Ballymulling

Tournes, Jean de, (1593-1669) printer

Teagan, sister of Conall and Lorcan

Archbishop James Ussher (1581-1656)

James Wadsworth, (1604-1656) son of Bedell's college friend

Waldron, Irish land owner

Thomas Wentworth, First Earl of Strafford (1593-1641)

Sir Henry Wotton, (1538-1639) diplomat, poet and politician

Introduction

My Lord,

I pray you will forgive one of so small and so scraped an acquaintance for taking the liberty of enclosing this letter with the translation of the Old Testament you have requested me to send. Since the document is of the highest value I have ventured to send it by the hand of the one most precious to me of all living on this frail earth.

I understand also that, beside the translation which your Lordship has expressed the desire to publish (and which I pray will dispel the darkness that hangs over your mother country), your Lordship was kind enough to request the story of my own involvement with the great and godly man who caused it to be made. I therefore present to your Lordship a full account of my life, thinking that perhaps so great a philosopher might take some interest in my meeting with those other lights of learning of my own younger days such as Signor Galileo and Brother Paul Sarpi and that above all you would be pleased to learn how God's Word was the fountain and foundation of their search for wisdom. Your Lordship, has perhaps heard something of this story from that great man Sir Henry Wotton, Provost of Eton College during your Lordship's time at that place.

Your Lordship has many calls upon your time and I will not be further tedious but commend you to the care of the loving Heavenly Father whom you serve and whose word you seek to spread abroad in the darkness of your own native country. That this translation should see publication is my greatest desire. Should your Lordship succeed in seeing it through the press I will be able to go with joy and comfort to that sure and heavenly country, knowing that the life's work God has set before me on this earth has been completed.

Your Lordship's, most ready always to do you service,

Samuele Paul,
lately professor of Hebrew at the Academy of Geneva
The Villa Diodati, Geneva
Dated the 3rd day of May 1679

By the hand of Mr Paul Mclure

Chapter 1: (Spring, 1607) The Account Begins

My pen cruised slowly across the ocean of white paper, each delicate tack charting information for some traveller who would come after: *"… per riuscire servitore non inutile a quest'Augusta Repubblica ed all' Eccellenze Vostre."* I sighed softly, having reached the end of the inky voyage. I put down my pen and stretched my tired fingers, glancing across as I did so at Brother Paul whose pen was still navigating diligently: Brother Paul Sarpi, the renowned, learned and enigmatic Provincial of the Servites in Venice whose kindness is my earliest clear memory.

My father had taken me to the Servites when he knew he was dying. He gave the monastery all his worldly goods and asked the brothers to take care of me, tiny as I was. I grew, and Brother Paul began to keep me always by his side trusting me with more and more of his work in Latin, Italian, French and Greek. Even his private ciphers were not secret from me. By means of these codes he corresponded with learned men all over the world—Francis Bacon, Galileo Galilei—anyone interested in searching for truth in any field of discovery. Little did these far away scholars realise when they received the great Sarpi's wisdom as a mere jumble of characters that the letters they held in their hands were the work of a small child scratching away at a desk beside his master. I soon learned to be trusty and efficient and it was I who ran with the original uncoded documents to the fire in the kitchen and watched while dangerous thoughts and ideas vanished in smoke up the monastery chimney, as though they had never been.

The day I copied that particular letter to the Doge for Brother Paul is fixed in my mind. It was during the year of the Venetian interdict. The cold spring rain was lashing the water of the canal in sudden showers which passed as quickly as they came. In between them the vivid light of the Venetian sky shone with almost turquoise brilliance into the little window of Brother Paul's cell, breaking into dancing wave patterns on the walls and ceiling as the water reflected it. Snug inside the cell, Brother Paul and I were concentrating on our work, hardly noticing the changing patterns of light, except as an occasional hindrance to our activity.

The grave, quiet, Servite brother, thin and lean beneath his black habit from years of spare and frugal diet, sat at his desk plying his pen. He was working hard and the prominent vein in his forehead stood out as he concentrated. To keep him warm, since the spring weather was still chilly, he had in the pockets of his habit two iron balls of his own invention which could be made hot in the fire. When they cooled down I would be sent to the kitchen to heat them up again. Brother Paul's chair and working area were screened from any slight draughts by pieces of paper constructed into a kind of box in which he sat and worked. This arrangement he called his "castle" and he believed firmly that protecting his head from the draughts that blew through the cell helped him think more clearly. And it was a time for clear thinking. Looking back now, I realise that only Brother Paul's active brain and steely logic stood between the might of Rome and Spain and the freedom of Venice.

From time to time Brother Paul raised his weary, slightly cynical eyes from his work to glance at the wall opposite. Here hung the only decorations (if such they could be called) that graced our cell. A small crucifix met his gaze and under it on a little shelf a human skull, dark with age. Beside these reminders of divine death and human mortality was a small picture in a plain wooden frame of Christ kneeling in the Garden of Gethsemane in his agony of prayer to his heavenly Father.

If anyone had seen the two of us I am sure I would have presented a great contrast to the thin and thoughtful Brother Paul. I was a lively and chubby child of about eight or nine years old with a mop of dark curls and I sat opposite the window, my chair raised on stone blocks to enable me to reach table height with comfort. I had just finished copying the letter to the Doge when a violent shower hurled itself out of the sky outside the window, dashing huge drops against the monastery's thick walls and blotting out the light that had been reflecting from the water. The rain hammered on the window and its shutter, rattling down the roofs and gutters.

I looked up as a thought struck me for the first time, "Brother Paul," I asked, "Does the rain never fill the canals until they overflow and flood the city?"

Brother Paul smiled, "Sometimes at a high tide the *fondamente* beside the canal is covered with water. You have seen that, Samuele, I know. But the water in the canals flows out into the lagoon and into the sea."

But the violence of the rain had bothered me, "What about a storm, Brother Paul or a very high tide?" I persisted, "could that not put the city in danger; perhaps destroy it altogether?"

"Samuele, Samuele," replied the Servite brother gently, "the most Serene Republic of Venice is not in danger from storms—not storms of that type at any rate. Doctor Galileo and I have had much discussion about the motion of the sea tides and we can tell when they will be high and why. But as for storms, alas, I cannot tell what will be the end of the storm the Pope in Rome would unleash on our beloved Venice if he could."

I was surprised, never having doubted for a moment that Brother Paul and the Doge could defend the city from *any* human danger. "But that is why you go to the Doge's palace every day to work isn't it, Brother Paul? You can defend the Republic with your pen by helping the Doge and his council to write wise words to the Pope in Rome. The Pope cannot hurt us in Venice just because we will not obey all his orders or let his priests go unpunished if they do wrong."

"Since the earliest times, Venice has governed her own affairs with a liberty and justice which is famous all over the world, Samuele," replied Brother Paul, "and I am glad that all the Venetian clergy have stood firm for that liberty. None but the Jesuits have obeyed the Pope's interdict and *they* have left the city. But as yet I do not see how things will work out. I thank God that I am so well lately; my old liver disorder hasn't troubled me for months. Perhaps I am being given divine strength for the work set before me now."

"But if the clergy stick to their posts and the Doge and his council still govern, how can the Pope harm us?" I persisted.

"You know that the Pope wants us to hand over priests who are criminals to be tried in the church courts rather than in our own. If we will not do this willingly he will take steps to make us. He could, for instance, ask the King of Spain to send his army to fight us and force us to obey," he replied, "but here is better news, look, I have had a letter today from someone who is a new neighbour of ours. Come here and sit in the castle and I will show you. He is from England and he wants to visit us."

I jumped off my perch and ran to where Brother Paul was carefully rearranging his draft-proofing to admit me. Settled by his side I felt comfortable and at ease. Venice could not be flooded by a storm; this I now knew because Brother Paul had just told me. That the Pope in

Rome could harm anyone in Venice while Brother Paul protected the city was something I still did not believe for a moment. His health was much better—I had noticed that too. He was free of pain and full of energy: as far as I was concerned all was well.

Brother Paul unfolded the letter and spread it out for me to see, saying, "The English Ambassador, Sir Henry Wotton, has a new chaplain just arrived from England. Here is a letter I have had from this chaplain who desires to meet me. I must confess I would like to meet an English chaplain. This one has a reputation for learning and he says he wants to improve his Hebrew pronunciation."

He studied the letter a little longer and I could see it was written in a bold, large yet neat hand and in excellent Latin, "Rabbi Leo of Modena would be the best person to give him help with Hebrew, not me," mused Brother Paul, "and you could go with the chaplain to show him the way and carry his books."

This sounded intriguing, "Perhaps I could learn Hebrew too," I ventured, wondering if this was my chance to add that language to those I already knew.

Brother Paul studied my face for a moment before replying as if weighing something up in his mind, "Well, yes—if you could do so just by listening to the Rabbi and this Chaplain—Mr Bedell I think his name is, yes Bedell—you must not utter a word you know, Samuele, if you are allowed to go," he said very seriously, "which reminds me: Brother Alessio was complaining to me that someone had been using monastery paper to make toy boats and sail them down the gutters and into the canal. That would not have been you by any chance?"

I leaned my head against Brother Paul's bony arm, "I won't even squeak if I can go with the chaplain," I replied earnestly, "and I'm sorry about the boats—it seemed such a good idea at the time—you should have seen them! They went down with such a whoosh and you could watch them for ever so long bobbing down the canal ..."

Brother Paul held up his hand to interrupt me, "Well, please go and apologise to Alessio this afternoon," he said with a sigh, "and try to behave in future."

Then before I could reply he added, "Samuele, I think *you* may be able to learn Hebrew just by listening. You do not realise it perhaps but you have a strange gift for languages. You seem to learn by listening and copying things that take others many years of study. This is a gift from God: it is nothing for you to be proud of. That is why I have always kept you by my side here in the monastery as my personal pupil. I have helped you nurture the gift but now you are nearly old enough to begin to take responsibility yourself for your talents."

At first I was rather surprised, "doesn't everyone learn languages?" I asked.

"No they do not," said Brother Paul with a smile, "and those who do generally have to spend much time in the patient study of grammar books and dictionaries before they can speak fluently in a new tongue."

My eye turned to the line of grammars and lexicons on the shelf and it dawned on me that although Brother Paul used them often, I almost never opened them, even when translating for him. I thought for a moment, trying to adjust to this new perspective on myself. Then I said, "Well, I never knew I had a talent! Except for those paper boats: I was good at making those ..."

"Paper boats are not allowed, young man," said Brother Paul, "I'm afraid that is a talent you are not going to be able to nurture."

"I know Sir Henry Wotton's Residence," I said, moving on from the difficult subject of the interdict on paper boats, "almost next-door to us along the canal, and the Ghetto where Rabbi Leo lives is very near the Ambassador's Residence. Are you sure the chaplain will need me to show him the way?"

Brother Paul smiled down at my eager face, "My son," he said, "he will need you." He paused as though thinking of something long ago. Then he continued, "When I first learned Hebrew my mother didn't ..." he stopped. Then, "We are both orphans you and I, Samuele. Do you remember your mother at all?"

"Not at all," I replied cheerfully; Brother Paul had been father and mother to me for as long as I could really remember.

"Can you not even recall her face?" he asked, a little sadly.

"I think she had dark hair," I answered matter of factly, "and I know that she sang to me because I can remember a little tune with some nonsense words that I know you did not teach me. It almost always comes into my mind at night when I am drifting off to sleep."

"What tune?" asked Brother Paul.

"Oh, it is just nonsense, probably a lullaby," I said, "like this:
Tras a na dont a dol sheer dol sheer
Slarness un wike less a slarn lies an gear ..."

After that the words ran out and I finished the little tune by singing "lah, lah" instead of words.

Brother Paul laughed his soft, cynical laugh, "No, I did not teach you that, nor did you hear someone who has just been to a great musical *opera con intermezzi* in the San Luigi theatre whistling it in the street! A very barbaric little nonsense ditty!" He seemed to shake himself mentally and his mood changed abruptly as he returned to our earlier conversation, "We have much for which to thank Sir Henry Wotton, the English ambassador. Since I am not officially allowed, as theologian and councillor to the Republic, to meet with foreign ambassadors themselves, I am very eager to meet Mr Bedell, his chaplain."

"Why do we need to thank Sir Henry Wotton?" I asked.

"He is a great friend of the Most Serene Republic of Venice, my son," replied the Servite, "and no friend to the Pope. He has many friends in other parts of the world who would like Venice to be independent of the Pope in church matters. The King of England, whom he serves wants this very much. Sir Henry Wotton has asked that great man, Signor Giovanni Diodati of Lucca, to come to Venice (from Geneva where he lives) to help us and he is a man of wisdom and learning. You remember it was he who translated the whole Bible into Italian. Signor Diodati has said he will come, although so far the winter weather and his own business (of which he doubtless has much) have prevented him."

"The man who translated the Bible!" I exclaimed.

Brother Paul had taken every opportunity to encourage me to read my Latin Bible and Greek New Testament saying that the book was not only true but very truth itself. I knew that the Italian Bible was on the Pope's index of forbidden volumes although it was a beautiful translation from the Hebrew and Greek; majestic and graceful yet simple. It was a superb way of reading the Bible—for any Italian who had the good fortune to get hold of a copy and was brave enough to keep it. Another question struck me as talk of the Italian Bible collided in my brain with the discussion we had been having about the Interdict, "Brother Paul," I asked "why does the Pope not like the Italian Bible?"

"Just as the Pope is concerned that only the church shall have the power to punish her clergy when they sin," explained Brother Paul, "so he is concerned that only the church should interpret the Bible to the people, lest they mistake its meaning. Now, I have a job for you."

He reached for his ink and pen and began to write a reply to the English chaplain on a clean sheet of paper. "Here Samuele," he said, sanding and folding the letter and sealing it with a little wax, "you may take this to Sir Henry Wotton's residence and wait for a reply. If Mr Bedell can come at once you may conduct him here. If not, I will send you when it is convenient to him."

I opened the door of the cell eager to go out into the delicious spring wind and sunshine.

"And do not forget," added Brother Paul, "you must speak to Brother Alessio as soon as you get back from your errand."

Brother Micanzio, Brother Paul's closest friend, appeared at the cell door as I left but I had so much to think about I hardly noticed him. I was glad to be allowed out in the fresh air. My life in the monastery moved in a very narrow circle but now I was to take a tentative step outside its circumference. The chaplain would speak English. Could I learn that too? Then there was also the prospect of going with him to the mysterious Jewish Ghetto behind the big iron gates where another and very valuable language was locked away. All remembrance of Brother Alessio and the necessary apology was soon gone from my mind. I ran, almost dancing in the wind, along the *fondamente*, to the grand Residence where the English ambassador lived. The spring showers had ceased but the wind was blowing huge clouds like sails across the sky. It was blowing into me, around me, over me, tugging me forward with the excitement of the new experiences that were beckoning to me, as though it knew that my life was changing tack and it rejoiced with me.

"And what are you doing here, young scamp?" Old Stefano, on duty at the Residence door was not welcoming. Without the carefully addressed letter to the chaplain I would certainly never have gained admittance to the cool hall with its windows onto the canal, its elegant furnishings, rich tapestry hangings, huge green arm chairs and big wall mirrors. In a cage in one corner was Beppo, the ambassador's pet ape. I say "pet" but actually the animal was rather bad tempered and inclined to bite. Only Sir Henry Wotton himself and one trusted servant, Henrico, could easily approach him without being attacked and when out of his cage the animal was kept on a chain or lead. Today he was huddled moodily in his cage and would not look at me although I spoke to him gently in Venetian, Italian, Latin and French in a fruitless effort to gain his attention.

A man entered the hall whom I recognised as Philippo, one of Sir Henry Wotton's *bravos* or "good-fellows."

"Samuele!" there was no doubt that Philippo was employed in a rough and violent trade but he greeted me kindly in the Venetian dialect, "You are abroad early today. What are you doing here? You should be off to the La Guerra Bridge where my son, Luigi, has his fruit stall. You should see the apples he has today! So red, so crisp yet juicy! They would do your skinny master good I'm sure."

Philippo may have been a ruffian hired to steal letters and to spy—that was a bravo's trade and all ambassadors and Venetian officials employed them—but like every Venetian he loved Brother Paul to the point of worship. Even the fruit-seller boy kept his very best wares for Brother Paul and Philippo was proud that I was sent daily to his son's stall to buy the fruit with which the Servite Brother augmented his diet of bread and water. Of course Brother Paul ensured that I had my share too, although I ate the normal monastery food in the refectory as well—not just bread and water. "I am on an errand to Mr Chaplain Bedell," I replied in my best Venetian, "but I am sure Brother Paul will send me for fruit later and I will remember your recommendations."

"I am sure you will," laughed Philippo, "boys are always hungry and I suspect Brother Paul does not eat all that fruit by himself!"

"Brother Paul is very generous," I said a trifle stiffly, for I did not like him to think that I ate any of the fruit before taking it back to my master.

"That's true," replied Philippo, still laughing, "no doubt he gives some of it to Brother Micanzio. But here comes Mr Chaplain. He is good; I am bad—so I will go before he sees me."

The man who entered the room was tall and his face was open and kindly. Brother Paul's face, though kind, shielded his thoughts from view but here was a man whose face and thoughts were united. Though young, he already stooped slightly as tall people often do, having to fit into an average-sized world. His twinkling eyes looked out over a flowing brown beard and his clothes, though plain to the point of coarseness, were not those of a churchman. He advanced towards me, his hand stretched out to shake mine, even though I was just a child and a servant. Obviously he was wondering in what language to address me since, as yet, he spoke little or no Italian. I hurried to put him at his ease saying in Latin, "Mr Chaplain Bedell, Sir? My master, Brother Paul Sarpi, the Servite, has sent me."

"I look forward to meeting him at once," replied the Chaplain glad to be able to use Latin with me, "I understand from his letter that he is free at the moment."

"Yes, Sir," I replied, "I can take you to him if you desire it."

***

There was no doubt that in Mr Bedell, Brother Paul found a kindred spirit. This was not just another learned man desiring to meet the famous Servite, in whose autograph book Brother Paul would write a few lines from the Bible before signing his name and saying a polite goodbye. The two men had an instant liking for one another. Although Mr Bedell was a quarter of a century younger than Brother Paul, they had studied many of the same theological problems and issues but often from different perspectives. They were thrilled to be able to compare their insights and findings. Where Brother Paul was cautious and wary, Mr Bedell displayed a disarming, almost breezy, frankness. Both loved their own countries very dearly and were eager to serve them. Both hungered for books more than daily food and Mr Bedell was delighted with the private library Brother Paul had collected in his cell. They also shared a great love for plants and botany but whereas Brother Paul's love was for the theoretical—

dissecting, describing and analysing, Chaplain Bedell loved growing and planting things, pruning and tending.

Brother Paul also knew that Mr Bedell had studied in depth theological books which he himself could not obtain but was keen to read. They agreed to meet every week under cover of language learning, for it would not do, even in Venice, for a Servite Friar to openly befriend a chaplain from England without some legitimate excuse. Mr Bedell was going to learn Italian and in exchange teach Brother Paul and Brother Micanzio English. I would not be slow to take advantage of that either! Now that I realised that my language gift was something unusual I began to seek for opportunities to exercise it. Together the three men began to plan what would be the best way to engineer in Venice a complete break from the Pope; perhaps even to bring the Reformation to the Most Serene Republic.

The Reformation! It is a strange fact that being able to translate from one language to another, to be a good, a natural linguist does not automatically guarantee a deep understanding of the words themselves—especially in a child. This *Riforma, Réforme, Reformatio, Μεταρρύθμιση*, what was it?

"Brother Paul," I began one warm afternoon as we worked away together, "what is the Reformation?"

"You should concentrate on your work and not idle away the time by asking about such things," said Brother Paul in a tone that surprised me by its uncharacteristic harshness and which was strangely loud. Then he got up, went to the window, which was open towards the canal, and closed it, fastening the stout wooden shutters. Silently he beckoned me over to the castle, moving the paper quietly and motioning me to sit beside him, a long slender finger on his lips. Narrow ribbons of light streamed in through the gaps in the closed shutters. As my eyes adjusted to the gloom, Brother Paul talked very quietly to me about John Huss of Bohemia; about John Whitcliffe of England.

"They preached that a man can personally know his Creator and Redeemer without going through a priest," came his quiet voice in the semi-darkness, "that a man can understand the Bible for himself and should study it in his own language." He paused, knowing that I would need to think. I asked no question and the hushed voice continued, "Huss was silenced. The damage done by Whitcliffe was controlled and limited. Then came Martin Luther whose burning determination that salvation from hell fire is by faith alone in Jesus Christ could no longer be resisted. But the church called no council, gave no consideration to the questions raised. Instead anyone espousing these ideas was branded a heretic and Europe crumbled into religious strife and bitter war." Again silence. I could not speak. It was as though in my head a jumble of ideas, snippets from books, tiny pieces of over-heard conversations were being sorted into a picture in which I had to find my own place. Brother Paul's voice continued, "People who read the Bible discover how far the church has departed from its teachings. They brave fire and sword in many countries in Europe in order that they can worship God in the way the Bible teaches. In Germany, Switzerland, the Netherlands and England they have managed to establish new churches, Protestant churches they are called after the protest of some German princes. In France the struggle continues and the Protestant cause is stumbling—perhaps towards defeat. In Spain the Roman Church triumphs. Italy is the Pope's own country; he is determined that the Reformation will not raise its head here. Spain will help him, as you know, if Venice looks as if she is wavering. Sir Henry Wotton has instructions from the King of England to promise help to Venice should she be attacked by Spain."

"And we Venetians ourselves are not idle are we?" I spoke now, thinking of the Doge, stately and solemn in his horned cap calmly ordering the navy to be brought up to full strength, ordering the building of more ships and the enlisting of more sailors and soldiers.

"Indeed," said Brother Paul, "but can we Venetians be encouraged not only to abandon the Pope's authority but also his teachings? Mr Bedell sees that as the most important thing of all—and the most difficult."

***

"Samuele," said Brother Paul the next morning, "I am sending you over to see Mr Bedell. He says he needs a language assistant to help him compile an Italian grammar. You would be just the person—and you will learn something more about grammar as well which will do you good! Go and clean your hands and face and then call at Sir Henry's Residence."

"A grammar!" I said in disbelief. I could not imagine why anyone would want to do such a thing, "I'm happy to help but it sounds a difficult way of going about things."

"Mr Chaplain Bedell seems to learn languages as quickly as you do," said Brother Paul, "he just has a different method, that's all."

Brother Paul's remark proved true. But not only did I learn from Mr Bedell: over the next few days I saw him often and grew to love him—and who could not love him? Gentle and thoughtful he did indeed learn languages with the same startling quickness that I did myself. However, whereas I listened and copied, understanding almost by an instinct, Chaplain Bedell had been through a rigorous grammatical schooling in his childhood; so rigorous in fact that a blow on the head he received from his strict teacher when he was about my own age left him partly deaf for the rest of his life.

"I always follow my old teacher's example," he explained without a hint of malice over the rough treatment he had had in his schooling, "he was a learned man though sadly short tempered. His method of learning any new language was to compile his own grammar textbook at once. I find it the quickest way."

So I sat by him (positioned beside his one good ear) in his study at Sir Henry Wotton's Residence answering his questions about the language as he wrote his grammar book. He finished his work in a very few days and having done so had virtually mastered the language at a stroke.

***

Chaplain Bedell had not been in Venice a year before he had amassed an impressive collection of plants. A strange medley of pots appeared on the windowsill of his study and I was delighted and fascinated to watch the plants in them grow and develop and to hear the stories of how he had acquired each one. Brother Paul, seeing that I was learning much from Mr Bedell, sent me to the chaplain's study more often and we became good friends. As I showed such interest in the plants and enjoyed helping him to care for them, Mr Bedell took the trouble to take some cuttings for me also and, finding some small pots, made me a present of some little shoots that he assured me would one day bear beautiful roses.

"Have you a little garden or even a yard at the monastery?" he asked.

"There is a little yard by the kitchen," I replied, "but nothing grows there."

"Excellent!" said Mr Bedell, "Can you remember in which direction in faces?"

The next day he called at the monastery with a servant carrying a long wooden box and a sack full of rich soil he had obtained from somewhere. In no time at all I had helped him to set it up in the yard and plant it with peas and lettuce. The brother in charge of the cooking was soon appeased when he heard that the contents of the box would be for his use in the kitchen and he gladly gave up the space for my vegetable garden.

"Nothing like fresh peas, Samuele," he said, smacking his lips at the thought of *pisi e risi* made of delicious young peas, rice and chopped ham, "which reminds me," he added, "you had better watch out for the sacristan—he's after your blood."

"Why?" I asked uneasily wondering which piece of my questionable behaviour had been discovered by the austere brother in charge of the stores.

"Because he found several pieces of string from the stores cut up for playing cat's cradle, and a big ball of twine, covered all over with something sticky that had obviously been used for playing ball games in the kitchen yard, that's why! If I were you I'd keep out of his way."

***

One morning not long afterwards I returned to our cell with Brother Paul's daily supply of fruit from Luigi's stall. Brother Micanzio was talking to Brother Paul as I entered.

"Do you think we could introduce Chaplain Bedell to the *Ridotto Morosini*?" Brother Micanzio was saying, "there is a meeting tomorrow at the *Nave d'Oro* in the *Merceria*. He would enjoy it."

"A society composed of all the thinking men of Venice should surely include him," replied Brother Paul, "he would find the rules to his taste—equality, informality, politeness and so on."

"Well, you are one of the most respected members," said Brother Micanzio, "it will be easy for you to arrange an invitation."

"Samuele could go with him," said Brother Paul with a smile in my direction, "would you like that, Samuele?"

"Yes please! But what is it?" I asked, hoping mostly that accompanying Mr Bedell might involve a gondola trip from the Residence to the *Merceria* where all the shops are in Venice.

"The *Ridotto Morosini* is a learned society," explained Brother Paul, "Galileo Galilei is often there. The members agree to treat one another as equals, whatever their calling or station in life, and with informality but with politeness. Everyone at the meeting is allowed to introduce a subject for discussion, whether literary or scientific, the only objective being to arrive at the truth about any matter. At the meetings Senators from the highest Council of Venice (the Doge himself is a former member), humble friars and wealthy merchants debate all kinds of things freely. Foreign visitors are welcome too. The *Nave d'Oro,* where the meetings are held, is a house belonging to a group of Flemish merchants."

And so it was that the next day, after Mr Bedell and I had finished our work together in his study, we prepared to make our way to the *Nave d'Oro.* Here we planned to meet Brother Paul, and at the end of the meeting I would accompany him back to the Servite monastery. However, today something in the chaplain's manner seemed disturbed and his eyes, usually so frank and open above the bushy beard, had a troubled look. He began to apologise that his concentration had not been as good as usual—and in truth I had noticed that his normally quick wits were elsewhere.

"What is the matter, Mr Bedell?" I asked in concern, "something is troubling you."

"I am worried about your master, to tell the truth," replied the chaplain, "Sir Henry Wotton has had very grave news concerning him."

"What news?" I asked, "How can Sir Henry have news about Brother Paul?"

"I cannot tell you that," replied the chaplain, "the information is very secret, I do not myself know fully what it is, only that it is important."

"Can't Sir Henry have an audience with Signor Scaramelli the secretary of the Venetian Council?" I asked, becoming worried that some danger was hanging over Brother Paul, "he would tell the Doge and get everything put to rights." My faith in the Doge was absolute.

"That is not allowed," explained Mr Bedell, "Sir Henry is an ambassador and ambassadors have to follow strict rules. One rule is that it is forbidden by the Council of Venice for members of the Venetian government to communicate with foreign ambassadors in any way."

I still did not understand what information Sir Henry Wotton could possibly have that he would need to pass on to the government about

Brother Paul but Mr Bedell's worried mood began to frighten me, "Is he in danger?" I asked, "now, this minute?"

"Someone like Brother Paul is always in danger," answered the chaplain earnestly, "but if only Sir Henry Wotton could speak to Signor Scaramelli the Senate could be warned! It is no use speaking to Brother Paul himself, he will never take action for his own protection even if he is able to do so."

"Brother Micanzio will be at the *ridotto,*" I said, "he will know what to do. He can speak to government officials and perhaps persuade them to hear Sir Henry Wotton, even although it is not allowed."

"I cannot divulge Sir Henry Wotton's information to Brother Micanzio," said the chaplain, "but perhaps I can give him a hint of how serious the matter is, that he could pass on to some member of the Venetian Council—there may even be a council member attending the *ridotto.*"

"Yes, yes, let's go at once," I replied in a frenzy of anxiety for Brother Paul. I almost tugged at the chaplain's sleeve in my eagerness to be off at once to the *Nave d'Oro.* Mr Bedell's face relaxed from its worried look and he smiled down at me from his great height as he said, "We need not rush. The meeting will not even be beginning yet. Besides, we have forgotten to do the most important thing of all to help Brother Paul."

It seemed to me that speed was what was most needed, "What have we forgotten?" I asked.

"God, who disposes of all things, and who is watching over his servant, Brother Paul, will answer our prayers if we pray to him," replied the chaplain simply, "we should do this now," and then in Italian, but like a man perfectly used to addressing his God in his mother tongue, he prayed, "Almighty and merciful Father in Heaven, we come before Thee to ask for the safety of Thy servant, Brother Paul. We pray that Thou wilt open up a route by which Sir Henry Wotton can speak to Signor Scaramelli and that those who would harm Thy servant will be thwarted. We ask these things in the name of our dear Saviour, Jesus Christ, knowing that what we ask in His name Thou wilt hear."

I was astounded. I had never heard anyone pray in Italian before. Brother Paul and Brother Micanzio always prayed in Latin. Sometimes they used the Lord's Prayer from the Bible or other prayers which they knew by heart. Although they never just mumbled a string of "Our Fathers," as many priests and friars did, they did not speak in *this* way, as though they knew God as a personal friend. "Mr Bedell," I said in astonishment, "you speak to God as if he were your friend!" As soon as the words were out of my mouth I knew what his answer would be.

"He is," he said.

***

We arrived at the *Nave d'Oro* by gondola but my worried state of mind prevented me from enjoying the ride to which I had so looked forward. The *ridotto* was well attended, quite crowded in fact, but when Mr Bedell was announced Brother Paul at once came forward to welcome him. There was to be a discussion on the movement of the blood in the human body, he explained, and he was going to present some of his ideas and discoveries with those of Signor Doctor Galileo Galilei. He whisked Mr Bedell off to meet a Dr Acquapendente from Padua who was at that moment talking to Mr Bedell's own Venetian medical friend Dr Despotine.

I slipped away to look for Brother Micanzio whom I found engaged in conversation on the other side of the room. I did not dare to interrupt and I was burning with anxiety as Brother Micanzio welcomed me silently with a pat on the head, continuing his discussion without further reference to my presence. Looking round the room I could see Brother Paul. He was talking to a priest with a long nose and a rather loud laugh. I was still wondering what I could do to gain Brother Micanzio's attention when one of the household servants approached us with a tray of refreshments. This he passed over my head, offering it to Brother Micanzio and the nobleman with whom he was talking. In my desperation I decided to create a diversion which might possibly give me a chance to whisper to Brother Micanzio. I bobbed up onto my toes under the tray, causing the contents to fly up into the air. There was a horrible crash and pieces of pastry flew everywhere spewing tasty fillings and delicate decorations in all directions.

Chapter 3: (1607) The Empty Church

The tray had only contained pastries and not drinks in costly Venetian glasses, but Brother Micanzio was surprised and angry, exclaiming at my carelessness as we bent down to pick up the fragments of pastry. Our heads were close together as we grovelled on the floor and the servant was momentarily engaged in recovering some pieces which were further away. Quickly I whispered, "Brother Paul is in great danger. Mr Bedell has serious information. Please come where I can explain." Brother Micanzio understood at once and said aloud, "Please excuse us, I must take this careless and insolent child where I can punish him properly," and grasping me by the ear he dragged me towards to door.

"Now what is this all about?" he said as soon as we reached the relative quiet beside the canal outside the *Nave d'Oro.*

As quickly as I could I explained and relief washed over me as Brother Micanzio took charge of the situation.

"Go back inside," he said, "and find Mr Bedell. As soon as you can, let him know discretely that he should return to Sir Henry Wotton's Residence. Say that I have told you to go with him. When you are out of ear-shot of the company explain that he should go straight to Sir Henry and ask him to await a request from Signor Scaramelli to attend on him—possibly this evening. Do not worry. God will take care of our Brother. You are a clever child to alert me in this way. I will go to the Doge's palace at once."

Although it was now quite dark, a gondola was approaching lazily along the canal towards us. Brother Micanzio called to the gondolier and to my amazement he sprang into the boat as soon as it was near enough to the stairs for him to jump across. He exchanged some rapid words with the gondolier who at once made off at a swift pace down the canal.

I slipped back into the *Nave d'Oro* and into the room where the *ridotto* was now in full swing. Brother Paul was addressing the meeting and Mr Bedell was sitting at the back with Dr Despotine. The doctor was drinking in all Brother Paul's words and earnestly taking down notes in pencil. I was overjoyed to find his spare paper and even a pencil on the floor beside his chair! Now there was no need to try to whisper into Mr Bedell's one good ear. Quietly I tore off a tiny corner of paper and wrote on it the words, "come out." Then, trying to look like a bored servant boy idling while waiting for his master, I casually moved round to Mr Bedell's chair and dropped the paper on his lap. It was good that Mr Bedell had had the foresight to station himself at the back of the room. Without even seeming to glance at my paper, he slipped it into his pocket and rose at once. Brother Paul's flow of eloquent Latin, describing the way in which he and Galileo had found valves in the veins which enabled the blood to return to the heart after travelling through the body, continued without wavering. I waited for a moment or two and then slipped out after Mr Bedell.

The English chaplain was delighted that I had succeeded so well and I think he was nearly as relieved as I that Brother Micanzio was on his way to the Doge's palace. He too praised my ingenuity until I was quite embarrassed but by this time we were in a gondola on our way back to Sir Henry's Residence.

When we arrived Mr Bedell left me in the hall with the caged ape for company while he went to find Sir Henry. After a very short time one of the ambassador's servants hurried past with a note on a platter and I had a feeling that Brother Micanzio had already been able to secure the interview that was so much needed. Minutes later Sir Henry and Mr Bedell appeared hurrying down the stairs. Sir Henry was not wearing his magnificent official robes but was quietly dressed. To my surprise he stopped when he saw me and spoke to Mr Bedell. Mr Bedell nodded, patted me on the head (something I felt I had had enough of for one day!) and then said to me, "Sir Henry commends you for your prompt actions and requests that you accompany him to carry his gloves and his papers. I will return to the *Nave d'Oro* so that Brother Paul is not worried about you." I was very taken aback. To accompany the English Ambassador! Sir Henry was obviously very pleased with me! I bowed my thanks to him, received his gloves and papers, gave Mr Bedell a nervous smile and fell in behind the ambassador at a suitably respectful distance.

Sir Henry's own gondola was waiting for us at the stairs: Philippo was acting as gondolier. In the presence of Sir Henry Philippo was not as chatty as usual but he favoured me with a very surprised wink as if to say, "Wait till Luigi hears about this!"

I imagined we might be going to the Doge's palace where Signor Scaramelli would receive the ambassador, unofficially and in private, but perhaps in the great council chamber itself. However, we disembarked at one of the city churches. The building was dark and empty at this hour but Sir Henry seemed to know exactly where we should go. Lantern in hand he entered through a small side door and I followed, our footsteps echoing eerily in the huge space. The candles twinkling in the distance on the high altar seemed to be miles away across a black void but there were smaller lights gleaming in a side chapel. Here Signor Scaramelli was waiting and some chairs had been placed. He received the ambassador with immense courtesy. There was a long exchange of courtly bows and the discussion began, the low voices of the two participants making a soft buzzing hum in the vast empty building.

I was still busy trying to take in whole situation when I heard Sir Henry saying, "I am sure, my lord, that you are aware that my royal master, King James, finds it necessary to maintain certain, er—contacts at the Court of Rome who keep him informed of matters that take place there."

I could see even by the dim lamplight that Signor Scaramelli's face twitched slightly at this delicate reference to spying and he replied, "Indeed, the Most Serene Republic also finds such, er—arrangements convenient."

Sir Henry continued, "From these sources we understand that the Court of Rome has determined certain measures to be taken against the Servite Brother Paul Sarpi, the Theological Councillor of the Most Serene Republic. These measures, if carried into effect, would result in the death of Brother Paul to the infinite satisfaction of the Court of Rome in general and Pope Paul V in particular."

"These are serious allegations, Sir Henry, which, if true, would cause grave concern to the Most Serene Republic," replied Signor Scaramelli, "they are also allegations which reflect very seriously upon the Holy Father in Rome and I would therefore ask you to produce some evidence for your accusations."

"I have here a letter, my Lord," replied Sir Henry turning to me and taking the papers which I held out for him, "which has, er, come into my hands. It is from the General of the Jesuits to the Jesuit Father Possevin, once of Venice but now in Ferrara, and it explains that there is a 'secret suit' being prepared against 'Master Paul of Venice' and gives the reasons for the Holy Father's extreme displeasure of which I am sure your Lordship is not unaware. You will notice that the cipher in which it is written has been decoded above the text. I can add details of the 'secret suit' which will allow the Most Serene Republic to be prepared and to take measures to protect her faithful servant and councillor. Apparently Brother Paul is to be tried in his absence secretly at Rome to justify these measures against him."

Signor Scaramelli, grave faced, took the papers from Sir Henry and scanned them quickly. Then he motioned Sir Henry to one of the chairs, sat down himself on the other and dropped his formal manner completely.

"We've been aware for sometime of the danger to Brother Paul," he began, "and have been taking some quiet measures to protect him but this is obviously very serious and we will take action at once. Can you give me all the details?"

"The Pope is well aware of what is going on here," said Sir Henry, "and he considers Brother Paul a great danger to his power. He knows also that, if he loses Venice, the Reformation which he so much fears will have a foothold in Italy itself."

"We are well aware of this," said Signor Scaramelli and I traced a hint of impatience in his voice, "although I would dispute your inference that should Venice be freed from the domination of the Pope, Protestantism would necessarily follow. The Republic of Venice has been exercising its liberty and justice within the fold of the church since its foundation. We only ask for this to continue. What we need to know from you is exactly what you know of the nature of the threat to Brother Paul."

"I do not have any names," replied Sir Henry, "or I would willingly divulge them to you. However, we know that some person or persons in holy orders in Venice have been instructed to capture Brother Paul and bring him to Rome for trial, or failing that, to murder him."

"Thank you, Sir Henry," said Signor Scaramelli softly, "you do not know of which ecclesiastical order these 'persons' are?"

"Only that they are not of his own order, the Servites," replied Sir Henry, "nor of the banished Jesuit order, although they would scarcely have much opportunity in any case."

I was very relieved to hear that the Servites were not involved. Brother Paul would be in grave danger if so and life in the monastery would be difficult indeed if everyone were suspect. The interview continued a little longer. Signor Scaramelli assured Sir Henry that the Council of the Republic would be informed immediately and would take action at the highest level to protect Brother Paul. Then he bowed Sir Henry politely out to the stairs where Philippo waited in the gondola.

When I finally arrived home at the monastery, I was almost shaking with excited reaction to all that had happened. Brother Paul, however, was as calm as usual and sat in his castle working away at his great *History of the Council of Trent*.

"What *have* you been doing, Samuele?" he asked wryly when I entered our cell, "Mr Bedell tells me you have been accompanying Sir Henry Wotton to see the Secretary of the Republic—about me!"

I explained as well as I was able but Mr Bedell and Brother Micanzio had obviously already told him as much as they could.

"Samuele," he said gravely when I had finished, "If God is all-knowing then He already knows the number of my days. If it is his will that I perish at the hands of the Inquisition in Rome, or some mad friar in Venice then the efforts even of the Doge to guard me will be in vain and I am content. I cannot die before God wills it. Now go and bring us some fruit from Luigi's stall before he goes home for the night and please do not stop at the stall to play with Luigi at throwing left-over rotten fruit at passing gondoliers—yes, I understand you were aiming at the gondolas last night not the gondoliers but the sacristan has received complaints and put two and two together. If it happens ever again you will be totally without my protection. Off you go!"

Chapter 4: (1607) Rabbi Leo and Escape of the Ape

Despite his own opinions, the threat to Brother Paul's life was taken very seriously by the rulers of the Most Serene Republic over the next six months. This meant that it became more difficult for him to receive guests. Also he could no longer walk unattended from the Servite monastery through the *Merceria* to the Doge's palace. All the *Sbirri,* the government police, were alerted and Brother Micanzio refused to leave his side for more than a moment. A bar was put on his window and a lock was put on his cell door—something he had never had before. The Servites themselves instituted their own watch, interrogating any visitor wanting to see Brother Paul and turning away most. All these changes, although they were undoubtedly stressful for Brother Paul, affected me little. I still worked in our cell, got occasionally into trouble with the sacristan, visited Mr Bedell and drifted off to sleep peacefully each night in calm repose with my mother's little nonsense song running through my head.

Only Mr Bedell still had completely free access to Brother Paul. His tall, stooping figure, burdened with books or plant specimens, was instantly recognisable and he was always admitted at once. He now spoke fluent Italian and Brother Paul had almost mastered English. I too could now converse quite well in the English language which I always used with Mr Bedell unless his Venetian friend, Dr Despotine, who spoke no English, was with him.

I had not forgotten about the Hebrew sessions in the Ghetto, that Brother Paul had spoken of. When would Mr Bedell be able to go there? When I saw Jews going about their business in Venice now I took more notice of them in their tall yellow hats and headdress. After sunset I rarely saw them.

"Why do they all hurry off to the Ghetto as soon as it begins to get dark?" I asked Brother Paul "and why do they always wear those yellow hats?"

"It is the law," he explained, "They must be back in the Ghetto before dark. A Jewish guard is posted outside the iron Ghetto gate at sunset. There are exceptions—Jewish medical doctors may stay out if called to treat patients who are not Jews, and merchants and others can get special passes because of the nature of their business. The yellow hats are a legal requirement too. The Venetian government wants Jews to be instantly recognisable."

Although we lived quite nearby I had never visited the Ghetto. Many Venetians did: the shops there were apparently crowded with gentile shoppers but I had never yet been sent on any errand there. Now it took on a new aspect to me: a mysterious, foreign place yet attractive because it guarded the secret of a language I had not yet mastered.

Brother Paul corresponded regularly with the young Rabbi Leo of Modena, the most distinguished Jewish scholar of the ghetto— perhaps of the whole world. I kept an anxious eye therefore on the to and fro of letters between Brother Paul and Rabbi Leo until the hoped-for day arrived when Brother Paul announced, "You will accompany Mr Bedell to the Ghetto today, Samuele, I have been able to arrange an interview for him with Rabbi Leo."

I hurried through my morning jobs and errands, buying our fruit from Luigi almost without looking at it, and then rushed off to wait at Sir Henry's residence. This morning the ape was out on his chain and I kept my distance, not wishing to be bitten, as I waited until Mr Bedell appeared. Together we walked up the *fondamente* to the *Ponte de Ghetto Nuovo* and through the iron gate into the *Ghetto Nuovo* itself. The cramped but bustling area was so overcrowded with residents that the buildings rose to six stories high and I gazed up at them with interest, staring round at the shops and the ornate synagogues with their foreign looking decorations. There were crowds of Jewish men in their yellow turbans and ladies, many of whom were richly dressed and wore tall hats or caps; still yellow in colour but decorated with gem stones. Everything had an unfamiliar aspect like nothing I had ever seen in Venice before.

Mr Bedell made inquiries for the *bet midrash,* or study house, of Rabbi Leo and we were directed to the door of a small building not far from the bridge. It seemed a strange little place for so great a scholar but I followed Mr Bedell who knocked boldly on the door. A servant, who evidently expected us, opened the door and conducted us to the Rabbi's room where he announced us and left.

When I first saw Rabbi Leo I was struck by the similarities, and also the differences, between him and Mr Bedell. They seemed about the same age and both had flowing beards. However, the Rabbi was already beginning to lose the hair on top of his head and his bald skull was just visible beneath his yellow turban. Their dress could not have been more different in one respect. Mr Bedell was dressed in very plain clothes made of serviceable but most unshowy fabric whereas the Rabbi was richly dressed in a velvet robe and wore a rich jewel in his turban. However, just as Mr Bedell did not care for his clothes and allowed them to become worn and unmended (although never dirty), there was a hint of neglect about the Rabbi's appearance also: the rich robe seemed untidy, the turban greasy.

He rose as we entered the room, greeted Mr Bedell politely in Latin and ushered him to a chair. He was evidently used to receiving scholarly churchmen who wished to study Hebrew and he wasted no time in getting down to work with Mr Bedell. He opened a Hebrew Bible at once, asking him to read so that he could judge how well he could already pronounce the language. At length he stopped him, asked him some questions and then got a little Hebrew grammar book down from a shelf. This was my opportunity and, manoeuvring myself so that I could see the book too, I settled down to learn everything I could from the great Rabbi.

That night, and for many nights afterwards, as I fell asleep my mother's song seemed to be accompanied by strange Hebrew characters that swirled around and danced to the little tune. Day after day we went to the Ghetto and Mr Bedell made rapid progress, so rapid in fact that I had a difficult job to soak up all I wanted to know quickly enough. The two men obviously liked one another and greatly respected each other for their learning. Rabbi Leo was often surprised and delighted with Mr Bedell's interpretations, especially of difficult passages. It became apparent to me that Mr Bedell's purpose in visiting the Rabbi was not just to improve his Hebrew. He began to discuss with him also the question of the Jewish Messiah and whether or not Jesus was he. The discussions were grave and polite and Mr Bedell seemed always to be able to answer the Rabbi's points.

***

One morning Brother Paul had sent me early for our fruit again so that I could go with Mr Bedell to the ghetto. Luigi had cherries and also luscious looking grapes. As I wavered, undecided over what to buy he looked round to see that no one was listening and then said very quietly, "Samuele, my father has a warning for your master. There is a man hanging about who my father knew once in Rome. He is a priest. A tall thin man with a very long pointed nose. He is here in

Venice and he has a job to do for the Pope. His job is to try to bribe your master to change sides in the dispute with the Holy Father. If he judges that he cannot do that, he must pretend to be a sympathiser with your master's way of thinking and gain information about who else in Venice is a danger to the Pope. This information can be used to bring such people to his court for trial. Your master should not talk to this man nor take him into his confidence." Other customers appeared before I could reply and Luigi continued, " I would take the cherries if I were you; they are fresh from the trees today."

I thanked Luigi for the cherries and pondered his words as I walked down to Sir Henry's Residence. As my mind went back to the evening at the *ridotto* I realised with a shock that I had seen the man Luigi was telling me about. He had been talking to Brother Paul when I was busy with Brother Micanzio and the ill-fated plate of pastries. Uneasy in my mind, I wondered whether I should return to Brother Paul and tell him, rather than meeting Mr Bedell as planned. However, as I reached the Residence, there was the tall chaplain at the stairs waiting for me.

Mr Bedell was now able to pronounce Hebrew entirely to the Rabbi's satisfaction and their conversations ranged very widely indeed. At our lesson that day Rabbi Leo and Mr Bedell were having a very enjoyable discussion on a point of Hebrew grammar. I was listening hard, trying my best to take everything in when, to my surprise right in the middle of the discussion and without the slightest warning that he was about to change the subject, the Rabbi suddenly stopped, hesitated very slightly and then said, "Mr Bedell, if Jesus was the Messiah, as you say, surely he should not have come in the strange way that you Christians say he did, leaving his own nation in doubt and suspense and scandalizing so many thousands. He should rather have come in a way that would have made it clear to all men who he was."

"My dear Rabbi Leo," said Mr Bedell at once, "you cannot prescribe laws for God, telling him how he should or should not act. What *we* think of the way in which God sent his Son is not relevant. God acts in accordance with his own will, not ours."

The Rabbi seemed agitated but Mr Bedell pressed on, more animated now and more excited than I had previously seen him in debate. He launched into a tour, as it were, of the Hebrew Scriptures picking out all those that made clear reference to the Messiah's coming, beginning at Genesis and going on through to the prophets. For each one he pointed out how Jesus exactly fulfilled the description given.

All the time the Rabbi listened, pale and silent, but when the Chaplain reached Isaiah chapter fifty-three where the prophet speaks of the Messiah bearing our griefs and sorrows and being wounded for our transgressions, he raised his hand and interrupted, "Dear Mr Bedell, I admit that I have often received more light in the letter and the sense of the Hebrew text from you than from all our Hebrew Rabbis, but on this matter they believe from the traditions of our fathers a different view from this which you are expressing and all over the world this is what our Rabbis teach."

The discussion ended with Mr Bedell kindly urging the Rabbi to reconsider and they returned to their talk about grammar. But the exchange lived on vividly in my memory: the calm but animated chaplain, his kindly face full of zeal and eagerness to persuade the learned Hebrew expert of the true interpretation of the Scriptures which he knew so well, and the agitated Rabbi in his rich oriental robes trembling on the brink of admitting something that seemed to frighten him to the depths of his soul.

***

When I reached my monastery home, however, I found that something had happened which eclipsed in my mind, for the moment at any rate, the strange discussion with Rabbi Leo that I had witnessed. Indeed it almost drove from my mind Luigi's message for Brother Paul.

For some days now Brother Paul had been at the Doge's palace almost day and night. I knew that he was deeply involved with negotiations with representatives from the King of France. This king had undertaken to act on behalf of the Pope over the question of the Interdict under which the Pope had placed Venice. The Pope insisted that there could be no end to the interdict all the while the Jesuit order was still banned from the city by the government. He also still wanted the Venetian government to surrender the two criminal priests to his authority. I knew that Mr Bedell was hoping and praying that Venice would stand firm, and never bow to the Pope. I think perhaps he hoped that the Doge would declare *himself* to be earthly head of the church in Venice rather as King Henry VIII of England had done years ago in his own country. This would make it possible for Venice to have an official reformed church—the first such church in Italy.

After leaving Mr Bedell at Mr Wotton's residence I had run down the *fondamente* to the monastery and dashed into Brother Paul's cell, hardly pausing to knock on the door and I was surprised to find Brother Paul sitting in his chair, looking very tired with Brother Micanzio in attendance. I looked from one to the other in surprise as the atmosphere in the cell was very far from the usual one of scholarly calm. Brother Paul spoke with an effort at maintaining his usual serene attitude as he welcomed me home.

"Come in, Samuele, how is Mr Chaplain Bedell and how is the Rabbi Leo? I trust you are making your usual good progress with Hebrew. It must be time for you to go to the refectory for a meal. The brothers will have almost finished but I have given instructions for something to be left for you. Brother Micanzio and I will join you later on when I have rested a little."

I was concerned to see Brother Paul looking so weak and exhausted, "Is everything well?" I asked, "you are not ill, Brother Paul?"

"Not ill, Samuele, just a little tired. I have had hard work for the Doge today and things have not turned out exactly as we might all have hoped."

I looked anxiously at Brother Micanzio and he smiled at me a little wearily, "All is well, Samuele," he said, "the Pope has lifted the Interdict."

"Yes!" exclaimed Brother Paul, "He has 'lifted' it, not 'revoked' it! At least we have had that satisfaction. And no Jesuits sneaking back into the city either."

"So the war of words has not become a war of swords and blood," I said, remembering Brother Paul's earlier words, but my heart sank as I thought how disappointed Mr Bedell would be with this news. There was to be no clean break with the Pope for Venice after all. This Pope too had been plotting to capture or kill Brother Paul himself. Was he safe now it was all over I wondered? I thought of the strange Roman priest with his long nose. I passed on Luigi's message adding as I did so that I was sure it was he to whom Brother Paul had been speaking at the *ridotto*. He nodded sadly.

"It was he I am sure," he said, "he was very loud in his condemnations of the Pope, so loud in fact that I was worried others would hear him. He seemed very friendly and a little foolish. A spy! Well, well, I am glad I told him nothing of importance."

The difference between lifting the Interdict and revoking it was, I confess, lost on my child's mind but it was important. Not till later did I understand that *revocation* would have assumed that Venice admitted that the Interdict had been deserved. *Raising* or *lifting* allowed the Venetians to say that they never deserved to be placed under an Interdict in the first place.

"All is well," repeated Brother Micanzio, "now go and get your food, Samuele."

Obediently I hurried off to the refectory—I was hungry. Brother Paul always took his bread and water in the refectory after the other monks had dined and Brother Micanzio often accompanied him. I tried to linger over my plate of cold sausage, bread and vegetables, hoping that the two Brothers would arrive before I had finished. It was a hard thing to do, however, for one so hungry and I had almost finished when they appeared. They were still discussing the day's events.

"No bells to be rung and no noisy public absolution with cannons fired off and all the rest of it," Brother Micanzio was saying, "and I hear the Doge had left the Ducal chapel and was with the rest of the Senate in the College before the French Cardinal Joyeuse arrived to pronounce absolution. Whether or not he tried to pronounce it, therefore, there was no representative of the Republic there to receive it. In fact, someone told me he made the sign of the cross secretly under his beretta!"

"Yes, we must be thankful. I have heard that Giovanni Diodati may be with us soon from Geneva," said Brother Paul, "and when he comes I think it is time we had a little *ridotto* of our own, you and I, Micanzio, and Mr Bedell and one or two others. Perhaps Sir Henry could join us too if it could be arranged without putting him in a difficult position. There are people who are concerned to follow the Bible more closely in Venice and they need help."

"At least you can get on with your work now, Brother Paul, without fear of spies and assassins round every corner," I said. Feeling content and full of sausage made me look on the brighter side of things.

"I'm not so sure of that," said Brother Micanzio, "I do not think we can drop our guard just yet. Especially if the plans you are outlining, Brother Paul, come to the ears of the Court of Rome."

***

As it happened it was Sir Henry and Mr Bedell, not Brother Paul who made the next move towards helping the Venetians to learn more of the Bible. I heard about their plans in the following way:

Sir Henry, as a special favour, was allowed to have his own chapel at his residence with services conducted by his own chaplain in English. My English had advanced very quickly thanks to Mr Bedell's lessons with Brother Paul and Brother Micanzio. One Sunday morning I was very surprised when Brother Paul said, "Samuele, I think you should go to morning service at Mr Wotton's chapel today. If anyone asks why you are there tell them I sent you to help you improve your English."

I was pleased with this suggestion. Mr Bedell was now my firm friend and I had often wondered what his preaching was like. Now I would be able to find out. "Thank you, Brother Paul!" I exclaimed with pleasure, "I should like to do that very much indeed. What a pity you can't come too!"

"It is a pity," said Brother Paul, "but you can tell me all about it when you come back."

I washed quickly and tidied myself up ready to go to the ambassador's chapel. I successful evaded the sacristan who was following up a report that a boy from the monastery had been seen by a lay brother engaged in a cherry-stone spitting contest with the fruit-seller boy on the corner. I walked briskly down the *fondamente* to Sir Henry's Residence.

When I arrived at the Residence I wondered where I should go. Had Brother Paul told Mr Bedell I was coming? Would I even be allowed in? I need not have worried, however, because the first person I encountered was my friend Philippo and he soon showed me the way up the grand staircase to the chapel.

"Not that I'd go myself, young Samuele," he said, "however much English I understand. I'd rather go to somewhere colourful like Madonna dell'Orto or San Marziale, not to hear good Mr Bedell going on about sin and death and other cheerful subjects—that is if I went to church at all!"

I slipped into the back of the chapel which was already quite full. Looking round I could see that most of those present were foreigners, not Venetians. However, I could see by their dress that many of them were not English but merchants and others from France and Germany. Dr Despotine was there although why I could not imagine since he spoke not a word of English. We were definitely not the *only* Venetians present, however, and I recognised some noblemen whom I had seen at the *ridotto* at the *Nave d'Oro*. Sir Henry Wotton had special seats at one side for himself and his household and Mr Bedell was standing beside a lectern.

I will pass over the details of the service because it was the sermon that interested me most. Mr Bedell's text was from James chapter 4: "... to him that knoweth to do good, and doeth it not, to him it is sin" and although his voice was not very loud and his manner was gentle rather than forceful, I remember quite clearly what he said. Looking round at his congregation he explained that they were in a privileged position compared to those around them. There were many good things out of the Scripture that they knew that those around them did not know. They knew, for instance, that their good works cannot merit heaven, that images should not be worshipped, that the Pope is not infallible, that there is no need to pray for or to the dead. They knew that only through the merits of the blood of Jesus could they have salvation and that the bread in the Lord's Supper is not miraculously transformed into his actual body. They had therefore great reason to take care in their behaviour. They knew the truth and they must be sure that they never denied it by word or action. He told them also to be very careful how they discussed such issues with those around them. "He that in matters of controversy shall bring meekness to his defence," he said, "shall overcome in the manner that he handles the discussion; and if he brings the truth as well as meekness, he shall prevail at last in the subject under discussion. Give me leave, beloved brethren and sisters," he continued, "to speak my mind freely to you. Too many people make railing and reproachful speeches using hot words and even misrepresent the beliefs of others and caricature them when we should remember that we are called to point out errors, not to disgrace with scolding words those who hold them."

My mind immediately went back to my monastery life. Perhaps the other Servite brothers were not aware of some of the false teachings Mr Bedell mentioned but I was and so was Brother Paul. I could see that Mr Bedell's warning could apply to us. We should be gentle but we should tell the truth also. What should I do when mass was celebrated in the monastery? I revolved these things round in my mind and resolved to speak to Brother Paul and ask his advice.

At the end of the service as I was slipping away, Mr Bedell came up to me. "Samuele," he said in surprise, "what brings you here?"

"Brother Paul sent me," I replied simply but very quietly for even in such a place I began to be conscious there could be someone listening who could make some sort of accusation out of Brother Paul's action in sending me to a Protestant chapel, where by rights I should not go.

"I am glad you are here," said Mr Bedell also speaking very quietly, "and be sure to come next Sunday if your master approves." Then he explained Sir Henry's plan, "We are going to use Italian in the service instead of English so you will understand everything with complete clarity."

***

The next day Brother Paul was very busy and went earlier than usual to his work at the Doge's palace. I was instructed to go along to Sir Henry's residence when I had finished tending my vegetable garden. There I was to await Mr Bedell who was going to visit Rabbi Leo for his regular Hebrew lesson. The matter of monastery mass and my worries over what to do, faded from my mind for the time being and I did not mention it to him.

When I entered the hall of Sir Henry's Residence I saw that Mr Bedell, sitting by the ape Beppo's cage, was deep in conversation with someone—a priest in fact. As I approached I recognised him. It was the long-nosed man that Luigi had told me about, the very man who had engaged Brother Paul in conversation at The *Nave d'Oro* and who had been so loud in his rude remarks about the Pope! Mr Bedell welcomed me with a pat on the head (by now I had begun to think of that as a sign of trouble brewing!) and I listened as they talked in Latin.

The priest was enthusiastic in his praise of Mr Bedell's learning and very interested in the services held in Sir Henry Wotton's chapel. "I would so like to come," he said, "it would be wonderful to hear so learned a man as yourself preach. No doubt you have many of the noble families of Venice in attendance."

I could see at once what he was trying to find out, the sneaking spy! Any minute now he might wheedle out of Mr Bedell the names of some of the Venetians who were running the risk of attending the ambassador's chapel.

"We have quite a large congregation, said Mr Bedell, smiling, "but you would be the first one to join us from among the ranks of those in holy orders."

"Alas, there would be little point in my coming," said the priest, putting on a sad and disappointed face, "I do not understand any English and I am sure your services are not conducted in Latin."

I could see what he was after in a flash. He had heard a rumour that the services were to be in Italian which was not really allowed. Sir Henry's chapel had only permission for English language services and the Pope had complained to the Venetian Senate about even that. This nosy priest was now going to get confirmation from Mr Bedell himself that Italian was to be used. I knew I had to act to stop Mr Bedell giving away what was going on and so, as he began to answer, I reached out to Beppo's cage and flipped open the door. Beppo leapt out, pausing only to bite me viciously on the left arm before racing for the door. Anything that Mr Bedell might have said was drowned by my genuine shriek of pain. We dashed to the door but Beppo was already out on the *fondamente* thoroughly enjoying his freedom.

"You silly boy," cried Mr Bedell in vexation, "go at once and find Henrico, he is the only one apart from Sir Henry who can handle the animal."

I hurried off to the servants quarters to find Henrico but when we returned a few minutes later Sir Henry himself was on the scene together with a very angry Venetian lady, a little girl and a very small boy whom Beppo had evidently bitten as they walked along the *fondamente*. His screams of pain and terror now filled the air. Mr Bedell was trying to calm the lady by apologising for such a dangerous animal being on the loose, the little girl was almost succeeding in her efforts to calm her baby brother and Sir Henry could hardly contain his anger at his chaplain when he heard him not only apologise but make an offer of financial compensation!

The uproar brought Philippo on the scene and as Henrico went off to catch Beppo Sir Henry said to him, "Take this infernal child outside and beat him soundly. He opened Beppo's cage, the animal got loose and now, thanks to my saintly chaplain, I am paying compensation for the damage it has done!"

Chapter 5: (1607) Dr Despotine

Philippo marched me grimly outside and unbuckled his belt, "You stupid boy! What did you do that for?" he asked as he made his preparations for a thorough punishment.

"Because Mr Bedell was talking to your friend the long-nosed priest. He was about to tell him that the chapel services here are to be held in Italian and probably also tell him the names of Venetians who are in the habit of attending," I replied with some heat, "I opened the cage to cause a distraction before he could say what your friend wanted to hear."

"Quick!" urged Philippo, all thought of punishment at once forgotten, "Did you see which way he went?"

But, alas, the priest had made off when the tumult started and I had no idea which way he had gone. "Well I must say, young Samuele," said Philippo with a wry smile, "you certainly acted promptly again there. If you ever change your mind about being a Servite monk when you grow up I can recommend you to a number of people who are looking for an astute young bravo. You'd obviously be an expert at the job in no time—with a little training from me!"

We looked up and down the *fondamente* but there was no sign of the long-nosed priest even in the distance. We reluctantly returned to the Residence where the uproar was now dying down. Sir Henry was still berating poor Mr Bedell for if there was anything he hated it was parting with money unnecessarily. "So I'm 'bound in conscience to make satisfaction' am I? and it's a 'slander to our religion to keep such harmful beasts and not repair the damage' eh! I have as good a conscience as anyone, Bedell, and I hope I have as good a hope of heaven as you," he was saying when we entered, "and I don't see why I shouldn't keep any animal I want to in my own home. Harmful beasts my foot! The child was not seriously injured." On seeing us he broke off and, surprised no doubt by my untearful expression, he enquired, "I hope he has had a thorough beating, Philippo?"

"He has had the punishment he deserves, Sir," said Philippo, "and if you please I need an urgent word with you and Mr Chaplain here."

When all the explanations had been gone into Sir Henry was full of apologies to me if not to Mr Bedell. "And look at your arm!" he exclaimed. In all the excitement I had almost forgotten the painful bite on my arm. "Off you go at once to Bedell's doctor friend—what's his name, Despotine—best person for that sort of thing. Philippo, get him one of those boxes from the kitchen that I had from Count Asdrubale and then take him to Despotine in my gondola."

I was hurried into the gondola, a small wooden box was put into my hands and Philippo began steering the gondola off to Dr Despotine's house at once.

The doctor gave me a thorough examination, tut-tutting as he did so about the ape and how it could have got loose. He cleaned the bite (which hurt), dressed it and told me I should return the following day to have the dressing changed.

When I returned to the monastery, Brother Paul was away at the Doge's Palace and in the quiet of our cell I started to examine the little wooden box I had been given. The lid carried the coat of arms of the Duke of Tuscany and it was sealed with tape and wax. I untied the tape, broke the seal and found inside, packed in thin paper, some little biscuits with a delicious smell. I sniffed them, "honey and almonds!" I thought in delight. I took one out of the box and tried to bite it—it was hard as stone! Thoroughly disappointed I set to work at the tasks Brother Paul had given me to do and was still writing away earnestly when he came in.

"Whatever, have you done to yourself, Samuele!" he exclaimed in alarm when he saw my arm in bandages. He listened gravely to my explanation which was rather rushed. I was by this time more eager to explain my disappointment over the little biscuits than to go over the history of the long-nosed priest and his activities. When I showed him the box of biscuits he smiled and said, "But these are Tuscan biscuits, Samuele, and you are not eating them in the correct way. Take one down to the kitchen and ask for a little bowl of milk. Then dip your biscuit in the milk as you eat it."

I sped off to the kitchen at once, very keen to try the experiment and I found that it produced a most satisfactory result. Once moistened the little biscuits were truly delicious, soft, sweet and fragrant with almonds.

When I went to bed that night the day's excitement filled my mind. Yet oddly enough the things that made me most concerned were not Beppo, Mr Wotton or even the long-nosed priest. Philippo's words, "If you ever change your mind about being a Servite monk when you grow up …" kept running through my head. Was I going to be a monk? Had I made up my mind? As my mother's song washed over me and sleep claimed me I saw the angry but kind face of the lady whose child Beppo had bitten and the little girl who so obviously loved her baby brother. It was a tiny glimpse of something my way of life meant I never experienced—a loving family—and it filled me with a curious kind of longing.

***

The next day Brother Paul again went off to his work in the Doge's palace very early. I went to Luigi's stall as usual and there being no one about I lingered to chat with him. You could always rely on Luigi for news and today was no exception.

"The house that caught fire in the Saliciati of San Lio is still burning," he informed me, "two whole days nearly and still they can't put it out. You can just see the smoke if you look over there," he added pointing. I was about to reply when he sighted some potential customers, "Cherries, all fresh from the trees today, all fresh!" he sang out.

"Have you been to see the fire?" I asked.

"Not myself," answered Luigi but one of my regular customers goes in that direction and said it is very spectacular. Nobody's been hurt but there was something stored in the house that burns well, tarry ropes or something, and they cannot put the blaze out. Crowds of people have been watching it burn."

"I could go in that direction with Brother Micanzio, when he goes to meet Brother Paul this evening," I said, "perhaps we could turn aside and have a look if it is still burning but I suppose it may be out by then."

Since the threats to Brother Paul's life had arisen, someone from the monastery always accompanied him on his walk to and from the Doge's Palace. I knew Brother Micanzio and one of the lay brothers would be going this evening. If I wished I could ask to accompany them.

***

Dr Despotine was in when I called and he greeted me kindly, "Hello, Samuele, have you come for me to look at that horrible bite? Has it been throbbing at all or giving you pain?" When I replied that, though it was a little sore, there was no throbbing and that I had slept well, he was pleased. "Good," he said, "I will not have to bleed you then. I had feared that the bite might go blue and swell; in that case you would need to lose some blood, however, a new dressing should put you right. Now, let me have a look."

As he unwound the bandages, to distract myself lest the unbandaging should be painful, I said, "I saw you at Sir Henry's Wotton's chapel the other day, Dr Despotine. Why do you go there? You do not speak any English do you? only Latin and Italian?"

To my painful surprise Dr Despotine gave the bandage a sudden involuntary jerk at this question and he seemed confused as he answered, "Were you there? Why did *you* go?"

"I went because Brother Paul sent me," I replied adding cautiously, "—to improve my English."

"I see. To improve your English," he said, looking at me strangely and pausing in his unwinding of the bandage, "You are not unaware, though, that only Sir Henry's immediate household are allowed to attend his chapel by order of the Doge and his council and that being found in attendance carries the risk of being handed over to the Inquisition. They have their own ways of finding out why one might risk going. I know that with three members of the State Council of Venice sitting on the Venetian Council of the Inquisition it is difficult for that, er, *holy* body to take the kinds of actions it would wish lately. Nevertheless it is not a wise thing to do for someone who wishes to be careful of their own skin." He recommenced his unwinding.

"But for someone who wished to be careful of their own *soul?*" I asked, "It might be wise then?" The bandage received another painful jerk, "Someone who had the good fortune to be sent by so illustrious a figure as Brother Paul Sarpi, Servite and Theological Councillor to the Venetian Republic in her hour of need, if discovered, would probably receive only a muted warning not to go again," the doctor said after another pause.

I did not consider this an answer to my question so, waiting until he had finished unwinding the bandage lest it receive another jerk, I said, "I can see that I am protected and you are vulnerable and so if you wish you need not speak but if you can trust me I would like to hear your reasons."

Dr Despotine examined my bitten arm in silence for some moments. Then he gently smeared the bite with some ointment and commenced re-bandaging slowly and smoothly. Then, just when I thought that he had decided not to tell me, he said, "You are a trustworthy boy, Samuele, and I can tell you my story:

"I was a good son of the church and I built up a profitable practice here in Venice, treating many of the nobles and senators of the Republic. Yet I became unquiet in my mind. I began to read more widely on religious matters. I read the Diodati Bible. Then my mind was more troubled, as I compared its teachings with those of the Roman church on some issues. Yet I tried to shut my mind to these problems especially since a change of opinion would mean danger for me.

"One day while I was in this undecided state, I was called to the bedside of a very noble Venetian lady. As she was extremely sick and also very rich she had called a conference of doctors around her to decide on a course of treatment. We doctors conferred together and decided among other things that we would take it in turns to be with her so that she would never be without a doctor present. Her condition grew worse, however, and it became known that she was near death. Accordingly her religious advisers, Jesuits and priests of other orders, began to flock to her bedside. It was my turn to be with her one evening—her last as it happened. She was sinking quickly and there was very little I could do for her. By this time Jesuits and other priestly confessors were in continual attendance on her and this evening in particular they did not stop from urging her to leave her money generously to their various orders. Each begged hard for his own order, waving a crucifix before her face and exhorting her to call upon 'Our Lady' who was (they said) the patroness of women in general and high born ladies in particular.

"These were all gathered on one side of the bed. On the other side was a single Capuchin friar. His approach was very different. He spoke to the lady in a few words, exhorting her to put her trust and belief in the Lord Jesus Christ and to look to him for mercy.

"Seeing that the flock of priests with their lighted candles and crucifixes were distressing the dying lady, I asked them as politely as I could to leave and allow the suffering lady to depart this life in some peace. They refused to move, however, or stop their clamour until the lady was dead.

"After the lady had died, it being the middle of the night, the servants asked us all to remove to other rooms in the house until morning and I found myself alone in a room with the Capuchin friar.

We began to talk about the dead lady and the friar was most indignant at the behaviour of the other priests, asking me if I did not think it was a terrible thing that they had continually pestered her to pray to Our Lady without even mentioning Jesus Christ. I was concerned lest he was trying to trap me into saying something indiscreet with which I could be charged later on. I tried to change the subject. He would not be put off, however, and continued in such a manner that I was convinced of his genuineness and opened my heart to him about all that had been troubling me. He too had many doubts about the Roman religion and had been studying the Latin Bible, finding it at variance in many places with what he had been taught. We talked long and earnestly, encouraging one another and comparing our experiences, until the sun rose and we had to be on our way.

"As we parted as daybreak he warmly invited me to visit him in his cell to continue our conversation. As soon as he was out of sight my doubts about him returned. He seemed to be exactly what he was—a Bible believer in a friar's habit—but could I be sure? If I did visit him would I be walking into a trap? I consulted friends whom I knew I could trust. They were sure it was a trap and so I have never seen that friar from that day to this. But the conversation I had with him made me sure of one thing. The Bible *is* right. It *is* the only true guide. Whatever priests, friars and Popes may teach, if it does not accord with the Bible we have *no* warrant to believe it. From that day I date my conversion. I had come to love the real Jesus Christ, not the dead figure on a crucifix but the living Saviour who spoke to me, not in the words of a priest or confessor, but in the words of the Bible. From that day I knew I could not push my belief to the back of my mind and try to deny it. As much as possible I withdrew from public society. I kept away from contact with people who could ask me dangerous questions. Not long after that I met Mr Bedell and it was obvious at once that he loved the real Saviour too. What a help he has been to me! That is why I take the risk."

For the first time in my life I fully understood what a privileged position I was in. Because of Brother Paul, I was running almost no risk in going to the English chapel. No one would ask *me* dangerous questions. No one would question my beliefs. No one that is except myself! I began to realise just how unsure I was about everything I had been taught. Thanks to Brother Paul I knew a lot of things—in theory—but how much did I know in practice? The thing that puzzled me most was that Mr Bedell and Dr Despotine seemed to *know* the Saviour. I just knew *about* him.

***

Brother Micanzio and I were late setting off to meet Brother Paul that evening; something had delayed him at the monastery. By walking briskly we could make up the necessary time but there was no chance of diverting to the Saliciati of San Lio to see the fire.

"You can come with me in any case," said Brother Micanzio, "we can pop over to see the blaze on the way back. I'd quite like to see it myself; everyone says it is very spectacular."

Together with the lay brother Marino we walked quickly through the *Merceria* and on to St. Mark's and the Doge's Palace. When we arrived Brother Paul was with his friend Signor Alessandro Malpietro who often walked home with him now that there was so much danger. He was an old man of grave and learned character whose conversation Brother Paul always enjoyed. It was starting to get dark by the time we left St. Mark's and walked to the *Merceria*. Here we stopped and Brother Micanzio explained about the fire in the Saliciati of San Lio.

"Go by all means," said Brother Paul at once, "Alessandro and I will continue home with Brother Marino and you can join us later and tell us all about it. I've half a mind to come and see it too but today has been busy and I have much work still to do. Samuele here deserves a little outing: I have not had a complaint about him from the sacristan for about a week!"

Brother Micanzio and I hurried off to the middle of the street leading from San Lio to the *Merceria* where the house fire was. The blaze had died down somewhat but there was still quite a crowd watching. People from the nearby houses were carrying water to throw on the fire lest it spread to their own. They were beginning to win the battle but it was slow work and to tell the truth a crowd of spectators like ourselves got in the way of their efforts. We stayed for quite a while watching the sparks and occasional flashes of flame light up the darkening October sky.

The scene was so picturesque with the firelight reflected in the shimmering water that I said to Brother Micanzio, "I'm sure Brother Paul would be sorry to have missed this sight; shall we run and catch him up and bring him back to see it?"

Brother Micanzio assented and we began to go quickly back through the *Merceria* towards the San Fosca square. The streets were unusually empty that evening because almost everyone in the area had crowded into the San Luigi theatre to witness a new *opera con intermezzi*. As we crossed the square we became aware of some sort of commotion on the far side of the La Guerre bridge near the Servite monastery. People were running and shouting and a gondola was moving away from the bridge down the canal at top speed. Women were screaming from the open windows of the upper floor of a house overlooking the bridge. Brother Micanzio suddenly exclaimed, "Brother Paul!" and started to charge across the square. I followed at a run; my heart in my mouth. Dashing towards us in the opposite direction out of the knot of people came Brother Marino.

"What is it, what is it?" shouted Brother Micanzio.

"Brother Paul has been stabbed to death," gasped Brother Marino, "Come quickly, oh, come quickly, whatever shall we do?"

Chapter 6: (1607) The Stiletto

Brother Paul stabbed to death! A heavy feeling came over me as if I could not move or hear properly what was being said. Stabbed to death! Brother Micanzio was speaking to me but I could not hear the words. To death! Brother Paul stabbed to death! Brother Micanzio was shaking me by the shoulder. His words came into focus, "Samuele," he was saying, "Samuele, run quickly to the monastery and fetch Brother Santorio the monastery physician; bring him to the bridge, go quickly, now, do you hear me? Now!"

I suddenly came to life; I sped off across the bridge; I pushed my way through the people; I burst into the monastery shouting as I dashed through the door, "Brother Santorio! Brother Santorio! Brother Santorio! Where are you? Come quickly, oh, come quickly!"

Brother Santorio appeared in the doorway of his cell on the floor above, "Samuele, whatever is the matter? Why are you shouting and making such a disturbance? How often must you be told of the need for a quiet demeanour? Less noise, please."

I dashed up the stairs, "Oh, come quickly," I gasped, "Brother Paul is dead—stabbed to death at the foot of the stairs by the bridge! Come at once!"

Brother Santorio needed no further urging. Although he must have been as shocked as I, he preserved a calm exterior. Methodically but quickly he reached for a bag and filled it with dressings and other medical equipment. I watched him gather his things. To death! Stabbed to death! Brother Paul! He descended the stairs with me and we started off towards the foot of the bridge. I was not walking, I was not running, I was drifting, floating. Brother Paul stabbed to death! To death! Brother Paul!

At the bridge the commotion had increased. Brother Santorio made his way through the crowd, saying loudly and calmly, "I am the monastery physician, let me through, please," as he shouldered people aside to reach the centre of the hubbub. I stumbled along in his wake; the terrible words hammering in my brain: stabbed to death! To death! Stabbed to death!

Signor Malpietro had managed to move Brother Paul to the house of a barber surgeon which was just by the bridge. As Brother Santorio and I neared the house I could see Brother Micanzio standing outside looking for us. He waved at Brother Santorio to show him where to come. I rushed up to him, "Is it true? It's not true, is it, is it? Not to death? Not stabbed to death, not Brother Paul?"

Brother Micanzio looked down at me, "He still lives," he said, "but he is gravely wounded. In here please, Brother Santorio. The barber has begun dressing his wounds and has staunched much of the flow of blood."

I must have fainted then. I remember nothing else until I found myself lying on a couch in the barber's house with old Signor Malpietro peering down at me anxiously with his short-sighted eyes. I was bewildered. What had happened? Where was I? Then I remembered: stabbed to death! But not dead! Brother Paul. Where was he? I tried to ask Signor Malpietro but my throat was dry and no words would come. The barber's wife appeared. "Poor child!" she said, "Has he woken? Good! Here, drink this, little one. You have had a terrible shock; it will help you feel better."

Something warming, strong and bitter-sweet trickled down my throat. My head cleared and I tried to jump up, "Where is Brother Paul! What has been happening?" I asked as I fell back onto the couch.

"They have carried him to the monastery. Brother Micanzio asked me to stay with you just until you were feeling better and to tell you that Brother Paul is still alive, though gravely ill from loss of blood and from his wounds."

I sat up carefully but slithered down again, "But who wounded him, Signor Malpietro? How did it happen?"

"We were at the last steps leading down from the bridge," said Signor Malpietro, "when a man rushed to the right hand side where Brother Paul was. He took aim at the Brother's face with a stiletto crying as he did so, 'Dog! Traitor!' I saw the stiletto fixed near the poor Brother's ear by his nose and the man standing by him. I turned back and pushed myself between the two of them and pulled the stiletto out. More men had appeared by this time and one of them held down Brother Marino so that he could not help Brother Paul. I shouted, 'Ah! You traitorous dogs, is this the way you assassinate men?' People had heard the commotion by this time and were running to the spot so I shouted, 'After them, boys!' At this the men stabbed the poor Brother many times and then ran off towards the church of San Marziale and jumped into a gondola."

"Brother Paul is at the monastery now you say? How did he get there? I should be with him!" I said, trying once more to get up from the couch and making a slightly better job of it.

"After his wounds had been dressed to stop the flow of blood Brothers Santorio and Micanzio put him in a gondola to carry him to the monastery stairs," said Signor Malpietro, "and I am as anxious as you to be with him."

"Who were they, these assassins?" I asked, "did you get a good look at them?"

"I have no idea who they were," replied the old man, "The first one was a tallish, square built man with a red face and a red beard but my eyes are weak and I can tell you nothing about the others, not even what they were wearing. No doubt the women who were watching from the windows by the bridge had a clearer view of them and will report what they saw to the authorities."

"The Doge will be furious," I said, thinking things out, "his great theological councillor wounded just when he needs him."

"Even if the Brother lives, he will be too sick to give council for a long time," he replied.

"If he lives!" I cried, "O surely, surely he will live, Signor Malpietro. God will not let him die; not now!" In a flash Mr Bedell's words came to my mind: *God, who disposes of all things, and who is watching over his servant, Brother Paul, will answer our prayers if we pray to him.* I sat up again and turned to Signor Malpietro, "We must pray for him," I said.

"Yes, of course," replied the old man reverently, "We will go to the monastery chapel and light many candles."

"No!" I exclaimed, "We must pray now!"

"Well if you wish," said the old man doubtfully looking round for a crucifix or a statue of Mary on which to fix his gaze, "I suppose we could," and he began to repeat the familiar Latin words, "*Pater noster qui es in caelis ...*"

"No, no!" I interrupted, "Not like that!" and, to the old man's astonishment, I began, "Dear Father in heaven, please watch over Brother Paul now and save his life. Our city needs him more than ever in these days. We all need him and I need him too. Please take care of him and do not let him die now. In Jesus' name, Amen."

Signor Malpietro was too astounded to say, "Amen." Perhaps he thought that my fainting fit had turned my head and so did not rebuke my strange behaviour. At any rate he said no more but helped me to stand and together we made our way out of the barber's house towards the monastery.

**

Brother Paul hovered between life and death for many days. News of the attempt on his life spread quickly through the city and soon the whole population was overwhelmed with grief and anger. When a rumour got about that the assassins were hiding in the house of the Papal Nuncio it took an order of the Venetian Senate to save the house from being pulled to pieces by angry Venetians. The Senators themselves were distressed beyond measure, the more so because, besides Sir Henry's warning, they had received a warning from the Venetian ambassador at Rome that a strong conspiracy was on foot against the Servite Brother.

Brother Micanzio was continually reproaching himself also for having gone off with me to see the fire. "I should have stayed!" he kept saying, "then this would never have happened." When I blamed myself for asking to go he replied, "No, no, you are just a child I should never have agreed to your request; my place was at the Brother's side."

The Council of Ten, Venice's highest authority, had met at once during the night of the attack to discuss the situation. They immediately took statements from everyone who had witnessed the attempt on Brother Paul's life. When, in due course it became known that the attackers had escaped to Rome they took steps to collate all the evidence from their ambassador there with that of the witnesses who were at the scene. They offered rewards for anyone who captured those responsible. At the same time they issued a notice proclaiming special protection to Brother Paul in the future, making it quite clear that anyone making a further attempt on his life could be expected to be hounded to the ends of the earth. They offered huge sums of money to anyone who brought future would-be assassins to justice, dead or alive. This scarcely needed doing, however, as every citizen of Venice was up in arms. That the Pope was at the bottom of the attempt infuriated them and increased the hostility of average Venetians to the Pope in particular and his court at Rome in general almost to fever pitch.

While all the investigations and recriminations were going on, Brother Paul lay in his cell, conscious, but only able to speak with difficulty because of the wound in his face. His bony body had received fifteen dagger wounds and the loss of blood left him dangerously weak. Small and thin as he was, he seemed like a pale skeleton, unable to move even to raise his hand. Round him was grouped the most expensive and experienced team of doctors ever assembled in Venice.

I say "team" but in fact there was little of team-work in their efforts. The Senate had spared no expense. Dr Acquapendente, the most senior medical doctor in Italy, if not the world, was rushed in from Padua and alongside him every other distinguished medical man that could be found was ranged. Poor Brother Paul himself would have much preferred to be left in the care of a young Doctor, Alviso Ragosa, who was very gentle and laid only the lightest of bindings on the wounds but this was not to be heard of. Instead the poor brother had to suffer the continuous wrangling of the various experts each of whom was sure that a different course should be followed.

"Treatment for a poisoned wound is urgently necessary!" proclaimed one, for instance, as I sat listening anxiously in our cell, "poison is clearly indicated by the fact that the edge of the face wound has turned black."

"No, no, with respect," clamoured another, "it is quite obvious that the blackness has another cause. We all know that this is exactly what happens when treacle is prescribed incorrectly. I warned you, my colleges, that treacle was a mistake—and now see the results!"

The continued wrangling caused the patient much distress but there was no respite from their advice or treatment. They cut and probed his wounded face deeply since it contained splinters of broken bone from the entry of the stiletto. Nevertheless they failed to find them all since, when the wound began to heal, inflamed abscesses formed through which the remaining splinters made their way out. Still, perhaps in spite of the learned doctors' treatments, Brother Paul slowly began to recover. The Senate and indeed the whole population of Venice, watched his recovery daily and with anxiety.

Chapter 7: (1608) The Hebrew Bible

For a long time I was too anxious about Brother Paul to leave the monastery. When he began to make some progress I relaxed a little but I was puzzled as to what I should do. The cell was now thronged with doctors at all hours of the day and night. Although I wished to talk to Brother Paul about the things that had been bothering me before the stabbing I could not have done so even if he had been well enough. I was left on my own to puzzle things out. Why did I sometimes feel as if I needed a family in spite of Brother Paul's love, kindness and care for me? Did I want to be a Servite? What should my attitude be to things I knew were wrong—things where the teaching and practice of the church were contradicted by what the Bible said? If I really wanted to follow the Bible, could I always just rely on Brother Paul's protection, knowing that no one would question my beliefs if he stood up for me? Most important of all, how could I know the living Saviour, the Christ of the Bible? Mr Bedell knew Him, Dr Despotine knew Him, perhaps Brother Paul knew Him.

All at once it occurred to me that the best thing I could do would be to go to Sir Henry's chapel. I would be quite safe, no one would interfere, especially after what had just happened, and Brother Paul was well enough for me to leave the monastery. I could not tell him where I was going in front of all the doctors but if I went out on Sunday morning he would surely guess where I was off to.

Accordingly, I set off for Sir Henry's residence the next Sunday. The chapel was much more full than it had been the previous time I had been there and there were many more Italian families present. I guessed that it was not only the fact that the service was now in Italian that had drawn them in. The stabbing of Brother Paul by the Pope's agents had caused a reaction in Venice that would have made it very difficult for the Venetian Inquisition to act against them. For this reason they had found the courage to come. Many who were waverers, as Dr Despotine had once been, were now brave enough to risk coming to a place which was not strictly allowed. Sitting at the back of this little throng of Venetian nobility and foreign merchants I was at the very limit of Mr Bedell's weak voice. Nevertheless, I heard much that encouraged me and I began to realise that not only could I pray for Brother Paul, I could pray for help to resolve my own difficulties also. As I sat there at the back of the chapel therefore I raised a silent prayer for help in my perplexed situation, never doubting that it would be heard just as my prayer for the life of my beloved Brother Paul had been.

After the service as I was leaving, Mr Bedell again came up to me, "Samuele," he said, "how is dear Brother Paul today?"

"He improves every day now," I replied, "the doctors are making him change his eating habits too: he has to have good broth as well as bread and fruit—and medicine."

"I am so glad," said the chaplain, "how good God is to us to spare his life in answer to our prayers. And what about you, Samuele, how are you? All this must have been so shocking for you."

I looked up at the kind face of the tall Chaplain and suddenly felt immensely small and lonely. "Yes," I began, "you see, Brother Paul is all I have in the world. I would have no family to go to if, if ..." to my horror tears were welling up in my eyes. I blinked and struggled.

The chaplain, seeing my difficulty, put his hand on my shoulder and said, "come along to my study, Samuele, I have something there that I have been wanting to show you for some time but Brother Paul's troubles have put everything else out of my mind."

He led the way to his study and waved me to a chair, "Now, look at this!" he said with the air of someone showing off a very great treasure. He lifted three large heavy brown volumes from a shelf and put them on the table before me. "Open it," he said encouragingly as if it was a treasure chest—which in a way it was. I turned the leaves and gasped in astonishment and delight. The book was the most beautiful manuscript of the Hebrew Old Testament I have ever seen. The Hebrew characters were very large and clear—astonishingly easy to read—and the pages were of thick durable parchment. In the wide margins were notes written in small Hebrew characters—I guessed by Rabbis who had owned the book in the past. No doubt it had passed through many such hands as it was obviously very old indeed. "This is beautiful!" I exclaimed, "How easy it is to read! It must be so old. Wherever did you get it?"

"Rabbi Leo helped me get it," said Mr Bedell, "he knew it was possibly for sale. I paid a huge sum for it. Can you imagine? It was priced at so much per ounce!"

I looked at the three weighty tomes, trying to calculate in my mind what they would weigh. I could understand that to Mr Bedell such a book would be beyond price.

"The pointing looks very exact," I commented looking at the little dots which stand for vowels in Hebrew, "and it must be very old."

Mr Bedell rubbed his hands in pleasure at my remark, "exactly!" he said, "therein lies a great part of its inestimable value."

Together we spent a happy hour gloating over the treasure and I quite forgot my sadness so it was a jolt when Mr Bedell suddenly said, "so you are an orphan, Samuele. I grew up among orphans, you know."

"How was that?" I asked, "you were not an orphan yourself were you?"

"No," he replied, "I had very kind parents and that is why I grew up among orphans! My father and mother were not very rich but being yeoman farmers they had enough. They could not bear to see a child in distress. Throughout my childhood there were always poor children living with us in the house, who had lost their parents and had nowhere else to go. My parents raised them as their own until they were old enough to earn a living for themselves. That is why I feel for your distress. Some of my best childhood friends were orphans: I grew up with them and I witnessed their sorrows and difficulties."

"Brother Paul has been so good to me," I said, "better than father and mother and until recently I honestly did not miss having a family to belong to. I cannot remember my mother at all except for part of a little song that she used to sing me and my memories of my father are very vague: I think that helped me feel settled in the monastery. I don't know why, but just recently things have happened that make me realise that I do not want to be a Servite monk when I am older (although what else I could be I cannot imagine) and when I see families together, helping one another or just playing I sometimes long for a mother to love me and brothers and sisters to romp and play with."

"Have you spoken to Brother Paul of all this?" asked the chaplain kindly.

"I was just about to, and some other things that bother me too," I replied, "but then came the stabbing. I cannot speak to him now because there are always doctors around him and such things need to be discussed when we are alone."

Mr Bedell nodded, "Of course," he said, "then you must just be very patient. It will not be long now I am sure before Brother Paul is completely well again and the doctors will pack their bags and go. Then you will be able to have a good talk to him. He is very wise and will understand how you feel."

"Do you think so?" I asked, "He was an orphan himself and yet he loves the monastery life. He does not seem to long for anything else."

"I am absolutely sure he will understand," replied the chaplain, "Just be patient, Samuele."

***

Soon Brother Paul began to be well enough to get out of bed. Still the doctors never left him unattended but they began to relax, taking it in turns to watch over him. The Senate still demanded a daily report on Brother Paul's condition but Dr Acquapendente returned to Padua, taking with him a silver cup engraved with the arms of St. Mark, a rich collar and a medal—the gifts of the grateful Venetian Senate. Some of the other senior Doctors were able to resume their usual practices and were also rewarded.

Although he had been persuaded to alter his very sparse diet, Brother Paul still sent me out to Luigi for daily fruit which he considered very necessary to health. Imagine my joy, then, when returning from Luigi's stall with some ripe pears I discovered that the doctor left in charge now was none other than Dr Despotine! Brother Paul seemed to improve greatly just from having Dr Despotine with him and I was so pleased to see him I could have hugged him! He greeted me with great affection and at once enquired after my left arm.

"Let me have a good look, young man," he said with a twinkle in his eye, "of course it may be necessary to bleed you!"

I laughed as I bared my arm for his inspection, "I don't think so, you can hardly see the mark now, look!"

"Hum," said the doctor with mock gravity as he studied the little scar, "nevertheless, Brother Paul is a good advertisement for the procedure; the villains that stabbed him let nearly all the blood in his body—and look at him now, almost fully recovered and much less of a bag of bones than he was before the phlebotomy!"

I was about to say that the enforced change of diet had more to do with that but Brother Paul cut in firmly, "No more blood-letting here, thank you, good Doctor. I am much less convinced of its efficacy than you."

We all laughed together and I think Brother Paul felt more happy and relaxed than he had done at any time since the attack.

"Can you get them to put you on duty often, Despotine?" he asked, "If I must be still surrounded with doctors."

"I think it was only through the offices of Mr Bedell and Sir Henry that I am here at all," replied the doctor, "but the good news is that I think they are so pleased with your progress that they will tell the Senate you no longer need constant attendance soon, especially once you are walking about more easily."

Brother Paul's response was to stand up at once from his couch, "walking takes practice," he said, "come, Samuele, Despotine, give me some help to get moving!"

Together we helped him walk round the cell and then out into the monastery. Here the other brothers hailed his presence with great delight. However, he became tired after a while and we returned to the cell.

"This stabbing has really set back our plans," said Brother Paul as he rested on his bed, "we were all set to begin our own little *ridotto* where we could make plans for progress in religion in Venice—Mr Bedell, Brother Micanzio and now also Archbishop Marco Antonio de Dominis of Split. He has retired to Venice because the Pope does not like his views of the church. I have a feeling that Sir Henry would come too if he could. But nothing like this can happen while I am in this condition, surrounded by meddling doctors—I beg your pardon, Despotine."

"Diodati of Lucca is the man we really need to help us," said Dr Despotine, "but he is not yet here. Perhaps by the time you are fully recovered he will have arrived."

"The Senate are pressing me to leave the monastery and come and live in a house they wish to provide for me in St Mark's," said Brother Paul, "they do not wish me to endanger myself again by walking across the city each day but I have lived here among the Brothers for so long I cannot change now. I told them I would stay here. So do you know what they are going to do? They are sending workmen tomorrow to make a start on making a little building communicating only with my cell here which will have a corridor to some stairs down to the canal where I must go in a gondola to St. Marks! If they have their way I will never walk again! I told them I will go in a gondola but only as far as the *Merceria*. I *must* walk from there for my health and it is completely open and public with no narrow alleys from that point."

Chapter 8: (1608) Speak Lord!

Over the next few weeks Brother Paul improved so much that the doctors were ready to relax their vigil. Dr Despotine came again but Brother Paul was soon on his feet and the happy time came when the doctors' attentions were reduced to a daily and then a weekly visit. Brother Paul was easily tired at first. A Servite Brother, Antonio, was appointed his official amanuensis and I was glad to relieve Brother Paul of any troubles by running every errand I could for him. Writing particularly tired Brother Paul now so being able to dictate to Brother Antonio was very useful. However, somehow Brother Antonio's presence made Brother Paul uneasy and he often dismissed him and asked me to write for him. I was quite happy when Brother Antonio obtained leave to go on a visit to Padua to study and visit friends and I cheerfully undertook to take his place. Not wishing to tire Brother Paul further with my own difficulties I worked away for him, writing from dictation and copying, and I kept my peace about the things that were bothering me, thinking to wait until he was completely back to normal.

Once day, out of the corner of my eye, I noticed him watching me from the security of his paper "castle" as I copied a letter for him, my head bent over my work.

"So what is it, Samuele?" he asked, "What's been bothering you all this time? This is more than just trouble with the sacristan for some misbehaviour or other. Come here and sit with me in the castle and tell me all about it."

I suppose I should have known that I could not keep my worries from him, that somehow he would know that all was not well in my mind, conscience even, and I ran joyfully over to his side. Carefully he admitted me to his paper protection, rearranging the sheets to shield us both, and I settled down beside my dear friend, full of relief that I could confide in him at last.

He took off the spectacles that he had needed since the stabbing, folding them carefully and laying them aside, and I looked up at his face, now scarred and distorted. There was a little black patch which he still wore over the place where the stiletto had pierced him. His face though kind and thoughtful, was as inscrutable as ever.

"Mr Bedell said I should tell you all the things that are buzzing about in my head," I said as I settled down beside him, "but now that you ask me I don't know how to start."

"Well just sit here for a little while while I finish this page then," said Brother Paul picking up the spectacles again, "you can sort out your mind while I work."

I watched the steady movement of his pen, neat and precise as his thoughts, and it helped me to gather the ideas that were churning in my mind. At length I ventured, "What will happen to me when I grow up, Brother Paul?"

"What would you like to happen?" he asked, putting down his pen again carefully.

"I don't know what I want," I said uncertainly, "but I do know that I don't think I want to be a Servite."

If he was offended, or thought me ungrateful he did not show it. Instead he said, "Well, to know what you do *not* want is a start. Have you any idea *why* you do not want to be a Servite brother?"

I thought hard, trying to get vague things into focus, "You have taught me things—and Mr Bedell has taught me things—which I think would make my life very difficult in a Servite monastery."

"That is true. But then, life is always difficult and you will have to consider what you would do about those 'things' even if you were not a Servite."

This was something I had not thought of before. I suppose I could not see beyond spending my life in the monastery. "How do *you* manage?" I asked suddenly, "You know that the Bible teaches that we should only worship God yet the Servites are dedicated to worshipping Mary also and praying to her."

Brother Paul's battered face did not change its tranquil expression, "I work away quietly always trying to improve things in the church. Many years ago I was in Rome. I will not tell you everything that happened to me there but I was able to petition successfully for some changes—reversions to earlier practices—in what the Servites recite in their chapels," he said, "my petition succeeded. For instance, we need no longer say the *Salve Regina,* which as you know is a prayer to Mary. It is good that the Servites no longer say this. I work on patiently hoping that one day *all* things that are not pleasing to God will be purged out of His church in this way. When I officiate in the chapel now I miss out parts of the Canon where prayers are offered to the saints. I never pray to saints myself and when we come to those parts of the office that go against my conscience I do not join in."

He paused here as if weighing something up in his mind. Then he said, "I cannot tell you now about some of the other things that cross my mind. How I am tempted to wonder about the very nature of religion itself ..." then he gave himself an impatient little shake, "no, Samuele, now is not the time for such discussion. I have been praying that God will guide you in life because I can see that you are a very thoughtful child. I too for some time have had no desire that you should become a Servite. Now I can see some answers to my prayers in that you yourself do not desire this." Then his poor injured face brightened and he said, "It may be that in a little while there will be great changes in the church here in Venice and perhaps in the whole world. It may be that we can go back to the ancient and pure state of the church where the things that are beginning to offend your conscience are done away with. Be patient a little longer, Samuele, and it may be that things will get better. Already there is much good preaching now in Venice and I have news that Signor Diodati of Lucca is well on his way here and we will be holding our long awaited *ridotto* soon."

There were so many things in all this that surprised me that I hardly knew where to start, "You do not want me to become a Servite?" I asked, "I always thought that you considered that, because I am able to learn languages so quickly, I would become a Servite scholar like you one day."

"When you were very small I thought so," replied Brother Paul, "but not now. I realise that God must have some other plan for you. But all this is only part of what bothers you isn't it? There is something deeper stirring up your mind."

I nodded. "I suppose so. You see I noticed something different in the way Mr Bedell prays—in the way he thinks about God. To him Jesus Christ is a friend. When he is in trouble or perplexed about something it is as natural for him to pray—just in ordinary words—as it would be for me to talk to you—Dr Despotine is the same."

Brother Paul paused again; weighing his thoughts with care. Then he said something which seemed strangely irrelevant, "Have you ever considered your own name or why you have it?"

"My name!" I exclaimed in surprise, "what has my name got to do with it?"

"You are named after someone, deliberately named by your father, after someone whose course of life he wished you to follow. This was the course of life upon which he set you when he brought you here to me."

I was staggered—what did he mean? "Samuele," I said, "my name is Samuele ... what do you mean, Brother Paul?"

"I think God is calling you," he replied to my immense astonishment, "these questions, these doubts, are not arising in your mind of your own accord but because God is dealing with you. He is arranging the very circumstances of your life for His purposes—which are good towards you. Samuele, my advice to you is: pray to God in just the way you have described to me, and say to him, 'Speak, Lord, for Thy servant heareth.'"

Now I understood, "Like Samuel in the Bible you mean?" I replied.

"Exactly," he said, "like Samuel, after whom you are named."

I pondered his words as I lay trying to sleep in the dark later that evening. So my father had intended that I should be a servant to a priest as Samuel was as a child! He had had this intention from the time of my birth and named me Samuele for that reason. In the Bible story Samuel had served Eli the old priest. How good that my Eli was Brother Paul! I remembered his advice. As the quiet lapping of the little waves on the canal outside the shuttered window turned itself into my mother's song I drifted towards sleep and whispered, "Speak, Lord, for Thy servant heareth."

***

Brother Paul was quite correct to say that there was now good preaching to be heard in Venice and not only in Sir Henry's chapel. There were several brothers of various orders, who had come to a clear understanding of what the Bible taught and were now not afraid to tell the people. They were very frustrated that the Italian translation by Signor Diodati was prohibited in Venice.

I was in the habit now of slipping out of Sir Henry's residence as soon as the service was over in the chapel and running as fast as I could to the church where Brother Micanzio was preaching so as to hear his sermon, or part of it at any rate, as well as Mr Bedell's. I think since I had begun to pray for God to speak to me that I made an extra effort to hear more sermons, supposing that perhaps God would speak to me through them.

Next Sunday morning the crowd in the church of St. Lorenzo was so large that I had a job to get in at all as a late-comer and I only just managed to squeeze through the door. Inside the atmosphere was tense with excitement. The crowd was standing listening very quietly. They had to be quiet if they were to be able to hear but it was not a drowsy silence; it was the silence of people straining to catch every word and drink in everything they heard. There seemed to be something in their souls that thirsted to hear. Brother Micanzio was preaching on the verse in Matthew chapter thirteen where the Lord Jesus challenges his hearers with the words, "Have ye not read?" and it was this little phrase that he was talking about as I pushed into the building between a very fat man in green stockings and a neatly dressed old lady who was listening with such intensity that she had cupped her hands behind her ears pushing them forward to catch every word.

"You all know the scornful words of Pontius Pilate, *what is truth?*" Brother Micanzio was saying, "Pilate thought there was no answer to this question and so it did not matter what evil he did, what injustice he committed. Well, I stand here today and I can tell you that Pilate was *wrong*. I have found that there *is* an answer to his question. I have been searching for truth for many years and I have found it. I can tell you all where you can find it too—here in this book," and before the astonished gaze of the congregation he pulled out one of Diodati's New Testaments in Italian and held it up for everyone to see. "But," he continued, returning the little book to his pocket, "the book is prohibited!" He paused and looked round before continuing slowly and deliberately, "If the Saviour were to ask the question *have ye not read?* to us all here today, the only thing we would be able to say would be: 'no, we are *forbidden—forbidden* to do so.'" These last words were thundered out and a murmur—no more—of approval ran through the congregation. The old lady, obviously short-sighted as well as deaf, whispered across my head to the man in green stockings, "What was he holding out?"

"A Bible," he mouthed back, "an Italian Bible."

Chapter 9: (1608) Another Ridotto

It was when the theologian from Geneva, Dr Diodati of Lucca, finally arrived in Venice that the longed-for meetings took place. I suppose I had imagined that Dr Diodati, Mr Bedell, the Archbishop of Split in Dalmatia and even Sir Henry Wotton would just come to Brother Paul's cell to meet with him and with Brother Micanzio. Of course that was out of the question. Instead the *ridotto* was arranged to be held in a certain amount of secrecy in a linen warehouse belonging to a Signor Cicchinelli who set aside a room for the use of Sir Henry's friends one evening after dark. I had been with Mr Bedell that day (Brother Antonio had returned to his duties and I was spending much of my time with the chaplain) and he was in a mood of very high hope when we set off together for the warehouse. He strode along on his long legs at such a rate that I could only just keep up. That afternoon he had been hard at work noting down three steps which he was going to present to the assembled *ridotto*. These steps were the plan which he thought would lead to the Reformed religion taking root in Venice. I told him about Brother Micanzio's sermon that I had heard on Sunday. "He actually held up a Diodati Bible," I said, "and told the people they should read it because it was the truth."

"It is a wonderful thing," answered the chaplain as he strode along, "how many of the nobles of Venice—some senators even—are on the side of Brother Micanzio on this matter. Did you notice what kind of people were listening, Samuele?"

"All kinds," I answered, "there were definitely some nobles and merchants there in smart clothes and I recognised some senators."

"Your Senate, with its excellent system of secret voting, protects senators since no one can know who has voted for any measure. If they vote for reformation they can do so in safety," he enthused, "each one can obey his conscience."

"What is Signor Diodati like?" I asked, knowing that the great translator had been staying at Sir Henry's Residence.

"I only met him yesterday," replied the chaplain, "but I must say we became friends at once. He is obviously an excellent scholar (his translation of the Bible makes that plain) also very logical and clear thinking and yet he is so modest—and he has a sense of humour."

"I am sure you must have shown him your wonderful Hebrew Bible," I said, thinking how such a man would appreciate Mr Bedell's treasure.

"I could hardly tear him away from it," replied the Chaplain, "he is full of ideas too for what could happen here in Venice and very willing indeed to do anything he can to help us. Did you know? he has brought some young members of his family with him from Geneva; a cousin and a nephew who is not much older than yourself!"

When we reached the linen warehouse other people were also arriving. Gondolas were moored up at the stairs and Brother Paul and Brother Micanzio were walking together across the bridge with Brother Antonio following behind them. I could see Dr Despotine hurrying towards the warehouse and who was the very fat man getting out of a gondola? Surely he must be the former Archbishop De Domini.

Signor Cicchinelli had appointed us a very cosy room tucked away at the back of the warehouse where he usually did his accounts. I slipped into a corner near Mr Bedell and took stock of my surroundings. The members of the *ridotto* were talking quietly among themselves as Signor Diodati had not yet arrived. Brother Paul welcomed Mr Bedell and gave me a cheerful wink. Brother Micanzio was talking to the fat man who I had noticed getting out of the gondola. I had been correct in assuming he was the former Archbishop of Split and it was not long before he and Brother Paul were discussing one of Brother Paul's favourite topics: the tides and what caused them.

"The tides are caused by the moon, Father Paul," the archbishop was saying, "which attracts all the water on the surface of the earth towards it. I have made a detailed study of the whole subject," Brother Paul was listening politely but I knew that he had worked with this problem with his friend Galileo and that they both considered the movement of the earth itself to be responsible. He winced too at being addressed as "Father Paul" although his position as head of the Venetian Servites meant he was entitled to this. It was typical of his modest character that he preferred to retain his old title "brother." The archbishop was just embarking on an explanation of the effect of the moon on the tides by means of a diagram when Signor Cicchinelli announced the arrival of Dr Diodati. I was eager to see what he would be like; would he bring his young relatives along?

Dr Diodati and the two young men had arrived in a gondola steered by Philippo. He turned out to be a very energetic man of about thirty with a thin but smiling face and a large nose; the sort of man who is used to getting things done and getting them done quickly. His cousin Geronimo, considerably older than I, was with him. His nephew, Carlo, who was only a couple of years older than myself had obviously found the journey from Geneva through territory which was hostile to followers of the Reformed religion very exciting.

"We were disguised as silk merchants for part of the way," he explained to me gleefully when we had been introduced and I asked politely about his journey to Venice, "and I learnt all about silk, where it comes from, how you can tell what is good quality and so on but in the end nobody asked me. I was quite disappointed."

"Just as well," said Geronimo grimly, "I would not want to trust to your knowledge of the silk trade to get me out of difficulties with the Inquisition!"

The arrival of a French Huguenot gentleman, M. Papillion, completed the *Ridotto*. As Signor Cicchinelli bustled away to find some refreshments the discussions got under way.

"So how is it, Brother Paul," asked Dr Diodati, "that Venice has become so much of a new world, where the sermons are, I am told, as good as those in Geneva and the people flock to hear them? How is it that the Inquisition is not able to act against such things? Surely they must object?"

"The Inquisition in Venice," replied Brother Paul, "is kept in check by means of one of its members being always one of the Senators. The Senate takes care to chose a man for this task who is a strong opponent of those who would give the Roman court powers which do not belong to it. He prevents any unfortunate decisions being made by the Venetian Inquisition."

"How splendid, Father Paul!" exclaimed the fat archbishop, "and your preaching is popular with the nobility here too."

"I rejoice that the *common* people hear the gospel gladly," replied Brother Paul with emphasis, "and that there are many eager for the truth."

"How many would you say are on the side of reform?" asked M. Papillion.

"As many as 12,000 would you say, Mr Bedell?" replied Brother Paul.

"Yes, indeed," replied the chaplain, "and I also rejoice that not only Brother Paul but Brother Micanzio and one of the Friars, Manfredi Fulgenzio, and others preach the gospel with great boldness. With your permission therefore I will outline a plan which I have formulated to take steps towards reform here in Venice."

Taking his piece of paper out of his pocket he began to read, "The first step. This must be to encourage the state here in Venice in good heart and courage against the encroachments of the Pope and the court of Rome and the power of Spain who is the Pope's backer. The second step must be to do all we can to increase the number of those who have received any light of the truth in religion. Towards these two objects a fair beginning—more than a beginning as we have seen— has already been made so that this evening we can consider the third step. This will be to gather together into a congregation at least some of those who are already alienated in their hearts and minds from Rome. I know that Brothers Paul and Micanzio desire nothing in the world so much as the reformation of the church and that many members of the nobility of Venice are on their side and even members of the Senate. With Mr Diodati here they can perhaps take this great next step."

"Your Doge and Senate are well known to be on the side of toleration in religious matters are they not?" said M. Papillion, "I remember hearing years ago that when Henry III of France visited Venice on his way home from Poland that as well as a lavish entertainment, your Doge Mocenigo gave him the wise advice that he should return France to mercy and a reasonable degree of tolerance."

The discussion continued. I could see that Mr Bedell and M. Papillion were thinking in terms of Dr Diodati remaining in Venice as the minister of a reformed church in the city. M. Papillion produced a list of names of people in Venice; Germans, Flemmings, French merchants and others who were not Venetians themselves but who were prepared to donate money towards the cost of having a Protestant congregation with its own minister in Venice.

Brother Paul was more cautious, "I think we need to have more meetings first," he said, "and those of the Reformed persuasion in Venice, whether Venetians or of other nations, need to talk together informally and grow in their knowledge of the truth more before we attempt your third step, Mr Bedell."

It was late when the meeting broke up. I went home with Brother Paul and Brother Antonio but not before I had been persuaded to meet Carlo the following day and show him round the city.

Chapter 10: (1608) Carlo

I set off early the following morning to meet Carlo at Sir Henry's residence and show him the sights of Venice. "For goodness sake don't get into any trouble, Samuele," said Brother Paul as I left his cell. You have been well behaved now for so long I fear you will get up to no good as soon as I take my eyes off you!"

Armed with apples from Luigi's stall, Carlo and I spent a happy morning wandering through the shops and stalls of the *Merceria.* Carlo had been given some pocket money by his uncle and he bought some slices of sweet *buccellato* ring cake for us when we got hungry. Feeling full of this delicious spicy fruit cake we carried on looking at all the grand buildings in St. Mark's square. Carlo was torn between admiration for the great churches (St. Mark's itself staggered him) and disgust at the statues and pictures of the Virgin Mary ("idols" he called them) that are to be found everywhere in Venice. While we were watching the boats on the Grand Canal (a sight that he found endlessly fascinating) a children's procession went by. A little lad much younger than us headed the procession chanting out the litany in a babyish voice and behind him came children all dressed in their best carrying brightly coloured little images of saints decked out like dolls in beautiful clothes. A troop of tiny children, some of them very small fry indeed, followed and their mothers and nurses stood by watching their little charges in admiration.

"What is this?" whispered Carlo in horror, "what are they doing?"

"The children? Well, they are going in procession to some nearby church where they will light candles and sing and say little prayers in front of the statues of the saints they are carrying," I replied, not without some embarrassment for such sights were so common to my eyes that I had never thought about them before, "every child in Venice is brought up in this way."

"Even you?" queried Carlo gaping in astonishment at the chanting toddlers, "did you do that when you were small?"

"No," I answered at once, realising for the first time that Brother Paul had never required me to join in such processions, "Brother Paul never made me—in fact I suppose he protected me from such things."

"Friend, this beautiful city of yours is an evil place. I wonder that your Brother Paul does not make his escape to somewhere where he could worship God in freedom."

***

Venice is a very beautiful city by night. Carlo and I had special permission from Dr Diodati and Brother Paul to stay out late that evening so that I could show him how enchanting the city was with the lamps in the houses reflected in the water and the little bobbing lights carried by the gondolas. It was a very clear evening with not even a breeze to ruffle the water. From the Rialto Bridge we watched the sun as it sank, turning the whole of the Grand Canal into a rippling medley of red, orange, purple, blue and black. As it grew darker the buildings became mere shadows. Then one at a time there were little twinkling lights, first in one building, then another as the householders lit candles or lamps in the windows. Carlo was quiet, taking in the scene. Everything was hushed, the bustle of the city was over, it was full of a great peace. The moon rose, a full silver disc, leaving a shimmering pathway on the water and then the silence of the evening was broken by the wail of a baby from a window nearby.

Carlo shook himself from his reverie. "It is very beautiful," he said, "but I stick by what I said. If I were in Brother Paul's shoes I would leave. But then," he added, "my family has always had to leave and start again so I am used to the idea I suppose."

A gentle crooning voice began to sing, not very tunefully, from the nearby window and the baby's cries became more subdued. I listened for a moment, wondering if it was a mother, a nurse or even a grandmother whose unmusical singing was so soothing to the baby in the house. I found myself thinking about my mother. Her song had soothed me when I cried as a baby yet I could not remember her—did not know who she was.

"What do you mean?" I asked, "about leaving and starting again?"

"Do you want to hear a long story?" asked Carlo, "because the history of my family cannot be described in five minutes."

"I have always loved stories," I replied, "and the longer the better."

"Very well, then," said Carlo, "you've asked for it!" and with the strange crooning still going on in the background he began:

"The Diodatis, in my great-grandfather's day were one of the oldest noble families in the city of Lucca right on the opposite side of Italy to Venice. The other great noble families of the city included two families, the Burlamachis and the Calandrinis, who were and still are closely tied to each other and to us Diodatis by marriages. My Uncle who is here in Venice now is married to a Burlamachi lady, for instance. Members of our families were often chosen to be in the senate of the Lucchese Republic and sometimes they were chosen as Chief Magistrate."

"Is that a person like our Doge?" I asked.

"Yes, very similar, I think," said Carlo, "but the important thing is that in those days there was a preacher in Lucca, rather like your Brother Paul. His name was Peter Martyr and he was very keen to see reform in the church. Many members of our families heard his preaching and agreed with what he had to say. They longed to be able to worship God freely, from the heart without all the superstitious rubbish that the church of Rome has added to Christianity. The Pope, did not like the ideas that were taking root in various cities in Italy. He decided to investigate. Peter Martyr was summoned to Genoa, nearly 100 miles away in the north, to explain his beliefs. He knew, of course, that once he got there he would find that he was interrogated, probably tortured and then put to a horrible death. He accordingly set the affairs of his priory in order, gave away his personal library to people who would make good use of it, and escaped to Switzerland."

"But what happened to all the people in Lucca who had been depending on him as their preacher?" I asked, "should he not have stayed to help them?"

"Staying in Lucca, was not an option," replied Carlo, "He had to go to Genoa as he had been ordered or get out before he was caught. Peter Martyr was of the Augustinian order. When he left there were other Augustinians who carried on his work and there was a little reformed congregation which met in private."

"Like the one Mr Bedell is proposing here?" I asked, interrupting again for the situation seemed so similar to our own in many respects.

"I suppose so," said Carlo, "but it was very difficult to worship God in this way in Lucca and so people began to think of leaving as Peter Martyr had done. My grandfather, after whom I am named, Carlo Diodati, was able to leave quite openly since he was going to serve an apprenticeship in a banking house in Lyons in France. My Great Uncle Nicolo also wanted to leave for Switzerland but my Great Aunt Elisabeta was not of the reformed persuasion. She kept him back. After he died, however, she changed her opinion and decide to go to Geneva with her two boys. However, she could not do this on her own. Persecution got more fierce in Lucca. Some relatives of Great Aunt Elisabeta's from the Calandrini family also wished to leave. Some members of the families managed to escape to Lyons in France and eventually a group of seven more people banded together to try to escape. They were too conspicuous, however. What would a group of Lucchese nobles be doing all travelling together to a Protestant town such as Lyons? While they lingered things became very dangerous for the leading member of the party, my first cousin twice removed, Pompeo Diodati. In desperation he fled alone to Lyons where he waited, full of anxiety for his mother and fiancée to follow. It was six months before they could join him. One of my other great uncles and one of the Caladrinis then returned to Lucca and helped the others to escape."

"Including your Great Aunt, I suppose," I said.

Carlo nodded. "My Grandfather moved to Geneva from Lyons but the other families went from Lyons to Paris. Here they stayed for a while but then the French Wars of Religion made Paris less safe for them and they joined some other exiles in a place called Luzzarches about twenty-five miles north of Paris where they rented a château—a kind of French castle—to live in. From here they had to flee again, this time from soldiers because the reformed party in the war was being defeated. They made a desperate journey to a place called Montargris. On this journey they had to travel nearly a hundred miles which took two months and winter was beginning. They had had to leave behind all their possessions which were plundered by soldiers and they suffered terrible hunger and cold. When they arrived at Montargris they were sheltered by a very kind widowed duchess. Two babies were born after the journey but only one lived. When the war seemed to be over the families returned to Luzzarches and Paris but the wars began again and they fled once more, this time to Sedan a hundred and fifty miles away and how they got there I have no idea! Another Duchess looked after them and then when there was another lull in the wars they went back again to Luzarches."

"How did they manage for money?" I wondered, "I know they were rich but could they take their wealth with them?"

"They were very rich and you are quite right they could not take much with them when they left Lucca. The Calandrinis left behind three magnificent palaces and *eleven* profitable estates of which they were the feudal overlords. I'm not sure quite how rich the others were exactly but their wealth was comparable. The Burlamachis lost all their wealth with one useful exception. They had investments in businesses in France and Holland on which they could draw. However, when they got back to Luzzarches after their time in Sedan everything there had been stolen or smashed. Some went back to Paris again but then came the terrible day of the Massacre of St. Bartholomew."

"I have heard about that," I interrupted, "the Protestants in Paris were all murdered at once weren't they? Everyone knew who they were because Romanists had been warned to wear white arm bands in honour of St. Bartholomew."

"That's right," answered Carlo, "but it was not just in Paris. The massacre spread to other parts of France as well. All those members of my family who were at the Luzzarches château fled with only the clothes they wore back to Sedan. Some of their relatives in Paris had a very narrow escape and nearly lost their little babies. They too set out for Sedan, completely destitute, their home having been ransacked. On their way it happened in God's good providence that they met a man who owed them a huge sum of money. They had no copy of the bond, of course, that was lost along with everything else, but God touched the heart of this man and he paid the debt there and then even without the bond! This gave them what they needed to continue their journey to Sedan and eventually after some years to Geneva. How pleased my Grandfather was to see them safe and sound at last!

"Other members of the family tried to stay in France but they found it impossible to raise their families in such a hostile atmosphere. My Aunt Madeleine, wife of my Uncle Giovanni who is here in Venice now, was one of the children born at this time. The families eventually braved floods and war to make their journey to the safety of Geneva. The Lucchese authorities proclaimed them all heretics and confiscated their property. They were in mortal danger all the time. If any of them were found by a Lucchese citizen in any province of Italy, Spain, France, Flanders or Brebant that citizen could kill them and claim a reward from the Lucchese government! Several children beside my Aunt Madeleine were born during the flight and wanderings of my family. They became used to having to make a new home in various places and to start a new profession in life since all their previous wealth and position was taken from them. Some went to England (I have another uncle who is a doctor in London) some became lawyers, some became merchants (yes, even silk merchants!) and gained great riches. Some were expert soldiers but one and all since my grandfather's time we have had it dinned into us that we must make our own way in the world, from nothing if need be, and do something new. My uncle Giovanni, for instance, is the first Diodati to become a Hebrew scholar and theologian."

"Would you like to be one too," I asked, thinking perhaps that this was why Carlo had come with his uncle to Venice.

"No!" cried Carlo, "Don't you see? That is not the Diodati way! I want to do something *different*. I have no interest in languages in any case."

"What are your plans then?"

"I love plants and gardens," was the surprising answer, "I want to be a gardener and grow fruit and flowers in places where they have not grown before."

"Mr Bedell loves growing things," I said, "he has books about plants which he often shows me. Did you know that his master, Sir Henry Wotton, has a house with magnificent gardens near Venice where he goes in the summer? Mr Bedell loves going there; he spends his time picking the gardeners' brains and they love him so much they are forever finding special cuttings of rare things for him. He has pots and pots on his windowsill in his study which he nurses with great care. I think he wants to have a garden of Italian plants when he goes back to England."

"Does he?" exclaimed Carlo eagerly, " I wonder if they could be made to grow there. Do you think he would show me his books and plants if I asked him?"

"I am sure he would; he is a very kind man. He helped me to begin gardening and now I have a whole kitchen garden in tubs and boxes in the monastery back yard! I must show it to you before you go home," I replied, "You know your family history very well, Carlo, and it's so interesting."

"Oh, I have not told you half of it," said Carlo carelessly, "but what about you? Where does your family come from?"

The crooning from the window had ceased and the baby was quiet. Silence and peace were around us again. I paused to listen to the lapping of the canal before I replied.

"I have no family," I said at length, "my mother died before I can remember really and my father not long after." Then I added, "but God has been good to me. Brother Paul is better to me than any father could be."

Chapter 11: (1608) The Whirlpool and Antonio's Secret

Carlo returned to Mr Wotton's residence full of thanks for the interesting day we had spent together. I should have gone straight home to the monastery but I felt troubled in my mind. I had been praying that God would speak to me ever since Brother Paul had told me why I was called Samuele. Why didn't He answer? I went and stood on the De La Guerra Bridge and watched the dark water of the canal. Cloud now covered the sky and the moon had sunk behind the buildings. The water was inky black. The lights in the houses were going out one by one. I turned over in my mind what Carlo had said. Suppose Brother Paul decided to leave Venice as Peter Martyr had left Lucca. What would I do? Would he take me? Perhaps that would not be possible. I knew that, like Peter Martyr about whom Carlo had telling me, Brother Paul had been summoned to go to answer for his opinions. He had refused to go, saying that such a request was not in the Pope's power. Of course, his case was different. The Doge and Senate protected him rather than forcing him to go, but that protection seemed such a slender thing. If it were ever to fail, Brother Paul would face death. In fact he already faced it: had he not been stabbed? He was not afraid of death, that I knew. I remembered his calm explanation that nothing could hurt him nor could he die before God willed it. I looked down at the black, cold water beneath the bridge. I felt alone and chilly. I tried to marshal my own thoughts. What did I think about death? I realised with a shock that I could not feel calm about it as Brother Paul did. Why? He was not afraid: what did I fear? I remembered a picture I had seen once in the Doge's palace when I had accompanied Brother Paul during his work. It was a very detailed and complicated painting with many figures hurrying about in it. I had stopped to look at it while Brother Paul talked to someone. I could see that parts of the picture showed heaven and parts showed hell. The scurrying, crawling figures came back to my mind. I realised with a jolt that the reason I feared death was that I was afraid of Hell! But surely I would not go there—I was a good Catholic … Even as I thought the words my mind brought me up sharply! I knew that meant nothing! Those who stabbed Brother Paul would claim the same! The black water swirled below me. My head swam with the thought; I knew the church could not save me! Who could then? Could I save myself? Could I be good enough for heaven on my own account?

Once again I knew the answer before I had even thought of the question. One stain would keep me out of heaven's perfection. I knew I had not lived a perfect life in every word, thought and action. Even the good things I had done were done for selfish ends. If I stopped to examine my life honestly I could see that my motives were self-centred. Even my desire to be unselfish was selfish in origin! If I tried to find good motives for my actions my thoughts went round and round always leading to myself at the centre. The dark eddy by the edge of the bridge seemed like an inky whirlpool. Was there no escape then? Would I be dragged down, down, a tortured scurrying figure into the depths? Terror seemed to whirl me round. I felt cold and horrified. Surely this was not true! There must be some escape from the sinful circle of myself. It was all horribly clear: good or bad whatever I did the motive was the same and it was not God's glory it was always for me. I stood shivering on the bridge horrified by the realisation that whatever my accomplishments, whatever my devotion *even to the Bible itself* I was a sinner through and through and I had no forgiveness.

Suddenly some words came into my head. I remembered a friendly voice saying, *God, who disposes of all things, will answer our prayers if we pray to him ... do this now!* and I remembered Brother Paul's words urging me to pray, *speak Lord, for Thy servant heareth.* Out loud I cried, "O Lord, please let me trust in you! Please let me be one of your people! I know I am not always good—not ever good—I do everything for myself not for Thee, but even with sin welling up in my heart, round and round and round, I know that Jesus died so that sinners can be forgiven. Could I not be one of those? I do want to be Thy servant. O speak to me, Lord!"

My tears fell into the black water of the canal and as I wept some some words from the Diodati Bible came to my mind with a force that was so powerful I almost fell into the canal with surprise: *Tutto quello che il Padre mi dà verrà a me, ed io non caccerò fuori colui che viene a me*—"All that the Father giveth me shall come to me; him that cometh to me I will in no wise cast out."

"Oh, then I will come," I cried, "I will come, I will come!"

***

As I ran back to the monastery in the dark I was so elated I felt I must tell someone what had happened or I would burst. Something was singing inside me for joy. God had spoken to me! He had spoken through the words of the Bible, bursting through the endless downward spiral of my sinful heart, and I knew I belonged to Him. Brother Paul would be asleep. I would creep into the monastery and into our cell and wake him up to tell him. I slipped into the darkened monastery, glad and a little surprised to find the front door ajar, and glided across the floor as far as the monastery vestry without making a single sound in spite of my excited state. At the open vestry door I paused for I could hear voices whispering, which was strange at this time of night and eerie in the darkness. I stopped, wondering who it could be. The whispering voices were quite clear and I recognised one of the speakers as Brother Antonio, "He has a grudge against everyone at Rome because he was never made a bishop, you know," he was saying, "the old atheist—you should read some of his notebooks of his *Thoughts!* I have read them while he has been out of his cell and I can tell you they are disgusting. He does not believe anything! I have been promised money to kill him before but in cold blood I could never do it. Poison would be easier and you would get the other one, Micanzio, at the same time then also since they always eat together and almost always alone."

"Two pigeons with one bean," came another whispering voice that I did not recognise, "The Holy Father in Rome has promised money and immunity from prosecution and I think I have something here hidden away in my stocking that will help you get the job done a better way." There was a very slight rustling sound like paper falling on the ground and then Brother Antonio began whispering again, "What is this? Wax? How will that help?"

"It is indeed wax, my friend," came the answering whisper, "and with it you can easily obtain an impression of the keys to the good Brother's cell. Get the impression to me and I will have some keys made from the impression. Then you can let anyone you wish into his cell at any time of the day or night. I am sure you can find some loyal *bravos* to do the deed for you and they will know how to do it quietly and then make their escape before the sad death is discovered."

I began to tremble. It was horribly clear what Brother Antonio was talking about but who was he talking to? Whoever it was, they were plotting together to kill brother Paul, right here in the Servite monastery. I shook until my teeth rattled and I was afraid I would be heard.

"It is very late," whispered the unknown voice, "I must leave, it would be better if I were not found to have come here."

"No, indeed," came Brother Antonio's answering whisper, "You know he has forbidden me to correspond with you. I can easily do as you ask. The old Jew we used to use as a go between has refused to carry my messages any more but I can still let you know when I have the impression."

The voices had begun to move towards the vestry doorway. In a moment I knew they would be making for the front door: no wonder it was open! Hardly knowing what I did but thinking that the unknown man must not escape whatever happened, I dashed to the door, slammed it shut, locked it, pulled out the key, threw it as hard as I could down the nearby cellar stairs and then began tugging with all my might on the rope of the bell that was used to summon the brothers to prayers. I had only managed a few pulls when I was grabbed from behind and received a stunning blow on the head.

Chapter 12: (1609) The Hero

Dr Despotine was bending over me. "What have you been up to now?" he was asking as he bathed my head with something soothing.

I stared up at him for a moment blankly wondering where I was and what had been going on. It was getting light. I was in the cell I shared with Brother Paul. Why did my head hurt? Then I remembered and asked urgently, "Have they caught him? Who was he? Where is Brother Antonio? The keys …"

"Keep calm, Samuele, Brother Antonio is quite safe. Someone got into the monastery probably to try to attack Brother Paul but Brother Antonio foiled him and he ran away down the back stairs when Brother Antonio rang the bell. I suppose it was the intruder that hit you."

"Dr Despotine," I exclaimed urgently, "That's not what happened! I rang the bell, not Brother Antonio; he's not telling the truth."

Dr Despotine looked surprised, "You have had a nasty bang on the head, Samuele," he said, "I dare say it has affected your memory of what happened."

At that moment Brother Paul entered the cell. He looked very weary. "We still can't find the keys to the front door and what I want to know is how did he get in, whoever he was?" he said, "How is he, Despotine?" he added looking at me.

"He's come round but he's a bit confused," said the doctor, "he says it was he who rang the bell."

"Brother Paul," I cried desperately, "I did, I did! There was a man in the vestry, he was talking to Brother Antonio and he gave him some wax …" I stopped, realising the seriousness of what I was saying.

"Wax!" exclaimed Dr Despotine, "Now whatever would he do that for in the middle of the night?"

But if Dr Despotine thought I was raving, Brother Paul certainly took me seriously, "Go on, Samuele," he encouraged, "tell us what happened."

"I came home and the door was open," I faltered, "I could hear voices in the vestry. A man was talking to Brother Antonio. He said that there was money offered by the Pope if, if …" I stopped as tears welled up in my eyes.

"We all know why the Pope has offered money," said Brother Paul very gently, "you don't need to go over that part just now, Samuele, carry on, please."

"He gave him some wax to make an impression of your cell keys, Brother Paul," I continued and as I spoke my head pounded, "he said that Brother Antonio could give the impression to him and he would get some keys made. Then Antonio could get some *bravos* and let them into your cell whenever he liked. They were going to escape so I ran back to the door, locked it, threw the key down the old cellar steps and started to ring the bell. Then something hit me and I woke up here."

Brother Paul looked grim, "What do you think, Despotine?" he asked, "I have never felt easy in my mind about Brother Antonio. He was too friendly with that character Francesco of Padua who is a known agent of Cardinal Borghese in Rome. I forbade him to meet with him and he laughed it off saying he was only friendly with him in Padua to get a good dinner out of him but I confess I suspected he was still seeing him from time to time."

Something stirred in my mind. I remembered the little rustling sound when the wax was being handed over. I wondered if some paper, perhaps a wrapping of the wax, had fallen to the floor in the vestry.

"Brother Paul," I said, "I know I did not dream all this. Send someone to look on the floor in the vestry. I heard something rustle when they handed over the wax, a wrapper perhaps. Maybe it is still there. That would be proof wouldn't it?"

Still grim faced Brother Paul went to call the sacristan and ask him to make a thorough search. He had not been gone more than a minute when Brother Antonio himself came into the cell.

"How are you now, Samuele?" he asked, "That was a very nasty blow on the head you had, although I dare say you can't remember much about it."

Dr Despotine gave me a warning glance, "He is only just coming round," he answered for me, "he should not speak just now. Would you wait here a moment, please, Brother Antonio? I believe Brother Paul wanted a word with you, he will be back in a few minutes."

Brother Antonio sat down on a chair. He shifted in his seat nervously and twisted his fingers round the edge of his habit. I wondered if he was trying to think of a good reason to go before Brother Paul came back.

Brother Paul reappeared, "Ah, Antonio," he said very gently, "the sacristan has something belonging to you, would you come with me to collect it?"

***

It was not a wrapper from the wax but something far more incriminating. It was not just wax that Francesco of Padua (for the stranger had indeed been he) had hidden in his stocking. A tightly folded packet of letters had been there also. The wax was sticky because it had not been properly mixed with the turpentine used to soften it. As Francesco pulled it out, the letters had stuck to it. In the dark he had not noticed and the little rustle I had heard was the sound of the letters dropping onto the floor of the vestry. The letters were ample proof of Brother Antonio's guilt. They were from a Brother Bernardo in Rome asking Francesco to persuade Brother Antonio to kill Brother Paul and telling him that money would be available as a reward. This time the conspiracy against Brother Paul *had* included Servites.

Brother Paul pleaded for clemency. Brother Antonio was simple rather than malicious he said. Nevertheless, the senate had him arrested and in no time at all had used threats and torture to ensure that he told where Francesco could be found. He also confessed the whole plot and once again Venice was swept by a wave of indignation at what might have happened to their beloved Brother Paul. The difference this time, however, was that overnight I found I had become the hero of Venice!

***

I was quite unaware of my status as hero at first as Dr Despotine was insistent that I rest in bed for at least a day after my blow on the head. Thanks to Brother Paul's intervention he was not permitted to bleed me, although he would dearly like to have done so to speed my recovery. The next day, when I was feeling very much better, Brother Paul received a message from the Doge asking to see me if I was well enough! I was so surprised I nearly had a relapse.

"What ever for?" I asked in terrified astonishment, "I haven't done anything wrong, have I, Brother Paul? The Doge isn't going to put me in prison is he?"

Brother Paul smiled, "Samuele, I think the Doge wishes to thank you for saving my life."

I took this in slowly. "Did I?" I asked.

"I rather think you did, although perhaps you did not intend to," he replied.

"I certainly wanted to save your life," I answered, "although I was not looking for an opportunity to do so at the time. Do you know, Brother Paul, I was creeping back into the monastery to tell you the most wonderful news. I was so excited I didn't even stop to be particularly surprised when I found the door unlocked. After that ..."

"After that, you were just in the place God in his providence wanted you to be at the time, Samuele," said Brother Paul quietly, "and I am very glad you were."

"So am I," I said fervently and glowing with excitement at the news I was about to tell, "But what I wanted to tell you was ..."

"That you have, as Mr Bedell would no doubt put it, found that the Lord Jesus Christ is your Saviour and that He has answered your prayer, giving your puzzled conscience sweet certainty," said Brother Paul, slightly sarcastic but totally perceptive as ever, "I can see it in your eyes."

***

I was very glad that I was not ushered into the presence of the Doge without Brother Paul at my side. He was used to meeting with the Doge and Senate: I was terrified. The Doge greeted us kindly and motioned us to sit down.

"So this is the remarkable child," he said to Brother Paul, "that has been so useful to the Republic. Young man," addressing me now, "I understand from Brother Paul that you are already an exceptional linguist and that in a little while will be ready to take up the study of Hebrew at university. I also understand from Brother Paul that you would wish to travel to do this," seeing the look of surprise on my face he added, "no, I do not wish to know which university—I quite understand that it would not be our university at Padua. The Republic of Venice wishes to express its grateful thanks to you. You probably know that since the barbarous attack on Brother Paul the Senate has offered various rewards for his protection and for the detection and capture of those who would harm him. The Senate has therefore decided (having consulted with Brother Paul as to what would best meet your needs) to enable you to further your studies by granting you a very small annual pension to be used for your education and maintenance—for the rest of your life. The Republic's banking contacts cover the whole of Europe and we will follow your academic progress (through Brother Paul) with great interest. I am assured that your future career will bring honour to the Most Serene Republic that has nurtured you."

I stammered out my thanks in an absolute maze of bewilderment and we were bowed out of the Doge's state chambers.

"I don't understand," I said to Brother Paul, "What does he mean? University? Travel?"

"He means, among other things," said Brother Paul, "that when you are ready to do so, you can go to study Hebrew in Geneva under Dr Diodati and the Senate will pay."

***

The money of which the Doge spoke was to be paid annually and, while I was still a child, administered by Brother Paul for my benefit. Brother Paul, it seems, had been contemplating having me eventually go to Geneva to study with Diodati for some time but had been unable to see how this could be accomplished. At first I was horrified at the very idea of leaving Venice, the only place I knew, the Servite monastery which was the only home I could remember, and Brother Paul who was father and mother to me. Even the prospect of studying Hebrew with Dr Diodati did not seem sufficient inducement. But Brother Paul was kind and patient. Rather than putting pressure on me, he simply recommended me to consider how I should best use the generous gift of the grateful Republic and to pray earnestly to God for guidance as to my future. This was sensible advice which I could hardly refuse and from that time I began to seek God earnestly as to what I should do.

"How do you think God will help me know what to do this time?" I asked Brother Paul.

"I don't know," he replied, "but I am sure He will." He paused and then added something that shocked me, "I think you should also begin to have more of Mr Bedell's company and less of mine. I will arrange it. This will be good for you in many ways not least because I may be a bad influence on you although you don't realise it."

"A bad influence! You of all people, Brother Paul," I cried in astonishment, "you are the best influence I have ever had!"

Brother Paul sighed. "I can see that the time has come for me to explain some things to you," he said, " and I can trust you not to breath a word about them to others, even to Mr Bedell himself, do you understand?"

I nodded dumbly and he continued, "Listen carefully to what I say then and I will tell you a little about myself.

"You must know that when I was young I served under Cardinal Boromeo in Milan. He was a pure living man who wanted to do the will of God and who hated the greedy, lax, immoral lives of the clergy around him. When the plague struck Milan you should have seen him! All the nobility and clergy that could get out of the city did so but not Borromeo: he stood by his post. A few clergy—fewer than thirty I think it was—remained with him. He fed the starving people out of his own purse, urging them to repent of their sins. He was at the bedsides of the dying seemingly without any care for his own health and he continued to preach in the cathedral throughout the plague. That man impressed me and I determined to imitate him for the rest of my life.

"Then I went to Rome. What a contrast! What an evil place, Samuele! So many churchmen with no thought of the church, only of themselves! So many priests and cardinals with no love even for their fellow men let alone God! The lives those ruffians led, the cunning deceiving scheming for money, possessions and every kind of evil vice! They treated those who devoted their lives in the way that Borromeo had done as if they were fools and they themselves lived as if *there was no God* to whom they would have to render account in the end.

"When I returned to Venice from Rome I was bewildered. I did not know what to think. Borromeo had devoted himself to the church—to reforming it along the lines of the Council of Trent. That council ought to have been the means of cleansing the church, bringing it back to the pure form in which it originated in the New Testament. It should have healed the rift between us and the Protestants. Instead of that, however, the Protestants were not invited to attend and certainly they had no chance to put their views on a equal footing. The abuses I had seen in Rome were just left unreformed and nothing was done to reconcile the churches under the Pope's power and those of the Protestants. The French had wanted some things allowed: services in the local languages not Latin, even bread *and* wine offered to the congregation rather than the wine reserved for the priest. They hoped, they said, that concessions such as these would heal the rift in their own country and prevent war. There was no question of this. And when I probed into its origins and precedents I began to realise that the Council of Trent had no legitimacy in any case. It simply did not represent the whole church as earlier councils had done because the Protestants were excluded. When I researched into the workings of that council I found it was all rigged with one end in view: to strengthen the power, might and riches of the papacy—of Rome.

"Then it began to dawn on me that perhaps in one way most of those in Rome whose behaviour had so shocked me were right—not in the way they acted but in the principal that underlay their actions—there is no God!" He held up his hand to prevent my astounded interruption, "there are no miracles; people believe in God through ignorance and because they want to escape from the harshness of life. Those in power, if they are good, use religion to help keep order in society and, if they are bad, to gain wealth and pleasure for themselves. There is no heaven, no hell: man's purpose—just as with other creatures—is to live."

"Brother Paul, Brother Paul," I cried in terror, "that's not what you think is it? Not now? That there is no God, that everything is … is … just a lie, just make-believe? You've never taught me that! You go to church, you write about theology, you must believe there is a God …" I trailed off into silence, stunned by the magnitude of what he was saying, and trying to grapple with its implications.

"For years I did believe what I have told you; and I will be plain with you, there are times when I find myself believing it still. Of course, I did not tell people what I thought. I studied mathematics, science, literature, church history even, but about my real beliefs I was silent. What purpose would there be in speaking? It would only get me put to death. In any case to live a lie was not a sin if there was no God: if there was no God there was no sin!"

I was silent, trying to take in what he was saying so he continued. I noticed that the vein in his forehead that always stood out when he was under stress seemed suddenly the most noticeable feature of his face:

"But my studies in church history led me to study the Greek New Testament very closely. I wanted to find out the exact origins of the church councils and also to examine the claims of the Pope to be the representative of God upon earth. I read the New Testament with close attention, marking each word that I had studied and weighed individually with a red pencil. There was not a whiff of the false about it. I went over it again and again until there was hardly a word that was not marked in red. I pondered. If there was no God where did this book, this New Testament, come from? Who wrote it and when and why? These were questions I had asked about other religious books and documents and I had always been able to answer them robustly— often to the embarrassment of the papal authorities. I had seen many fakes and fairy-stories before—*The Donation of Constantine* for instance—but this book was so different. It was plainly an accurate record of people's actual experience and who would be prepared to pay with their life for spreading such things if they knew them to be untrue? The apostles were put to death because they said they were witnesses of Jesus' death and resurrection. Who would go to such lengths for what they knew to be a falsehood? Yet I was still baffled. The church as I experienced it was *nothing like* that described in the New Testament. Even my youthful hero, Borromeo, for all his devotion and charity, had beliefs that had no place in this book. Where was the church then? Had it died out to be replaced with this monstrous parody? I delved into church history yet further. I began to see glimpses of something more like the church of the New Testament. Every time, of course, it was stamped on. Often, after it had been wiped out, its beliefs were distorted and reported as heresy by the writers of the histories—who all came from one place! But I became more expert in reading the truth into what I saw on the page. It was not long before I fitted Martin Luther into the picture and the pattern became complete."

Somewhat relieved by this explanation, I asked, "But I do not understand. Why would all this, terrible as it is, make you a bad influence on me?"

"Because," said Brother Paul, "I do not always feel as convinced by the arguments I have just given you as I do now. Because sometimes a black mood comes over me and I still find myself thinking that all that matters is that I live and can serve my beloved Venice. That if, by skilfully playing of Romanist against Protestant, France against Spain, heretic against orthodox, I can enable the Venice that protects me to remain unharmed, nothing else matters. That maybe there is no God who cares …"

"But there is!" I cried, "There is! I know Him!"

"And I," answered Brother Paul, "having no dramatic experience like yours, often fear that perhaps I do not."

And so Brother Paul saw to it that I spent more and more of my time with Mr Bedell. He also arranged to use some of the first instalment of my money to pay for me to study for a short time with Rabbi Leo. In this way I could improve my Hebrew in a more formal way than I had been able to do when merely accompanying Mr Bedell. I continued also to attend the chapel at Sir Henry's residence. The services were quite crowded with Venetians now and I found Mr Bedell's sermons seemed to speak to my soul, ministering comfort when I worried. And I often was worried about the constant danger Brother Paul still faced from his enemies and also about his strange states of mind.

One Sunday Mr Bedell had been preaching on some words at the end of Mark's gospel where Jesus, about to return to heaven, gives his disciples instructions that they should go into all the world and preach the gospel to everyone. He explained how the church spread as Christians travelled through the world and he was very emphatic about Jesus' instruction that the gospel should be preached to *every creature*. "Here in Venice," he said, "there are many of God's creatures who are in need of the gospel and who cannot be reached by a preacher such as myself since they do not come to listen. Are they to perish because no one will tell them the way of salvation? Even the feeblest of us here must know someone to whom we can communicate the truths of the gospel."

I felt challenged—guilty even—on considering this. Compared to an unprotected Venetian such as Dr Despotine, I could do what Mr Bedell was suggesting without much danger. I thought about Luigi. How often I had stood at his little stall, chatting with him about all the Venetian news and yet I had never mentioned to him anything about his spiritual needs! I had wondered about him coming to the chapel at the Residence but had never even asked him to come with me. I decided to do something about it.

The next day there was to be another *ridotto* at the linen warehouse. Since the previous one the Frenchman, M. Papillion, had been active among the foreign merchants in Venice. He went around telling them that if they helped the cause of the Reformation in Venice by putting up money for a reformed church here, the Doge and Senate themselves would be very grateful. They had responded magnificently, thinking that they were doing something endorsed by the government of the Republic and that they would thus be in no danger. M. Papillion had hurried back to France full of joy, telling his Huguenot friends that Venice was about to fall from the Pope's grasp. The news spread through France like wildfire. Meanwhile it became clear to the foreign merchants in Venice who had originally promised the money that things were not at all as M. Papillion had described. The Doge and Senate were by no means about to make a break with Rome. Most of them hurriedly drew back when they realised that they would be in danger of losing their goods and even their freedom. The Senate of the Republic of Venice was somewhat shocked to learn that in France it was confidently believed that Venice was about to embrace the Reformation. This situation caused great embarrassment to the members of the *ridotto* and they now had to decide how to proceed.

On the day of the *ridotto*, however, there were other tasks for me to do. My kitchen garden now covered every available space in the monastery yard and was quite productive. Brother Paul sent me to spend some time tending it before going to Luigi for fruit and then to Mr Bedell's study. As I worked away weeding, hoeing and watering my improvised containers I wondered how to broach the subject of the gospel with Luigi. "It's going to be difficult," I thought, "I don't suppose Luigi will be expecting me to talk about religious matters." I had learnt now that the best resource when I needed courage or wisdom was prayer and as I worked away among my plants I prayed for Luigi, asking for help in speaking to him.

Since my exploits with Brother Antonio and the foiled attempt on Brother Paul's life, Luigi had frequently teased me about my status as hero of the hour. Today he greeted me cheerfully, "And how is the Protector of the Republic today? Will it be apples or plums?"

"I am not the Protector of the Republic, Luigi," I replied, "although I do know him."

"Ah ... that would be your chum the Doge, then," teased Luigi, "and no doubt you are on the way to the palace at St. Mark's for a quick bowl of *risi e pisi* with him before getting down to a few more deeds of valour."

"The Doge is not the protector of Venice either," I said, hoping to lead the conversation in a more serious direction. "There is only One who protects the city for the sake of His children who live there."

"My word!" exclaimed Luigi, "You are in a sober frame of mind today—must be because it is Monday and you were in Mr Bedell's chapel yesterday listening to all that cheerful stuff about sin, death and hell."

"Why don't you come too next Sunday?" I asked, "It would be quite easy, your father works for Sir Henry after all."

Luigi looked astounded, "Me?" he asked, "Chapel is not for the likes of me! I think that bang on the head you had the other day is not quite better yet, Samuele, or you would not be saying such things. What on earth would I do coming to a chapel?"

I felt lost for words. I paid for the fruit and returned to the monastery feeling disappointed that I had not made any progress with Luigi.

***

That evening as Mr Bedell and I made our way to the linen warehouse I told him about Luigi. Rather to my surprise he seemed pleased. "Keep speaking to him, Samuele," he advised, "you never know how God may work in his heart. It may not be long before Venice is resounding with the gospel and perhaps Luigi will be one of the first-fruits."

The *ridotto* was held in the same comfortable room and when we arrived Brother Paul and Dr Diodati were already there. Brother Paul beckoned us over to him. "I am keen that Samuele here should study in Geneva under your direction one day," he said to Dr Diodati, "but as yet he is young and does not wish to leave Venice."

"Perhaps he will be able to continue his studies here in Venice or even Padua if he waits a little longer," said Mr Bedell, still full of enthusiasm for the coming Venetian Reformation, "if God prospers all our plans."

"Perhaps," said Brother Paul, "but we have much to discuss this evening."

"And little to thank M. Papillion for," put in the Archbishop de Domini who had just arrived, "imagine spreading such ideas all over France at this stage!" and he waved his fat arms to show his exasperation with the situation.

"At least some beginnings of a congregation could be started," said Mr Bedell, "even if it were to be very small. It would be like a little snow falling from the top of a hill which gathers more and more over time as it rolls down until it is a huge mass. Recent events have made the people of Venice less and less happy with the Pope. Every time he tries to have you done away with, Brother Paul, the people here love him even less."

Mr Bedell had been working away hard at an Italian form of service which he had translated from French. He had found a confession of faith in Italian which dated from before the Diodati Bible and was a good summary of Bible teaching. He brought out these documents to show the members of the *ridotto* now.

"This was actually printed in Venice with the approval of the Inquisition," he explained spreading out a printed sheet of paper, "It is a plain summary of Scripture and I'm not sure how it got past them but it did and so should not endanger anyone who subscribed to it."

He passed the paper round but as the room began to fill up with the members of the *ridotto* everyone's eyes were on Dr Diodati. Would he consider it possible to start a reformed congregation here in Venice? After all, the implication was that he would be the minister if so.

"I must be frank with you all," he said when everyone was assembled, "I think the hope here in Venice is very small. You do not have enough nobles or any Senate members who are willing to join in a reformed church and you have no one to serve as minister. I am willing to try, of course, if you still wish it but you must know that my skills are in divinity and Hebrew rather than preaching and pastoral work. I may not be the best person."

"I am very willing to minister to such a congregation myself," offered Mr Bedell, "if it would help."

Brothers Paul and Micanzio exchanged anxious glances. I could see that this was not their idea of a practical way of proceeding. "I think that would make great trouble with the Senate. They could hardly turn a blind eye to it as they do to the services in Sir Henry Wotton's Residence," said Brother Micanzio, "and it would create difficulties which even Sir Henry could not solve. Indeed even your being present very often at *ridotti* such as these makes for problems. We need to proceed with great caution. We are still permitted to preach the gospel ourselves—as I intend to do freely again this coming Lent—but without the Council of Ten behind us I think we cannot go much further."

"You brothers need to take stronger measures," urged someone from the back of the room, "you cannot keep stalling and putting things off for ever. The time for the Venetian government to break with Rome was while we were under the interdict. If the Doge and Senate could not be persuaded to break with the Pope then, they are not likely to do so now. You have to face the fact that you may have to act without your Council and Senate if Mr Bedell's avalanche is going to get started."

"God has not given me the spirit of Luther," replied Brother Paul.

After this remark the *ridotto* seemed rather to lose its way. Diodati tried his best to encourage Brother Paul into stronger action. "When I return to Geneva," he explained, "I can send some young scholars to Venice who could be employed as tutors in the homes of sympathetic Venetians. They could teach—and teach not only the children—the truths of the Bible. They could assist the families where they were employed by holding daily family prayers. I can think of some already who would be willing to volunteer for the task."

"I thank you," said Brother Paul cautiously, "that might be the best way of moving forward."

Chapter 14: (1609) At the Stationer's Shop

It was not long after this that I was busy helping Mr Bedell one morning when we came to an unexpected halt. We had been hard at work, Mr Bedell translating King James' book the *Premonition* into Italian. I acted as a sort of language assistant, being a native Italian speaker while he had but lately learned the language. Reaching for another sheet of paper, the chaplain found he had exhausted his stock, "Now where is the best place to buy supplies of paper?" he asked.

"I know," I said, "there is a little shop not far from here, shall I run and get some for you?"

"A good idea," replied the chaplain, "but I need some exercise; let's both go."

Old Guiseppe the stationer was very pleased to see an important person like Mr Bedell come into his little shop. He found his best quality paper and wrapped it up carefully for his customer, chatting away as he did so, "Now tell me Mr Chaplain, Sir, if I might be so bold as to ask, what is the difference exactly between your Church of England and us Catholics?"

"None in respect of name," said Mr Bedell, "except we in England count ourselves good Catholics you know but not *Roman* Catholics. Catholic means 'worldwide' so Roman Catholic is rather a contradiction in terms."

"Well now, there is a bigger difference though to be sure, Mr Chaplain, whatever you may call yourselves," said Guiseppe, unwilling to be put off with such a general answer.

"You know the Apostles Creed I am sure. Well, we believe all twelve articles—but not the thirteenth article put to it by the Pope."

"Thirteenth Article!" exclaimed Giuseppe, "I never heard of it! What is it?"

"It is that article whereby Pope Boniface defined it to be *altogether of necessity to salvation, to every human creature, to be under the Bishop of Rome*—the Pope in other words," replied the Chaplain, "We consider that to be rather an extravagant claim and we do not believe it."

"Well I never did!" exclaimed old Giuseppe, "Is that really so? I'm sure there are many in Venice would agree with you then. Just imagine adding that to the creed!"

Before Mr Bedell could explain more, another customer entered the shop. Giuseppe bustled off to serve him, leaving the shop boy, a lad of my own age, to bow us out of the door. As he did so he smiled at me and said very quietly, "Message from Luigi, Young Sir, he says, 'See you on Sunday.'"

"Whatever does that mean I wonder?" I thought as we strolled back to the Residence, "and I've seen that boy somewhere before! Now where was it?" But by the time Sunday arrived I had forgotten the mysterious message completely.

***

That Sunday I hurried of to the chapel in the Residence as usual. By now I had to squeeze in at the back if I was at all late so I made sure I was in good time. The service was as beneficial to me as usual. Mr Bedell dwelt on the need to know the Saviour and to pray to him from the heart. He explained very clearly that forgiveness from our sins is not by our own works or religious observances or by the merits of other people—dead or alive—but only through faith in the Lord Jesus Christ. How I enjoyed now being able to worship God in Italian! As we recited the creed together in our own language *"Credo in Dio, Padre onnipotente, Creatore del cielo e della terra ...* I believe in God the Father Almighty, Maker of heaven and earth ..." I thought what a difference it must make to Dr Despotine, and others like him, to be able to come to the chapel at the Residence. How lonely he must have been before, trying to keep what he knew to be true to himself and avoiding people who would want to discuss religion with him in case they were out to trap him! Now we could sing together in Italian too. Carlo's Uncle Giovanni had finished his metrical translation of the psalms into Italian and so we could use them in the chapel. The poetry was beautiful. I made a mental note to ask Carlo whether this was another Diodati "first" or whether there were already any poets in the family.

When the service was over I made my way towards the door. The room was quite crowded as many people had arrived after me so I had to wait where I was towards the middle of the room for a moment. As I watched the people making their way out, I spotted the lad from the stationer's shop.

"Of course that's why I recognised him the other day," I thought, "I must have seen him here before." I smiled to myself at the sight of him in his Sunday best without his shop apron and with his black hair neatly combed. Then as he turned to go towards the door I was amazed to see that by his side was Luigi!

It was all I could do not to wave and shout his name! So that was what the boy had meant by his strange message! I hurried as fast as I could in the press of people but they were through the door before I could reach it. I went down the stairs as fast as was possible without being rude and out onto the *fondamente*. I looked up and down outside the Residence but although there were quite a few people about I could not see my friends. Although I was disappointed, I knew where I would be able to find Luigi on Monday of course, so I trotted home to the monastery to tell Brother Paul all about it.

Brother Paul had just returned from the monastery chapel when I arrived and he was very pleased to hear my news.

"The ordinary people of Venice are hearing the good news gladly it seems," he commented, "that is how it was in the days when Jesus himself was on earth. Do you remember the words in Saint Mark's gospel 'the common people heard Him gladly' when He taught in the temple, although the rulers and religious leaders despised Him."

I nodded, remembering the passage, "Things don't change much do they, Brother Paul, people are still the same aren't they? Rich and powerful people not listening to the truth but poor people, like Luigi..."

"Rich and powerful people, like to keep their riches and power," said Brother Paul, "and they also still tend to despise something that poor, uneducated people can easily understand." Then he changed the subject, "You had some good news for me, now I have some for you," he said, "would you like to go on a summer holiday?"

"A summer holiday?" I repeated in surprise, "I don't know— where?—when? ..."

"You know that Sir Henry always moves out of Venice during the hot summer months and goes to live in his country villa at Noventa near Padua," began Brother Paul, "Mr Bedell has to go with him and so do all the other members of his household. He will be leaving Venice for his villa in a few weeks' time. I have had an invitation for you to accompany Mr Bedell when Sir Henry goes there this summer. You will act as a ... er ... language assistant to the chaplain."

My mind was in a whirl at this unexpected announcement and questions crowded into my head. I had never left Venice before so Noventa, although only some twenty or so miles away, seemed like the end of the earth. On the other hand my apprehension was conquered by the thought of the gardens. Mr Bedell's descriptions of them had been so glowing that I longed to see them for myself. I knew too that travelling to Noventa would mean a leisurely boat ride along the Brenta Canal, its beautiful route lined with graceful villas and punctuated by fascinating locks. In the end all I managed to stammer out from this whirl of conflicting ideas was, "Oh! What about Luigi?"

"Luigi?" asked Brother Paul in surprise, "What has Luigi got to do with it?"

"If I go off to Noventa, and worse still if Mr Bedell goes, who will help Luigi to come to faith?"

"I imagine God will," replied Brother Paul, and there was a trace of irony in his voice, "but in any case it will be a few weeks before you set off on your travels so there will be plenty of time to talk to Luigi."

Images of beautiful trees, fruit and flowers, lakes and statues filled my head as I lay in bed that night and tried to imagine what Noventa would be like. My mother's little song spun round in my head as I tried to pray for Luigi and then drifted off to sleep.

***

The next day Luigi was serving a customer when I arrived at his stall and I stood waiting patiently, wondering what to say. The lady walked off with her apples and Luigi smiled at me, "You see I came!" he said.

"Yes," I answered "and I am so glad. What made you change your mind? Was it that nice lad from the stationer's shop?"

"Not exactly," said Luigi, "you see I kept thinking about something you said. You said you *knew* the One who protected Venice. If you had said you knew *about* Him I would not have been so intrigued. What caught my fancy was that I had been talking only that day with young Lorenzo from the stationer's shop and he used the same sort of words, trying to explain to me that you could *know* Jesus Christ. I told him I thought that was a barmy idea, Jesus Christ has been dead for years, but Lorenzo insisted that he talked to Jesus when he prayed. Not just *Pater Noster* or *Ave Maria et cetera, et cetera* but just talking, telling Him things and asking for His help. I said that I couldn't see what he was driving at and then, just like you did, he asked me to come to the chapel to find out for myself. I pooh-poohed the suggestion but afterwards I wondered. 'It can't do any harm to pray how Lorenzo says he does,' I thought to myself, 'and see if anything happens.'"

"So did you pray?" I asked bursting with curiosity.

"Yes I did," said Luigi, "I asked God to guide me—which is what Lorenzo suggested I should ask—and I'd just finished when you popped up! I'm coming again with Lorenzo next Sunday. I still don't understand what it's all about but I realise it's important now; as Lorenzo said you can't go on laughing off important matters forever."

***

It was when I visited Mr Bedell that I learned some of the reasons behind my holiday invitation. Carlo, it seems, had been fascinated by my brief description of the gardens and plants at Sir Henry Wotton's villa in Noventa. When he heard that Sir Henry's household would be moving to the villa shortly, he was seized with a desire to visit Noventa before returning to Geneva. His uncle was uneasy about the idea at first although Mr Bedell assured him it could be arranged. For diplomatic reasons Carlo's safety would not be compromised if he was a member of Mr Wotton's household. Even so Dr Diodati was concerned about how Carlo would return to Geneva at the end of his stay if he and Geronimo set off first without him. Again Mr Bedell came to the rescue, finding a member of Sir Henry's household who was travelling home to England via Geneva later in the year. Carlo could travel safely with this young man. A letter was sent to Carlo's father requesting permission for him to go and Carlo was on tenterhooks until the reply arrived some weeks later giving him permission. Mr Bedell had asked Mr Wotton if I could go also as company for Carlo.

Mr Wotton, since the affair of Brother Antonio, would refuse me nothing. When he found I was interested in plants and gardens he was delighted, "Plenty there to amuse you," he told me when I was called to see him about the invitation, "bowls, pallone games and whatnot. I always take care that I am there at the grape harvest too. Plenty of grapes in the vineyard by the house. Bedell tells me you grow vegetables at the monastery. Very commendable! We'll see if we can get you a good cutting from one of my vines to grow up a trellis in a nice big pot by the monastery back door."

Later I asked Mr Bedell, "What about Luigi? He's coming to the chapel every week now. If the chapel is closed while we go away he will have nowhere to go."

"Yes, that's awkward," agreed the chaplain, "and it's not just Luigi, you know. There are quite a few people who will miss the chapel while we are in Noventa."

***

A few days later I was talking to Luigi again. I had gone to get our fruit as usual and Luigi's usually cheerful face was troubled. I chose my purchases and then asked him what was worrying him.

"Do I look worried?" he asked in surprise, "well, perhaps I do, although in my job it doesn't do to have an unhappy face. You have to be cheerful to sell fruit to passers-by. I've been thinking about what I hear in the chapel more and more and Mr Bedell makes it all so plain. I'd love to read the Bible for myself but there is a problem. I can't read. I've never been to school or anything. Not that Bibles are easy to come by, although Lorenzo has one."

"Would he let you read it?" I asked, knowing what a valuable and dangerous book a Diodati Bible was.

"I think so," replied Luigi, "he showed it to me."

"Maybe I could teach you to read," I volunteered, "It's not really difficult."

"Do you think you could?" asked Luigi, "I always thought it would be too difficult for me to learn."

"Yes, I'm sure you could," I said, "in fact I think you could almost teach yourself."

"How would I do that?"

"Well, each day before I come to get the fruit, I will write a short lesson for you. When I come for the fruit I will give it to you and show you how to read it. You can practice it over when you have quiet moments during the day. I will come over in the evening and listen to you say your lesson. Then the next day I can give you a bit more."

"I'll try it!" said Luigi, "When shall we start?"

"Right away," I replied, "I'll go and jot down a little lesson for you now and bring it back."

I hurried off to the monastery and sat down in the cell. Brother Paul was out at the Doge's palace and had left me some small jobs to do before going to Mr Bedell's study. I found a scrap of paper that even the sacristan would not miss and wrote on it the first few letters of the alphabet. Beside each letter I drew a crude picture of something that would help Luigi remember the correct sound: A is for *ape* (bee), B is for *barca* (boat), C is for *cane* (dog) and so on up to F. Pleased with my work I hurried back to his stall. I waited until he had no customers and then I showed him my work, explaining the sounds as I did so.

"Hooray!" he cried, full of enthusiasm, "is that all there is to it? How many of these letters must I learn before I can read?"

"Twenty-one," I replied, hoping that he would not think it too many.

"Good," he said, "I can manage that. Come back this evening and see if I can still remember these." He propped the paper up on his stall, wedging it in place with an apple and took up his usual cheerful cry: "*Frutta fresca,* fresh fruit—F is for fruit, fresh fruit, all fresh!"

"Well done, Luigi," I said smiling, "You will learn in no time!"

***

Luigi did learn the alphabet in no time. My next problem was how was he going to put this useful knowledge into practice by starting to put the letters together and read words? I wrote a few words for him to sound out each day and he could soon read them all quickly. Now he was ready for something more and I wondered how I could give it to him.

One Monday morning when I arrived at his stall he was very excited. In fact he saw me coming along the *fondamente* and waved at me with both arms, jumping up and down as he did so. "I did it!" he shouted, as soon as I was within hailing distance, "I did it! I can read!"

"Well done!" I shouted back and trotted along the *fondamente* at top speed to where he was.

"I went round to Lorenzo's little room after chapel yesterday," he explained, "and he showed me his Bible. We opened it up right away and I said 'shall I try to read something?' Lorenzo said to go ahead so off I went with the beginning of St. John's Gospel, *Nel principio la Parola era*—in the beginning was the Word—and I never looked back! I can do it! Lorenzo had to help me sometimes but I am going to go every Sunday and practice."

He stopped to draw breath and I slapped him heartily on the back. "Congratulations!" I said, "there will be no stopping you now."

Luigi became more serious now, "I couldn't have done it without your help," he said, "thank you so much, Samuele."

"I'm so glad I could help, Luigi," I said, "but Lorenzo helped too, you could not have done it without him either."

"No, that's true," he said, "and do you know what? We are going to meet together every week for me to practice as I said and then when Mr Bedell goes to Noventa and the chapel is closed, Lorenzo and I are going to meet in his room and read and pray together and learn as much as we can all summer."

"That's wonderful," I said beaming with happiness, "I can remember a time when I could never have imagined you doing such a thing."

"I never forgot what you said you know, Samuele, about knowing God yourself. I long to know Him too now."

"Keep praying to Him, Luigi," I said earnestly, "and I am sure you will."

Chapter 15: (1609) Noventa and The Perspective Glass

Carlo had said good by to his Uncle Giovanni and to Geronimo who had set off for home. He was now under Mr Bedell's care at the Residence. One morning Mr Bedell sent him round to the monastery with a message to Brother Paul that I should be ready to start for Noventa in two days' time. Now that Lorenzo and Luigi had something planned for the time when the chapel would be closed and also now that I'd had time to get used to the idea, I was looking forward to going to Noventa.

"Venice is a disgustingly smelly place," said Carlo, wrinkling his nose at the unpleasant aroma that was stealing in through the cell window, "now that the weather is getting hotter."

"I'm afraid so," I replied, "the canals are not just the highways of the city, they are the sewers as well! You and I will enjoy being out of the city now that summer is here. We will be safe from the plague too; it often seems to haunt the city in the summer time. I'm glad we are really going at last. I hope these wonderful gardens we have heard so much about come up to your expectations."

"I am sure they will," said Carlo, " and Mr Bedell is going to introduce me to all the gardeners! I'm going to pick up all the hints and tips I can."

"Good for you," I said, "the only thing that worries me now about leaving Venice is who is going to look after the kitchen garden Mr Bedell and I have created here at the monastery?"

***

In the end I had to be content with the assurance from the brother who was in charge of the kitchen that it would be watered regularly. "But don't expect me to do the weeding, Samuele," he said, "I don't know a weed from a plant; I'd pull up all the wrong things!"

Sir Henry Wotton had already set off for Noventa when I arrived at the Residence on the day we were due to depart. He had gone the day before along the canalized River Brenta in the luxury of his ornate *burchiello* with its beautifully decorated wooden cabin.

I had seen many a *burchiello* being rowed on the canals or under sail on the lagoon but I had never even peeped inside one.

"Have you been in it?" I asked Mr Bedell, "what is the inside like?"

"Very comfortable, I believe," replied the chaplain, "on the Brenta it will be pulled by a horse who walks along the *alzaia* beside the canal. But such vessels are only for important people like Sir Henry, we will be going in an ordinary *padovana.*"

So Mr Bedell, Carlo and I boarded a humble horse-drawn *padovana.* As they glided past, the scenes on the bank were totally new to me. I gasped in astonishment. I had lived all my life in Venice and had never seen anything except buildings, pavements, bridges, wharfs, docks and water. The sight of fields of ripening wheat, vineyards, orchards, and of little farmhouses with their vegetable gardens amazed me.

Carlo smiled as I gazed about me, "You've never seen anything like it before have you?" he asked.

"No," I admitted readily, "all that land, the fields going on and on … it's so different from what I've ever been used to before. Is your country like this?"

"Well we do have fields of wheat and so on a bit like this," replied Carlo, "but this is all so flat! Switzerland is famous for mountains and high pastures where the cattle and goats graze in the summer. The pastures are full of flowers and there are little streams that run down icy cool from the tops of the mountains where the snow never melts. You can lie in a meadow and listen to the bells ringing round the necks of the cattle and eat wild strawberries …" his voice faltered.

"Poor, Carlo," I said softly, "I believe you are feeling homesick!"

Carlo smiled, "Yes," he said, "a bit. I don't know why—I am so looking forward to Noventa."

"Will we be able to see mountains when we get to Noventa?" I asked looking round at the flat fields of wheat.

"I think we will," he answered brightening up at the prospect.

The villa itself when we arrived fully came up to our expectations. In fact it was even more remarkable than I had expected. At least, not the villa itself—I was used to quite grand houses in Venice—but the gardens! From the steps that led down from the terrace in front of the villa the eye was led down a long vista with a central gravel walk edged with miniature hedges. This led to a graceful fountain from which radiated other gravel walks like the spokes of a wheel. The main walk continued beyond the fountain until it reached the canal.

Between the spokes of the wheel were set formal gardens in geometrical patterns full of flowers, statues and elegantly shaped trees, all the walks and borders being edged with miniature hedges. Beyond the formal gardens were orchards, vineyards and fields stretching away as far as the eye could see towards the distant mountains.

That summer at Noventa was such a happy time for me. Carlo and I became very firm friends. Together we roamed the fields, orchards and vineyards—and grew healthy and strong eating so much fresh food. We ran races (I always lost at first having had little exercise and no practice in such things), climbed trees and spent almost all our time outdoors. I even learnt how to ride a pony and Carlo and I rode bareback and stirrupless through the sunny countryside. We also had the use of a little rowing boat which we became adept at using on the canal. There are locks on the Brenta at Noventa to enable the boats to go up to Padua and we spent much time watching the busy scene at the lock-side as the laden barges, *burchielli* and *padovani* passed up or down the canal.

We often went with Mr Bedell who spent much of his time outdoors talking to the gardeners. They adored him and were never tired of answering his questions and showing how they did things. They even gave him some tools such as they used in grafting fruit trees and showed him how to use them and they found him many cuttings and seeds. These he squirrelled away carefully for his collection back in Venice. By the end of the summer Carlo knew everything there was to know about the soil, climate, native plants and local crops in Noventa and I was not far behind him in knowledge.

The university of Padua is not far from Noventa and here many English students went to learn medicine. They would often visit Sir Henry and some also attended the chapel services Mr Bedell conducted at the villa on Sundays. To my special delight there were also daily prayers morning and evening for the whole household conducted by Mr Bedell. In England, he explained, it is the custom for everyone working in the house down to the lowest servant, to attend prayers. To make this a duty in Italy would have caused difficulties and in any case the workers on the villa estates could not speak any English. However, Mr Bedell made sure that they all knew they were welcome if they *wished* to come, and when some began to attend he used Italian for at least part of the service. This was good for Carlo too since, although he was fluent in Tuscan, Italian and French he spoke no English.

I have said that the summer was happy. But it was not totally unclouded by anxiety. News reached us from Venice from time to time and some of it was very disturbing.

***

"Letters, letters, letters!" stormed Sir Henry, "they are always getting into the wrong hands, being stolen, being misinterpreted, passed to people who should not read them! Letters! They are the bane of an ambassador's life!"

I smiled inwardly, remembering the darkened church where he had met with Signor Scaramelli. Sir Henry happily made use of other people's letters when it suited him.

"Has there been some bad news from Venice then, Sir Henry?" enquired Mr Bedell.

"Well it's not usually good news when intercepted letters are involved," said Sir Henry, "Someone got hold of some of Diodati's letters to a friend in France and made a digest of them. They included a description of some of the things that have been going on involving Diodati in Venice and they mentioned Micanzio's involvement, especially his preaching."

I pricked up my ears at the mention of Brother Paul's friend.

"Someone passed the digest on to the Venetian authorities," continued Sir Henry, "with the comment that Micanzio was a Trojan horse, letting Protestantism into Venice. Now the fat is really in the fire!"

"Was it someone who heard him preaching at San Lorenzo?" enquired Mr Bedell, "he certainly was very bold in what he said."

My mind went back to that Sunday when I had seen Brother Micanzio hold up a Diodati New Testament and astound the congregation by thundering out, " ... we are *forbidden—forbidden* ... " If that was not "letting Protestantism into Venice" what was?

"My informant does not know who it was," replied Sir Henry, "but the Doge is not pleased. If he feels he has to act in order to show that Protestantism is not about to take over Venice things could go very badly with Micanzio."

Sir Henry stalked off taking his complaints elsewhere.

"What will happen to Brother Micanzio?" I asked Mr Bedell, full of concern.

"I don't know," he replied truthfully and with a worried look, "but I hope I have not led Brother Micanzio into any kind of trap."

"You led him?" I asked.

"Yes, you see those were sermons we planned together. He did the preaching but I am afraid many of the ideas came from me."

"Mr Bedell," I said as a comforting though struck me, "they were not your ideas really were they? I mean they came from the Bible— they were God's ideas."

Mr Bedell looked down at me and his eyes were now twinkling again above the bushy beard, "quite right, Samuele, and God will take care of Brother Micanzio. We will pray for him together right away."

***

It was hard not to let the news about Brother Micanzio cloud the holiday. But for me at least it did have one good effect. Whenever I felt the worry of the situation back in Venice welling up inside me I tried to stop and pray quietly in my head. Gradually the problem faded from the foreground of my mind.

One evening Sir Henry was sitting on the terrace with a group of English students from Padua and other young men from his household. Carlo and I had been on a long ramble through the fields that day and were now sitting drowsily content beside Mr Bedell's chair.

"I hear that Galileo and Sarpi are making some interesting discoveries in optics," remarked one of the students, and I at once pricked up my tired ears at the sound of Brother Paul's name, "Galileo brought an amazing instrument to the university recently. He had it from somewhere in the Netherlands and made some improvements to it himself. It enables one to see things clearly at a distance."

"Like spectacles?" asked someone.

"Not exactly," replied the student, "but when you look into it—it is a kind of tube—you see an image of the object at which it is pointing but which is larger, clearer and nearer. Suppose you pointed it at that shed over there," and he pointed to a little hut away out in the fields, "you could see clearly the face of a person standing outside."

"That's unbelievable," said Sir Henry, "how is it done?"

"I'm not an expert in optics," said the student, "but I think it is an arrangement of lenses and mirrors inside the tube."

"A very useful device in time of war," said one of Sir Henry's young men meditatively, "any army that had one would have a great advantage being able to see the enemy's dispositions, manoeuvres and movements at a distance."

"Well, if Sarpi has anything to do with it," said Sir Henry, "you can be sure the Doge is already looking into one right now!"

The company laughed and the conversation turned to other topics. One of the Italian students had a friend whose cousin was a young Jesuit priest. This cousin had joined a Jesuit Missionary, Matteo Ricci, who had reached the Forbidden City, Peking, in China where the Chinese Emperor lived.

"My friend's cousin has managed to get a letter home," he said, taking a piece of paper out of his pocket, "and I copied these characters from it, look," he held out the paper, "these are Chinese characters. They each represent whole words."

"Do the Chinese have a character for each word?" asked Mr Bedell, suddenly full of interest.

"Yes, indeed," replied the student, "this is a bird, and this a house and so on."

"Seems a clumsy way to go on," said another student, "so many different words and no way of knowing how to say them by looking at them."

"Ah yes," said Mr Bedell, "but an end to all translation problems."

"What do you mean?" asked Sir Henry.

"Well imagine," said Mr Bedell "that not just the Chinese, but all of us used characters for words—the same characters whatever language we spoke. After all, we already do this with mathematical terms. For our numbers and for plus, minus and so on we use the same symbols whatever language we speak. I have often thought that it is time, at least for scientific works, that we developed some way of writing that used a universal character, so to speak, in order that translation would not be needed."

"Latin does the job well enough," said someone else.

"No doubt, that is true up to a point," said Mr Bedell, "but in practice I find myself needing to learn new languages in order to communicate nevertheless."

The rest of the conversation was lost on me. I was so tired after my day's ramble that I was almost beginning to hear my mother's song in my head. I found myself wondering if the words of the song were Chinese: *Tras a na dont a dol sheer dol sheer ...*"

"Samuele," said Carlo, "Samuele, you're going to sleep!"

***

Summer and harvest passed into autumn. Sir Henry was determined to stay until the grape harvest in September and he personally supervised the pressing of the grapes grown in the villa vineyards. Picking the grapes involved the whole villa staff and we boys joined in, putting the grapes into wicker baskets and carrying them to the presses until we ached all over with tiredness and heat. After the grape harvest Sir Henry planned to travel on to Lake Garda before returning to Venice. Carlo would leave at the same time with the young man from Sir Henry's household who was going back to England via Geneva. As the grape harvest progressed I found myself wishing it would go more slowly. I had become used to having someone of my own age to play with and talk to. I had come to be very fond of Carlo.

When the time came for Carlo to leave for Padua on the first stage of his journey home I went with him down to the canal to wave him off.

"I shall miss you," I sighed as he stowed all his beloved plants carefully in the waiting *padovana*, "but I am sure you will be glad to get home to your family."

I shall miss you too," he said, "but cheer up! It will not be long now before you are coming to Geneva yourself to study at the university with Uncle Giovanni, then we will have some fun I can promise you! I can't wait to introduce you to my brothers and sisters. We will go rowing on the lake, hiking in the hills and I'll have such a garden to show you—*if* I can manage to get all these treasures home in one piece!"

I laughed, "What a pity you can't go all the way in a *padovana*, then they'd be fine. As it is I don't see how you are going to manage on a horse with all those pots."

"Well, I'm just going to get them as far as I can," he explained, "and hope that if I have to abandon the pots I'll be near enough to home to carry cuttings from the plants. Or maybe I can take some of them out of the pots and wrap the roots with damp sacking; we'll see anyway. If I don't start out with the plants I certainly won't end up with them: if I start out with them I might manage to end up with them—who knows!"

"How long will you stay in Padova?" I asked, wondering where the pots would go when Carlo had to stay in a inn.

"I'm not sure," he replied, "but I am going to beg my hardest for a trip round the botanical gardens there before we leave."

"Oh no," I teased, "more specimens! You'll never get home, Carlo!"

The rest of the passengers soon arrived, the boat man cast off and the horse began its easy motion along the *alzaia*.

"Goodbye," I shouted, "I'll write!"

"Goodbye, come soon!" replied Carlo.

***

Noventa without Carlo was much less fun and I was not sorry when a few days later Mr Bedell and I were seated in a *padovana* ready to go in the opposite direction back to Venice. As I surveyed the collection of pots that Mr Bedell had with him, which was even larger than Carlo's, I mused that he had a better chance of getting them back to Venice than Carlo had of arriving safely at home with his botanical burden. But then Venice was not the end of the journey for *these* pots.

"However will you get all those home to England in the end?" I asked the chaplain when all was settled and we began to move off.

"I don't suppose I will get a fraction of them back," said the chaplain composedly, "but I will enjoy their company while I am in Venice and," he patted a large parcel affectionately, "I am sure I will get my wonderful garden tools back home in safety. We have nothing at all like this in England."

When I arrived back at the monastery it was as though I had never left it. I slipped in through the front door and hurried to Brother Paul's cell just as if I had only been to fetch fruit from Luigi's stall. As I knocked on the door I suddenly wondered if Brother Paul would be there. What about Brother Micanzio? All my worries about the letters came rushing back. And would Brother Paul be at the Doge's Palace working? But no, there he was seated inside his castle quietly writing as if I had never been away.

"Samuele," he cried in delight as I put my head round the door, "Home again, how wonderful! You are just in time to look at something truly amazing, come here!"

As he moved the sheets forming the castle aside I saw that beside his books and papers lay a long black tube.

"I have heard about that," I exclaimed, recognising the new optical instrument, "someone from Padua was talking about it to Sir Henry."

"News travels fast!" said Brother Paul, "would you like to see how it works?"

"Yes, please," I answered, "it sounded like magic from the description I heard."

"Not magic," replied Brother Paul, "but the science of optics by which we are just beginning to find out the wonders of all that God has put together in the universe. Come on, we'll take it up on the roof and I'll show you."

Puzzled by such a vast claim from the usually cautious Servite, I followed him up the stairs and through the little door which led by a small ladder out onto the leads of the monastery roof.

Here Brother Paul had rigged up a stand onto which the tube could be fixed to steady it while in use. Brother Paul looked through the eye piece for a moment and then motioned me to look.

"Do you see those boats over there?" he asked, pointing to a line of gondolas moored in the distance, "I've focused on the centre one, look."

I put my eye to the end of the tube but could see nothing clearly.

"You may need to shut the other eye," Brother Paul explained.

I covered my left eye with my hand and gasped in astonishment. Every detail of the gondola was clear including the delicate carving on the prow, which should be totally invisible from our present distance.

"I can see everything," I gasped in astonishment, "even ... oh!" and here I jogged the tube in my excitement, throwing it slightly off its mark and leaving me with a view only of sky.

"Ah, you have to keep it very steady," explained Brother Paul, "that's one of the things that has given us most trouble, making a good mount for it: here let me find the boat again for you."

We descended the stairs again after I had gazed my fill though the wonderful tube.

"We will come up again when it is dark," said Brother Paul, "so long as the sky stays clear, and I will show you an even greater marvel."

Brother Paul was keen to here all about my time in Noventa and I chattered away to him as we went down. He seemed very pleased that Carlo and I had become such good friends.

"God, has worked out everything, for your good you see," he said and I was glad to notice that his smile now had none of its old cynical look as he spoke, "you will go to Geneva happy now with a good friend already there to meet you when the time comes."

"Yes, that's true," I said, "Now I can look forward to my travels without so much apprehension although I will still miss you, of course."

***

In the refectory, to my delight there was Brother Micanzio to greet me.

"Samuele," he cried in delight, "you have grown about six inches!"

Indeed my appearance had changed since I went away. Never before had I had so much fresh air and exercise coupled with good food and the result was a spurt of growth that rendered me taller and stronger in every respect. I was hungry after my travels and was glad to find that there was some of my favourite *risi e pisi* left that I could enjoy with Brothers Paul and Micanzio.

"Just like old times," said Brother Micanzio contentedly as we settled down to eat, "have you been looking through the famous 'tube' then, Samuele?"

"He has," answered Brother Paul, "and he's coming up again to have another look after dark—no don't give the game away, Micanzio, I want it to be a surprise."

"What has been going on in Venice while I've been away—apart from the tube that is?" I asked.

"Diodati's young scholars have started to arrive for one thing," said Brother Micanzio, "several families now have them as tutors and they are doing a good job by all accounts."

"That's good news," I said, tucking into my dinner with relish.

"But we have had a set-back in another direction," said Brother Paul, and Brother Micanzio's face fell as his friend spoke, "Some letters of Dr Diodati's to friends in France fell into the wrong hands and the French ambassador has been complaining to the Doge that Brother Micanzio is responsible for letting Protestantism into Venice."

This was the news I already knew and I paused with my food halfway to my mouth, anxious to know how the situation had developed, "That's serious, do you know what will happen?" I asked.

"Not for certain, yet," replied Brother Paul, "but most probably he will be forbidden to preach any more."

"That would be bad," I said, "but perhaps not the worst that could happen."

"We don't fear the absolute worst," said Brother Micanzio cheerfully, "I'm too close an associate of Brother Paul here for that and in the meantime I've been making the most of the opportunity to preach as much as I can in case I am stopped."

The thought of preaching jogged my memory to ask, "Does anyone know what's happened to Luigi?"

"Luigi?" said Brother Paul, "Luigi's been distinguishing himself but I'll let him tell you about that!"

After dark that evening Brother Paul took me once more onto the monastery roof. He carried a lantern, "Don't look at it, Samuele," he commanded, "or your eyes will not get used to the dark."

We made our way across to where the telescope could be mounted. In the clear dark sky above the city the moon had not yet risen and there was nothing to dim the glory of the stars. "Now look," commanded Brother Paul, "do you see that star there? Well that is the planet Jupiter. Look at it carefully. Do you see it? Good. Now I will train the tube on it and you tell me what you see." He moved the tube on its mount until it pointed directly at Jupiter. He paused to gaze for a few moments and then, "here, now you look. Be careful not to jog the tube."

I put my eye to the tube and cried out it surprise, "I see a disc, a round disc and ..."

"Yes, yes and what else?"

".. and some bright white dots, two on either side—what are they?"

"Now," said Brother Paul ignoring my question for the moment, "let's look at the milky way, Samuele, over there," and as I glanced up at the familiar light band in the sky he moved the tube for me. When I looked I could not believe my eyes.

"Where did all those new stars come from?" I exclaimed, "I never saw those before!"

"Come back down and I'll explain," he said.

We made our way back to the cell and, settled once more in the castle with a lamp beside us, Brother Paul began his explanation.

"The tube reveals that there are many, many stars in the heavens which we cannot see without its aid," he began, "the milky way it seems is in fact composed of stars! Of all the bodies in the heavens only the planets appear as discs through the tube. Jupiter is most interesting because of the little dots, as you called them, which can be seen. Galileo and I have been watching those dots very closely now for some time and we have discovered that they do not stay in the same place. They move round Jupiter—they are, as it were small planets, circling the large one!"

"Now I understand what you said earlier about the wonders of God's universe," I said, "these discoveries are going to shake up the map of the heavens aren't they?"

"That's very perceptive, Samuele," said Brother Paul, pleased, "and the interesting thing is that the church of Rome has made all sorts of pronouncements about the heavens, the planets and so on in the past, pronouncements based on the ancient pagan writers, which this tube is going to prove are quite, quite wrong. The church has insisted that she and her Pope and not the Bible are the source of truth. Now she will be forced either to admit she has made a mistake, which will be the end of her authority, or to continue to deny a truth which will soon be plainly visible to all eyes."

***

The next day I settled into our normal routine and I made it my business to go out to get our fruit as soon as I could.

Nothing could conceal Luigi's delight at seeing me again, "Samuele!" he shouted, "you're back! Hooray!"

Before I could answer a customer arrived and he turned away to attend to her politely. He helped the grave elderly lady to select some pears and apricots and then to my astonishment I heard him say, "lovely fruit, madame, and all fresh as God made it and have you thought about the state of your soul today, madame? No? Well it's an important matter, very important. Why don't you go to the Convent chapel of St. Lorenzo and hear Brother Micanzio preach on Sunday, you'd benefit I'm sure. Good day to you madame, enjoy your pears!"

Before I could speak another customer came up and received similar advice along with his purchases and then another, who had obviously met with the advice before and commented, "Well you are a good advertiser, young man, what makes you so keen that we should all go and hear this preacher then?"

"You need a Saviour, Sir," was the ready reply, "so do we all: best way to hear all about it is to listen to a good preacher who knows the Bible and there's none better than Brother Micanzio at present in Venice. A very good day to you, Sir, and enjoy your apricots."

There was a lull in trade and I seized my moment, "Luigi! It's good to see you again! What have you been up to? You are very brave telling all your customers to go to the chapel of San Lorenzo!"

"Samuele!" he cried in delight, "don't you see? I must do something for my Saviour!"

Between customers Luigi told me his story. His conversion had been dramatic and had caused him many problems, not least with his father, Philippo, the *bravo*. However, he had stood firm and in a kind of radiant defiance he had determined to say some word of witness to all his customers at least until they declined to listen. He had fully expected this tactic to reduce his custom but on the contrary he was busier than ever. In fact, I suspected his new found zeal was such a novelty that word had got round and people came and bought fruit just to hear what he would tell them!

I returned to the monastery full of joy at the news. I had been worried that Luigi would suffer when the chapel closed and Mr Bedell had to go to Noventa but now God had overruled and Luigi had flourished as never before!

When I returned to our cell I found Brother Paul preparing for a visitor.

"Galileo arrives from Padua today," he announced, "and tomorrow we take the tube to demonstrate it to the Doge. Would you like to come? We are going to show him what it can do from the top of the *Campanile.*"

"The great bell tower at St. Mark's?" I was excited, "Oh I'd love to go, I've never been up there! You must be able to see for miles!"

Dr Galileo arrived later in the day, a broad shouldered man with red hair and a red beard, active and energetic, full of ideas. The following day we made our way to St. Mark's early to make sure the tube was set up and working well before the Doge arrived. I was delighted with the view from the top of the tower and exclaimed in delight, moving from window to window in wonder as I examined the scene. Brother Paul and Galileo, however, had seen it before and were more concerned with setting up the tube. It was a very clear fine day and below I could see the great square with people moving about like ants, all the fantastic cupolas and roofs of St. Mark's Basilica itself and beyond them the red tiled roofs of the houses in the city lay before me. The Doge's palace, the Lagoon, the Lido and beyond it the Adriatic Sea itself, all was spread out before my fascinated gaze. I did not tear myself away until I realised with a start that the procession of important-looking people I could see crossing the square from the palace was the Doge in his horned cap and some senators on their way to the *Campanile*.

"They're coming!" I cried in excitement and Galileo and Brother Paul glanced out of the window.

The Doge mounted the stairs and Galileo and Brother Paul received him with ceremonious bows. The senators arranged themselves around the little room and Galileo politely motioned the Doge to the only chair, in front of the tube which was set in an ornate brass mount on a table covered with a rich blue carpet.

Galileo pointed out a ship which was just visible as a dot on the horizon, "can your highness see the ship far out to sea?" he enquired.

The Doge graciously nodded his assent and Galileo dexterously focused the tube upon it and invited him to peer through it. There was a moment of hushed suspense and then the Doge drew back from the tube and said quietly, "A Levant trader of moderate tunnage, under full sail, moving away at speed." There was a gasp from the assembled senators. "I congratulate you, Doctor," he continued looking at Galileo, "this is nothing short of miraculous. Venice must have such instruments at once. That vessel is two hour's sailing away from the city. In time of war we could identify any enemy and be prepared to meet them well before they arrived."

The Doge was so pleased with the tube that Galileo's post as professor of mathematics at Padua was made perpetual and his salary was doubled. Highly delighted with his success, Galileo was present at a *ridotto* at the *Nave d'oro* the following day where he demonstrated the tube to everyone. Mr Wotton himself was there and at once wanted to order a tube so that he could send it to the King of England. It was clear that Galileo could sell as many tubes as he could make and for a very good price. As a scientist and also a businessman, he was delighted. The moon rose above the city and Galileo trained the telescope on it. The assembled members of the *ridotto* eagerly peered at its surface not smooth and perfect, as they had been taught by the theories of the pagan philosopher, Aristotle, but pock marked and pitted. When they had all seen their fill Galileo embarked on a description of what he had seen when looking at Jupiter. His concluding remarks were shattering in effect:

"Gentlemen, we can conclude then, since there are planets moving round Jupiter in orbits of their own, that everything in the universe does *not* rotate around the earth. This is an idea that has been propounded before by Copernicus and Kepler. We are now seeing real evidence that the earth and the planets move around the sun!"

Chapter 16: (1610) Farewells, A Death and The Starry Messenger

Things forged ahead with Galileo's ideas after the *ridotto*. He and Brother Paul spent much time together especially when the sky was clear at night, sketching the view they had of the moon and watching the little planets that circled Jupiter. I settled back into my studies with Mr Bedell (theology), Rabbi Leo (Hebrew) and Brother Paul (Greek, church history and logic) working as hard as I could to prepare myself for the day when I would depart for Geneva. At first I carried on going to the chapel at Sir Henry Wotton's on Sundays and I exchanged letters also with Carlo. He had arrived home safely, although most of his plants had succumbed to the hardships of the journey. "Do come soon," he wrote, "my cousins are looking forward to meeting you and Uncle Giovanni already has a very high opinion of your talents at Hebrew. Don't you think Brother Paul might let you come next year?"

Not only had Dr Diodati's scholars arrived in Venice to act as tutors in various families, but also through diplomatic and other channels, Heer Lenk and Heer Vandermyle had been sent to Venice from the Dutch Republic. The idea was that not only would they be preparing the way for the opening of diplomatic relations between Venice and the Dutch Republic but also (much more quietly) they would help the Protestants in Venice to start their own church. And start it eventually did with help from Brother Paul, Brother Micanzio, Sir Henry Wotton and Mr Bedell. The long awaited congregation of believers began to meet on Sunday mornings. One of the noblemen who had a large house not far from us in the Cannaregio area of Venice allowed a room to be used and the families, their tutors and others like Lorenzo and Luigi gathered together with some foreign merchants. I was delighted to be able to go. At last a proper church of our own in Venice!

I was working away with Mr Bedell one Monday morning, telling him all that had gone on in the Venetian congregation the previous day. He beamed with pleasure at my description, "That is so good to hear, Samuele. Now I will feel happy when I have to return to

England soon. The believers in Venice will have made a start and I am sure that God will bless them."

"Are you going back so soon?" I asked in surprise and disappointment.

"Yes, in a few weeks I'm afraid," replied the chaplain, "Sir Henry Wotton is going back as his term of office is over and another ambassador, Sir Dudley Carlton, will be replacing him. Sir Henry is going home via Constantinople—you know how he enjoys travel—but I am going straight back to England."

"I don't know how we will manage here without you," I said sadly, "Brother Paul loves your company and conversation and as for Dr Despotine …"

"Dr Despotine is thinking of coming with me or with Sir Henry—of course you won't breathe a word—it could be awkward for him if it gets out that he's going."

"Dr Despotine as well," I cried, "Oh dear, all my friends are leaving Venice."

"Cheer up, Samuele," said Mr Bedell, "Brother Paul is still here and so is Luigi for that matter and besides you will be off to Geneva yourself one of these days."

"Only to study," I replied, "Venice is my home. I will come back here when I have finished my studies."

As I said the words I realised for the first time how naïve and impossible they sounded. What would a Geneva-trained Hebrew expert be able to do in Venice for the rest of his life? He would be risking the Inquisition and would have to work quietly, almost under cover. A change of Doge, of mood in the city or in Brother Paul's standing could mean the Inquisition and death. But Mr Bedell saw no incongruity in what I had said.

"Yes, of course," he beamed, "the Venice congregation will have a Geneva trained minister who is a native Venetian perhaps!"

Somehow I could not share his confidence. My heart felt heavy.

"I have never thought of myself as becoming a minister," I faltered lamely.

***

Brother Paul was sympathetic when I talked to him that evening about what Mr Bedell had said.

"Things are not as simple as people sometimes think," he mused, "take Galileo now. He's all ready to publish his little book *The Starry Messenger*. He thinks he will get away with it all because it is demonstrably true. He even talks of going back to Florence. Yet I am sure that if he leaves Venetian territory—leaves Padua—he will face the Inquisition in the end. They will not let go, Samuele. They consider themselves to be the very creators of truth and if the 'tube' disagrees with them, well, the 'tube' must be wrong—and so must its inventor!"

"So you consider Venice *is* safe—I could come back?" I asked.

"It is safe enough *now*," he replied, "but you have seen what has happened to Micanzio even now—forbidden to preach. I am here to protect him from worse but I am not immortal. Micanzio and I are old: you are young. I do not think Venice is the place for a young man like you—not in the long term."

"But I don't want to leave you, Brother Paul," I burst out, "not for ever. I didn't mind going for a holiday to Noventa, I don't mind going to Geneva to study—but if I can't come back … can't come home again ever …" I was close to tears.

"Samuele," said Brother Paul very, very quietly, "Micanzio and I may not stay here either: we have been invited to go to England and we may go. Archbishop De Domini is thinking of going also."

"Not with Mr Bedell?" I asked, whispering.

"No, not yet. We could not travel with Mr Bedell in any case, we would have to go secretly. But you must see that it would be hard for you to come with us—not from Venice. From Geneva you could join us if you wished."

Suddenly I felt better. I might not be able to return to Venice but I would not lose Brother Paul for ever. We would be together in England in the end. Geneva no longer seemed like a painful separation which was hanging over me; rather it was a means of rejoining Brother Paul and Brother Micanzio when they left Venice. Mr Bedell would be in England too and Dr Despotine—all my dearest friends would be together!

***

The *Starry Messenger* was published and became an almost instant success. Galileo boldly advanced the ideas of Copernicus—that the sun and not the earth was the centre of the universe—believing that opposition from the Church of Rome would fade away in the face of the facts. He stoutly maintained that he was not intending to cast doubt on the Bible by what he wrote. Anything which could be observed as a fact could not contradict the Bible since the Bible was true, he explained. However, he pointed out, it was possible for the Bible to be misunderstood and misinterpreted. This was what was being done by those who insisted that the Bible taught that the sun revolved round the earth. By the time that Sir Henry Wotton returned to England the revolutionary idea was well on the way to being accepted in Protestant Europe where Papal authority could not delay its acceptance.

I said goodbye to Mr Bedell with sorrow. He and Dr Despotine left Venice quietly, for the doctor's sake, and few people knew they were departing. Brother Paul was very sorry to lose his friend from whom he had learned so much. As he was leaving he presented him with a beautiful little Hebrew Bible and Psalter and also with his own portrait done in miniature to remember him by. Mr Bedell was moved. "We must keep in touch by letter," he said, "although the post is slow and uncertain it may be that I can get some letters through via the new ambassador."

"I will be anxious for you until I hear you have reached home in safety," replied Brother Paul, "and you will be in my prayers daily."

***

Sir Henry's Residence was now empty. I accompanied Mr Bedell and Dr Despotine to the River Brenta to begin their journey.

"Work hard, Samuele," were the chaplain's parting words to me, "I look forward to hearing from Brother Paul all about your achievements in Geneva."

"Yes, work hard," echoed Dr Despotine, "you are sure you would not like me to bleed you before I go, just in case your old war wound on your arm still troubles you?"

We all laughed together and I said, "I will keep praying for your safety and I will be glad when Brother Paul hears that you have got safe home."

"And we will pray for you," answered the doctor at once, "what a blessing that we can pray for our friends!"

And so I waved them goodbye as they set off in a *padovana* for the first stage of their journey, a few possessions and many pots of plants carefully stowed away in the bottom of the boat. I felt lonely and small as they disappeared but at least I now had hopes of seeing them again one day.

***

In fact I did not set off for Geneva for a couple of years. Brother Paul, busy with affairs of state, gave up the idea of going to England for the present, even though he received a personal invitation from the King of England himself. Through Sir Dudley Carlton the ambassador he received very pressing messages that he would be most welcome to make England his home but he chose to remain and serve his beloved Venice. He found it more and more helpful to have me to act as scribe and general assistant. Now I accompanied him to the Doge's palace, sometimes daily, or else remained working at the monastery while he attended on the Doge's business.

The monastery garden flourished as never before under my care. Mr Wotton had been true to his word about the vine cutting and a delightful shady plant now grew about the back door of the kitchen. It did not seem to mind in the least that its roots were only in a pot— albeit a large one—and after three years I fully expected it would produce some grapes. The yard itself was filled with peas, beans, carrots, some new vegetables called potatoes and anything else that could be grown in some kind of container: every inch was productive. I wondered whether I could add a beehive to complete the usefulness of my little plot and I began reading about bee-keeping.

During this time, my involvement with the Venice congregation increased and my friendship with Luigi grew ever stronger. We also heard from the new ambassador that Mr Bedell and Dr Despotine had reached England safely. I longed to find out what had happened to all the plants that set out with them in the *padovana* but Sir Dudley Carlton did not know and no letters from Mr Bedell ever reached us. I still heard from Carlo from time to time and I received not only letters from him but plants also. Alpine strawberry seeds survived the long trip from Geneva and began to produce a delicious crop as did various new types of lettuce.

When Mr Bedell departed Brother Paul and the Archbishop De Domini became closer friends, Brother Paul having few of his opinion that he could safely talk with and De Domini being in the same position. Brother Paul trusted De Domini, even lending him the manuscript of his great book *The History of the Council of Trent*. To lend this was a sign of great confidence since the book was so critical of the Roman church that, had its contents leaked out, Brother Paul would have been in great danger. As it was when the book was published (and how that happened you will hear later) Brother Paul never admitted to being its author. I, however, try as I might could not get to like the Archbishop.

"I find him so strange, almost eerie," I said to Brother Paul one day as we were working and talking about the book, "he seems to agree with everything you say and yet somehow I feel that there is something held in reserve, something ... I don't know ... not quite right."

"We must be generous to him," said Brother Paul, and I heard that old world-weary tone creeping into his voice as he spoke, "remember he has been nurtured in the dungeons of the Jesuits, as it were, there in Dalmatia and has extricated himself from their darkness by his own efforts. If he were, for instance, from France where there is a little more free exchange of ideas, I would feel as you do but coming from where he does I feel we should give him credit for his ideas and accept him at face value."

"I'm sure you know more about these things that I do," I said, "but your book is a dangerous thing. If the Archbishop is not what he seems you could be in trouble from which the Doge himself could not easily extract you."

"I'm sure he *is* what he seems," replied the Servite with all his old weary sarcasm now, "what we have to decide is whether what he seems is an honest man or a rogue."

And there the matter rested.

***

Philippo continued to work at his old profession of *bravo* for the new ambassador, Sir Dudley Carlton. Although I still often saw him in the *Cannaregio* he passed me by without his usual friendly word and wave. This was I supposed because he held me responsible for what had happened to Luigi. When I asked Luigi about his father he hesitated before answering.

"To tell you the truth, Samuele," he said after a moment, "I would like you to pray for my father. You see, he wants me to follow him in his profession as a *bravo*. When I was young I always assumed that was what I would be as soon as I was old enough. Now that things are different I cannot bring myself to enter into a way of life that involves stealing letters and spying as its better aspects and murder and violence as its worst. What makes matters worse is now I am old enough to join my father in some of his darker exploits but I have been refusing to go with him. He complains that I will never learn my 'trade' as he calls it, without this 'training' and hardening to deeds of violence."

I looked at Luigi and wondered whether "complains" was a euphemism for something more harsh. Philippo would not be the kind of father who hesitated to beat his son if he refused to obey his commands. I remembered the belt with which he had been about to punish me on the day the ape made its escape and I felt pretty sure Luigi had been having a taste of it recently. "Poor Luigi," I said, "I will certainly pray for your father, and for you too. What a pity that Mr Bedell has had to go home to England, perhaps he could have spoken to your father."

"I don't suppose my father would have listened," said Luigi sadly, "he always laughed at Mr Bedell and called him gloomy, although in reality you could not find a more cheerful person could you?"

"God will find a way, Luigi," I said, but as I spoke I felt guilty. Who was I to advise Luigi how to withstand his father's beatings with patience when I did not suffer myself? Luigi clearly did not see it that way, however.

"He will, He will," he said reverently, "thank you so much for your prayers, Samuele, "things are not easy for me at the moment."

***

The way in which our prayers were answered was strange—so strange in fact that at first we did not recognise the answer for what it was.

Philippo had been set to work by Sir Dudley on some job or other the exact nature of which neither Luigi or I ever found out. What was clear was that it involved some equally cunning ruffians on the other side with whom Philippo had to deal in order to carry out whatever Sir Dudley's wishes were. He was absent night after night from the little rooms that he and Luigi shared on some business or other. Luigi took no great notice since this was the usual pattern of his father's "work".

One night, after Brother Paul and I had retired to bed there was a great commotion outside near the monastery stairs, with screams and shouts, and fighting which sounded as if it were taking place in the water. Brother Paul and I listened but of course, due to his circumstances, he did not go to investigate—that would have been quite against the Doge's rules and could have involved him walking into a trap. We knew, however, that someone else from the monastery would go to see what was going on and that if needed Brother Santorio the convent physician would be on hand. We heard the monastery front door open and the sound of various brothers investigating and then more noise, Brother Santorio being called, noises as of someone being helped or carried into the monastery and then silence again.

"Some drunken brawl," murmured Brother Paul, "Santorio, is patching up the remnants that have lived to fight another day. Go back to sleep, Samuele."

When I woke the next day I had forgotten about the incident until Brother Paul came back from the refectory before going over to St. Mark's.

"The fellow that was rescued last night is in a very bad way," he said, "Santorio thinks he will not last much longer. Santorio asked him if he wanted a priest but he said 'no' and is insisting that he will only see me."

With that he went off to visit Brother Santorio's cell but then returned quickly.

"Samuele," he said, "it is one of Sir Dudley Carlton's *bravos*. He is desperate for someone from the ambassador's residence to come over before it is too late and he is also asking for you."

"For me!" I said in astonishment, "Why me?"

"He knows you or you know his son or something. I've sent to the residence—you'd better go up to Santorio's cell."

"It must be Philippo," I exclaimed, "Luigi's father! I'll go at once."

***

Philippo was laid on a bed in Brother Santorio's cell and as I entered the brother motioned me aside.

"He is not long for this world, I'm afraid," he said, "and he seems to be rambling already in his words. Do you really know his son?"

"Yes," I said, "and somebody ought to send for him at once. He is the lad that sells the fruit on the corner of the *fondamente* not far from here."

"I know him," said Brother Santorio, "I'll have someone fetch him now," and he hurried off leaving me with Philippo.

Wondering what on earth I should say, I approached the bed where Philippo lay. Brother Santorio had done a good job cleaning and dressing his wounds but his breath was painfully laboured and his faced was a deadly pale colour.

"Philippo," I said bending over him, "it is Samuele."

"Samuele," he said in a low croaking voice, "Samuele, there is not much time. Tell me, what must I do?"

"Do?" I echoed in surprise.

"Yes, quickly tell me ..." he stopped and began breathing very heavily, "what must I do to be saved like you ... like Luigi, quickly!"

"You must repent," I began earnestly, too overwrought by this time to be surprised, "and you must trust the Lord Jesus Christ to save you. He died for sinners, Philippo, to take their punishment instead."

"How ..." faltered Philippo, "how ... do ... this?"

"Pray!" I urged, "Pray—not *Pater noster*, not *Ave Maria*, not words you do not understand but ask in your own words to be forgiven and tell the Saviour you are trusting in Him."

"Will he do this? Even for me?" the words were only a whisper, " ... very wicked life ..."

"Yes," I answered, "tell Him that!"

"I am a sinner, Lord forgive me," he began, then there were words so quiet and laboured I could not catch them. Then louder again, "I trust in Thee, only in Thee to save me. I have been wicked, vile even to my own son, but I know that Thou canst save me," this last phrase was loud and emphatic.

Brother Santorio returned, "the son is being fetched," he said and then bending over Philippo he asked, "would you like the last rites, my son?"

"No!" came the decided answer and quite clearly, "no priest, nothing—only Jesus!"

Brother Santorio looked at me in bewilderment, not knowing how to proceed.

"I would grant him his last request if I were you," I said quietly.

***

The representative from Sir Dudley arrived too late for Philippo to pass on any message he may have been hoping to give, although papers were later found on his body that were passed to the ambassador and (Luigi subsequently found out) proved that Philippo had carried out his orders (whatever they had been) faithfully.

Luigi also arrived too late to speak to his father and after he had spent some time weeping in great distress over the body, I led him gently away to the privacy of Brother Paul's cell. I shut the door carefully and then I said, "Luigi, do not weep. I have some good news for you. What were you talking to your father about when you were last with him?"

Luigi wiped his face with his sleeve, "I refused to go with him last evening. He was very angry. He … I told him I trusted in Jesus only, whether I lived or died, that I was going to heaven one day, that …" here he was stopped by fresh tears.

"Your father has gone there," I said quietly.

"No," said Luigi, "Please don't tell me that, Samuele. You know as well as I do that he hated the Christian religion and mocked it continually."

"I know that," I replied gently, "but I was with him when he died. He asked me what he should do to be saved like you. I told him to repent and trust in the Lord Jesus. I am sure he did so although his voice was low and I could not hear all that he said. He confessed that he had lived a wicked life. He prayed earnestly for Christ to save him. He died refusing the last rites from Brother Santorio and with the words 'only Jesus.'"

Chapter 17: (1613) Departure

By the time the grape vine over the monastery back door began to flower in May, Luigi's existence was as fragile as the subtle fruit scent of its clustering spikes of greenish white flowers. As I buried my nose in them I wondered how much longer he could go on supporting himself with his little stall.

"What can he do?" I asked Brother Paul, "he has no training in anything."

"Do?" asked Brother Paul, "Do? oh, don't be concerned. I've got something he can do—or rather you have."

It was a time when political events in Europe made Brother Paul gloomy and withdrawn and I had learnt by experience to let him tell me his ideas rather than to ask. I waited patiently for an explanation.

The son of the King of England, Prince Henry, of whom Brother Paul had had great hopes had died the year before. The old spirit of intolerance was strong in France. Here in Venice one of Brother Paul's close friends, the theologian Giovanni Marsilio, had died, probably from poison administered from afar by the hand of the inquisition. Galileo had written three letters—in Italian to give them the widest possible circulation—setting out his ideas on the positions of the sun and the earth in the universe. They had not been well received by the Pope, and Galileo was now locked in a controversy with the Court of Rome.

Altogether it was not a hopeful time and I wondered if Brother Paul's thoughts were once more turning to leaving Venice for England. If they were he gave no sign of it. He laid down his pen, pushed aside the sheets of paper forming the castle, took off his spectacles and said:

"Luigi would make an excellent young gentleman's servant, especially for someone who is travelling abroad. He is resourceful and a good Christian. Anyone travelling for their education or health would be glad to employ him."

All this seemed sensible enough, although how Luigi would find such a gentleman puzzled me.

"Do you know of a young gentleman like this then, Brother Paul?" I asked.

"Indeed I do," he replied, "a young man who is about to set off for Geneva to study and has a handsome pension from the senate and some savings to enable him to travel in comfort."

For a moment I did not know what he was talking about. Then I saw it! "You mean I could go to Geneva this year and take Luigi with me as my servant?"

"Exactly."

Any last doubts I had about going now seemed to melt away at this prospect, "Oh, that would be wonderful! With Luigi I would not feel lonely or strange anywhere!" I said.

"That's just as well," said Brother Paul, "because I think you should go now. Things on the world stage do not get any brighter. Hopes of reform and regeneration from within the church seem further away than ever. Shall I write to Dr Diodati and tell him you are on your way?"

"Yes, please do," I said, "but how will we get there? I mean we will need a guide or something won't we?"

"I think you can hardly get there by following your noses," said Brother Paul dryly, "I will find someone to guide you from Padua. Now I need to explain to you about your financial arrangements."

The senate had been paying my little pension to Brother Paul who had been laying a small amount of it out for my education and prudently banking the rest. I did not know much about banking but apparently, although I would be wise to take some of my money with me, Brother Paul would be able to ensure that I could draw on the rest through bankers in Geneva. He could forward the subsequent annual payments also by this means.

The next morning I hurried off to tell Luigi the news. He was busy at his stall as usual and it was a few moments before I could speak to him. He looked thin and ill I thought as I watched him selling his apples and peaches and it struck me that there was no reason for him not to become my servant right away even before we set off for Geneva. He would need to recruit his strength for the journey and as my servant he could have regular good food.

"Luigi, I've got some news for you," I said as soon as he was free, "would you take a job as a paid servant to a young man travelling to Geneva?"

"It would depend on who he was," said Luigi, rather startled by the proposal, "I couldn't go off with just anybody!"

"It would be me!" I explained.

"You! You! Well that would be … well it would be … when can I start?"

***

Our main difficulties on the journey, Brother Paul explained, would be to pass through Italy once we had left Venetian territory. If we were wise, he said, we would try to keep quiet about our views on everything and even about our ultimate destination. In the end Brother Paul decided the best way would be for us to travel with some merchant bankers who were going to Lyons in France. At Milan two of them were leaving the party to travel into Switzerland across the Great St. Bernard pass. They would leave us at Villeneuve in Switzerland on the edge of Lake Geneva where we would have to find a boat across the lake to Geneva itself on our own.

We were not to tell anyone about our departure, even our friends at the Venetian congregation. Brother Paul seemed to me to be very anxious about our journey, although probably no one else would have noticed it. I too was anxious, although not about Luigi and myself. I was worried about Brother Paul. He was still hated by the Court of Rome and was still the object of plots and intrigues aimed at dragging him off to Rome or failing that to murder him. He would be in danger in that respect until his dying day. But even this was not my main concern. By now I could read his moods well. Of late I had sensed a return to the old uncertainty in his mind that made him doubtful about even the existence of God.

The night before Luigi and I were due to leave for Padua, Brother Paul and I were sitting working in the cell as if nothing different was going to happen the next day. I went over to a particular bookcase, opened it and reached out Brother Paul's worn little Greek New Testament.

"Brother Paul," I said, "dear Brother Paul, I can never thank you enough for all you have done for me. You know as well as I do that it is possible we may never see one another again in this life. Will you make me a promise? Keep reading this book. Read it with all your mind and strength with all your heart and I will pray that God will speak to you as you do so."

Brother Paul took off his spectacles and, to my utter amazement, tears were streaming down his face.

"I promise, Samuele, my son, I promise," he said.

***

No one saw us off as we joined the *padovana* for our journey to Padua. Luigi had almost nothing with him except some warm clothing I had bought him for our crossing of the Alps and I had not much more. We had instructions as to where we were to find the merchant party that were leaving Padua in a few days and that was it—we were on our own.

The details of our journey to Geneva, the adventures we had en route, our difficulties with the merchants, the climbing of the great pass, our crossing of the lake; all these things would make a book in their own right and I don't propose to relate them here. I can say, however, that the journey cemented our friendship for ever and that during our travels I grew from a child to a man—with Luigi's help. He may have been the servant and I the master in theory but in practice it was I that relied on him in every crisis—and he never failed me.

Chapter 18: (1614-23) Geneva

It took me a long time to get used to life in Geneva but that was not because I did not like it. When you have grown up looking over your shoulder to see if the Inquisition is watching you, living in a free atmosphere is almost shocking. Both Luigi and I found it hard to adjust to a life where we could speak our minds—and hearts—freely and ask whatever questions we wished without fear.

It was just as well that when we arrived in Geneva many of the students were away for the summer break. This enabled me to settle into a new way of life before I enrolled for my studies.

Carlo was overjoyed to see us and very eager to find out what we thought of his home city.

I found it difficult to answer his questions, "It will take some getting used to," I replied, "I've never lived with a family before—and the students as well! The house is overflowing with young people. There seem to be so many children and I can't even remember all their names. All my life I have lived with grave quiet Servites, all this noise and fun is quite difficult to deal with!"

"Well believe me you are lucky to be lodging with Dr Diodati and the Signora Madeleine," he said, "you have a comfortable billet there and very good food—although I expect it's very different from the menu in Venice."

"After what we have eaten—and haven't eaten—on the way here, any well cooked regular meals are heaven," I said, "whether or not the food is familiar! But I wish I could get the hang of all the different family members—all the students staying there confuse me as well. Half the time I can't remember who is a student and who is a Diodati and also I'm finding myself very clumsy in a family situation. In a monastery everyone knows their place and I know mine. This is all new and I'm sure I'm saying the wrong things to the wrong people all the time."

"The Diodatis won't mind if you do," said Carlo, "the house is always full of students from all over Europe. When they first come I expect they mostly feel just like you."

I had my private doubts about this. How many of the usual students at the Geneva Academy had grown up in a monastery, I wondered? "The children certainly make me welcome," I said, "Dorothée is the eldest, is that right?"

"Yes," said Carlo, "a second mother to the little ones, so gentle but a disciplinarian too! She virtually runs the household nowadays. Then there's Charles, he is the studious one and very serious—not like Marie."

"Which one is Marie?" I asked, making a determined effort to sort out the children in my mind, "not the little girl with the pigtails who follows Dorothée around and is obviously devoted to her?"

"No, no," said Carlo, "that's Elizabeth; she's only five. Marie is the cheeky one; full of fun and mischief—about nine years old. Between the two girls comes your namesake Samuel. He's the one who likes mechanical things. I can see the first ever Diodati engineer in the making there!"

"I remember the little one's name, he's Theodore, isn't he? He sits in a high chair at the table, telling anyone who can listen that he is big brother to the baby!"

"Yes, that's him," said Carlo, "and the baby is Marc, just a few months old. Now you've got them all sorted out!"

It was the Signora Madeleine who helped me most to adjust to my new way of life. From the first she treated me like one of her own sons. She made allowances and gave me hints, understanding that sometimes I had no idea what to do. Often, as I drifted off to sleep, it was her face that filled in the details of the shadowy image of my mother singing the quaint little lullaby of my babyhood.

It was not long before Carlo took both of us to see his garden.

"You were my inspiration, at least in part," he explained, "that garden of yours at the monastery was so tiny yet you managed to use every inch just by growing things in pots and boxes."

Carlo's garden had grown from a plot not much bigger than the one at the Servite monastery. Here, he explained, he had grown vegetables, fruit and even a few flowers for his own family. He sold a few things here and there to neighbours and saved some money to buy a little more land when it became available. That enabled him to expand and market his produce a little more widely. This led to further expansion until his plot was big enough for some sizeable fruit trees and rows of vegetables.

You will be so surprised when you see it, Samuele," he chuckled, "because … well, wait and see."

He opened the gate in the high wall with a flourish and as Luigi and I looked in, I gasped with surprise. The trees were set out in ordered walks which provided shade and some peaches had been trained along a south facing wall. Beds of herbs edged the vegetable plots and neat gravel paths intersected the whole like the spokes of a wheel.

"Noventa!" I exclaimed, "you've copied the garden at Noventa, but in fruit and vegetables! It's not just productive—it's beautiful!"

"I'm glad you like it," said Carlo with quiet pride, "My only problem now is I am producing so much that I can't sell it easily. I don't want to spend time traipsing the streets trying to sell fruit and vegetables: I want to be here growing them."

"Can't sell it," said Luigi meditatively, "How do you say 'fresh fruit, all fresh' in French?"

"Why, yes!" I cried, "You need a fruit-seller and Luigi is a professional!"

"Come into my little shed," said, Carlo, "this is an idea that needs thinking about."

He led the way past bee hives and a lavender hedge to a tiny stone two-room building at the back of the garden. It was surrounded with beds of flowers and herbs and had a grape vine, rather like my own back in Venice, trained up over the door. The shed plainly did duty as a store room, tool shed, office, dining-room and even a makeshift bedroom for Carlo.

"I'm never really happy unless I'm in my garden," explained Carlo, as he moved aside a wheel barrow to make space for us, "so I tend to spend more and more time here. It is so peaceful that if the plot behind the garden ever comes up for sale I think I'll extend the shed and move in here altogether!"

He pulled some chairs round his little table and fetched a bowl of strawberries for us to help ourselves.

"I wonder if it would work?" he said.

"Try it out," I suggested, "Luigi is officially my servant, but now I am safely in Geneva, I don't really need him to look after me—not all the time at any rate. Perhaps he could divide his time between you and me."

"You need not pay me," said Luigi, "we could work on a percentage of what I sold."

"Watch out, Carlo," I said, "he is an expert salesman, he'll make his fortune and sell more than you can keep up with!"

***

The time came for me to register as a student at the university. Dr Diodati accompanied me to the Rector's rooms where I was to be entered solemnly in the Rector's Great Book. I had to give my name and sign that I agreed to behave modestly and do my duty, living in the fear of God and in the ordinances of the Church. Since the *only* name I had was "Samuele," Brother Paul had advised me before I left Venice to take his name if I ever needed any other. This I now did, giving my name as "Samuele Paul" and my date of birth as "about the year 1600." I was then asked to promise to live piously according to the Word of God and to "renounce all papal superstitions and all heresies." This struck me as an enormous task—to live according to God's Word at all times seemed to me beyond human competence. I looked at Dr Diodati and he smiled encouragingly. Then I thought of Mr Bedell and the answer came to my mind, "Sir, God helping me I will attempt it; pray for me that I will be given strength to do so."

"Amen," said the Rector reverently and he added my name to his book with a flourish of his pen.

As I settled into my new life as a student I still spent much time with Carlo in his garden. Happy as I was with the bustle of family life at the Diodati home I often felt I needed peace, especially to study. Carlo always welcomed me and understood my need for quiet perfectly. In fine weather I would sit beneath his shady apple and pear trees working away at my books while he dug, planted, weeded, pruned and harvested in the garden. Luigi would wheel off his barrow of produce every day, whistling cheerfully as he went. When he returned at the end of the day the three of us would spend some happy time together reading the Diodati Bible and praying before the sun set. We found we each naturally had something to contribute as we talked together about how God's word worked out in our daily life; I, from my study of the words themselves in great detail; Carlo, from his keen observation of God's work in the natural world and Luigi, from his interaction and conversation with all types of different people as he worked his way along the city streets.

This was a period of delightful peace and calm in my life despite all the new experiences but it was not to last for ever.

***

At first I drank in everything the University of Geneva had to offer until I could almost feel my mind expanding. Having grown up in a monastery in Venice I set myself the task of consciously comparing everything I believed with the Word of God itself in order to fulfil my promise to "renounce all papal superstitions and all heresies." I had made this promise in good faith and fully conscious that to do so was to make a turning point in my life. From now on I was not a son of the Roman church. From now on I was not destined for the Servite monastery. From now on, by virtue of my promise, I was a declared and open Protestant. What would Brother Paul think of this? He must have known that something like it would be required. I remembered his words, "I work away quietly always trying to improve things in the church ..." he too was aware that there were superstitions and heresies in the church of which he was still a member. He too renounced them—at least inwardly. Yet he remained in Venice. Was he still patiently waiting for change to come within the Roman church? Would he waver and give himself up to the unbelief that sometimes plagued him? To my relief I found I could correspond with Brother Paul quite regularly. The English ambassador at Venice, Sir Dudley Carlton, occasionally exchanged letters with Dr Diodati and I was allowed to send my news with these letters. Brother Paul was well, was serving the Doge in his usual capacity and the vine over the monastery back door was bearing fruit. But even in cipher—and we had arranged one for our use before I left—I dare not discuss more important issues with him by letter. For myself I would have to think them out alone. For Brother Paul I would have to trust that God would answer my prayers.

***

During my second year in Geneva Sir Henry Wotton returned to Venice in place of Sir Dudley Carlton but the most startling news that year concerned someone else.

"Have you heard the news from Venice?" said Dr Diodati as we sat at the dinner table one day.

"What news?" asked the Signora Madeleine without pausing in her attempts to spoon soup into little Marc without spilling too much.

"The Archbishop De Domini has made his escape to England: apparently Mr Wotton and Sir Dudley Carlton arranged it all for him," said Dr Diodati, "did you know him, Samuele?"

"Not well," I answered, "although Brother Paul thought highly of him."

"Well he's gone to England via Heidelberg where he has published a very strong attack on the Roman church I'm told—once he was safely out of its clutches. I hear that King James has welcomed him with open arms."

"I have not had any letters from Brother Paul for a little while," I said trying to picture the fat archbishop sneaking out of Venetian territory on his way to England, "perhaps he will tell me about it when I next hear from him."

In my own mind I pondered over why the archbishop had gone and yet Brother Paul had stayed. Did this mean he had decided he would not leave Venice after all? I knew this was something it would be difficult for him to write about safely to me. A letter discussing a move from Venice could easily fall into the wrong hands as had happened with Dr Diodati's letter that once caused so much trouble for Brother Micanzio. Then Brother Paul would be in danger since the Doge would not be pleased to hear that he had been even thinking of such a thing. Yet I longed to know. All our plans had been founded, so it seemed to me, on his leaving. If he stayed in Venice I would never see him again.

I must have been staring absently, my spoon poised on its way to my mouth, because Marie, sitting next to me, nudged me, "Samuele, eat up, please," she said in a good imitation of her mother's voice when reprimanding the younger children, "no cake otherwise." There was so much going on at the table that no one noticed this cheeky remark except Dorothée who frowned sternly at Marie and said to me sympathetically, "Poor Samuele, you still miss your dear Brother Paul very much don't you?"

"I do," I said, "I hope that one day he too can go to the safety of England because otherwise I might never see him again."

"Perhaps there will be a letter soon," said Dorothée comfortingly, "Who is this archbishop? We have two uncles in London, Uncle Theodore and Uncle Philip—and some cousins we have never met— do you think they will meet him?"

"Archbishop De Domini is a strange man," I replied, "to be honest I never liked him very much. He is a fat man, rather greedy in fact, and he has hard little eyes. I could never understand why Brother Paul took him so much into his confidence but he is a good judge of character so perhaps I am mistaken. As to whether your uncles and cousins might meet him, I can't say. I do not even have any idea how big a place London is."

***

You cannot go on being a student for ever. The following year I received my certificate from the Geneva Academy.

"Well, Samuele," said Dr Diodati, when the excitement of the ceremony was over and I was sitting at the fireside with him and the Signora Madeleine, "what are you going to do with yourself now?"

I faced this question with a heavy heart. Many of my contemporaries were going back to their homes in France, where they would pastor Huguenot congregations who were facing troubled times of war and persecution. I could join them if I wished—my French was good—and there was much to be done. I dreaded the prospect, however, not because I was afraid of persecution (although of course I was) but mainly because I felt I could not preach. I was relieved when I found that Dr Diodati agreed with me.

"You are no preacher, Samuele, you are a scholar and a linguist, "he said.

"I had always imagined that when I finished my studies here I would rejoin Brother Paul in London. There I could continue to assist him as I had done in Venice—only much more ably thanks to my studies," I said, "but no news of this has come from Brother Paul directly and certainly no hint that he is about to leave Venice for London."

"There is no reason why you should not stay here if you wish it," said the Signora Madeleine, "you are one of the family here and we would all miss you if you went to England."

"I think the academy here would offer you an appointment if you wish to stay," said Dr Diodati, "your Hebrew is excellent, you have showed yourself very diligent and I notice that the younger students already look to you for help. You could perhaps lecture here in Hebrew under me. I have often to be away and it would be a relief to me to know you were here to stand in for me. And then you know, I am working on a French translation of Brother Paul's *History of the Council of Trent*. I would be happy to have you at my side while I do this work. You know Brother Paul so well and were with him when he wrote the book."

Talk of Brother Paul reminded me that I had very great cause to be grateful and not just to him. The old Doge's words came back to me: "we will follow your academic progress (through Brother Paul) with great interest. I am assured that your future career will bring honour to the Most Serene Republic that has nurtured you." Without my Venetian pension I could never have come here to study. Venice had certainly nurtured me well. How could I show my gratitude? The old Doge was dead but Brother Paul now worked for his successor Doge Memmo. When I returned to the quiet of Carlo's garden shed I sat down and wrote to Brother Paul, pouring out my thanks to him, to Venice, to the Doge and to the good God who had so ordered my life that I could serve Him in so pleasant a place of learning. I left it to his discretion how much of what I said, if any, was passed on to others in Venice.

***

I was pleased and complimented at Dr Diodati's offer. Although I had no burning desire to be a University lecturer, I relished the prospect of helping translate the famous *History of the Council of Trent.* Accordingly I was received into a lectureship at the academy that year. I offered to move out of the Diodati household to make way for younger students but the Signora Madeleine would not hear of it. "We cannot allow you to leave, Samuele," she explained, "the children love having your company. Who would take them for games in Cousin Carlo's garden if you were elsewhere?"

"My wife is afraid *she* will have the job if you go," explained Dr Diodati, "you are too useful to us here, Samuele!"

Visits to the garden with the children were a great pleasure to me. Having never had the luxury of much playtime in my own childhood I enjoyed making up for the lost time with the young Diodatis. Carlo never minded them coming provided they did no damage and they were too fond of their visits to risk losing the privilege by damaging fruit or trampling on crops. Samuel had grand ideas of how water could be carried into the garden from the lake by means of a pump. Carlo was interested in this because carrying water from the well was hard work but, although Samuel worked happily for many hours at various constructions in the garden, he never succeeded in moving a drop of water anywhere useful! Charles was happy to sit under a tree with a book but Marie and Elizabeth were energetic, devising many games of tag and chase in the garden. Little Theodore and Marc stood no chance of winning unless Dorothée, always concerned to see fair play, insisted on a handicap or "start" that would render things more even. The new baby Renée often came too in the capable care of her big sister Dorothée. The fact that I was now a university lecturer did not inhibit me in the least once inside the walls of the garden. I raced and chased with the best of them, sometimes with Theodore or Marc on my shoulders ready to be plumped down at whatever winning post had been marked out—well ahead of the girls.

***

In the end I remained in Geneva for over twelve years! There is no space to tell of all that happened during that time: Carlo's marriage; new additions to the ever growing Diodati family; the publication in England of Brother Paul's great *History of the Council of Trent*; Archbishop De Domini's return to Rome and his death in the Inquisition's prison; a host of other things personal and universal. Instead I will confine myself to relating two events that were very important to me and which led eventually to my leaving Geneva.

My correspondence with Brother Paul, though not frequent was more or less regular. His letters were, however, watched by spies which meant he had to be very guarded in what he wrote, even in cipher. He had managed to convey to me his surprise at the publication of his *History of the Council of Trent* in London under the supervision of the Archbishop De Domini. A copy of the manuscript had been smuggled out of Venice at the request of the English Archbishop, George Abbot, and had reached him via a network of Dutch merchants. For safety the whole manuscript was not sent at once but in separate pieces. Every time Archbishop Abbot received a packet of its pages he wrote back to say that he had received the *canzoni*—Italian songs—safely! De Domini had written a preface to the book in language quite lacking in the moderation Brother Paul himself used throughout the rest of the work. The King's printer in London had printed the book with the royal coat of arms on the title page. Brother Paul's name was not mentioned, of course. Instead the author's name was given as "Pietro Soave Polano" which was an anagram of his name.

In that same year also he wrote to me about the decisions of the Synod of Dort in which Dr Diodati had been greatly involved and about which you will hear later. He described Dr Diodati's conclusions at the synod as "cogent and thorough" and heartily approved of the Synod's findings and actions. I took this as evidence that his old doubts were not torturing him and that my prayers for him were being answered. But although I felt at ease about Brother Paul's mind and spirit, I was anxious about his health.

"You know I never catch colds or fever," he wrote, "this year I have had fever almost all the time."

He told me also that he had been granted the extraordinary privilege of free access to the secret archives of the state which he was to examine and put in order for the government. He also had the task of scrutinizing canon law—the church law—and ensuring that any new laws that the church issued were in conformity with the law of Venice. "There never will be a perfect peace between the Apostolic See and Venetia, except such an one as Brother Paul Sarpi chooses," complained the new Pope Gregory XV angrily. Later that year I began to receive hints in his letters that he would leave Venice, old and ill as he now was. He feared that his continued presence there would cause friction and difficulty for the Most Serene Republic that would lead to war with Rome or its agents. He made preparations to depart and it was with alarm that I heard he intended to travel not to London but to Constantinople! However, the Senate would not hear of his leaving and I was relieved to hear that he had agreed to stay.

At the end of 1622 I received a letter in which his clear handwriting was no less firm than usual but in which he wrote, "We are near the end of the day, and I look forward with joy to a long rest after a weary journey. In my next letter, I will send you some papers that I have here of your father's. They are but trifles, I fear, scraps of tattered papers in a barbaric tongue but it is right that I should send them on to you. Continue with your studies. Your teacher [he meant Dr Diodati] is an excellent man. My advice to you, when you are ready, is to seek out your *old* teacher who is now far from you and whom I will never now join." As usual Brother Paul mentioned no names, not knowing who would possibly see the letter, but it was clear that he was referring to Mr Bedell in England. He was also making it plain that he would not leave Venice for England himself. He spoke of a "long rest," and I was anxious. I was puzzled that he seemed to want me to go to England and seek out Mr Bedell. I wrote expressing my concern for him and asking in guarded terms why he had advised me to do this. No reply came. I began to be more anxious.

"Should I write to Sir Henry Wotton?" I asked Dr Diodati, "perhaps Brother Paul is too ill to write."

Dr Diodati offered to make enquiries but before he could do so I received a letter from Brother Micanzio.

"My dear friend Samuele," he wrote, "our dear Brother Paul went to his eternal rest a few days after the feast of the Epiphany. To the last he was serene and comforted by the Holy Scriptures which he constantly repeated. Do not grieve for him: it was his wish that no one should express extravagant sorrow ..."

Do not grieve! I felt utterly bereft. However kind the Diodatis were to me I had no relatives or anyone to call "father" in this world. My only "brother" was Brother Paul. I grieved for him as a son would grieve for a father and I was doubly sad because I had neither been with him at his death nor visited him before the end. I felt guilty too. He had done so much for me, surely I could have risked the journey back to visit him just once! I poured out my grief to the Signora Madeleine who listened quietly and patiently, laying aside her needlework as she concentrated on my troubles.

"Poor, Samuele," she said, when I paused for breath, "What a sad thing to happen to you, to lose your dearest friend! I know how hard it is to rejoice when those we love pass on to glory and leave us behind —especially when we are far from them at the time."

"I should have been there," I complained, "at least I should have gone to visit him. I knew from his last letter that he was not well."

"He may not have wished it," she replied, thoughtfully taking up her needlework again, "how good that he was comforted by the Scripture at the end!"

"Yes," I said, remembering my parting conversation with Brother Paul, "Brother Micanzio says," I opened the letter again, "'... towards the end I read to him from the *Gospel of John* the Passion of our Saviour and he spoke of his own sins and his strong confidence in the blood of Christ. He repeated often a text from St. Paul's epistle to the Romans: *quem proposuit Deus propitiationem per fidem in sanguine suo*—whom God hath set forth to be a propitiation through faith in his own blood.' No atheist would say that would they?"

"No indeed!" she replied in surprise.

I hurried on quickly lest she should ask the meaning of my remark for I did not wish to disclose what Brother Paul had often felt about his doubts, "Do you think I should go and see Brother Micanzio? He is old also and has perhaps no one left in Venice to share his faith now that Brother Paul is gone."

"Write and ask him," she replied practically, "and tell him how you feel about Brother Paul's death too, just as you have told me," then she paused and added, "Brother Paul always gave you wise advice didn't he? Well, a good way to honour his memory would be to read his last letters looking for any words of advice and be sure to follow them."

***

Brother Micanzio's reply came quickly. He assured me that Brother Paul would have done his utmost to discourage me from returning, "The place you mention in your letter is not wise for you to visit now, nor would the person you mention have wished the risk of a visit," he wrote. Then followed details of the funeral and a reassurance that my pension from the Venetian government would still be forwarded to me as he had taken charge of the matter on Brother Paul's death. To be honest I had not even considered this aspect of the situation before. Finally, he wrote, "I bless you for your kindness in even thinking, dear Samuele, of visiting your old friend's friend. It will not be necessary. If you can find time to write now and again that would bring joy. I will continue to pray for you. Remember me in your prayers also and on that glorious day we will all meet again." There was a postscript promising to send on some papers when they were located and explaining that there was a great deal of Brother Paul's correspondence and papers to go through.

So I met with my first loss. The next was in some ways even harder to bear.

***

Carlo, having married, no longer spent all his time in his little "shed" in the garden and so I was able to use it as a study and even as a bedroom in the summer as the Diodati household was crowded. Luigi continued to sell everything Carlo grew, both in the garden and in the many other plots which he now occupied outside the city walls. The expansion meant that other sellers were employed and Luigi was in charge of them. He too had married—a girl who was the daughter of a good old widow woman who came to help prepare the vegetables and fruit for sale. They lived in a tiny house not far from the garden. Here the widow also found shelter and helped the business along by baking fruit pies from garden produce to be sold hot in the streets by some of Luigi's vendors. Although the three of us were still very good friends, the marriages of my two companions changed our relationship and made Luigi and Carlo necessarily closer to each other than I was to them.

Young Charles Diodati was now a student at the university and Samuel already had various business ventures in the city supplying water via wells and conduits. The older girls, however, still came to the garden bringing the new additions to the family, seven year old Renée and the toddling Philippe, to play in the garden as they themselves had done when they were younger. Carlo's young family also played in the garden for much of the time and he joked that he would have to have done with fruit and vegetables and grow a lawn for them all.

Marie Diodati took to inviting her friend Adrienne to join in the fun. Adrienne was a little older than Marie but the two had become close friends as they shared a tutor and often had lessons together. Adrienne was a motherless girl with no brothers or sisters and her father was glad that she was able to spend time with the Diodatis. Unlike the Diodati girls who were quite plain to look at, having inherited their father's prominent nose and large features, Adrienne was dainty and delicate. She seemed almost to dance about the garden when playing with the little ones. The Diodati girls dressed in serviceable plain frocks and aprons especially when taking their younger siblings to play in the garden. Adrienne, on the other hand was a picture in graceful silk and lace which she contrived to keep clean and neat however much running about was called for.

When the younger children were being put to bed by Dorothée and their mother, Marie, Elizabeth and Adrienne would sometimes come to the garden looking for flowers for the house or simply to walk in the cool evening air. I began to find myself looking forward to these visits. There was something so sweet and yet mischievous about Adrienne—so mischievous in fact that I could tell that Dorothée did not quite approve of her as a companion for Marie. But then Dorothée was very straight laced, not like Adrienne herself who was always laughing, teasing, singing or joking over something or other.

One evening after a warm spring day I was sitting under the oldest apple tree after finishing my supper and my preparation for the next day's lectures. I was thinking about stretching my legs with a walk in the fields and orchards outside the city walls. I was just standing up and brushing the crumbs from my lap when the garden gate opened and Adrienne came in.

"Hello," I said cheerfully, "where are Marie and Elizabeth?"

"They have to help with the children," replied the girl, "Dorothée has a headache, so I came alone."

"I was thinking of going for a walk through the orchards outside the walls," I said, my heart suddenly racing at the thought of pretty Adrienne accompanying me, "would you care to come too?"

***

Days of heady delight followed that evening stroll. Adrienne came again. And again. We walked together often through the orchards and fields that form such a pleasant landscape outside the city walls of Geneva. Soon she was never out of my thoughts. I drifted off to sleep now, not with my mother's song in my thoughts but with a vision of Adrienne, skipping, dancing over the orchard grass, Adrienne laughing, singing, chattering, teasing me for being the "monk of the garden", Adrienne, Adrienne, Adrienne …

Before, when I envied Carlo his happy family or mourned my own loneliness, I had never considered that I could do anything about it or change my situation. Now it dawned upon me that here was somebody who had the power to banish my loneliness for ever. I began to make plans.

Summer came. Adrienne and I walked in the fields and orchards almost every evening. I made up my mind.

It was a particularly lovely evening in late summer and Adrienne and I had walked through the fragrant orchards and fruit gardens along the edge of the River Rhone. We turned to go back to the city gate and crossed an apple orchard where a stile led from the riverside path. I crossed first and then took her hand to help her over. When, light as a butterfly, she crossed the stile I did not let it go.

"Adrienne," I said, as we walked slowly together through the young trees, "I must speak to your father."

Her face turned deadly white and she stopped in her tracks, dropping all the flowers she had gathered on the grass.

"My father," repeated Adrienne in a whisper, and her laughing tone was quite gone. I did not answer for a moment and she seemed to get her breath back. When she spoke again there was the old teasing tone in her voice but it shook as she spoke, "Why would you speak to him, Samuele?"

"I think you know why, Adrienne," I answered quietly.

"I'm sure I do not," she replied the teasing smile playing round her lips but not in her eyes, "you must tell me."

"Do you not know that I want to marry you, Adrienne?" I answered.

There was silence for a moment and then like a clap of thunder she exclaimed, "You!" her voice took on a mocking tone, with a hard edge to it now, unlike her usual teasing, "the garden monk! You want what? Tell me, Monk, what is your name? Go on! Your name: all of it!"

"My name?" I asked, "What do you mean, Adrienne?"

"Mademoiselle Adrienne De Lange, if you please," she said haughtily, "and you are …?"

"Samuele," I replied pained and puzzled, "Samuele Paul."

"Oh no you are not," came the sharp retort, "you only call yourself Paul because that was your monkish master's name. You have nothing to offer me, Monk, not even a name!" and to my astonishment she wrenched her hand from mine, picked up her skirt and ran from me through the field, along the lane and out of sight.

Utterly bewildered and shocked I sat down on the grass. I do not know how long I sat there beside the fallen flowers but it began to grow dark. My mind, previously so full of happy thoughts seemed completely empty, destitute, numb. Like something from another world I heard Luigi whistling as he pushed home his hand cart on the other side of the hedge. He hailed me cheerfully when he saw me, "Hey, Samuele, out for a stroll? Are you going my way?"

I forced myself to gather my wits and answer him but my reply seemed to come from a long way off. Whatever I said cannot have made much sense for he replied by leaving the empty cart and crossing to where I sat.

"Are you all right, Samuele?" he asked peering at me in the gathering gloom.

I shook myself, "I'm fine, Luigi," I replied, "are you going home? I'll walk with you."

***

It was Dorothée who wheedled the story of my misery out of me, gentle Dorothée who could not bear the sight of anyone in distress and who was so sensitive to the feelings of others. I do not think anyone could have hidden a grief of heart from her. Her shock was almost equal to my own but she was also very, very angry.

"How long has she been walking alone with you in the evenings, the minx?" she asked in a tone I had never heard her use before.

"Don't be angry with her," I protested.

"Don't be angry!" she exclaimed, "I don't think I have ever been so angry in my life before!"

And then she told me. There were two young men, students at the university whom I knew slightly, who had gone together to France for a period of two years to aid the Huguenots. One was a very able preacher, Arnaud Lamarche, to whom she was herself betrothed although no announcement would be made until his safe return. The other, Léon Simoneau …

"Léon is similarly betrothed to Adrienne and an announcement is to be made when they return," she said, "no one except myself, my parents and her father, of course, know this yet. Now you know why I feel so angry with her! How dare she behave as she has done! Poor Léon! He deserves someone better—and so do you Samuele!"

I protested feebly and did my best to offer my congratulations to Dorothée on her engagement.

"But what is to be done now?" she asked, greatly concerned.

"O please do not mention this to anyone, least of all her father, M. De Lange. I would hate her to get into trouble," I urged.

"That is all very well, Samuele," said Dorothée, gently again now, "I do not wish to see her punished but you must understand she should not be allowed to associate with Marie any longer."

I saw the point at once. The boisterous Marie was fond of Adrienne and inclined to follow the older girl's lead. The thought of her being led astray by Adrienne's behaviour was not to be borne.

Dorothée bent down to little Philippe who was playing with some twigs and leaves on the gravel path. I answered giving her the permission she sought to speak of the situation to her mother and begging her to protect Adrienne from trouble if at all possible. At that she stood up, took Philippe by the hand and said, "How could she be so cruel! Of all the things to reproach you with! You have a *good* name Samuele, a good name for honesty, scholarship and Christian living. What does any other name matter?" And with that she left the garden.

***

It was a long time before Adrienne's face began to fade from my dreams and my mother's gentle, "*Tras a na dont a dol sheer dol sheer,*" came back to lull me to sleep at night. The Signora Madeleine contrived to settle the difficult situation by speaking herself to Adrienne and also to Marie, telling her only that Adrienne had misbehaved and that she was no longer to see her.

"Poor Samuele," she said to me as she sat in the garden with little Philippe and some of Carlo's children, "you have been very spitefully used."

I could think of no answer except to thank her for her concern.

"Did you re-read any of Brother Paul's last letters?" she continued referring to our earlier conversation.

"I did," I replied, "and do you know, I had almost forgotten what he advised me to do."

"What was that?" she asked.

"He told me to seek out my old teacher, Mr Bedell, who is now in England. I wrote to ask him why he wanted me to do this but I never had a reply from him. I know my last letter reached him, Brother Micanzio told me, so I suppose he was too ill by then to reply."

"And do you think it was wise advice?" she asked, "Will you follow it?"

"I cannot see how it would help me, although, of course, I loved and respected Mr Bedell deeply," I answered "but I must admit, after what has happened, I do feel like travelling and leaving Geneva, at least for a while."

***

A few days later Dr Diodati called me to his study, "Do you think it is time you made a *peregrinatio academica*, Samuele?" he began, referring to the journey to visit the most famous seats of Reformed learning which those students who could afford it often undertook, "I am going to visit the Huguenot Academy at Saumur in France, then I plan to travel down the Loire River and then by sea to the Dutch Republic and the University of Leiden. I was wondering if you would like to come with me. I expect your skill in Hebrew would make you feel at home with the scholars at Saumur and I understand from the Signora Madeleine that you feel you would benefit from a change of scene."

"It is kind of you to invite me," I replied eagerly, "I would love to come if I can be spared from the academy here without difficulty."

"I'm sure that could be arranged," he replied and I knew that as he himself was now the Rector, no problems would be put in my way, "we could travel to Basel first and visit Johannes Buxtorf before crossing to France."

"Oh, I'd love to meet him!" I exclaimed, "no one on earth knows more about Hebrew than he does!"

"Louis Cappel of the Saumur Academy thinks he does," remarked Dr Diodati dryly, referring to the controversy over the age of Hebrew vowel points that had occupied the two men, "I wonder if we can somehow manage to fit in a trip to the academy at Sedan as well—or maybe you could go on there on your own from Leiden."

"It all sounds very exciting to me," I replied, "whatever you think best will suit me!"

"It is a great pity we cannot travel the same route that I took when I went to the Synod of Dort," he said sadly, "you would have enjoyed travelling from Lausanne to Basel and Strasbourg and then to the academy at Heidelberg and then on the Rhine to the Hague. But the area is now torn by this terrible war over the Palatinate and would not be safe. When I travelled that route to Dort for the synod I met the Elector Palatine at Heidelberg and his English wife, Elizabeth, the Winter Queen. They were so kind to me and so concerned for the spiritual welfare of their people in the Upper and Lower Palatinate. They are truly godly rulers."

"And now the Elector has been defeated by the Catholic forces of the Holy Roman Emperor," I said, "his territories ransacked and taken over by the forces of the Catholic Counter-Reformation and the Elector and his wife are exiles in Holland."

"What has happened there is a great tragedy," said Dr Diodati, "refugees from the Palatinate are fleeing to any place where they can worship in freedom: Bayreuth, and Nuremberg, are overflowing with people who have lost everything."

"Let us hope and pray that help will come to the Elector—perhaps from England—then all these poor people can go back to their homes," I said.

"The Signora Madeleine's brother in England is helping to collect money for them to ease their difficulties," replied Dr Diodati, "but I fear military aid for the Elector himself will be another matter."

* * *

I was sure the Signora Madeleine was at the bottom of this kind invitation to travel and I was grateful to her. I had no strong ties to anyone in Geneva now that Luigi was happily married and the best way to escape my sorrow, it seemed to me, was to leave it behind. Now here was a chance to set out with Dr Diodati, an experienced and expert traveller, on a very different journey from the one which Luigi and I had accomplished with so much struggle to reach Geneva in the first place.

"You'll be travelling in style this time," joked Luigi, as I made my preparations to depart, "no skulking about trying to look as if we were not Venetians on the run, no looking for merchants who had received money to look after us and really hoped they could set off without us, no getting lost in the snow, no climbing the wrong pass for miles, no …"

"Stop, stop," I laughed, "did we really do all that, Luigi?"

"All that and more," he replied, "it is a wonder we ever got here at all!"

"Do you remember the time we ran out of food and it was miles to go to the place where that oldest merchant—what was his name—Nadat—told us to meet him? Why was he so keen we were to go ahead alone I wonder?"

"I never trusted him," said Luigi, "I expected him to give us away at any moment if there was money available for doing so!"

"I would never have had any idea who to trust and who not," I said with a laugh, "without you I am absolutely sure I would have ended up dead on the road somewhere between Venice and here!"

"I'll miss you, Samuele," said Luigi, "take care of yourself and come home safe and sound."

"Remember me in your prayers, please, Luigi," I asked.

"I will, of course, my friend," said "Luigi, "and as for Carlo he's green with envy—I understand the Dutch are expert vegetable gardeners!"

Chapter 20: (1626-7) At Sea

If I had known when I set off on my *Peregrinatio Academica* how long it would be before I returned and what would happen to me on the way I would have been shocked, perhaps even dismayed … but things must be told in their proper order and set out according to their importance so I will begin at the port of Nantes on the River Loire.

At Nantes we were to transfer from the river-boat from Samur to an ocean-going vessel bound for the Netherlands. We arrived at the quayside in lashing, torrential rain that almost blotted everything from view. In any case I was not in a condition to take much notice of my surroundings. After our travels to Basel and on to Saumur my head was almost bursting with the new experience of interaction with scholars and experts from different traditions and with different opinions. By the time we reached Nantes I was beginning to wonder how much more of the *academica* part of my *peregrinatio* I could cope with. I definitely needed some time for quiet reflection to sort things out in my mind and I had my doubts as to whether I would find it on an ocean voyage to the Netherlands.

We were hoping to sail on a *fluyt* called the *Dolphijn* and we found her with some difficulty due to the pouring rain. We were welcomed aboard by the part-owner, Captain Doomer, with whom Dr Diodati had sailed before. He was delighted to see his old friend but concerned as to where he could accommodate me in the ship.

"You can shake down with me in the cabin," he said to Dr Diodati, "but I am afraid the only other space is in the aft quarters with the crew: my brother, his sons, a couple of fellows from the Hague—you've met one of them already I think, Piet, he is the one with the good French—and my own son who is on his first voyage."

"His first voyage! He was a little lad still at home playing with toy boats in the canal when I last sailed with you!" said Dr Diodati.

"Ah," said the captain proudly, "Hans has been playing with boats and in boats since he was able to walk. He is turning out to be a good seaman. Of course I have to treat him exactly the same as the others on board and he does not shirk doing his share. A *fluyt* such as the *Dolphijn* needs only a small crew but everyone must play his part even if he is only learning his craft. On a *fluyt* one must take every chance to learn from the others and the best way to do that is to seize every opportunity to work—and work hard."

"I can't imagine a lazy Doomer," said Dr Diodati with a smile, "When do we sail, Captain?"

"The *Dolphijn* is still loading her cargo of wines," explained Captain Doomer, "and when that is finished as soon as the weather improves and the tide is right we will be leaving—with the help of a river pilot."

"What were you bringing to Nantes?" asked Dr Diodati, "the usual naval stores?"

"Yes, and good Dutch cheeses," replied the tall Captain, "they are very popular here and fetch a good price."

I had seen nothing of the elegant little *Dolphijn* or her crew as I scrambled aboard in the lashing rain. Glad to get below out of the wet I was unaware of everything except the need to stow my few possessions and clothes in a tiny space aft and to dry myself out. There would be no time for quiet reflection here, I thought ruefully, squeezed in with the crew of six who already shared a space barely big enough for two. Not that there would be many times—if any— when they were all there together I reasoned. Crew members would surely have to be on duty day and night on a sailing ship. Although they were all on deck now, I supposed that once out of the river they would be taking turns to sleep and go on deck. I hoped they would not resent my presence and the extra discomfort I would cause.

"Dinner with the Captain this evening," said Dr Diodati putting his head into the little space some time later after the pilot had come on board and the *Dolphijn* was moving downstream, "and by then we will be well out at sea I hope—the sky is brightening up already."

After stowing everything as well as I could and taking stock of my new surroundings I decided I would dry off much better on the deck in the sun and breeze. I made my way up to find the pilot had already left in the little boat that the *Dolphijn* had been towing. It was strange, I mused, that I had grown up in Venice, that great sea trading city, and yet had never before made an ocean voyage. My only experience of sailing stopped at gondolas and padovanas! I kept out of the way of the sailors working the square sails on the two tall masts, fascinated as the land slipped away behind us.

I soon identified the captain's son, a lad of about twelve, who was happy to talk to me but kept a wary eye open and an ear well tuned to any order that another crew member—and they were all his superiors —might give. In answer to my questions he told me that the *Dolphijn* was eighty feet long and roughly pear-shaped. "That gives her a nice big hold," he explained in halting French, "and everything is set up so that she only needs a small crew. Her shallow draught lets her to come up to ports like Nantes with ease. When we get to Amsterdam ..."

"*Hans! Hans! Waar is de jongen?*" came a cry from somewhere astern and my informant shot off without apology.

Now we were out in the open sea, carried along sedately by our four sails in a gentle breeze and bright sunshine, I wondered if I would be sea sick.

"What in this weather!" laughed Dr Diodati, when I voiced my fears, "wait till the weather gets choppy out in the Bay of Biscay or the English Channel!"

That evening in the captain's cabin I was introduced properly to Captain Doomer.

"From Venice!" he said, when Dr Diodati had explained exactly who I was, "What a city for ships!" and to my embarrassment he began to quiz me (Dr Diodati acting as interpreter) on exactly what types of vessels I had seen in my home city, where they were from, what cargo they carried, their rigging, size ...

"Oh dear," I said to Dr Diodti, "you had better tell him I did not have much to do with ships in Venice. The best I can do apart from gondolas and padovanas is describe watching the Doge go in his state barge to drop the golden ring into the water during the ceremony when Venice weds the sea each year. Would that interest him?"

But the explanation did not satisfy the captain who clearly thought I must have gone about Venice with my eyes shut, "you scholars are in danger of having your heads too much in your books!" he exclaimed, "it is the same with Dr Diodati here; he does not know one end of the ship from another!"

***

That night, unable to sleep (for the little space aft seemed stuffy) I came up on deck for some air. The night watch on board consisted of just two or three sailors if the weather was fair and not changeable. Tonight there were two: the helmsman, at the vertical whipstaff on deck which was connected to the tiller below and another sailor, Piet from the Hague, the lookout, his gaze fixed upon the dim blue vacancy ahead.

Piet was singing softly to himself, *"Het ruime hemelrond Vertelt, met blijden mond, Gods eer en heerlijkheid,"* and the familiar Genevan tune for the nineteenth psalm with its gentle measured pace seemed to fit the night perfectly. The *Dolphijn* was only moving through the water very slowly, and since there was no swell she was so steady that her progress was almost motionless. To port was the pure calm disc of the full moon, her silver glow dulling the stars nearby and spreading a glittering way right up to the ship. All over the rest of the heavens the stars were shining in the clear sky, except just around the horizon's edge, where there was a border of fleecy clouds. What a contrast to the hectic and intense time I had been having on my travels! With a mind unexpectedly restored to peace I joined in softly with the Psalm-singer but in the French I was accustomed to sing in Geneva, *"Ce grand entour espars, Publie en toutes parts, L'ouvrage de ses mains."*

"Mr Paul?" said Piet, quietly so as not to break the enchantment, yet without taking his eyes off the view ahead, "have you come up to enjoy the night air?"

"I have," I responded in a low voice, "and if this is sailing the ocean, I am enjoying it greatly."

He laughed quietly, "it won't be like this all the way to Amsterdam, you know," he said, "have you been to the Netherlands before—with your teacher to the Synod at Dort a few years back perhaps?"

I explained that I had never been to the Netherlands before.

"Were you in the Netherlands yourself at the time of the synod?" I asked.

"I was," he said, still looking straight ahead, "and during all the troubled times before it. Mud-beggars they called us!"

"Who called you such a name and why?" I asked in some surprise.

"Has your teacher not told you?"

"I know about the actual proceedings of the Synod," I said, "and, of course, I've studied the Canons, but I know very little of what led up to it all," I replied.

"It was nearly civil war," he began, and then stopped, "what are you doing on deck young Hans?"

I looked round. The captain's young son had joined us.

"What a night!" he exclaimed, "and you are going to begin a yarn. How can I stay below? I was wide awake with Jitz's knees digging into my back and old Pieterzoon snoring."

"Very well then, but if you are tired and slipshod on the morning watch you'll have to answer to your father, not me!"

"How could the discussions of the academicians at Leiden University lead to civil war?" I asked as anxious as Hans to hear the "yarn".

"Your teacher has told you what Arminius had been teaching at our university of Leiden?" continued Piet, still looking ahead of him.

"Yes," I replied, "God does not choose who will be saved but he knows who will decide to be saved; man has free will to do good; our salvation is achieved in part by Christ's sacrifice on the cross and in part by our own good deeds; a Christian can be saved and then lost again if he goes back to his sinful deeds and … was there anything else?"

"Yes, *and* the state, the government, is in charge of church affairs," finished young Hans Doomer.

"Surely people in Holland did not take up these ideas, did they?" I asked, thinking as I did so that the last idea was one which would have perhaps appealed to the old Doge, "I mean, they had been fighting to be free of Spain because Spain forced them into a church which had many of these kinds of ideas. They would not want to go back to them would they?"

"You are right, as far as the common people are concerned," replied Piet, "but the prominent, the distinguished, the powerful people, the leaders and governors of the land mostly swallowed Arminius' teachings, especially in the important provinces of Holland and Utrecht and in Overijssl. These people demanded toleration by which they meant that Remonstrant preachers—those who agreed with Arminius—should be tolerated in the churches but any preacher who took the opposite view—Counter Remonstrants they were called —should *not* be allowed."

"A strange kind of toleration!" I remarked.

"Indeed," said Piet dryly, "very strange. Under the guise of this 'toleration' they forced preachers and people who clung to the old teaching out of the churches."

"Where do the 'mud-beggars' come into it then?" I asked.

"I was one!" said Hans proudly, "although I was only little at the time. You see we had to walk to church miles away in Rijswijk on a Sunday if we wanted to hear a good Counter Remonstrant preacher like Herr Rosaeus. Our own church in the Hague had a Remonstrant in the pulpit. If it was wet and muddy, well, *we* got wet and muddy— all seven hundred of us. Then they laughed at us and called us names like 'mud-beggars'."

"Seven hundred people, marching off to church in the rain and mud! You must have seemed like an army. What did the government do?" I asked.

"The provincial government, the States of Holland, was asked to call for a National Synod. The Counter Remonstrants asked them to call for one to thrash out the theological issues in the light of the Bible," said Piet, "They refused. If a National Synod—a synod of the whole country—was called, the Remonstrants would never win the argument. The States of Holland were only prepared to consider a synod of the province of Holland alone—where the Remonstrant ministers were in large numbers."

I began to see the seeds of civil war in the situation. Would one provincial synod sanction the teachings of a heretic that were repugnant to the country as a whole?

"Even our great Land's Advocate Oldenbanenveldt sided with the Remonstrants," Hans chipped in, "he lived in The Hague and he demanded that Prince Maurice, the head of our armed forces, stop us all walking to church in Rijswijk."

"Civil war a step nearer," I thought.

"Yes but the Counter Remonstrants themselves *also* petitioned the Prince," said Piet, "asking to be given a place to worship—a house, a barn, anywhere—in the Hague so that the women and children did not have to walk to Rijswijk and back on Sundays."

"What did he say?" I asked, "whose side did he take?"

"He agreed with us!" said Hans gleefully, "and he even offered his *own* house for our use as a church until an old monastery which had been used as a munitions factory could be prepared for us."

"How did that go down with Oldenbarnenveldt?" I asked.

"He went back to the States of Holland and Utrecht and persuaded them to enact a resolution refusing a national synod to debate the issue," said Piet, "he got them to empower the cities involved to raise a militia or local defence force."

"Two armies then," I thought, "Prince Maurice and the local forces. Hard to avert civil war when that happens," out loud I asked, "did it come to fighting then?"

"No!" said Piet, "thankfully the States General of the United Provinces now intervened. Because the States General consisted of members from *all* the provinces, not just Holland and Utrecht it had many Counter Remonstrant members. They ordered a National Synod to take place."

"But what about the militias?" I asked, "they were still there and armed ready to stop the mud-beggars."

"The States General empowered Prince Maurice to disband the militias. What a Statesman! He did it—and all without bloodshed, praise the Lord!" said Piet.

"So now the doctrinal question could be settled in the light of the Bible without force being used," I said, "I suppose the Remonstrants knew all along that only force would enable them to foist their ideas on the people."

"Indeed," said Piet, "any synod of the whole country would decide against them. And so … well, your teacher saw how they behaved at the synod. No wonder poor John Bogerman the chairman ended up losing his temper with them!"

"They were disgraceful," said a voice behind me and I saw that Dr Diodati too had come up on deck to enjoy pleasant night air, "they would not engage in any discussion or set out their beliefs. For days and days they simply stalled the proceedings with endless complaints about the existence of the synod, its right to judge their doctrine and also a host of minor matters deliberately put forward to stop the synod getting down to an examination. I remember it was agony to listen to them going on and on day after day and never stating their beliefs or teachings!"

"How did it end then?" I asked, knowing that the synod *had* examined Remonstrant ideas and unanimously condemned them as unscriptural.

"Well, in the end John Bogerman could not stand it any more," said Dr Diodati, "he banged on the table and said, 'enough! You have deliberately stalled as long as you can. We now send you away! Go away! Go! Go!' and he pointed to the door. After that we examined their beliefs by means of studying their published books and came to our conclusions without them."

"I do not understand why you were there at all," I said, "I seems to me the affair was wholly a Dutch one."

"Because the issues involved were so important, participants were invited from the rest of Reformed Europe," explained Dr Diodati, "Tronchin and I were the delegates from Geneva, Dr Samuel Ward— Mr Bedell's old college friend—was one of the English delegates and there were delegates invited from France also, although at the last minute the King of France forbade them to attend."

This made sense to me, "You mean it was a kind of reply to the Council of Trent which had excluded the Protestants?" I asked, "No wonder Brother Paul always spoke of its conclusions, the Canons of Dort, with approval!"

"Indeed it was!" he replied, "That is a very Venetian way of looking at it, Samuele."

"And what happened to Oldenbarnenveldt in the end?" I asked.

"The Canons of Dort shot off his head!" replied Dr Diodati with a grim laugh, "having brought the United Provinces so near to civil war, he was executed."

***

The next day we made good speed and the weather was fair—not a cloud in the sky and a good breeze. I stayed on deck as much as I could, enjoying the new experience of being at sea and out of sight of land. The *Dolphijn* was a complete world of her own out there on the ocean, her competent little Dutch crew a tight-knit community in which everyone knew his place and could do his job—even young Hans.

"It reminds me of the Servite monastery where I grew up," I said to Dr Diodati, "everyone has his job, his duty and his place in a chain of command."

"A monastery!" exclaimed Piet, in horror, overhearing my remark, "begging your pardon, Sir, however did you come to be in such a place?"

"I not only grew up there, but Dr Diodati here was a regular visitor to one of the Brothers who brought me up," I replied, adding, "and he wrote him friendly letters until the day he died."

"Well, I can't believe it!" exclaimed Piet shaking his head in perplexity as he walked away to take over from Pieterzoon at the whipstaff.

I began to imagine that I was a born sailor: I was so happy on the deck in the sunshine. I had already started to learn Dutch from the crew in readiness for our arrival in Holland and I could communicate quite well. Dr Diodati's remarks about the choppy sea of the Bay of Biscay seemed quite unfounded.

And then we entered the English channel. The sky clouded over and the wind became stronger. Rain again lashed the decks and I realised that my stomach could cope with the horrible motion of the ship no better than that of any other landsman at sea for the first time. Feeling wretchedly sick I lay below moaning while my new-made friends, the Dutch sailors, struggled to keep the vessel on a safe course. Dr Diodati, a seasoned traveller and a very good sailor himself, tried his best to look after me but in the whole of my so far healthy life I had never felt so ill. I no longer knew or cared whether it was day or night: I simply longed for some kind of end to it all.

At one point I was conscious of Dr Diodati making his way on deck and returning. "The captain does not like the look of the weather," he said, "and is proposing to make for an English port for shelter before continuing to Holland."

I remember saying that I didn't care if we sheltered on the Barbary coast in a nest of pirates so long as I could get off the ship. From the horrible motion of the *Dolphijn* I assumed the weather was worsening. After a while there was much shouting and bumping about above and Dr Diodati went on deck again. When he returned he reported that we were making for an English port but he was not sure which one it was. After a while there was a change in the ship's motion, and he went on deck again.

"They are going to anchor in the Downs until the storm is passed," he said but I hardly heard him and would not have understood if I had. But before morning the storm had abated and I dozed off into a fitful sleep, my mother's little song lurching round in my head broken and disturbed by the movement of the ship.

***

It was bright daylight before I awoke. The storm had blown over completely and, as I staggered up on deck, I could see blue sky over head and gulls wheeling. The *Dolphijn*'s sails were furled and there was not a breath of wind. Dr Diodati came in view with old Pieterzoon.

"Where are we?" I asked.

"We are at anchor off the coast of England in the Downs, Sir," said Pieterzoon, "there are treacherous sand banks in the English Channel called the Goodwin Sands and between the sand banks and the coast there is a sheltered anchorage where we are now, called the Downs."

"So what happens now?" I asked.

"The sea is a sheet calm, as they call it here, Sir," replied Pieterzoon, "but the Captain will have us set sail again for Amsterdam as soon as there is a favourable wind."

"But what about a change of plans?" said Dr Diodati, "Having arrived right outside the English port of Deal how would you like to go ashore, Samuele, and break our journey to Holland by visiting London?"

Chapter 21: (1627) Travels to London and Onward

Although its position in relation to the Downs makes Deal a busy port, it has no harbour. We said goodbye, therefore, to Captain Doomer on the deck and clambered into the little boat towed by the *Dolphijn*. Old Pieterzoon and Hans Doomer rowed us ashore. They had a list of commissions from their fellows and the captain himself to be obtained in Deal and as they bent to their oars and the *Dolphijn* faded from view I am ashamed to say I felt only relief as the ship and my new-found friends on board grew smaller and smaller. My seasickness had, at least for the time being, obliterated everything else about the voyage from my mind.

We thanked Pieterzoon and Hans, wished them Godspeed and made our way to the clean, comfortable kitchen of the Carpenters' Arms near the beach at Deal. Here I found, to my surprise after what I had been through, that I was hungry. I managed to tuck away a large plate of good English bacon and fresh eggs and began to feel much better. The *Dolphijn* was not the only vessel to have run into Deal to shelter from the storm. I gathered from the conversation around me in English, French and Dutch that a number of vessel were riding at anchor in the Downs. The bad weather had brought extra business to the Carpenters' Arms and the little kitchen was crowded.

"Feeling better?" asked Dr Diodati.

"Much better, thank you," I replied.

"That's good," said Dr Diodati, "because we need to discuss our plans."

"Whatever they are," I said with feeling, "if they involve staying on dry land for a while, I'm all in favour of it!"

"Exactly!" smiled Dr Diodati, "and since we are here in England, and not that far from London where I have both a brother and a brother-in-law settled, it would seem foolish to miss the opportunity of visiting them. We can carry on to Holland by another ship later. We may be able to look up your old friend Mr Bedell also—he must be at least a bishop by now I should think!"

I tried to imagine Mr Bedell in the lawn sleeves and linen neck ruff of an English bishop and totally failed to do it. "I think that would be an excellent plan," I answered, "did you know that in his last letter to me Brother Paul urged me to seek out Mr Bedell?"

"Well now you will be able to carry out Brother Paul's advice," said Dr Diodati, pleased, "in that case we will definitely look up Mr Bedell or Dr Bedell or Bishop Bedell or whoever he is by now!"

We paid our bill and sauntered out into the sunshine on the beach, "I'll go to the post house and see if I can hire some horses to take us to London," said Dr Diodati, "then we can decide when to start."

***

How Carlo would have enjoyed that ride through the orchards, cornfields and hop gardens of Kent! Remembering how much as boys we had enjoyed riding about the countryside round Noventa, I made a mental note to write to him as soon as I could and tell him all about it. The fine early spring weather continued and we made our way onto the Dover Road—the highway that leads to London. The Kentish villages each with their cottages grouped round a green with its flint-walled church fascinated me and I was pleased to find that my English, though rusty, was quite adequate. My accent began to improve as we travelled. I was very pleased when we stopped at the sign of the Green Man in the little village of East Wickham to be told by a serving girl that she was certain I must be "a lad from the North country or round those parts," by my speech!

The good roads and fair weather carried us speedily on towards the city. Whenever we reached high ground now the squat tower of St. Paul's was visible dominating the London skyline, the air being still rain-washed clear. We entered London and, crossing London Bridge and disposing of the post horses, we made our way on foot through the crowded streets towards the great cathedral itself. A dark, brooding building, I could not help contrasting it with the sun-drenched magnificence of St. Mark's in Venice.

"I can't imagine two more different cathedrals than St Paul's, and St. Mark's can you?" I asked Dr Diodati but I had no reply. My friend's concentration was taken up with trying to remember the way through the maze of streets and alleyways to his brother's house on the corner of Doolittle Lane and Knightrider Street.

Theodore Diodati was a medical doctor and his home was one of the many timber houses that lined the London thoroughfares, their upper stories overhanging the street so that they almost touched. Dr Diodati succeeded in finding the house without too much difficulty

---

and we knocked at the doctor's door, tense with excitement at the surprise we were about to deliver. The doctor's wife herself answered, thinking that we were come to find the doctor for a patient.

"The doctor is in, you are lucky, please to step inside," she said politely.

"Don't you recognise me, Eliza?" said Dr Diodati with a smile.

She stared at him for a moment and then sat down quickly on a bench, "Giovanni!" she cried, "Giovanni! Theodore come quickly, your brother is here—your brother Giovanni from Geneva!"

The joy and delight of Dr Theodore's family at seeing his brother was unbounded. There was so much family news to catch up with since Dr Diodati's last visit after the Synod of Dort that we stayed up half the night talking. One of the boys, John, was still at the nearby St. Paul's school but the older boy, Charles, was home from his studies at Oxford.

"I'll show you round St. Paul's cathedral in the morning," he promised, "my old school friend John Milton—he's up at Cambridge —will love to meet you, he's a master of languages rather like you: we'll all go together."

The next day Dr Giovanni Diodati went to pay a call on Philip Burlamachi, brother of the Signora Madeleine, who lived in a grand mansion in Putney about seven miles away up the river. I watched him set off in a Thames wherry rowed by a waterman (the London equivalent of a gondolier) after a careful consultation about the tides. Then I went off to look at St. Paul's with Charles and his friend John Milton.

There was no doubt that St. Paul's was an imposing building and not just from a distance. The two boys were eager to show it off to me. "In other parts of the world," I mused, "such a massive cathedral would have a spire on top of the tower. I wonder why St. Paul's does not have one?"

"It used to," replied John Milton, "but there was a fire—years before we were born—and it burned down. The building was repaired but the spire was never rebuilt."

We entered the churchyard through a narrow passage, St. Paul's Gate, that squeezed itself between the houses. "Our old school is over there," said Charles pointing to a long building right up by the end of the cathedral, "and that's St. Paul's cross where public sermons are preached."

The boys wanted to know all about Geneva and we were still chatting as we entered the building. The inside was crowded with people and the boys warned me to be careful, "plenty of pickpockets in here," said John Milton.

"I'm quite safe," I replied, having left most of my money at the Diodatis' house, "there's nothing in mine!"

The noise inside the building was amplified by its shape into a kind of loud hum or buzz of voices. "This is *the* place to be in London for news or gossip," explained Charles, "everyone comes here to talk. Business deals, meetings of friends, this is where they take place. Everyone comes here to find out what is going on in the city."

As we strolled down Paul's Walk, the long nave of the cathedral, I joined in the hubbub and explained my connection with Brother Paul in Venice to the boys.

"Now I'm hoping to meet up with my old friend Mr William Bedell again," I said, "do you know of him?"

"Bedell … Bedell," said Milton, "no, I think not. Was he an Oxford man perhaps?"

"No Cambridge," I replied, "You must have heard of him he is such a scholar, especially in Hebrew."

"I don't recall the name," said Charles, "but if Uncle Giovanni asks about, someone will know him I'm sure."

***

Dr Giovanni Diodati returned from his visit to Putney looking rather grave. All through dinner he was unusually quiet and it was easy to see that he had brought back something other than friendly greetings and cheerful family news from his brother-in-law's home.

"I am afraid the Signora Madeleine's brother is heading for trouble," he said in response to my questions later when we were alone.

"Trouble?" I queried, "what sort of trouble?"

"He has lent a huge sum of money to King Charles. It looks as if he may not be paid back."

"Not be paid back!" I exclaimed in horror, "how much money is involved?"

"A vast sum. Enough to ruin him," replied Dr Diodati, his face very serious. "For a merchant banker he is a very quiet and obliging sort of person, not one to turn away appeals for help. The King has taken advantage of him. And that is not the worst of it."

"Not the worst!" I exclaimed, already feeling sorry for the kindly banker.

"No. You see, this will ruin the other family members who have lent him money in their turn—you know how we Lucchese do things. His brother-in-law Philippe Calandrini (another one of us Lucchese exiles) is heavily involved as are a number of Dutch merchant bankers all related by marriage to us in one way or another."

"Why does the king need such loans?" I asked, "surely he can raise the revenue he needs to govern by means of taxes."

"The King of England cannot legally raise taxes without the sanction of his Parliament," explained Dr Diodati, "and Parliament will not grant the king the revenue he needs."

"Why not?" I asked.

"Back in Geneva, we think of King Charles as the Brother of the Winter Queen and we remember his father sending delegates to the Synod of Dort—even if he did give them instructions to mediate between the two sides!" said Dr Diodati, "We remember his predecessor, Queen Elizabeth, the champion of Protestantism in Europe and we appreciate the wealth of puritan scholarship that comes from England. You have to realise, though, that when you are in England, you see things from a different point of view. Charles is king over a keenly Protestant nation, that is true, but he himself and many of those he puts into powerful places are not so keen. Charles is married to a French princess, Henrietta Maria, and she is a Romanist. Parliament contains many puritan sympathisers and it does not like this at all. It does not like the queen having her own chapel and her own priests. It has made King Charles withdraw his promise to France that he will grant more freedom to Romanists here in England. This puts him in danger of war with France. King Charles tries to rule without parliament by resorting to taxes that are not legal or are barely legal and even that does not get him enough money. When he calls parliament because he has run out they refuse to grant him money until he has put things right. They hate the king's close friend and advisor Lord Buckingham and every time parliament is called they ask for his dismissal. So far, every time the king has called parliament he has ended up sending it away without granting its demands and without getting any money."

"How can this go on?" I asked, "the king cannot govern in this way, surely one side must give in?"

"I do not know how it will end," replied Dr Diodati, "but I cannot see that the king will ever repay his debts to the Signora Madeleine's brother: he simply cannot raise the money to do so."

"And who are these puritans who have power in the parliament?" I asked.

"Very good men, for the most part," he replied, "men who want the Church of England to move further away from her somewhat compromised origins in a more reformed direction. Many of them have spent time in Geneva for various reasons. They are often merchants though not always; some are great scholars."

"Have you had any news of Mr Bedell," I asked, changing the subject.

"I have asked everyone I've been introduced to and all those I know from the last time I was here," he replied, "and no one has heard of him. I can't understand it! A man of his learning and experience and yet unknown in his own land! Perhaps his puritan tendencies have caused him to forfeit any advancement."

***

We had been staying with Dr Theodore and his family for over a week. Dr Diodati and I were walking down one of the streets near the doctor's house when, as we turned the corner into Cheapside, I saw a tall stooping figure carrying a pile of books approaching us. Dr Diodati saw him at the same moment, "Bedell!" he cried in amazement.

Mr Bedell (for it was indeed he) dropped his books in astonishment, "Diodati!" he shouted joyfully, not even recognising me, "what are you doing here?"

"Looking for you mostly!" replied Dr Diodati as he embraced his old friend, "and I had almost given up. Where have you been hiding? And who do you think this is?"

"Not Samuele!" said Mr Bedell, seizing me by the shoulders with both hands and looking me up and down with tears of joy in his eyes, "This is truly wonderful. However do you come to be in London?"

We gathered up the fallen books and proceeded to Dr Theodore's house all of us talking all the way as hard as we could. The London Diodatis were very glad to meet our dear friend and we were soon settled round the fire talking together.

"For the last twelve years or more I've been the rector of a small Suffolk parish called Horningsheath," Mr Bedell explained, "and I'm afraid I'm very out of things down there. I'm not surprised no one has heard of me. It is a good place, however, for me—not too big. You know my voice is not really powerful enough for a large congregation such as the one at St. Edmund's Bury nearby where I was originally. They are dear people in Horningsheath, it is a joy to minister to them."

"But your talents are buried out of sight in such a place!" exclaimed Dr Diodati, "I thought you would be a bishop at least by now! I will see what can be done to get you promoted now I have found you. I will have to introduce you to Thomas Morton—he's Bishop of Lichfield and Coventry now but I've known him well since my last visit to London."

"I'm not sure I want to move up in the world even if I could, my dear friend," replied Mr Bedell, "I'm a married man now with a family—I have others to consider and consult with who would have to move if I received any promotion and had to move my home."

"Married!" I said, struggling to take in this new development which somehow I had never imagined.

"Yes, indeed," he replied, "my dear Leah and I have been married now for about fifteen years. What a godly woman! How I would have managed without her I have no idea. And the blessing of it is that being a widow she brought with her two sons and a daughter, my beloved Nicholas, young Leah and Edward so I had a family ready made!"

"And have you any other children?" enquired Mrs Theodore politely.

"Oh yes," we have a full set of six altogether still living," he replied, "Our dear daughter Grace is with the Lord—she was only ten. William is fourteen now, John is three years younger and Ambrose is nine—full of life and energy all of them and set fair to be scholars all three."

"And is your wife from er ... where was it you said you lived?—Horningsheath?" asked Dr Giovanni Diodati, no doubt thinking that it might be his wife's ties to the parish that made Mr Bedell seem reluctant about promotion.

"Not originally," replied Mr Bedell, "her family came from Ersham in Norfolk about forty miles away but her first husband was from

Saint Edmund's Bury very nearby—where my first parish was. And of course you will not know that Despotine is married now too—and become quite a famous doctor. At first he got into terrible difficulties because he could not speak English at all—I had to translate for him all the time. Now he speaks fluent English though his accent always marks him out as a foreigner. That is no disadvantage for a doctor in England where everyone thinks a doctor from abroad must be better than an English one. It was so hard for him to learn English that I almost despaired of him ever getting hold of it!"

"Dear Dr Despotine!" I cried, " does he still live near you? Oh how I would love to see him again!"

"He does indeed—with his wife Susan (I married them myself) and their three daughters in my old parish, St. Edmund's Bury," replied Mr Bedell, "he became quite famous in court circles when the late King James was ill. He was called in to consult with the king's own medical men and the king was so pleased with him that he sent him home in one of his own carriages! As to seeing him again, why should you not, if the Lord wills? Come and stay with us in Horningsheath. Leah would be so please to meet you both and the things I've told the children about you, Samuele! What a surprise we could give Despotine!"

My heart leapt with joy at the idea and I looked at Dr Giovanni Diodati to see how he would react. He shook his head sadly. "I've already stayed in England far too long for my original plans," he said, "though I would dearly love to go with you." My face must have fallen at this remark because he said, "Poor Samuele, I can see you are longing to go. But wait! Why should you not go if you wish? You have no need to continue with me to Holland. You can stay here as long as you like!"

"Can I truly?" I asked in delight, "well, yes of course I can! I suppose my pension from the State of Venice can be paid to me here as well as anywhere else and Brother Paul did specifically tell me to find Mr Bedell …"

"Your pension from the State of Venice!" exclaimed Mr Bedell, "I had quite forgotten that! They are still paying it? Excellent! And did Brother Paul really ask you to come seeking for me? How extraordinary!"

"I can see I have some explaining to do," I said with a smile and launched into a brief life history beginning with the death of Philippo and then going on to my travels to Geneva. "You'll never guess who accompanied me to Geneva as my servant and right hand man," I said, but Mr Bedell knew at once, "Luigi!" he said, "it has to be Luigi! Is he here with you now in London?"

"No," I said, "Luigi has made his home in Geneva. He is a married man now. He began by selling Carlo's fruit and vegetables for him on the city streets from a hand cart. Young Samuel Diodati painted it up in bright colours for him and soon everyone in Geneva had heard of the Italian fruit-seller who dispensed wit and homely advice with every purchase! Carlo could not fail after that. He had to employ quite an army of street vendors with Luigi in charge. Luigi's old mother-in-law makes the best fruit pies I have ever tasted out of Carlo's apples, pears, apricots and what not. They are snapped up by the citizens of Geneva as soon as Luigi's underlings can get them onto the streets."

"Remarkable!" cried Mr Bedell, "and just like Luigi: I still remember his cry of '*Frutta fresca*' floating over the summer evening air and er, smells of Venice."

"We must make some plans," said Dr Giovanni Diodati practically, "I will send a messenger to Bishop Morton at once. I am due to dine with him this week and I know he will not want to miss the privilege of meeting you, Mr Bedell, when I explain to him who you are and how well you knew Brother Paul. When are you due to travel home to Horningsheath?"

"The day after tomorrow," replied Mr Bedell, "although I can stay longer, of course, should the Bishop require me."

"Leave it to me," replied Dr Giovanni, "I'm sure he will want to see you."

***

And so it fell out. Mr Bedell went with Dr Diodati to dinner with the Bishop who was charmed by his learning and quiet erudition and I made plans to accompany Mr Bedell back to Suffolk.

"You have managed to follow Brother Paul's advice," said Dr Diodati, "here you are in England where he himself had often considered going and with Mr Bedell whom he urged you to find. I think you could do a lot worse than continue with Mr Bedell who can teach you much. If you keep in touch with me I will see to it that your pension is forwarded—though not through the agency of the Signora Madeleine's brother. I'm afraid," he added sadly, "that might be taking a risk."

Mr Bedell insisted I lodge with his family. I think he was more highly delighted with the prospect of this than with all the hints about promotion that Dr Diodati had made. We set out on the Great North Road towards Suffolk the following week. For this we had to hire post horses and a guide (although Mr Bedell knew the way perfectly well) in order to return the horses to the post master. As the three of us wended our way out of the city I felt quite a seasoned traveller. Ever since my Noventa days I had been happy on horseback and other travellers on the road fascinated me.

"Who were they and why were they off to London?" I asked Mr Bedell after a couple rode past, she riding pillion behind her husband, with a fresh faced youth on another horse following them.

"Probably taking their son to be apprenticed to some trade in London and going to do some sight-seeing while they are there," guessed Mr Bedell.

"And who was that?" as a well dressed rider overtook us swiftly.

"A doctor responding to an urgent message, I expect," came the reply.

As the city gave way to fields and orchards the company and conversation of my old friend made me feel contented and I continued to quiz him on everyone that passed us on the busy road. He identified a smart new chariot attended by two liveried horsemen as, "newly-weds going to buy new furniture for their home maybe," and a woman on a horse with panniers was "a farmer's wife carrying butter and cheese to sell." Wagons loaded with market produce, a flock of geese, a litter of pigs, and a herd of cattle, all these passed us on their way to London.

When we had the road more to ourselves we spoke much of Brother Paul.

"I still have his picture—the one he gave me when we parted—hanging up in my little study," said Mr Bedell, "and I dedicated my Latin translation of his *History of the Venetian Interdict* to the king—the late King James you know—and my translation of his *History of the Inquisition*. The king was gracious enough to say that he was much pleased with both translations."

"What about De Domini?" I asked, knowing that it was Archbishop De Domini who published Brother Paul's great *History of the Council of Trent* in England and that Mr Bedell had been responsible for translating some of the volumes of that vast work also.

"Poor man!" exclaimed Mr Bedell, rather to my surprise. I had little sympathy for a Romanist Archbishop who could run away to England to become a Protestant, write many books about the evils of Romanism and then run back to Rome again to denounce the Protestants.

"He was completely deceived, you know, by the Spanish Ambassador Gondomar—what a man! He rivalled Machiavelli himself for trickery!"

"How tricked?" I asked, "I always assumed his old school friend the new Pope offered to pay him better than King James as well as make him a cardinal and he was fool enough to believe the offer to be genuine."

"There may be something in what you say," replied Mr Bedell, "but I corresponded with him even after he left England. I am sure he had been told that not only would the new Pope make him a cardinal but would also listen to his complaints about the corruption in the church. He told my friend Dr Hall that he was reluctant to leave England but felt he should go because of this good work he thought he could do. Instead he found himself trapped and tried for heresy before the Inquisition. All his wealth brought with him out of England was confiscated and he himself was done away with by poison in prison."

I did not wish to contradict my friend though I still felt little sympathy for the Archbishop so I changed the subject by asking about Brother Paul's *History of the Council of Trent*.

"What a piece of scholarship!" enthused Mr Bedell, "you have studied it, of course?"

"Indeed," I replied, "I have read it through many times. It is a masterpiece; a true example of how history should be researched and written."

"Without it we could only guess at the proceedings and machinations at the Council," said Mr Bedell, "Brother Paul had access to precious documents and he laid it all bare. What was supposed to be a return to the pure form of the church and a purging of abuses was turned instead into a tool for tightening the Pope's grip on the church."

"Indeed," I agreed, "it is as useful a book on church history as Calvin's *Institutes* is on theology."

"Ah, you've mastered that book at the University of Geneva, no doubt," said Mr Bedell, "now there is a book Brother Paul spoke of very highly."

Our conversation was interrupted by a whole party of coaches each pulled by six horses lumbering towards us. We reined our horses to the side of the road to let them pass. Well attended by servants in smart livery, Mr Bedell identified them from the arms on the coaches as they passed. "Dons," he said, "but from Oxford, not from my old university."

"Have you ever felt inclined to take up an academic post?" I asked, thinking of his immense scholarship and ability in languages.

"I would go wherever God calls me," he replied, "but I must admit I am very happy in my little parish."

Chapter 22: (1627) Horningsheath

Horningsheath was a pleasant little village straggling along a street leading to the gates of Sir William Hervey's grand house. Just outside the gates stood St. Leonard's church where Mr Bedell was the rector. As we went down the little street we were greeted by everyone we met, rich or poor, and it took quite a while to pass along the road: Mr Bedell stopped to converse with almost everyone. Mr Bedell's patron, Sir Thomas Jermyn was Sir William's brother-in-law and lived at Great Horringer Manor. Turning down the lane leading to his patron's home we arrived at the rectory. Our arrival was greeted with whoops of joy and cries of, "Hooray here's Father!" from a lad who was playing in the lane. "Ambrose!" cried Mr Bedell dismounting to hug his son. The noise brought his older brothers William and John from the little barn beside the house. The general commotion that ensued meant that other members of the family were soon on the scene and I found myself in the centre of an enthusiastic welcome before I had even been introduced.

"And who do you think this is?" asked Mr Bedell when the hubbub had died down.

There was silence and the family looked at me intently. "Welcome, dear friend, whoever you are!" said Mrs Bedell holding out her hand to me.

"We can't guess, Father!" said Ambrose.

"This is Samuele—all the way from Venice! Samuele, Brother Paul's protégé, who helped me learn Italian!"

***

The post horse guide was paid off and departed with the horses and the Bedell family accepted me into their home warmly. I had to tell almost my whole life story and Leah and Edward Maw, the step-children, quizzed me in great detail about Brother Paul. Mrs Bedell bustled about organizing space for me in the room the older boys shared and getting the servant to take up my little bit of luggage. Her neat, almost elegant appearance—though it was not showy— contrasted with Mr Bedell's very plain clothes which seemed chosen mainly to give him freedom of movement and to be long lasting. Leah Maw her daughter likewise was dressed neatly and elegantly, although her clothing was of a sort to allow her to help in the house and kitchen. Supper time was approaching by now and just before Mr Bedell began to prepare for family evening prayers, a servant entered and spoke quietly to Mrs Bedell. She rose and went over to her husband, "My Lord," she said, "there is a beggar come to the door. Will you have him sent away or will you examine his pass?"

"Come with me, Samuele," said Mr Bedell getting up, "and we will see who this fellow is before we have supper."

I followed him to the kitchen door, outside which stood a young man, short, sun-tanned and barefoot, in seafarer's clothes somewhat ragged and very ill-fitting with a stout stick in his hand.

"Now my good man," said Mr Bedell cheerfully, "I understand you are asking for shelter for the night and a little food, is that right?"

"Yes, Sir, if I may, Sir," the reply was ready and smart but the voice sounded tired.

"Let's see your pass then," said Mr Bedell, kindly and the young man pulled a carefully folded paper from the battered cap which he held in his hand.

"This is to certify," read Mr Bedell, "that Richard Lovelady, fisherman, of the Parish of North Meols, in the County of Lancashire is lawfully returning thither after the loss of his boat in storms and to request that he be furthered in his journey. Signed Edward Blye, Churchwarden, Felixstowe in the county of Suffolk this fourteenth day of March sixteen hundred and twenty six."

MrBedell surveyed the man, "How long have you been on the road?" he asked as he handed back the paper.

"Three days, Sir," came the reply.

"And where did you stay last night?"

"Brettenham, Sir, the farmer let me sleep in his barn, Sir."

"What happened to your boots?"

"Took 'em off, Sir, afore I had to swim off the boat."

"What happened to your shipmates?"

"Drownded, Sir," said the young man quietly.

"Poor souls! Jane! Find this poor fellow something to eat, please. He can stay in the barn. His pass is in order and he'll be on his way tomorrow. Make sure he has food to take with him on his journey. Do you know your road, young man?"

"Thank you very much, Sir, and no, Sir, I'm better at finding my way at sea, Sir, and I'm not familiar with these parts."

"You have a long way to travel, young man, the whole width of England in fact! After you've had your supper I will give you a list of towns and parishes through which you can pass. Can you read?"

"Yes, Sir, indeed I can, Sir! My father had me learned to read so I could read God's Word, Sir."

"A worthy man he was then!" exclaimed Mr Bedell, "now go to your supper and I'll see you later. Oh and, Jane, see if you can't find him some boots. He looks about Edward's size and there may be an old pair."

I was intrigued about the pass.

"Do all wayfarers have to have one?" I asked.

"If they want to avoid being taken up as vagrants by the constable, whipped and then sent back to their own Parish by means of a pass, yes they do," replied Mr Bedell. "No one is supposed to go begging around the country. Each parish is responsible for looking after its own poor and its own poor only. Mind you, there is a brisk trade in stolen or counterfeit passes. Plenty of people who should know better will write out a false pass for some rogue who is willing to pay with his ill-gotten gains."

"How can you tell if a pass is genuine, then?" I asked.

"Almost always if it is not there is something that will give it away —something in the person or their answers to relevant questions that does not quite add up. Not, I admit, usually as much as in the case of one stout fellow who came here a while back, however. He gave me a pass (stolen at some point, I guess, though probably sold on to him by some trickster who knew he could not read it) which said he was, "Moll Jenkins making her way by pass to her home village of Bartestree in Herefordshire after visiting her daughter!"

**

It was Mr Bedell's habit to rise at four in the morning. He went straight to his study and allowed no interruptions until it was time for morning prayers. "Never disturb him then," warned William, "he gets very angry if he's disturbed in his study in the mornings."

"Yes," added Ambrose, "And it's not just me and William or Edward or John who get shouted at but even Mother. 'I insist that I am left in peace!' he said to her and once when she went up there because Mrs Blagge called about something he said …" and here this revelation was terminated because Ambrose caught young Leah's eye. Clearly whatever Mr Bedell had said to his wife in his wrath was not something Leah wanted communicated to someone outside the family!

"I'll be sure not to interrupt him then," I promised.

After dinner I was invited into the study myself, however, and as soon as I entered the comfortable little room I was reminded of my childhood days in Mr Bedell's study in Sir Henry's Residence in Venice. There were the pots of plants on the window sill, the shelves of books and a copy of the Diodati Italian Bible on the table, obviously in regular use. On the wall near the desk hung Brother Paul's portrait that had been his parting gift to Mr Bedell.

"I almost feel home sick for Venice seeing all this," I said, "and a Diodati Bible too! Do you use it regularly still?"

"Every day!" he replied, "it is such an excellent translation that I find it constantly useful."

As I gazed at the treasure trove of theological books, grammars and dictionaries a thought struck me, "Where did you get all these wonderful books?" I asked, "it must have taken years of time and much expense to build up such a library."

"Have you ever heard of William Perkins?" he replied, "no?" as I shook my head, "well he was my teacher at Cambridge and a very godly man as well as a great scholar. His *Exposition of the Lord's Prayer* is a model of simple and yet profound writing. You should read it—here it is—truly excellent. Mr Perkins, sadly, died when he was quite young. I was still at St. Mary's in St. Edmund's Bury at the time and I was able to buy his library. Of course, I have added to it as you can see."

I looked round the shelves. Not only theology was represented. Botany, Mr Bedell's great practical interest, also featured and I noticed a well-used copy of Gerard's *Herball*.

"I am in correspondence with a Mr Thomas Johnson," said Mr Bedell when I showed an interest in the book (surely not one that had been Mr Perkin's) "who is engaged in a complete revision of Gerard. It is to be greatly expanded and—this will interest you, Samuele—will include the Welsh names for plants found in that region as well as the English and Latin."

"Welsh!" I exclaimed, "well why not? Now there is a language I would like to learn!"

"I do wish," mused Mr Bedell, "that at least for scientific works such as a herbal, we could have a universal character that would represent the idea not the sound of a word—as the Chinese do."

I had never had much faith in this idea since I first heard of it in Noventa years ago but did not say so. Instead I continued to study the shelves looking for a certain old friend in three heavy leather bound volumes.

"Ah! here it is! The wonderful Hebrew Bible you bought in Venice, safe and sound in England," I said, "do you know, I was telling Johannes Buxtorf about it when I was in Basel."

"You met Johannes Buxtorf!" exclaimed Mr Bedell, "the Master of the Rabbis! What a scholar!"

"Indeed he is," I agreed, "and I also met Louis Cappel at the Samaur Academy."

"Ah!" exclaimed Mr Bedell, "and which of them, in your opinion, is correct about Hebrew vowel points, Buxtorf or Capell? Were they there at the beginning or were they added later?"

"Well," I began, "At Geneva, everyone is behind Buxtorf ..." and we settled down to a comfortable discussion that lasted until Mr Bedell, looking out of the window and seeing that the rain had stopped (it had been pouring all morning) announced a conducted tour of his beloved garden.

We left the study and I carried Mr Perkins' book with me, ready to escape to a quite corner and read it later. Mr Bedell took me all over his little plot. It was very well managed and he himself did most of the hard labour.

"So are any of these plants that were brought back with you from Venice?" I asked, "I often wondered how many of your precious pots and cuttings reached home."

Mr Bedell smiled sadly, "almost nothing!" he said, "there is a fig tree at St. Edmunds Bury that I planted and there are some roses in that bed over there but apart from that nothing survived the journey."

"But the tools arrived safely?" I asked.

"Oh, yes, indeed: they are most useful and they came home quite undamaged."

We arrived at some delightful peach trees trained up against a south facing wall. Mr Bedell was very proud of these as they were great rarities in England. He was about to explain to me how he came by them when there was the sound of a horse turning in at the gate.

"Hulloo, *C'è qualcuno in casa?* anyone at home?" called a voice that I recognised at once though I had not heard it for so long.

"Despotine, welcome!" cried Mr Bedell, running to the gate and motioning me to stay where I was, "William, Ambrose, John, come and take Dr Despotine's horse! Despotine, we have a visitor who has been asking to see you. He's through here in the garden: do come and meet him."

The doctor came in through the garden gate and I rose to greet him, "Dr Despotine," I said and then in Italian, "how are you after all these years?"

He stopped still in his tracks for a moment and then with a cry of amazement he flung himself on me and embraced me, "Samuele!" he cried, "is it really you? What on earth are you doing here?" Then holding me away from him to inspect me closely, "I know! Your old wound in your arm has been giving you trouble and you've come all the way from Venice for me to bleed you!"

We all laughed heartily at the old joke as I settled down to tell the good doctor all about my adventures. Leah came out of the kitchen accompanied by a kitchen maid who managed a tray of fresh baked cakes and home brewed refreshments very dexterously despite having only one arm. The two boys appeared having dealt with the horse. In no time at all we were all sitting in the porch, enjoying the thin spring sunshine and good baking straight from the oven.

"So what are you going to do with yourself next?" asked Dr Despotine after I had finished recounting my travels.

"I suppose I shall continue my *peregrinatio academica* and eventually return to Geneva," I replied, perhaps with less enthusiasm than I should have shown, given the great privilege I enjoyed in being able to choose such a course of action, "I have made tentative plans to rejoin Dr Diodati in the Netherlands."

"You might do worse than go to Cambridge, if you could stretch your *peregrinatio academica* that long, you know," suggested Dr Despotine thoughtfully, "there would be many opportunities for you there."

"How far is Cambridge from here?" I asked an idea forming in my mind.

"About thirty miles, maybe less," said Dr Despotine, "certainly not a hard journey."

"What are you thinking, Samuele?" asked Mr Bedell.

"When you left Venice, Mr Bedell, Brother Paul, as you know, sent me to Geneva to study. He did this at least in part because he and Brother Micanzio were considering leaving Venice for London. The plan was that I would join them there from Geneva. Brother Paul, however, died and Brother Micanzio has remained at Venice. Before he died, Brother Paul's last advice to me was to come and find you, Mr Bedell. Although I took no active steps to follow this advice I am here now by what seems to be an accident of the weather!"

"There are no accidents with God!" remarked Dr Despotine who was listening very intently.

"Exactly," I said, "I have prayed most earnestly that God would guide me and I am conscious that he has done so. I feel that I should stay at least *near* you, Mr Bedell. Do you not think that God is leading me in this way? If so, Cambridge is not very far and I could continue my studies there. It would be a good use of my Venetian money."

"That is a wise suggestion," replied Mr Bedell, "I have tried to make it a rule in my own life that I would never seek promotion or a move from where I have been put. In that way if such a thing should come to me, I can be sure that it is not through my own desire for glory or worldly position but because God would have it so. When I was sent to Venice with Sir Henry Wotton, for instance, it came as a complete surprise—a shock even. Many times in my own life, and in the lives of those around me, I have seen that those who wait quietly under God's will have their prayers answered and are put into the place He has prepared for them."

"Amen," said Dr Desoptine, "wait here, follow your gift for languages, study (at Cambridge or wherever it may be) and see what God has in store for you, Samuele. He has brought you back to Mr Bedell, so stay with him until God moves you somewhere else. Now, I am afraid *I* will have to go somewhere else! I have not finished my rounds. I have calls to make in Chevington, Hargrave and Denham before I go back to St. Edmund's Bury tonight."

He got up, brushing the crumbs from his clothes and William rose to fetch his horse.

We saw him off at the gate and resumed our tour of the garden. It was not long, however, before we were interrupted again.

"More visitors!" exclaimed Mr Bedell in surprise as another rider turned in at the gate, "now who can this be? Go and find out, please, boys."

Ambrose returned in a moment with the rider while William and John looked after the horse, "Letters, Father!" he cried in excitement, "by special post."

"I have letters for the rector, Mr Bedell," explained the rider, "and also for an Italian gentleman, Signor Samuele Paul, who I am told will be here."

"This is Signor Paul," said Mr Bedell and the rider handed over a letter to me and two to Mr Bedell.

I broke the seal and found another letter inside the first. I began reading at once. The outer letter was from Dr Diodati who explained that he was proceeding to Holland at once with the aim of returning to Geneva more quickly than he had originally planned; in part because of some sad news that had reached him from home. "The enclosed letter from the Signora Madeleine will explain what it is," he wrote, "I must let you know also that some moves are afoot regarding Mr Bedell's promotion. Should you wish to remain with him longer than we originally anticipated you can write to me through the Signora Madeleine's brother. The messenger who brought this can take any replies."

I broke the seal on the inner letter and read:

"My Dear Samuele,

I am writing to you because some sad news has reached us from the island of La Rochelle in France where the French Huguenots are holding out against their persecutors. During the siege last autumn, Arnaud Lamarche and Léon Simoneau, students from Geneva, were assisting their Huguenot brothers and sisters. News has now reached us that both young men lost their lives at some point in the action, although it is not yet clear exactly how. Dorothée has submitted to the Lord's will with wonderful calmness and patience. She mourns Arnaud but not as one without hope. Adrienne, however, is distraught. No one can comfort her and her poor father, not knowing (as we do)

---

the probable cause of her extra misery, is very worried. Please
remember both girls in your prayers.

"The children send their very best wishes,

Madeleine Diodati"

I thought of Adrienne, not as I remembered her, dancing and laughing in Carlo's garden, but weeping inconsolably because she could
never now ask Léon's forgiveness for her flirtatious behaviour. I could
imagine Dorothée also, continuing in her daily duties of help to her
parents and care to her brothers and sisters while laying all her grief at
the feet of her Lord. I stood up. "Please excuse me," I began, "but I
must go and answer this at once ..." I looked round. No one was
listening. Instead they were staring at Mr Bedell who, the colour quite
gone from his face, was clutching his letters and staring straight ahead
as though transfixed.

Chapter 23: (1627) The Call

"Father! What is the matter?" cried Leah anxiously, "is it bad news? Shall I fetch Mother?"

Mr Bedell seemed to gather himself together, "Yes, please," he said calmly, "please ask your mother to come out here, Leah."

As Leah went indoors he said, "What was it we were speaking of with Despotine? Never moving or seeking promotion but rather letting the Lord move us?"

"We were," I agreed, "I am afraid your letter brings bad news."

"Not exactly bad news, more rightly strange news. Ah here is Leah ..."

Mrs Bedell came out of the house, wiping her hands on her apron, "Is all well?" she asked, "Leah says there is a letter ..."

"Sit down, my dear," said Mr Bedell making room for her beside him on the bench, "I have two letters here from a secretary of Archbishop James Ussher, the Lord Primate of Armagh, asking me whether, if the Archbishop were to obtain it for me, I would accept the post of Provost in a college."

Mrs Bedell looked puzzled and alarmed. She plainly did not know who Archbishop Ussher was or where Armagh was either, and, in fact, at the time I mistakenly thought it was in Scotland.

"Provost of a college, which college? Where? We would not have to move would we?" she asked in some confusion.

"Trinity College," began Mr Bedell.

"That's thirty miles or more away in Cambridge!" she cried, "we would have to move ... but it would be a great promotion to you ... that is you could do much good there ... and we could come and visit our friends often ... and Dr Despotine often rides out that way ..."

"Trinity College in Dublin, my dear," said Mr Bedell very gently.

Mrs Bedell sounded relieved, "Oh," she laughed, "Dublin! Ireland! Well you would never accept a post like that! We could not possibly go there ... could we? Could we?"

"It may be that the statutes of the college require a single man," said Mr Bedell, "in which case I could not be appointed. If not, I do not think I can dismiss the matter out of hand. This may be God's call to us, my dear."

Mrs Bedell's face went white as her own clean apron, "I have never left my native country," she said, "Ireland is a foreign place. I should be afraid of such a journey—to cross the sea in a ship—nevertheless, my Lord, I will be content with whatever God shall appoint," and with that she bowed her head and put her face in her hands.

I stole away to write my own letters and read Mr Perkins on prayer, leaving them to console each other.

***

The following day was Sunday and Mr Bedell refused to allow it to be spoilt by worries over Trinity College, Dublin. "I will go to Bury tomorrow and consult with Despotine and also with my patron, Sir Thomas Jermyn, to have their advice," he said, "today we will serve the Lord in our usual fashion without pondering this matter."

He rose early that morning as usual and retired to his study in his normal way while Mrs Bedell was busy making sure the children and servants were ready and neatly dressed ready to go to church before he came down for family prayers. After prayers the whole family together with the servants formed into a kind of procession to walk to the church.

The service was of the plainest. Mr Bedell did not deviate a whisker from what was set down in the Prayer Book in word or in gesture. His sermon was exactly as I remembered his preaching to be long ago when I was in Venice. It was characterised by the greatest simplicity—a child could understand it as I remembered having done as a child myself—and every word he said was derived exactly from the Scriptures. Listening to him I could understand why he had not been promoted before. His style was different from the eloquent rhetorical style of fashionable English pulpits, which was laced with classical quotations and designed to impress rather than to teach. Instead of long sentences and flourishing words he used simple expressions and began by explaining the exact meaning of the Greek words of the text he was dealing with. Then he carefully compared the text with other passages of scripture by which means he brought out the meaning clearly. Having seen his wonderful library I was surprised at first that he did not quote from any learned books. Instead he seemed to have given his whole mind to the text in hand, as a whole and word by word and in the context of the whole of Scripture.

If Mr Bedell's style would not have gained him any worldly advancement, however, his parishioners clearly enjoyed it very much indeed. Ever since the time at Noventa when I had mastered the Piedmontese language just by talking to a humble gardener from Piedmont every day, I had made a habit of talking to ordinary people —peasants and artisans—as often as I could. After the service I made sure I had the opportunity to talk with some of the congregation as they made their way through the churchyard. Explaining that I had come from "foreign parts" to study I was soon able to get them to talk to me warmly about their minister.

"I am sure you cannot study with anyone better, young sir," said a man I recognised as the local thatcher, "the minister we had before, though I don't say he wasn't a very learned man, made the plainest passages of Scripture seem hard to understand but Mr Bedell now, he makes everything, even difficult passages, easy to understand."

"You'll come to the catechising this afternoon, won't you, Sir?" urged another who I think was a farm lad, "one from papistical lands such as you've doubtless come from will learn a great deal from Mr Bedell's catechising."

I promised to attend and then quickened my pace slightly to catch up with the minister's family and servants who were making their sedate way back to the rectory.

The catechising preceded the evening service and was officially for the benefit of the children. Mr Bedell was careful to make sure that the children did not just answer like parrots. When they had given the rote answer they had memorised, he followed up the catechism question with supplementary questions of his own designed to help the children understand what the catechism meant. Carefully he drew the correct answers from them and with gentleness corrected them when they were mistaken. The adults present—and there were many of them—were obviously as eager to learn as the children.

***

The next day Mr Bedell set off early for Bury. He returned after a short time very frustrated. Neither Dr Despotine nor Sir Thomas were at home—or likely to be at home that day. He decided to consult his old friend Samuel Ward at Cambridge by letter but there would be no chance of a reply from Dr Ward in time to help with any decision. He seemed heavy hearted as he went up to write his reply.

"I never looked for this," I heard him complain to his wife at the bottom of the stairs that led to his study, "and now—all without consulting my friends—I will have to answer this meddling letter. How I wish people would mind their own affairs!" and with that he stumped up the stairs and banged the study door behind him.

At length he came down looking calmer and sent William to organise someone to take his letters.

"I have written to the Archbishop's gentleman explaining that I am married and therefore may not serve if a single man is required by the college statues," he began, "I have also explained how little we all as a family desire such a move. Nevertheless, I have told him that if this matter proceeds from God I must close my eyes to all my personal objections and if I may be of better use to my Country, my King and my God I will cheerfully go not only to Ireland but even to Virginia if the Lord wills it!"

Mrs Bedell shuddered, "There is little difference, I have been told," she said, "between the wild savage Indians and the wild savage Irish, save that the Indians are pagans and the Irish are papists."

"All in need of the Gospel," replied her husband.

"Have you said what you will consider to be God's call?" I asked, feeling sure Mr Bedell would not have left the matter vague.

"Oh yes," he replied at once, "I have said that I will make no moves myself either for or against the idea. But if those whom it concerns—the fellows of the college, the Archbishop and William Laud the Bishop of London—are able to put their case to those who have the power to *command* me to go and they do command me, I shall of course go."

"And who could command you to go?" I asked.

"The King," he replied.

Chapter 24: (1627) Sir Henry Again, Dublin

We none of us had any idea of it until much later but there had been something of a quarrel over who should be Provost of Trinity College, Dublin. The tugging and pulling of the different parties in the Church of England which had been hinted at by Dr Diodati when describing the difficulties of his brother-in-law became much clearer to me when I found out what had happened. The puritans Richard Sibbes, Joseph Mede and also Mr Bedell's friend Samuel Ward of Cambridge had all been discussed as possible Provosts. The Irish Archbishop Ussher had put them forward knowing them to be godly men. For these very reasons the powerful Bishop of London, William Laud, would not accept them, being anything but a puritan sympathiser himself. The fellows of Trinity therefore on his advice rejected all three suggestions. Mr Bedell's name, when suggested (presumably by Bishop Morton after Dr Diodati's efforts) produced a more favourable reaction. Laud had heard little or nothing about Bedell except that he was a scholar, had been in Venice and was a friend of Brother Paul.

This last fact was significant since Laud took the view that the legitimacy of the Church of England rested not on the extent that its prayerbook and catechism were in line with the Bible but on its direct descent from the Church of Rome. Mr Bedell's connection with Brother Paul therefore appealed to him. Brother Paul had been a life-long member of the Church of Rome—though a critical one. This was just how Laud would have liked to see the Church of England itself! Here at last was a candidate for the job who was a scholar, yes, but surely not a meddling puritan like Ussher's other suggestions. Little did he know! He recommend Mr Bedell to the fellows. The fellows, no doubt glad that the two men could agree on someone, asked old Sir Henry Wotton (now the Provost of Eton College) to write to the king telling him how suitable Mr Bedell was for the post.

Sir Henry at once wrote to the king, explaining who Mr Bedell was. King Charles was no lover of puritans either. Sir Henry therefore emphasised Mr Bedell's connections with Brother Paul and how highly Brother Paul regarded him. He also was careful to describe Mr Bedell as the fittest man in the whole kingdom for the post because (among other good qualities) of his "conformity to the Rites of the

Church." This was intended to sway the king who would not want any advancement to be given to anyone who wanted to change the church in a more puritan direction—any more than Laud did. On the other hand, what the letter did not mention was that Mr Bedell was a stickler to the letter of the Prayer Book in *all* matters and *all* directions. Mr Bedell was careful not to introduce any innovations in a puritan direction however much he might privately have wished for some changes. He was equally firm against innovations in a "papistical" direction—as my friend the Horningsheath farm lad would have described it. He was firm against altar rails round the communion table, bowing towards the table as though it were an altar, and elaborate music with musical instruments. These were all things that were not allowed in the Prayer Book but which were enjoyed and quietly overlooked by Laud and his party. The King was pleased to listen to Sir Henry's advice and the fellows elected Mr Bedell.

***

Of all these things we were only very dimly aware at the time. The result was dramatic, however, and swift. A messenger arrived at the rectory with a letter for Mr Bedell from a Mr Temple, one of the fellows of Trinity College, Dublin. It was a while before sense could be made of its contents because it arrived before other letters which the writer assumed Mr Bedell would have received already, informing him of the fellows' choice and the King's command. Mr Temple was at that time in London, and planning to return to Dublin and wondered if Mr Bedell would wish to accompany him on the voyage.

Mr and Mrs Bedell both accepted the King's command as a clear demonstration that the call to Dublin was from God. When Sir Henry's role in the affair became known Mr Bedell sighed, "It is one thing to give me peach trees and books on botany," he lamented, "but *this* is a gift I have not looked for."

To the Bedells the move had come just when they began to feel at their most settled in Horningsheath. "After all these years of litigation," said Mr Bedell somewhat sadly, "just when everything is sorted out and I have no more legal battles."

"What legal battles?" I asked.

"Some encroachment of church property here in Horningsheath," he replied, "I learned so much law in order to defend the church's cause myself that local people come to me for legal advice now!"

"The thing that worries me most, my Lord," said Mrs Bedell anxiously considering the plan for Dr Bedell to travel with Mr Temple, "is your going over to Ireland on your own ahead of us to make things ready."

"Don't be afraid," he replied, "the servants here are very trustworthy and Dr Despotine is within call."

"No, no, my Lord," she replied, "I am not anxious for myself: I am among friends here. It is you I fear for, alone in a strange place. Who will take care of you, my Lord?"

"Sir," I replied, to set her mind at rest, "if you would accept my company, I would be only to happy to extend my *peregrinatio academica* to Ireland. I have been doing some research and I find there is a new language to be learned across that little bit of water!"

"Would you really go with him?" she asked looking very relieved and when I replied she at once launched into a detailed description of the laundry, medical and dietary needs of Mr Bedell which she wanted to put into my hands before we departed!

Mr Bedell held up his hand and the list of instructions died away, "My dear Samuele!" he exclaimed, "I can think of no better companion. And when I get to Trinity College, things there are bound to need much work since they have had no Provost for so long now. What a help it would be to have you with me!"

***

Mrs Bedell need not have worried that her husband was going to be hurried off to Dublin in the next few days. It was not until July that we made our journey in the end and the whole family did not join us for almost a year. During that year Mr Bedell encountered so many difficulties at the College that he was on the point of resigning and going home to Horningsheath.

***

My arrival in Dublin was so unlike my arrival in London. There was no friendly John Milton or Charles Diodati to show me round and in any case I had no leisure for sight-seeing. Even Mrs Bedell's list of necessities could not be properly attended to as Mr Bedell threw himself into his work, grateful to have me at his side to help, copy, listen and even advise. From the start he was a whirlwind of energy hardly pausing to sleep and only pausing to eat because his presence in the college hall at meals was part of his scheme for transforming and revitalizing college life.

At first to me the contrast between life at Trinity College and life at the Geneva Academy where I had studied was painful. Despite being set up as a college for training men for the Church of England ministry many of the students were reluctant to study divinity at all! The college chapel itself was used for debates in all manner of other subjects and some of the students were in the habit of laying aside their academic gowns and going into the town *incognito* to enjoy themselves. But worst of all there was a violent division in the college between the Irish students and the English which hindered any united action and sometimes came near to open war and even blows.

The very statutes of the college themselves could not even be found at first. Mr Bedell eventually discovered them; a loose bundle of papers stuffed into a drawer, unbound and for the most part unobserved. He set them in order and took steps to have them carried out together with some very important additions of his own.

The statutes required topical weekday sermons ("commonplacings" they were called) and certain theological debates and disputations to be held regularly as academic exercises.

"Debates, Samuele!" Provost Bedell exclaimed, "they must have debates! The statutes require it and they are vital. How will they hold their own in debates and discussions later on if they don't practice here and now?"

"I agree," I said, "debate is of great importance in Ireland: the conflict between Catholic and Protestant theology is so keen. What are you going to do about it?"

"Well, it's useless to force them into debates if the standards are not high," he replied, "so I do not intend to just leave them to debate among themselves. I shall take part in the debates myself. I will make them work hard to defeat me! That should soon rekindled their enthusiasm."

From now on it was also the rule that the students wore their gowns in college or in the town so that everyone knew who they were. The new provost also insisted that on Sundays they went to church in the town with him in a body.

"What about mealtimes, Samuele? They are a shambles at present."

"Something needs to be done," I agreed, "to improve the atmosphere and guide the conversation onto spiritual subjects."

"I've looked at the statutes and I think it would be good if before the main course is brought in, one of the scholars reads a chapter of the Bible in Latin and gives thanks for the food."

"Yes, and then after the food is served perhaps he could go up to the high table where you and the fellows sit," I suggested, "and recite a few verses of the chapter just read with the aim of providing you all with something good from the Bible to discuss as you eat."

On Sundays between the two church services Provost Bedell held catechism sessions in the college chapel. These, once word got round of their quality, were thronged not just by the students but also by people from the town. For my part, I was struck by the similarity of these sessions to those catechisings I had witnessed at Horningsheath where the well-taught children had often been more advanced in their knowledge than some of the students at Trinity.

But the area where Mr Bedell made the most difference was the one that concerned and interested me most deeply of all—the Irish language. We had not been in Dublin very long under his new regime when Mr Bedell, pushing back his chair and laying down his pen said, "Well, Samuele, what do you think of it all? Am I doing the best for the college? Come, give me your advice freely. How does it compare to your experiences in Geneva?"

"At first," I said, "I despaired. It was so different from Geneva that I wondered why most of the students were here at all—until, that is, I discovered that here in Ireland becoming a minister of the church is a way to a good living with little work attached! Now, I can see that you are making progress. Those who are here because they truly want to serve God as ministers are very grateful whether they are Irish like Murtagh King or English like Thomas Johnson. I think with time you will get the place under control. But one thing is still missing without which even the best of your students will struggle to reach the Irish with the gospel and that is the Irish language."

"Exactly!" he exclaimed, "This is vital and I knew you of all people would see it. Now here is my plan: tell me what you think. One of the fellows, Murtagh King, you mentioned him, well he is a vital man. He is from an old family of Irish bards and is an expert in the language and not only in its poetic aspects; he has also had training in drafting legal documents. I am going to employ him here to teach me Irish and to teach the students also. Those students who come here from an Irish background can take their skills further under his direction—many are quite deficient in writing the language—and those who are from an English background can learn the basics of the language in order to communicate with their parishioners. The meal time readings from the New Testament must be from the Irish Bible—alas there is no Old Testament in Irish—what an appalling state of affairs! I can find no one here—absolutely no one—who can explain the grammar of the Irish language; even King is hazy. We will start having compulsory training in Irish daily and I will put King in charge of it."

I could see what a problem the lack of grammar was for him, given his method of learning languages, but although it surprised me that so old and dignified a language lacked codification, it would not hinder my learning. In fact, I had already made a good start by listening to Murtagh King. But I wanted to learn more and I knew that just as in Noventa I had learned Piedmontese from an old gardener or on board ship I had picked up Dutch from the sailors, the best way to do so would be to go out and speak to ordinary Irish people going about their daily work.

"I think that will be an excellent plan," I said, "but I also think it will arouse some opposition especially among the English faction in the college. I think it would be good to get some backing for your plans. Would Archbishop Ussher be supportive?"

"He is a native Irish speaker himself," replied Mr Bedell, "and loves the language. He collects Irish manuscripts, you know, and is an avid reader in Irish. He knows that the problem out in the parishes is lack of Irish language among our ministers but he has to be quite careful in what he does these days—the puritan party is out of favour at court. Bishop Laud and his faction do not want to see the Irish natives advanced in any way and as far as they are concerned the native Irish only exist to provide the tithes that make up each church living. What language the natives speak and whether they remain in the darkness of ignorant Roman superstition or not seems to be of no importance to Laud. It is Laud, not Ussher who has the ear of the King and as far as Laud is concerned the natives must forget Irish and learn English. I have written to Archbishop Ussher and told him what I propose to do and I know he will support me—as far as he dares."

"I wonder," I said, almost thinking aloud rather than proposing a course of action, "whether it would be possible for me, perhaps accompanied by a Irish speaking servant to ride on some sort of tour of Irish livings. It is obvious that here in Dublin we don't have a clear picture of what life is like out there in the wilds. I could use my wits, learn Irish quite quickly and maybe even make some notes towards a grammar. Having grown up in Venice as a Servite might give me entrance to some places that would be closed to you, an English clergyman, and I think I could stretch the terms of my *peregrinatio academica* to cover the study of Irish even if this suggestion is a rather unconventional method of study."

"What a good idea!" said Mr Bedell at once, "you can go from one living to another by means of letters of introduction from me at the college..."

"You mean you will provide me with a vagabond's pass!" I laughed, thinking of the sailor who had presented his credentials at Horningsheath on the day I arrived.

"Exactly!" said Mr Bedell, "although I hope you will not end up sleeping in the barn too often. I'll make some enquiries today and see if there is anyone who knows the roads in the area who could act as your guide and servant."

***

If Mr Bedell was too much of a puritan for the likes of Bishop Laud he had problems in the opposite direction with some of his colleagues at Trinity College. The Divinity Professor at Trinity was a godly and erudite man, Dr Joshua Hoyle. Dr Hoyle was inclined to be hot headed and he took great exception to one of Mr Bedell's characteristic attitudes when it came to the Romanists. Mr Bedell was always careful to make a distinction between the *church* of Rome and the *court* of Rome. His experience in Venice and especially his regard for Brother Paul and Brother Micanzio made him refuse to admit that there could be no true believers in the Roman *church* although they groaned under the yoke of the Roman *court*. From this he concluded that it was not right to refuse to allow that the *church* of Rome was in some sense a true church since it contained some true believers. This Dr Hoyle could not stomach and he was not a man for any kind of compromise or smoothing over of differences. Dr Hoyle was the type who, once he found a point of disagreement, would take every opportunity to bring it to the fore, mention it and provoke some argument.

It happened one weekday that Dr Hoyle was preaching in the college chapel. In order to emphasise his difference of opinion with

Mr Bedell he chose to preach on Revelation chapter 18 verse 4 "Come out of her my people" which he took to be a command to all believers to disassociate themselves from the Church of Rome. As he preached he kept directing fiery looks at Mr Bedell which it was easy to see were intended to indicate that he considered he was preaching to the Provost with the intention of putting him right on this important point. Mr Bedell listened mildly to the sermon without giving any indication that it disturbed him. As I watched him I thought of his old teacher William Perkins whose treatise *A Direction for the Government of the Tongue According to God's Word* contained a whole chapter on *Silence* which he was fond of quoting and which was probably standing him in good stead now. After the chapel service he went to Dr Hoyle's chambers with him. Here they held a private debate in Latin without anyone else being present except a sizar (a poor student who had to work to pay his way through college) whose job it was to make up the fire and fill the log basket. No one knows to this day what they said to each other (the sizar kept his mouth firmly shut) but they parted the very best of friends. Dr Hoyle afterwards described Mr Bedell as "the purest Ciceronian I have ever discoursed with" alluding to the ancient Roman orator, Cicero, famed for his eloquent prose. I conclude from this remark that Mr Bedell definitely won the argument!

It took more tact and careful management than even Mr Bedell could provide, however, to stem the tide of constant wrangling between the Irish students and the English. Before I set out on my trip things had reached such a pitch that even he found it difficult to manage. It was now that he began to wonder if instead of making arrangements for Mrs Bedell and the children to come over and join him he should give up being Provost and return to Horningsheath. A letter of encouragement from Archbishop Ussher persuaded him to stay at his post, however, and he found time also to look out an Irish guide for me and furnish me with the letters of introduction I needed. I left him writing, organising and putting in order and set out in quest of the Irish language. He had urged me to go but I was feeling guilty that not only had I not attended properly to Mrs Bedell's list of his needs to begin with, but now I was deserting him altogether.

Chapter 25: (1627-8) Wild Ireland

Dear Carlo,

I take the opportunity of enclosing this letter to you with one for Dr Diodati and I am writing in a hurry because a messenger is leaving today for London who can take letters to the Signora Madeleine's brother. I have just returned from the most remarkable journey I have ever undertaken—and that includes my crossing of the Alps with Luigi! I set out with an Irish servant to find out as much as I could about the country (and especially the language) and report back to Mr Bedell, partly in order to help him in making sure that what Trinity College provides is the training best suited for ministers who are going to serve in the wilds of Ireland.

I was totally unprepared for what I found. Ireland is a strange place. The mountains are all at the edges and as a result the lowland in the centre of the country is very boggy and full of lakes and swamps. I think even you would be hard put to find a way of growing things successfully here in soaking wet acidic soil. My mind went many times to young Samuel Diodati. What scope there is here for someone who enjoys planning waterways and drainage systems! Who knows what could be grown here if the land was properly drained? To give you some idea, we set out early from Dublin on a bright, clear spring morning and my guide told me that he would take me to a view point where I would be able to "see all Ireland." This turned out to be the top of a strange hill about a day's ride from Dublin to the North West. The hill is surmounted by huge piles of glittering white stones placed there (for what hideous purpose I can only guess) by pagan savages in ancient times. The whole hill, in fact, is riddled with holes and passages dug by these heathens and my guide told me that the place is considered so haunted by witches and the like that the Irish will not come near it. He, however, had no fear of witches or spectres, at least by day, and having climbed to the top we were rewarded with a prospect which stretched for miles in all directions.

It was not a cheering sight. Distant mountains could indeed be just descried to the north and to the south, but the prevailing landscape below us was one wild bogland broken by lakes or pools of water. The inhabitants who eke out a living as best they can in such a country, cut, stack and dry turfs from the bog for their fuel. Their homes are miserable cabins cobbled together from whatever can be found and which shelter not only the people but their animals as well.

And what of the inhabitants of such a place? Well, they are miserably poor. Where they do have some land to settle and graze their animals their troubles are not over. The whole country is divided into parishes each of which is allocated a minister by the Church of Ireland but does this mean that there is regular gospel preaching all over the place? Oh no, far from it! Almost all the inhabitants cling to the Roman religion except for settlers who have come over from England or Scotland. The Irish have their own bishops and priests who celebrate mass for them in every parish. Almost none of the inhabitants come to the Protestant services at all. The clergy who are sent out to the parishes collect the tithes from the inhabitants of course, whether they come to church or not, so the poor deluded Irish are paying tithes twice, once to the minister and then again to their popish priests.

And that is not the worst of it. The ministers, finding that they can collect the tithes and yet have almost no one in their churches, do not usually inconvenience themselves by living in the parishes remote from civilization but rather live elsewhere in comfort. Those to whom they are supposed to minister the gospel are left in darkest ignorance and superstition. Many of the ministers are incumbents of more than one parish (and so receive more than one lot of tithes) and never visit them let alone live in them! The tithes are collected by tithe-farmers often by brutal methods. The clergy are mostly unable to speak Irish and their parishioners mostly speak no English so they are totally unfit for their work in any case. Everywhere I went I found church buildings in ruins. No one uses them, no one bothers to repair them and so they fall down! The people get no crumbs of help from their Roman priests either. You won't find a Brother Paul or a Brother Micanzio here! The priests are very ignorant and lead the people on in superstition without ever telling them of the Bible—which in any case is not exactly widely available and of which the priests themselves seem to know little or nothing. There is no translation of the Old Testament at all in Irish and no concern (even in places where the Protestant churches are still standing) to place even a New Testament in Irish in church for people to read—not that many of the Irish can read in any *language.*

When we travelled further to the North East of the country, however, there was a great change. Many Scottish settlers have come to this area and it is a cheering contrast to what we had seen in the centre of the country: neat little farms, meadows and cornfields even some work on drainage well begun. And that is not all. There is gospel preaching here and in many places the people are as well taught and cared for by their ministers (most of them also from Scotland) as Mr Bedell's own flock at Horningsheath in Suffolk.

But I have not yet mentioned to you the greatest discovery I made during this journey. We were returning from Antrim in the North East and staying in Ballymulling, a tiny scattered settlement in County Cavan ...

My pen fell listlessly from my fingers as I wondered how on earth to describe my experiences to Carlo. To be honest I had made not one great discovery but two and both had left me in a state almost of shock at least to begin with.

***

Mr Bedell had found me an excellent guide, one Conall, a lad of about fifteen who was travelling back from Dublin to his home in County Cavan. A lively native Irish speaker full of conversation and ever willing to correct my accent and construction he was just the person I needed to progress rapidly in the language. He was from a family which I think had originally been very important in Ireland but had fallen on hard times. He was also unusual in that his parish was one in which one of the very few Church of Ireland ministers lived who tried to fulfil his duties conscientiously and to reach the native Irish with the gospel. Although this minister could not speak Irish himself he went to the trouble of finding a translator who could translate his sermons for him as he preached and by patience and generosity he had gradually won the respect of many people in the parish. It happened that the Roman priest in this parish was such a drunkard and a bully that the people noticed the contrast at once. Conall, his father, mother, sisters and brothers had all listened to the minister and over time had come to see the truth of what he so patiently taught. Recently Conall had had the opportunity to travel in the North East of Ireland to Antrim where there were settlements of Scots and he was bubbling over with joy at what he had heard there— of which you will hear more later in my narrative. He was more than willing to take me to this area also before returning to Cavan.

So I set out, a seasoned traveller by now, in high spirits on a young but steady dark brown mare (called for some unaccountable reason *Sneachta*—Snow) with my guide and a little pack of food—ready for any adventure.

"I assume you will wish to ride English-style, Sir, not Irish-style?" asked my guide as he led the horses towards me.

"I learnt to ride Irish-style, as you call it, as a boy in Italy," I said, recalling the far-off happy days at Noventa with Carlo, "but since then I have travelled many miles through Italy, Switzerland and France using a saddle and stirrups like the English and I have become used to it. I'd better stick to that, I think."

In England (and on my travels in Europe for that matter) I had generally stayed in inns. Standing on top of the weird old hill of Slieve na Calliagh (that I mentioned in my letter to Carlo) near the end of our first day's ride and gazing at the desolate bogs and forests spread out before us, I realised that inns in this part of the world were very few and far between.

"Where are we going to stay tonight, Conall?" I asked as *Sneachta* bent her head and tried to crop at the coarse scanty grass, "and how on earth do we find our way across that boggy waste?"

"We'll not be going much further today, Sir," he replied, "some of my mother's family live a few miles from here; we can stay with them. As for finding your way, Sir, don't you be fretting over that now! Isn't that why you have me with you?"

And with that I had to be content. Conall seemed to know paths through this waste and having descended the hill we progressed roughly North West as far as I could judge.

It was with some trepidation as night began to fall that I saw that we were making for a small hut, sheltered by some alder trees. "My Aunt's house," said Conall pointing cheerfully and he urged his ambling horse to a trot. I followed with less enthusiasm as the place hardly looked inviting. I was beginning to wonder how we would be able to feed the horses—never mind ourselves. As we neared, however, some more or less cultivated land came into view behind the hut and I could see a bony cow grazing.

"Hullo Auntie!" called Conall as we approached and an old lady appeared at the door of the hut. Small in stature but neatly dressed, though bare foot, she ran to embrace her nephew and there was a torrent of Irish which I could not follow until it slowed down and introductions were made.

When Auntie found out who I was she seemed wary and ill at ease, "She's thinking the priest will be angry with her for looking after you," Conall explained, "and she's expecting him to visit her at any moment!"

Sure enough just as Conall had finished his explanation a ruffianly looking man strode up to the hut. He wore nothing that would identify him as a priest but Conall's Aunt's agitation made it plain who he was. I stepped forward and introduced myself politely in Latin, "Good evening, Sir. I am a student of languages from the City of Venice and am touring your country to learn the Irish language."

"From Venice! That's a long way to come to learn Irish!" he said, looking me up and down suspiciously, "and what were you in Venice, then?"

"I grew up in the Servite monastery there and studied under Brother Paul, head of that order in Venice," I replied trying out my Irish now, thinking that this would put him at his ease. He shrugged his shoulders, "Never heard of him," he grunted, "does the bishop know you're here?"

"I should not think so," I replied, thinking it very unlikely that the titular Roman bishop (or the church of Ireland bishop to whom I had letters of introduction, for that matter) would have heard of me, "I only arrived today from Dublin and will be departing tomorrow."

The news of my departure seemed to please him more and he relaxed a little, "Where to tomorrow?" he asked.

"My guide is taking me round to see the countryside and study the language; where would you recommend I go?" I asked not wishing to let this unhelpful character know exactly where we were planning to visit.

"See the countryside! Learn the language!" he exploded, "You seem to be pretty good at speaking the language already, young man! You clear out of here tomorrow sharp back to Dublin."

"Why are you so angry, my friend?" I asked.

He replied at once, "Because there are people who go around spying for the English oppressors and prying and spreading heretical ideas."

"I have no intention of doing that," I replied, "My teacher, Brother Paul, insisted that the people be taught the pure gospel out of the Bible."

"The Bible!" he scoffed, "What would they want with that! You are on strange—dangerous—ground for a Servite!" and with that he turned on his heel and strode into the ramshackle cabin.

Conall shrugged and showed me a field at the back of the cabin where the horses could be turned loose to graze. "I'll take care of them," he volunteered, "and make sure the saddles and other valuables are stowed somewhere out of sight. You go in and Auntie will find you something to eat."

I hesitated, not wishing to encounter the hostile priest again but as I turned round he came out of the door of the cabin clutching a bulging covered basket which obviously contained some of the best food Auntie had to offer. Auntie herself came out behind him, curtseying reverently. She watched him disappear down the track and then turning to me she said, "You are very welcome, Sir, please come in."

The tiny cabin was a very humble dwelling. A peat fire burned on the open hearth and the smoke found its way out of a hole in the roof. The furniture was a bench and the floor was hard earth strewn with rushes. In spite of this, however, Auntie made me very welcome now that the priest had gone. Since I was hungry with a day's riding, potatoes with butter washed down with butter milk was a feast fit for a king and Auntie served up a generous helping from her little store. After dinner I asked if she would like me to read a little from the Irish New Testament and she asked me what that was.

"The Scripture, God's Word," I replied, "it is God's message to all his creatures."

She looked doubtful. "I get God's word from the priest, sure I do. Wasn't he here just a while ago giving it me?"

"I am very glad if he did," I said, "but if he did indeed give you God's word he was only telling you something from this book. What did he tell you?"

"Sure and how would I know?" she asked in great surprise, "I cannot understand a word of that rigmarole."

"Then how can it have been God's word?" I asked gently, "since you cannot believe or act on something you cannot understand."

"I believe the priest right enough," she replied somewhat sulkily now, "but have it your own way and read your book if you will."

I got out my Irish New Testament and wondered what I should read. Poor Auntie seemed so ignorant of anything to do with the Gospel that I wondered where to start. Had she heard about the fall of man into sin and his punishment? I asked and her blank shrug made me long to be able to read her something from the beginning of Genesis—alas, not available in Irish. In the end I settled for reading her the third chapter of John's gospel, which tells of the visit of Nicodemus to Jesus by night and Jesus' amazing answer to his questions.

She seemed as genuinely perplexed by Jesus' words, "ye must be born again" as Nicodemus himself had been and when I read the wonderful words of Jesus, "for God so loved the world that he gave his only begotten son that whosoever believeth on him shall not perish but have everlasting life" she broke in with, "Ah sure, now that's the mass is it not!"

I tried to explain what the words meant but she seemed to have difficulty understanding me. To Conall, who could speak her language so much better than I, she would not listen at all; how could her little nephew know more of these things than the priest?

Conall and I slept on a pile of rushes on the floor by the dying embers of the peat fire that night. As I arranged my saddle bag into a pillow I wondered if the grand letter of introduction with which Mr Bedell had provided me would ever need to be taken out of it! The light from the embers grew fainter as my mother's song ran round in my head and I drifted off to sleep.

***

I woke next morning very stiff and cold, to find Conall already busy kindling the fire.

"We have a long day's ride ahead of us today, Sir," he explained as I turned over on the hard floor with a groan, "but I know you will be encouraged. Ulster is very different from this place—just you wait and see."

Auntie came in from outside with fresh milk and that, together with cold potatoes left over from the night before, made our breakfast. Conall reported that the horses were ready and we set off in good spirits in weather that Conall described as "very fair" but which I would have called drizzle.

As we rode along a track through the bog I asked Conall about himself.

"I never realised truly that I was a sinner myself until it dawned on me that I was afraid to die," I told him, "I thought that as a son of the church I was bound for heaven. When my master, Brother Paul was attacked and nearly died, I realised that he was not afraid of death and I could see I *was* afraid. Did you have a similar experience?"

"Not quite," he said, "I understood all sorts of things in my head thanks to the minister of our parish—gradually—but it was not until I heard Mr Glendinning preach that I understood how serious sin is."

"Mr Glendinning? Who's he?" I asked.

"He's the minister in Oldstone near Antrim," he replied, "and he's a terrifying preacher. He only has one message—but I'm hoping you will hear him for yourself, Sir, his preaching defies description and it is the strength and horror of it that God has used to wake up a powerful lot of sinners in that region. After that, Sir, they didn't know what to do because Mr Glendinning could only tell them of their sin, Sir, and not of God's mercy to the repentant."

This sounded a very strange situation but Conall seemed unable to describe it any better. I had to wait until we reached the County of Antrim before I could get an explanation.

***

Antrim was something of a contrast to the wild boglands of Cavan. Stone built farm houses dotted the landscape here, neat and trim, and the land had already begun to be drained by means of ditches. There was corn, there was flax, potatoes planted, seaweed stacked up for manure, orchards of apple and pear trees and gardens. Houses, cottages, townships, water mills, churches—all were in good repair. A huge lake (which the Irish call a lough) as big as an inland sea was in the centre of the land and flowing into it a river called Owen-na-view beside which was the place where Mr Glendinning ministered. In a nearby parish a tidy inn awaited us—a welcome contrast to the previous lodging I have described. Here the horses were fed on oats and we ourselves on oatcakes, bacon, wheaten bread and fresh eggs. I was glad to see Sneachta well cared for. She and I had now become good friends and she was an excellent animal, steady and careful but strong, tireless and willing. Between Dublin and Antrim she had become devoted to me and I would be sorry to part with her when we returned.

Conall was seemingly well known at the inn: he was obviously a regular courier between north and south and I found to my surprise that he carried a budget of letters to various people from Dublin.

As I passed through the kitchen I heard snippets of conversation between him and the motherly cook, "and what of your soul, Conall, lad," she was saying as I passed, "are you spending much time in prayer in secret now?"

Conall's face lit up as he recounted how warmed his heart had been in prayer and how God had blessed him. Later I heard him telling her about his Auntie and how she would not listen to him. "The hearts of my own people are so hard!" he mourned, "and it is so difficult! As far as they are concerned the English and the Scots have taken their land away and they are in no mood to listen to anything that such 'robbers' have to say about religion. They would much rather listen to their own priests who can never tell them the truth."

When we had eaten I took my letter of introduction from Mr Bedell to the house of the minister, Mr John Ridge which was a neat little dwelling beside the church. He received me with civility, but when I gave him my letters from the Provost of Trinity College, Dublin he became almost as wary as the priest I had met at Auntie's cabin in Cavan.

"So why is the Provost sending you here?" he asked.

"I am interested in languages and want to learn Irish," I explained, "and the Provost was anxious to find out what the best training would be for the young men in the college to bring the gospel to the Irish."

Even this explanation did not seem to allay Mr Ridge's anxiety and it was not until I had explained that I was myself a member of the Geneva Academy and was in Ireland as part of a *peregrinatio academica* that he thawed out.

I began to realise that as a Presbyterian he was nervous about anything that smacked of an investigation by the English church hierarchy with its bishops and archbishops. Once he saw that I had a Genevan, and therefore Presbyterian background myself, he lost his reserve and began to explain to me the things I wanted so much to know. Yes, I would be able to hear Mr Glendinning preach—the next day if I wished—yes, it was true that Mr Glendinning was able to preach only the terrors of the law—he was a very strange man—and yes, many of his people spoke the Irish language since it was very similar to the Scottish Gaelic of their native land. He also explained the delicate compromise by which Archbishop Ussher's "Irish Articles" had managed to enable Presbyterians to minister in the Irish Church. He expressed his fears that this happy situation might not continue much longer now that Bishop William Laud was in the ascendancy in King Charles' court.

"Laud will be an enemy to the Provost's plans to make sure that the gospel is preached to the native Irish too, when he comes to hear of them," I said and he nodded his head in sympathy.

"That's true enough, but they are hard people to reach, you know, the Irish," he said grimly, "some of them have settled down as tenants on the land around here but they are sullen and united in their hatred of the Scots. I am sure they are biding their time in the hope that one day they will be able to cut their landlords' throats and grab back for themselves the land they have lost."

"One at least I have met who is a true Christian," I answered, "my young guide, Conall, is as godly a lad as you could wish."

"Oh, I have met him," replied Mr Ridge, "he carries the letters from Dublin doesn't he? A real Christian lad, as you say, with a heart for the gospel. I hope he does not pay too dearly for his faith when he is among his own people."

***

At the appointed time we filed into the church where Mr Glendinning was to preach. The building was very full and the expectant hush of the people made me remember that time long ago when I had heard Brother Micanzio preach in Venice and he had held up his New Testament to the people.

The clerk led the people in singing some psalms and the passage of Scripture for the day was read. Then Mr Glendinning entered the pulpit to begin his sermon. He was a very thin man with a pale face and lank grey hair. But the most noticeable thing about his appearance was his eyes. They were piercing eyes and they glittered and sparkled and held your own eyes so that you could not look away from them. I tried to glance around the congregation, to look at Conall next to me, but it was useless: I could not take my eyes off Mr Glendinning.

His text was from Luke's gospel, "whatsoever you have spoken in darkness shall be heard in the light," and he held our attention in an iron grip from the first words that he said. Not that his voice was loud —at least to begin with—he spoke quite softly but clearly—oh so clearly. He soon had the congregation, myself included, anxiously recalling all the unwise, careless and down-right sinful things we had said, out loud or silently, when we thought that nobody was listening.

"Mark those words, my friends," he said in a voice soft with menace, "mark them. You thought no one heard them: they were spoken in the darkness. In the darkness when no one was there. But there is no such time! Always One is there! His eye all-seeing, his ear all-hearing! Mark those words for they will drag you down to hell, hell, hell."

As he pronounced those last three words, slowly, quietly, and each successively lower in pitch, the congregation let out a groan.

At that groan Mr Glendinning's voice changed as though it had been the signal for which he was waiting. Now he thundered. He described the torments awaiting the damned and I saw before my eyes again that painting I had once seen as a child in the Doge's palace: the agonised scurrying figures spiralling downwards in a whirlpool of guilt, shame and torment, on and on for ever …

Then abruptly his tone changed. He became calm, reasonable, as full of cold logic as he had been of hell fire. Anyone who listened to him would be in no doubt of the justice of God's condemnation of sinners in general or of himself in particular. The reasoning was crystal clear but it flowed in the same inescapable whirlpool as before: guilty, guilty, guilty …

I found I was trembling. In the agony of this sermon I almost forgot my Saviour who had died to save me from all this terror. Held in the powerful grip of Mr Glendinning's unblinking eyes I could think of nothing but my guilt; that I was fitted only for Hell.

Then he returned to his opening discourse on the text again. "My friends, whatsoever you have spoken in darkness shall be heard in the light—the light you cannot bear, the light of God's justice. And those words, those same words spoken in darkness will deliver *you* to darkness, eternal darkness!"

By this time the congregation was in agony. Many were crying openly, shaking with fear and terror. In desperation I managed to shut my eyes to escape from that terrible burning gaze in the pulpit. When I opened them Mr Glendinning had vanished. The pulpit was empty and the clerk was trying to lead the people in singing a psalm. I could not see where he had gone and for a moment I wondered if he had been real at all.

Amid the confusion Conall and I stole quietly out of the church and back to the inn.

"What do you think of him?" he asked.

"I'm glad the people here have him to preach to them," I answered, "and I'm gladder still that they have Mr Ridge!"

"So am I," he replied, "he and the other ministers hereabouts have arranged special meetings for the people on Fridays where they preach the *whole* gospel to them—not just the terrors of the law as Mr Glendinning does. The meetings are packed and hundreds of people have turned from their sins to find the love of the Saviour: Jenny the cook at the inn—she is one of them."

***

We left to return to Cavan after a few days but I never forgot that rich valley of county Antrim with the river flowing through green meadows and fertile cornfields, the peaceful farms and churches. It gave me a vision of what all Ireland might be like—if only things were different.

We travelled a roundabout route on the return journey for Conall had acquired more letters to deliver in the little market town of Belturbut before visiting his own home and then returning to Dublin. This suited me, as I was able to see more of the countryside. It was a few days before we arrived at Conall's home in the parish of Ballymulling. I was warmly welcomed by his family and taken almost at once to visit the kind old minister, Mr Smale, who lived nearby. He was eager to hear all I could tell him of Venice, Geneva and my travels on my *peregrinatio academica*. He had heard of Provost Bedell and was thrilled with the news I was able to give him of the Provost's plans for improving the training of ministers at Trinity College.

"The Irish language is one of the keys to the whole thing," he said, "I'm trying hard to learn it myself but I still cannot preach in Irish. I have to use a translator and it is a great blessing that I have one whom I can trust."

"Have you any advice for the Provost that you think would help him?" I asked and he looked very thoughtful.

"I'm sorry to say that I have little advice to offer," he said at last, "the situation is fraught with problems that the Provost will not be able to solve, I'm afraid."

"You mean the non residence of most of the clergy in their livings?" I asked.

"That's a problem but it is not the only thing," he said sadly, "have you any idea how the ecclesiastical courts—the church courts—here function?"

"The courts!" I exclaimed, "what have they got to do with it?"

"A great deal," he sighed ruefully, "you see, if the Irish can't or won't pay their tithes they are excommunicated as a punishment. Now that means little to them since they do not come to the church in any case, they go to the Roman priest, but as excommunicated persons they are then brought before the ecclesiastical courts. The courts are not run by the bishops themselves but by their chancellors who are lay men. These men pocket the fines from the courts. They fine the Irish and imprison them until they can pay. Many can't pay. They die of starvation and disease in the prisons or else escape before they are brought to the court by running away to the hills where they live as bandits. This situation makes such a hatred of the church exist among the Irish that evangelism seems almost impossible and I don't see what the Provost can do about it."

I was aghast at this fresh revelation and my mind immediately went to gentle Archbishop Ussher, an Irishman himself. How could he allow such a state of affairs to continue?

"Does the Archbishop allow this?" I exclaimed.

"He cannot prevent it since the courts are in the control of the greedy laity—the commissioners—who would fight all the way to the crown itself to preserve their interest," he replied sadly.

"Can nothing be done then?"

"That is a question for your Provost and for the Archbishop; I cannot answer it," he replied.

***

Although it was by no means as prosperous as the farms I had seen in Antrim, Conall's family were clearly working hard on their little plot of land and had begun some primitive drainage work. I spent a pleasant evening with the family who were delighted to hear me read from the New Testament and were proud that Conall had taught me Irish so well. In order not to cause any embarrassment to them I offered to sleep in the hay stacked for fodder in the tiny barn-cum-stables adjoining the cabin. They accepted my offer with signs of relief—they were obviously wondering where to put me among so many brothers and sisters.

The morning dawned, rarely bright and sunny. Although there is so little fair weather in this part of Ireland, when the sun does shine the land is truly beautiful. I stood looking out of the barn door at a smiling landscape. Water was everywhere. Ditches, puddles, little streams, all reflected the morning light. New-washed by overnight rain everything was fresh and every surface reflected the sunshine. Drops of water sparkled on the grass and on the leaves of the alder trees like tiny jewels. Not far off the water of the lough spread out as far as I could see, reflecting the early sunlight with an almost blinding brilliance. There was a strange familiarity about the scene; I was looking at a kind of emerald green Venice—as it might have been before the hand of man drained and built and canalised! I had grown up surrounded by water and sunlight and this landscape seemed almost familiar now I saw it in the sunshine. I thought of taking Sneachta for a drink of lough water. A well-worn path wound through some trees towards the lough and I thought I would explore it to see if it led to a suitable place for watering horses. Pulling the hay out of my hair as I strolled down to the water, I stretched my stiff limbs, enjoying the immense calm. There was not a breath of wind and no one seemed yet to be stirring in the little cabin. A robin started singing somewhere in the hedge, almost deafening in the sweet, sunlit silence.

As I neared the lough another sound crept into the silence so gently that I was only aware of it gradually. In fact, so familiar was the sound, I did not realize at first that it came from outside my own head at all. As I strolled nearer my mind absently registered that someone was singing. I moved lazily forward still enjoying the peace and the sunshine. Suddenly my reverie shattered with a shock that was almost physical. Every note of the song seemed to sting me with a sweet pain of recognition. Without thinking I broke into a run towards the unseen singer. I knew the song! I had always known it!

Trasna na dtonnta, dul siar, dul siar,
Slán leis an uaigneas 'is slán leis an gcian;
Geal é mo chroí, agus geal í an ghrian,
Geal a bheith ag filleadh go hÉirinn!

A girl's piping voice is mixed with the splashing and slapping of water. I slow down. I must think before I encounter the singer as well as the song. I stop. This is my mother's song. Every night I hear it in my dreams. But it is an *Irish* song! Now I even understand the few words of it I remember from my distant early childhood. *Over the Waves, Going West, Going West, Goodbye to loneliness* ... Who was my mother then? If this was her song, she was Irish! And so am I therefore—at least in part. A huge struggle to come to terms with all this goes on in my head as the singer continues—verse after verse. My eyes fill with tears. I know who I am—and I am not Venetian. Irish is my mother tongue! I force myself to become calm. The singer sings on; extolling the joys of coming home to Ireland over the sea. I steady my nerves. She sings of fair weather for sailing home. I blink my eyes free of tears and feel an overwhelming happiness: I *have* come home.

Chapter 26: (1628-30) Beside the Lough, The Bishop of Kilmore

I had grown up in a place where beauty itself and images of beauty were all around me. The Doge's palace where my master, Brother Paul, had worked every day was a treasure-house of priceless pictures and statues, and was itself a masterpiece of architectural splendour. In Venice I had seen finely dressed noble ladies every day wearing silk, brocade, jewels, lace. The whole city, in fact, was itself a radiant jewel sparkling in the sun of the Adriatic Sea. I never imagined therefore, as I forced myself to walk calmly through the alder and birch trees to the edge of an Irish lough, that it would be here that I would see the most beautiful sight I had ever set eyes on: a sight that would live in my memory for the whole of my life. Nor would I ever have imagined that a poor Irish girl in faded, darned, mended petticoats and apron, washing coarse linen on some stones at the edge of the water could be such an overwhelming vision of beauty.

The singing voice was indeed that of a washer girl hard at work slapping linen clothes on flat stones where a little stream entered the lough. She stood in the water, her skirts kilted up to her knees her arms bare and her hair damp and tousled. As she slapped the linen on the stone she sang in time to her vigorous actions. On the grass in the sunshine, linen was spread out to dry. A bucket of lye and two baskets of clothes still to have this stern treatment meted out to them stood on the bank. Drops of water flew up in the air, a shower of living diamonds scattered before the sun, as she worked. The powerful mixture of the mundane and the exquisite: the washing and the jewelled sunlight, the laborious work and the sweet song; together with my already overwrought emotions fixed the scene on my mind as though it had been painted there by Veronese or Tintoretto.

As I reached the edge of the lough not far from the singer, Conall came down another path towards the water leading the horses. The girl stopped singing, splashing and slapping and hailed him, "Conall, lad, don't you be bringing the beasts near my washing, now!"

Conall laughed and then seeing me standing by the loughside trees he waved, "good morning to you, Sir!" and then coming closer as the horses bent their heads to drink, "You did not meet my eldest sister last night did you, Sir? Teagan, this is Mr Samuele Paul from Trinity College in Dublin; Mr Paul, this is my sister."

I replied with something confused and muddled in I know not what language while Teagan, hastily putting her skirts to rights and stepping out of the water, dropped a courtly curtsy.

"Forgive me for interrupting you work," I said, feeling as if I was babbling some kind of nonsense, "but I heard your singing. Where did you learn that song?"

"Oh, my mother sang it to us all as children," she replied, "it is a very old song I'm sure, Sir."

"My mother used to sing it to me too," I said.

"Did she indeed, Sir?" she said politely as though that was the most natural and unremarkable thing in the world.

But Conall's eyebrows shot up, "Your mother sang that song to you in Venice? Sure, I did not know that Irish songs could travel so far! She never sang it in Irish now did she?"

"She did indeed, Conall," I said gravely, "and I suppose it is the only Irish song ever sung there."

"Well, it's a rare song right enough for someone to sing if they are far from their home—as you mother must have been if she was an Irish woman in such a place," said Teagan, "for it is all about coming home and I am sure that is what anyone would long for if they were in foreign places, England or Dublin or—where was it you mentioned? —Venice, or the like."

Two of Conall's younger sisters now appeared to help with the washing and, saluting me cheerfully proceeded to tuck up their skirts and paddle out into the water. "My mother has some food ready for us I think, Sir," said Conall, "and the horses have drunk their fill, would you be coming back to the house for a bite?"

"Can you join us, Miss Teagan?" I asked, "I would like to hear more of that song."

She looked at Conall and then shyly at me, dropping her eyes and hastily smoothing stray wisps of hair under her linen cap as she prepared to go with us.

**

Once in the cabin by the peat fire with some food before me and Conall's kindly parents listening, I found the words to explain my strange discovery.

"I grew up an orphan in a Servite monastery in Venice," I explained, "I can remember nothing of my mother except a little song that she sang to me when I was tiny. When I heard Miss Teagan this morning I realised that it was my mother's song she was singing. That means that my mother must have been Irish. No one but an Irish person would sing an Irish song in Irish."

"But what would she have been doing in Venice?" asked Conall's mother in astonishment, "I never heard of anyone going to such a place."

"Irish people have been all over the world, Mother," said Conall, "Why I've been as far as Dublin and Antrim myself!"

"I have no idea what she was doing there," I said, "and I know nothing about who my father was, not even his name."

"Talking of travelling and the like, Sir," said Conall, "When would you be wanting to start back for Dublin? With the weather so fine we could make good progress if we made a start today."

I was shocked to find that I did not at all want to start back to Dublin and leave Teagan for ever here beside the quiet waters of Lough Mulling.

***

It was many weeks before I returned to Trinity College. Just as I had forced myself to become calm that morning by the lough when I discovered my Irish identity so I forced myself to remain calm and patient when it came to Teagan. I knew that the most sensible thing to do would be to get to know the whole family well, understand her place in it and then woo her (for I knew of a certainty that woo her I must) with the utmost gentleness and tact or else even my new-found Irishness might not be enough to bridge the gap between us. Fortunately the minister of Ballymulling, Mr Smale, came unwittingly to my aid. Finding that I had been sleeping in the barn he at once invited me to stay at his little house. At his house I was able to write to Mr Bedell at Trinity College, sending the letter with Conall who decided to return with his various commissions before I did. I gave Mr Bedell a report of my discoveries about the situation in Ireland both among the Irish and the Scottish and explained that I had decided to stay at Ballymulling for a little longer. At Mr Smale's house also I made some attempts to turn what I had learned of Irish into some kind of grammar but it was slow and uncongenial work for me and as I struggled I thought how much better Mr Bedell would be at the task.

Every day I visited Teagan's family. My excuse was linguistic—at least at first.

I soon discovered that Teagan was not only quick witted (although quiet and often slow to speak) but immensely hard working and with a sense of humour that was borne of quiet observation. Her beauty did not rely on fine clothing: what she wore, though neat, was of the coarsest. It was rather the strange combination of daintiness and strength, intelligence and practicality which made her such an attractive character. Her knowledge of Irish literature was extensive and she could quote beautiful poetry at great length—while plucking a fowl or gutting a fish. Her figure was small and slender and her hands tiny but she could wring out linen clothes so that no one could squeeze a drop more water from them. Her little feet were beautiful—and impervious to the coldest lough water. Something in her ancestry, the long line of Irish chieftains to whom her family laid claim, gave her the grace and the earthiness of a princess in a legend who is beauty personified and yet buys cattle and doctors horses.

Teagan's parents had earned the disapproval of their neighbours by going to the little church where Mr Smale preached. Giving up any claim to the lands around them (which others said had been stolen from them by English settlers) they lived as best they could on their little rented plot. They were waiting, not for revenge, but for the great day when they would see their Saviour come in clouds and glory and go to dwell in his everlasting mansions. Besides this an earthly inheritance was of no significance.

Family prayers in the little cabin was a wonderful experience. Before and after the day's hard labour Conall's father drew his family together round the peat fire. Their lack of a whole Bible in their own language was pitiful; the more so since Conall's father could read Irish and had taught his children to do so. Conall's father prayed with simplicity and his exhortations to his family were wise and always derived from the passage he had read to them. The story of his gradual conversion was touching. Conall's Mother had clung to the old superstitions long after her husband but his example and newly gentle way of life had won her over.

The time came when I could not spin out my visit any longer. Conall had returned from Dublin and was ready to conduct me back home to Trinity College. I decided I must speak about Teagan to her father before I returned.

When I returned to Trinity College I found Mr Bedell very glad to see me but strangely agitated. Mrs Bedell and the rest of the family had been safely brought over from England and were settled at the college (which was a weight off his mind) so it was not family matters which concerned him. It was not long before I discovered what was worrying him. While I had been away his patron Sir Thomas Jermyn back in far-off St. Edmund's Bury had been busy on his behalf. He had worked hard, using all the influence he could command with the King and the results of his labours had just been made known to Mr Bedell. Much to his surprise, and not at all in line with what he would have wished, Mr Bedell was offered the Irish bishoprics of Kilmore and Ardagh by the King.

"I never wanted to be a bishop!" he lamented, "There is work enough here in the college to last me for years. Now I, who never wanted or dreamed of any bishopric, am being offered two bishoprics at a clap—when I am not sufficient for one!"

"You could do much good as a bishop," I mused, "from what I have seen, although it would be a very hard and thankless task."

"That is exactly what Archbishop Ussher says," he replied, "he says there is much good to be done. But, you know, I am hesitant. Already here at the college I have seen how Laud and his friends hamper the Archbishop. I am willing to obey the excellent Articles of the Irish Church and follow the Book of Common Prayer to the letter but I will not go beyond them nor yet fall short of them. If I am to do the good that the Archbishop speaks of I fear I will fall foul of the King's advisers sooner or later."

"But that could happen here at the college too," I said, "Laud and his fellows will get the Irish Church Articles replaced by something more to their taste if they can, which you would find it hard to accept."

"I know, I know," he sighed, "what you say is true and we must trust our Heavenly Father for today and not fear tomorrow. Despite my fears and hesitations I have already decided to accept. But what about you? You have come back to the college in a high state of excitement. Whatever did you find in the wilds of Ireland to bring such colour to your cheeks and give you such a brisk, purposeful stride? There has been more to your journey than your letters speak of —they tell of rain, peat bogs, hovels, ignorance, oppression, ruined churches and mad preachers, the whole enlightened only by some

Scottish settlers and a couple of decent English ministers. Surely all this would not bring such a light of happiness to your eyes!"

I smiled at this, having been quite unaware of my changed attitude and appearance.

"Well, I have found myself for one thing!" I answered and told him the strange story of my mother's song.

He digested the tale with raised eyebrows, "Remarkable!" he exclaimed, when I had finished my account, "but there is more to it than that, young man. Even the discovery that one is at least partly Irish does not bring such radiant and obvious joy. Come, who is she?"

***

My main worry on leaving Ballymulling was the problem of how I was to travel back there again to visit Teagan and her family. I had taken careful note of the way we took when I returned with Conall and, of course, I would have travelled to China or Newfoundland if necessary to see Teagan again. However, you can imagine my joy when I discovered exactly where Kilmore was. The sparse little cathedral with its bishop's residence (palace was far too grand a word for the little house) was about a mile and a half at most from Ballymulling!

Mr Bedell smiled when I asked him whether I could serve him in any way when he became bishop, knowing full well how it would fit in with my plans to be near Ballymulling. However, he was also pleased at the suggestion from a practical point of view since he was determined to start work on a translation of the Old Testament into Irish. Not that he could do the job himself, of course, as he spoke Irish only moderately well. But he had worked out a plan of action which involved Murtagh King and others to form a kind of translating team which would be headed by himself. He was more than happy to have me join it as a Hebrew expert with an interest in Irish. I was certainly passionate about the idea, having seen first hand how much the whole Bible in Irish was needed. Mrs Bedell was very willing to have me lodge with them again and as soon as she heard of Teagan she wanted to know every detail I could tell her.

"In rank she is a kind of princess in Irish society," I said beginning my description grandly, "but of course in Ireland a princess is different from a princess elsewhere."

"Ah! That is how it should be!" said the practical Mrs, Bedell, "Every lover woos a princess. But tell me is she handy? Can she manage a house? I'm afraid you menfolk with your 'princess' ideas often neglect these important things!"

"If you had seen her dealing with linen or milking a cow you would have no doubt of her capabilities!" I explained, "that is what I meant about the difference between an Irish princess and any other, you see in Ireland ..."

"But we are beginning at the wrong end!" interrupted Mrs Bedell, "Is she a godly young woman? Quiet and obedient to her parents?"

I thought of Teagan as I had seen her on the last day of my stay at Ballymulling, a shaggy Irish mantle cast over her head, kneeling with her parents, brothers and sisters by the peat fire at morning prayers. I thought of the very last glimpse I had had of her, after I had spoken to her father and gained his consent to woo her. She was standing between her parents, each with an arm around her at the door of their little home. They had both waved to me as Sneachta carried me away. Before waving to me herself I had seen Teagan glance up at her father, waiting for his approval of this gesture of friendship on her part. Only when he smiled his permission did she raise her hand in farewell salute.

"Yes," I said, "she fills that description and goes beyond it."

***

In the event it was quite some time before Mr Bedell was consecrated a bishop and moved from Dublin with his family to Kilmore. Why this tiny place was a bishop's seat was lost in the mists of time. There was certainly little enough there in 1629. The nearby town of Cavan was small and the nearest neighbours of any standing were a mile away.

As soon as he arrived, Mr Bedell threw himself into his work as he had done at Trinity College. Riding tirelessly round the whole diocese regularly he soon found out what the problems were and set to work to right wrongs and redress grievances. He set in hand work to rebuild the ruined churches of the diocese, saw to it that benefices were no longer sold and made all new ministers sign an undertaking to live in their parish when they received their benefice. He allowed no new minister to take on more than one parish. Since there were difficulties for ministers who wished to live in their parishes as their glebe lands (on which they depended for their living) were scattered all over the place and not necessarily in their own parishes, he set in motion a scheme whereby they could get together and petition for their glebe lands to be exchanged.

The bishop began the work of spreading the gospel among the Irish at once by publishing a little single sheet in parallel Irish and English called *The A.B.C., or the Institution of a Christian.* This contained the Apostle's Creed, the Lord's Prayer and the Ten Commandments together with some selections from the New Testament arranged to form a summary of the Gospel, and some Scripture prayers. This he had printed in Dublin and distributed it throughout his diocese. You cannot imagine what a revolutionary thing this little sheet of paper was or how much good it did; the Irish being for the first time able to understand these things and digest them in their own language. They had often been told by their priests that Protestants believed horrible and ridiculous things. The little sheet went a long way towards reassuring them that this was not so.

"Samuele,"said Bishop Bedell as we worked away in his study one morning, "I have just been on a visit to a monastery!"

"A monastery!" I echoed in surprise.

"That's right! There is a monastery not far from us here in Kilmore and I find that its priests and friars are, some of them at least, much more learned than those you encountered on your early travels. Many of them have been trained in seminaries overseas. So do you know what I did?"

I was quite unable to answer this question so he carried on, "I prayed for wisdom and then took my courage in both hands and requested that they put down in writing everything they could think of on behalf of their own religion and every objection they could raise to the reformed religion."

"Did they agree to do so?" I asked wondering what the point of such a request might be.

"They did indeed," he replied, "and as soon as I receive it I intend to settle down in my study and produce an answer, going through every point they make, answering it clearly and satisfactorily."

I had my doubts as to how this would help the situation. "Are they likely to listen to reason?" I asked.

"I think they might," he answered.

***

After a few days the bishop received a reply from the monastery. The monks had set to work and produced all their ideas and arguments in the most learned form they could. Bishop Bedell set to work using all his skill in debate. His extensive knowledge of church history and of Brother Paul's *History of the Council of Trent* stood him in good stead as he worked since he was able to show where many of the false ideas presented in the document had come from. As well as being forthright, he pursued what was his ordinary policy of never exaggerating the differences between the Romanists and the Protestants and showing any points of agreement if he could and of always adopting a polite and friendly tone. I smiled to myself when I read his mild and yet trenchant document, imagining what his old friend Dr Hoyle of Trinity College would have thought of it. When this answer was ready it was presented to the priests and friars for their scrutiny.

It was a fortnight before anything more was heard of the written debate. By then I was sure that nothing more would come of it. But then, when everyone except the bishop had given up any hope of further progress he called me to his study.

"Look, Samuele, look! this message has just come from our dear friends at the monastery. They did not dismiss my defence! They have studied it with great care."

"And what do they say?" I asked with great interest.

"That I am correct! Right in every particular!" he exclaimed, tears of joy running down his cheeks.

The priests and friars, almost to a man, had renounced the Roman religion! The Bishop was utterly delighted and overflowing with gratitude to God. He welcomed them with open arms, and they in their turn were very willing to learn from him. In due time, when he was sure they were well weaned from their errors, he found some of them parishes in his diocese where they ministered faithfully to the people in Irish. Their background gave them an entrance into Irish society that was quite unique.

All this activity made the Bishop many enemies. There were not a few who lost money from his reforms. Some resented his promotion of the Irish whom they would have preferred to see ground out of existence. Others lost power and influence, particularly the lay chancellors who operated the ecclesiastical courts. It was not long before Bishop Bedell was locked in legal wrangles which not only took up his time but moved him a step nearer the dangers he had feared when offered the bishopric in the first place. His skill in legal matters (acquired during his difficulties at Horningsheath) stood him in good stead now. Whenever he had to appear before his enemies in court his erudition and his fair-minded approach left them looking ignorant, greedy and unfair—which they frequently were. Like Daniel before Nebuchadnezzar, Belshazar and Darius he stood protected by his God. Not only did he often succeed but even when he failed and his enemies won the day, they were sometimes so ashamed of opposing so godly a man that they never claimed the money awarded them by the courts and slunk away rebuked, never to bother him again.

One thing that worried Bishop Bedell greatly was the fact that he was the bishop of two dioceses. He was waging a war against clergy holding more than one living and yet he could be accused of doing he same thing himself! The two dioceses were very small, which was one reason why they had been joined together. The entire living of each amounted to less than that of one wealthy English parish but he was very relieved when he was able to assign the bishopric of Ardagh to a Dr Richardson and remain himself only as Bishop of Kilmore. Dr Despotine wrote to him, concerned that he would not be able to manage on the revenue of Kilmore alone but the Bishop was cheerful and convinced that "the Lord would provide" if he took the right course of action.

***

Above all, Bishop Bedell had set his heart on the translation of the Old Testament into Irish. He worked harder than ever to learn Irish himself once he was at Kilmore, embarking on his usual method of compiling a grammar of the language as a means to learning it. He found it a struggle.

"I must inure myself to the Irish characters and observe the difficulties as I go," he said stoically, "have you heard of Roger Ascham, Samuele?"

"The inventor of the double translation method?" I answered, "yes, Ascham's method provides an excellent way of checking ones work, in my view. Were you thinking of using it in translating the Old Testament?"

"Yes," he replied, "and I will need your help. I was thinking that I would send for Murtagh King. There is a vacant living in the diocese which would suit him and he could begin translating. Then there is Mr James Nangle. He is a skilled man in Irish, and I was thinking of assigning the Psalms to him. Mr King could work from the English Bible, as he has no Hebrew but then we would have to review his work as it progressed against the Hebrew Bible."

And so the bishop followed a set method which involved the use of the Great Hebrew Bible brought back from Venice, the Greek Translation of the Old Testament, the English Bible and Diodati's Italian Bible as well as two copies of the pages of Mr King's new Irish translation. Every day after dinner we would set to work. Bishop Bedell himself first made a general comparison of the newly translated sheets with the Hebrew Bible, noting any difficulties onto the sheets. Then Ambrose Bedell slowly read the relevant chapter from the English Bible while Bishop Bedell followed in one copy of the Irish translation and the Bishop's chaplain, a Scotsman, Mr Alexander Clogie, followed in the other. I also followed in the Diodati Bible, ready to offer its reading when any question arose and again any necessary corrections were made. The final stage was for Bishop Bedell to read a verse from the Irish translation but not in Irish. Instead he translated as he read into Latin. Mr Clogie followed with the next verse in the same way until the end of the chapter was reached.

"This is congenial work for me!" I exclaimed when my part in the enterprise was settled.

"But it is what you have been trained for all your life," said the bishop, "not just congenial work, it is God's planning and he never makes mistakes."

When the translation team reached the end of the sheets and were satisfied, it was my job to write up the results by making a fair copy of the newly translated sheets incorporating all the corrections. My heart overflowed with gratitude to God for how he had led and prepared me for the work he had given me to do. Here I was doing what I had been brought up by Brother Paul to do from my childhood. I was doing it in a newly acquired language and yet that language (as I now knew) was in a sense my mother tongue. Above all I was sure that what I was doing was the Lord's work. How I had admired Dr Diodati who had translated the Bible into Italian! Now I too was able to help translate God's Word into the language of people who had never heard it in their own tongue before.

When I had finished each day's copying I set to work again and made a copy for my own private use. As these personal sheets grew in number I bound them loosely with tapes so that, although it was cumbersome to use, I began to have an Irish Old Testament of my own to read and study.

My letters to Dr Diodati at this period were overflowing with joy in my work. A regular exchange of mail continued via Conall to Dublin and thence to the Signora Madeleine's brother in London, and in this way I was able to keep the far-off Doctor and therefore the University at Geneva and my old colleagues informed my continuing studies. "Stay at the Bishop's side," urged Dr Diodati, "How right Brother Paul was! He must have realized that Mr Bedell would always be an excellent guide to your studies."

From Carlo too, came letters with little packets of seeds—would I try this or that in the Irish soil? Did I think such and such would grow?—and as it turned out they were often useful.

But it was not just my work that made my heart sing with joy at this time. What of Teagan while all this activity was going on in Kilmore?

***

When I first returned to Ballymulling I was puzzled. Where was the happy girl, splashing in the lough washing linen, telling legends to her little brothers and sisters, singing while she churned the butter or planted potatoes? Like the robin in the hedge who will only stay fearlessly near you all the while you do not betray any interest in his presence, Teagan seemed to have fluttered to a branch just a little farther off. But that vision I had once seen of her never left me, never wavered for an instant. I had seen the real Teagan and nothing could take the sight away. The difficulty was how to reach out to her without her taking fright and I pondered over the problem endlessly. It was her voice that sang the little song to me now as I drifted off to sleep at night and it was her face I saw in my mind's eye. I was utterly determined that I would not lose her but I was also aware that, as with many delicate precious things, it would need care not to crush her even as I reached out to her.

I carried on going to Conall for help in improving my Irish and it was not usually long, once I appeared at the little cabin, before his younger brothers and sisters had enlisted my aid in some game or practical project. One morning I walked to the cabin with some of Carlo's seeds in my pocket. They had arrived that week: strawberries, lettuce and some dried peas ready for testing in the Irish soil. Teagan was nowhere in sight when I arrived but two of the young brothers hailed my arrival with delight and were soon busy helping me make a bed for the seeds I had brought them.

"The peas will want sticks to grow up when they come up," I explained, "hazel twigs are best; the pea tendrils seem to love to reach out to hazel twigs and they rush up them in no time and start growing and flowering."

"How long will it take for the peas to grow—I mean when will we be able to eat them?" asked one of the lads.

"They will be ready in the summer; the sun will swell the pods and ripen them and then you can have delicious fresh peas. I used to like them with rice and ham—*risi e pisi* we used to call it—but I dare say they will go well with potatoes and butter."

"What a pity you won't be here to enjoy them," he mourned.

I was rather surprised, "Why ever not?" I asked.

"Sure, you'll be going back home to Venice or Geneva or wherever before then won't you?" he explained.

"But this is my home!" I exclaimed, "My mother was as Irish as you are. I have no intention of going anywhere away from here."

"That's good!" he replied with feeling, "I thought—well everyone said—that you would have to go back soon."

"That's *very* good," piped up his younger brother, "We don't want to lose you or Teagan!"

"Shush!" rebuked his brother, "You know what Mother said about that—not to talk. Why she may not even …"

"What is all this?" I interrupted before the discussion got out of hand, "I don't know who's been telling you all this stuff but I have no intention of going back to Geneva let alone Venice at the moment!"

"Ah, but you will one day then," said the bigger one, now much interested, "Teagan said …"

I interrupted again to prevent him disclosing speculations not meant for my ears, "We none of us know what God has in store for us, and where he will put us. But he plainly has work for me here just now. I have never had a place I can truly call home before. Venice was where I grew up but I don't even know now whether I was born there. It might even be dangerous for me to return there. I can go back to Geneva whenever I wish but I am as much an exile there as you would be yourself. No, if God sends me travelling in the world again now I am sure my heart will always be longing: *Trasna na dtonnta, dul siar, dul siar ...*"

"Well that's a relief!" said the older boy practically, "come on, I know where there are lots of hazel twigs."

The boys rushed off towards the little paths beside the lough quite unaware that they had furnished a key to Teagan's change of attitude. How could she commit herself to me without risking being torn from everything she had ever known and thrust into some strange sphere she was unable to even imagine? As I made to follow them I was conscious of someone behind me. When I turned round Teagan herself was standing there—Teagan, no longer wary or cautious but still every inch a princess—with a brace of dead wildfowl in her hands and blood stains on her coarse apron.

"Thank you, Samuele," she said quietly, "I overheard your talk and I am very grateful for your discretion." She seemed to hesitate. I waited for her to continue, as one would wait without movement not to startle the robin that would sing again, but she looked steadfastly towards the lough. I moved to stand beside her and follow her gaze but I could not look at the bright water, only at her regal face.

"Teagan," I began, taking the birds from her and laying them on the wall, "Teagan, if you had me beside you always ..."

"The sun rises at this side of the water," she said pointing, "and sets at that side."

"I will not willingly go," I said understanding her, "but if I do, if God calls me, would you follow?"

She lifted her eyes from the dancing water of the lough and looked directly at me, "To the end," she answered firmly standing very straight, "to the end."

Chapter 27: (1631-7) Home, A Wedding

Teagan and I were betrothed before the peas were in flower. All the space that held us apart seemed to have vanished like mist over the lough in the early morning and she no longer held back when I reached out to her. My shy robin no longer fluttered fearfully out of reach and it was as though a burst of sunlight had appeared from behind a cloud, lighting up everything I saw, everything I did.

Conall arrived from one of his journeys with the mail. For the bishop there were some winged sycamore seeds which he had requested Dr Despotine to send.

"Excellent!" he exclaimed when he unwrapped them, "I intend to plant one just there, Samuele, by the graveyard but of course I will raise them in pots first and select the strongest one that germinates."

I was a little surprised that such an ordinary tree would excite his enthusiasm but when I asked why he was going to such trouble he explained at once and I was ashamed of my lack of observation.

"But there are no sycamore trees in Ireland—I certainly have not seen one have you?" he asked.

"Now that you mention it I don't think I have," I answered but my concentration was now elsewhere as I noticed a little packet had also arrived for me from the Signora Madeleine via her brother in London. There was a kind letter accompanying the packet full of congratulations. "Although I know that you will be staying with Bishop Bedell now," she wrote, "if ever things change you will both be so very welcome here."

Curiously I opened the tiny packet—smaller even than the one containing the bishop's seeds. Inside was some ivory coloured silk. Gently I unfolded it. Fold after fold opened out, until there seemed to be yards and yards of the stuff! I was amazed that such a huge expanse could be folded into such a small space. When I had finished I realised that what I had draped over the study table was a beautiful bridal gift.

"For Teagan, I think," laughed Bishop Bedell as I struggled to fold up the billowing fabric, "better take it down to Mrs Bedell, she'll know what to do with it."

But the letter and packet were accompanied by another letter. It was from Dr Diodati and it explained that not long after writing to me and packing up the silk with her own hands the Signora Madeleine had passed to her rest after a short illness. It was a few minutes before I could read the rest of the letter. The Signora Madeleine had been like a mother to me while I was in Geneva—and now Teagan would never meet her. How would Dr Diodati manage without her? No doubt the capable Diodati girls could carry on running the household smoothly but there would always be a gap now that warm-hearted and gentle lady was not there. The rest of Dr Diodati's letter went on bravely with news of Charles Diodati his nephew from London whom I had met when staying with him at Dr Theodore Diodati's house in Doolittle Lane. Charles had decided to study theology and had chosen not to go to Oxford or Cambridge to do so but to travel to Geneva.

"He is a promising student and has been here nearly a year," wrote Dr Diodati "he reminds me of you in his desire to help the younger students. He asked me to remember him to you. His friend John Milton, who I gather you also met on your visit is still studying at Cambridge and is very undecided as to what to do in the future. We are hoping that perhaps he will pay us a visit while Charles is here."

As rector of the university Dr Diodati had also written formally releasing me from my post but also emphasising that I would be welcome in Geneva should I ever wish to return. "We never have enough experts in Hebrew here at the Academy," he lamented, "so someone of your accomplishments would always find a place here."

I could not imagine myself going. More than ever I felt that Ireland was my home.

***

Mr Bedell agreed with me that a parish in his diocese was not the best option for me: I was no preacher—in Irish or any other language. Instead we had managed to find a little plot of land as yet unclaimed by any settler from England. I was to claim it, build a house on it and farm. This would enable me to stay near Kilmore and continue to help with the work of translation. At first I was worried. To farm I thought I could manage, especially with the back up of my Venetian money: to build was quite another question and I had absolutely no idea of how to go about it. It was clear that Teagan and I would have to have somewhere to live when we were married but even a simple cabin would have been beyond me. However, just as I was beginning to despair of the Bishop's wonderful plan, Mr Johnson arrived from Dublin.

Mr Johnson had been one of the Fellows of Trinity College when Bishop Bedell was Provost. Brother of Thomas Johnson of Chester with whose work on Gerard's *Herball* the Bishop was well acquainted, he was a great enthusiast for the Bishop's ideas of a universal character. At Trinity they had discussed the idea often and Mr Johnson was confident he could write a book setting out the whole idea if he had some help from the bishop. The bishop was keen to find him a parish in his diocese where he could combine his parish work with writing the book which would contain a complete universal character for scientific use based on his brother's herbal. The herbal would be translated into this universal character as part of the project. Mr Johnson had other qualifications, however, which were of much more interest to me. He was also something of an engineer, an expert who could lay out a house and gardens or plan drainage work. He arrived in Kilmore just when I was beginning to despair of building any kind of dwelling and he was only too happy to be employed to build me a little house on the plot well within the time scale I needed. Meanwhile Bishop Bedell drew up the whole outline of the proposed book on the universal character, ready for Mr Johnson to complete it according to his plan.

"This land has definite possibilities," he mused when I took him to look at the building plot, "I think you could do quite a lot here with good drainage."

"Do you think so, Mr Johnson?" I asked, "I'm afraid I know nothing about drainage. I just assumed that the boggy land you are looking at was useless."

"I don't think so," he mused, "Where were you thinking of building the house? Water that's not useful in one place can be very handy in another!"

When the house was finished, I took Teagan to look at it. Mr Johnson considered it a rough and ready little piece of work but I was very happy with it. Under a neatly thatched roof were two downstairs rooms, a kitchen with a good fireplace and a stout chimney; and a little parlour. These were supplemented by two rooms upstairs, a bedroom and a storeroom, the latter with a good outside access by steps; this formed the total accommodation. The windows closed with only wooden shutters to keep out the weather, except for the parlour window. For this window Mr Johnson had somehow managed to find some glass. The front entrance was sheltered by a porch, outside which was a huge stone trough that Mr Johnson had salvaged from somewhere or other. Into this flowed a continuous stream of fresh water, diverted from the stream as part of the drainage works. I was particularly proud of this feature (not that I had had anything to do with its design) and was looking forward to showing it to Teagan. From the outset of the building plan I had told her that I wanted the house to be a surprise—my wedding present to her—and she had been most careful to keep away from the site. The boys, however, were forever sneaking off to look at the work and I could only hope that they would not give the game away.

"Keep your eyes shut!" I commanded as I led her towards her new home, "no peeping!"

Laughing and clinging to my hand as she stumbled along the path, Teagan did not notice, and neither did I, two of the boys quietly following at a discrete distance. At length we reached the little paved yard outside the front door.

"Here we are!" I said as we stood in front of the door, "you can open your eyes now."

"Surely not!" she exclaimed, "I can hear running water just by my feet—you are teasing me, Samuele!"

"Open your eyes and see," I replied, watching her face intently. Her eyes opened slowly and then wider and wider.

"But this is a proper house!" she exclaimed in wonder, "and so big! Stone walls," her eyes travelled upwards, "a chimney—no, two chimneys—and there is an upstairs floor. A window with glass in it! And the stream is flowing right here outside the door in a trough!"

"So you like it?" I asked, but she was already off exploring the inside exclaiming with pleasure at all the features, opening the shutters, admiring the chimneys and the little ladder by which the two upper rooms were reached from inside.

I stayed outside, allowing her to do her own exploring of her new home, basking in her happiness with everything I had had done. At last she reappeared, having explored every inch and descended by the outer stairs from the store room.

"I can't believe it's for me!" she exclaimed, in absolute wonder, "Thank you, Samuele, thank you! Now I know you mean to stay here for ever: who would build such a solid stone house if he intended to leave?"

"Who would marry a beautiful Irish princess," I replied drawing her towards me, "beside a sparking green lough and then carry her off to some dreary city like Venice or Geneva?"

Before she could answer there was a whoop and the boys burst out from their cover full of excitement and noise.

Teagan leapt like a startled deer, "You bad boys!" she exclaimed, "how dare you follow and then jump out at us! A good thing it will be when Samuele and I are married and we can shut this fine stout door behind us and keep you out!" There was no anger in her voice and the boys knew it: she was too happy to be cross. They dragged her away to look at the little barn, still under construction beside the house, pointing out all its convenient features and chattering like magpies.

I waited quietly beside the water trough, thinking about her words. At the moment, the thought of Teagan in Geneva or Venice was somehow as incongruous as a robin in a bookcase, yet I knew that in time my practical princess would be able cope with life in the most civilized part of the world just as well as here in the wilds. Now she might be afraid, unable to visualize any other kind of existence, but if I were able to help her to share my own experiences, the fear would go and the capable part of her personality would take over. But why had I wandered down this pathway in my mind? Why would I ever want to leave this place? Something chilly, like a shadow seemed to pass over me again and at the same time the little song sang itself in my head, *Trasna na dtonnta, Trasna na dtonnta ...* across the waves, across the waves ...

***

Every year the bitter Irish winter descended on Kilmore. If the Bishop had made enemies among the church hierarchy he had also made many friends among the Irish—a very unusual thing for a Church of Ireland bishop. At Christmastime it was his custom to give a feast in his house for the poor from the surrounding area and Teagan spent many hours helping Leah and Mrs Bedell prepare a huge quantity of food for the guests. All were invited without question of religion. What a joy it was to see the Bishop, grave and dignified, surrounded at his table by men and women in rags eating a good wholesome meal while he conversed with them about the Scripture for all the world as if they had been lords and ladies in fine clothes.

That year, as the great log fire crackled in the hearth and Leah and Teagan waited with hot food under covers while the Bishop said grace in Irish, there was a knock on the door. Thinking it might be a party of late-comers from more distant parts, I waited until the Bishop had finished and then went to open the door.

Instead of the poor peasants I was expecting, a well-dressed young nobleman in a fur riding habit stood outside in the freezing night air. He had dismounted and held his horse by the bridle. "Is this the residence of Bishop Bedell?" he asked in English but with a slightly strange accent.

"It is indeed, Sir," I replied, "Come in and welcome. I will find someone to look after your animal."

"I thank you," he said and shaking the snow from his garments and stamping his fashionable riding boots he entered the house, "Praise God I have found it. This benighted country is a foul place to travel in winter."

"Few travellers are abroad on such a night, Sir," I replied, "Do you have business with the Bishop? He is in the hall entertaining the poor of the diocese at his Christmas feast. Pray come and warm yourself."

He followed me into the hall and I sent a lad to look after the horse. "My name is Wadsworth," he explained as we made our way towards the Bishop, "and I am sent to see him by my late father who was his friend."

"Mr Wadsworth, my Lord," I said as we approached the Bishop's chair, but I was on his deaf side and I do not think he heard what I said. He stood up and gazed at the stranger in astonishment for a moment and then said,

"It looks like—Wadsworth—no, it cannot be—he is dead!"

"I am his son, my Lord," said Mr Wadsworth, kneeling before the Bishop (something I knew Bishop Bedell did not like), "and I am come on his express instructions to thank you for your letters which he read constantly and kept ever by him. On his death bed he insisted that I make my way to you at all costs, saying 'I will save one, yes, I will save one.'"

Bishop Bedell's eyes filled with tears. He raised the young man up and put his arm round him, leading him to a seat among his beloved Irish poor, and sat down beside him. I could see, even from a distance, that the well dressed and haughty young stranger was rather surprised to be seated next to a ragged old man who was scoffing food very noisily despite his lack of teeth, but the Bishop did not appear to notice his discomfiture.

"Who is that sitting talking so earnestly to my father?" asked Leah pausing as she carried dishes from the kitchen were she had been helping her mother.

"A Mr Wadsworth, or rather his son," I said, "he's just arrived."

"Mr Wadsworth's son!" she exclaimed, nearly dropping the food she was carrying, "Never! Surely he has not come here—and all the way from Spain!"

"Who is he then?" I asked full of curiosity about the young stranger.

"His father was a great friend of Father's when they were at Cambridge together," replied Leah, "At about the same time that Father was sent to Venice to be Mr Wotton's chaplain, this Mr Wadsworth was sent to Spain as chaplain to Sir Charles Cornwallis, the ambassador to Spain."

"What happened then?" I asked, "Surely this Mr Wadsworth did not stay in Spain?"

"Oh, but he did," explained Leah, "because while he was in Spain he turned Papist! The Jesuits persuaded him to change his religion."

"Why would he send his son here then?" I asked, "and what is all this talk of letters?"

"Why he would send his son I know not," she answered, "but the letters you mention must be those that my father wrote to Mr Wadsworth. They exchanged many letters; Mr Wadsworth putting points in favour of the Roman religion and my father answering them."

I began to understand. "The Bishop's letters must have had a great effect," I said, "the young man says his dying father insisted he go to see him. He says he used the words, 'I will save one.' I suppose he meant that your father would be able to speak the truth of the Gospel to his son and prevent him making the same terrible mistake that he himself had made."

***

I was much puzzled as to how to furnish the little house now that it was built. Teagan's wants were very modest but I was concerned to provide for her as well as I could. Although my own ideas were not grand, a chair or two and a table and dresser struck me as more or less essential. At last, however, Mr Johnson was able to recommend a carpenter, Richard Castledine, who was engaged on work for a drunken old English squire called Waldron who lived near Belturbet. Castledine was not only an excellent carpenter—far too good for the master he served so well—but also a wonderful Christian man with a reputation for being an amazingly fast and most accurate taker of sermon notes. These he squirrelled away, after reading them to his family, until he had a wonderful collection, including many of Bishop Bedell's. He got leave from his master to come over and look at the house and find out what I wanted.

"I can make you everything you need and I have a good supply of timber," he told me after looking round."

"And your master will not object?" I asked, knowing that he served his master faithfully despite the fact that Waldron took no interest in his lands and spent his time only drinking and roistering.

"My master will not object—nor will he be my master much longer, if God wills it," he replied.

I raised my eyebrows, "How so?"

"He is going back to England," he replied, "He takes no interest in anything now that his eldest son has died and with what God has prospered me I am able to purchase the remains of his ruined estate for my own!"

"You will not be doing carpentry any more then," I said, thinking that as a landowner he would not be following his old trade any longer.

"I will be glad to do this last job for a friend of the good Bishop before I lay aside my tools," he replied, "I have heard how you are helping him with the Irish Old Testament—although not how a Venetian comes to be here in Ireland after studying in Geneva!"

"It is a complicated story," I said, sitting down with him on a log by the lough.

"But one I would love to hear!" he answered.

I launched into the story of my adventures and he listened keenly, asking interested questions as I went along. By the time I had finished we were good friends and I was very glad Mr Johnson had put me in touch with him.

As to Mr Johnson himself, a parish was eventually found for him and he settled down to his duties and also to his book on the universal character, reporting back to the bishop by letter at regular intervals on his progress.

The house was ready and furnished, the garden and vegetable plot were fenced and planted and I had set Swiss strawberry runners in a sunny spot not far from the edge of the lough. I purchased a cow, some hens and a few sheep to set us up. Conall had brought me some pots and pans back from one of his trips to Dublin and Mrs Bedell had made us a wedding present of some beautiful linen from her own store chest. Teagan was very grateful for all the good things we had been given but she was disquieted also.

"I am afraid being your wife means living a different kind of life from my parents," she said, "all this will seem very grand to them, Samuele."

"A different kind of life but not necessarily a better kind," I reminded her, "God has indeed blessed us with many good things but he has blessed your parents too, Teagan, with long life, a healthy family and most of all the light of the gospel which does not shine as brightly in some other parts of Ireland. I am sure they would say the same thing themselves."

"They do, they do," said Teagan earnestly, "Father was saying almost exactly what you just said only this morning but I am afraid, Samuele, perhaps I will not be able to live properly in such a grand house with such grand people around me. I will not know what to do, what to say …"

"Teagan, Teagan," I said, "You are forgetting yourself! You are a princess!"

"In your eyes, Samuele, I may be but my father's family has fallen very low. Even a princess can fall into poverty."

"And face it *like* a princess," I replied my mind going back in a flash to that conversation with Dorothée Diodati all those years ago, "your high birth would be nothing without your attitude. I remember once when someone was very hurtful to me they accused me of having no name."

"No name?" asked Teagan in surprise.

"My surname, Paul, is not the name I was born with. It is the name of my dear master, Brother Paul, who allowed me to use it because I did not, do not, even know my father's name. But when I was feeling wounded by … by someone's hurt, I was reminded by someone else that a good name for honesty and Christian living is far more important than any other kind of name. I have never forgotten it."

"I shall be proud to take your name, Samuele," said Teagan, "wherever it comes from."

"It is not a noble name like yours," I said, taking her hand and drawing her to me, "I am no prince; so you see, Teagan, in marrying me you are taking a step down not a step up in society!"

***

Marriage is always a big step in life; one that both opens and closes doors—doors from the past and into the future. For me the step was huge, and some of the doors that shut behind me were ones which I had imagined I had closed many years before. The door of the Servite monastery where I grew up closed to me with marriage, of course, but that was not all. I was surprised to find, in the recesses of my mind a door behind which stood the laughing, dancing figure of Adrienne and another behind which (and this shocked me even more) stood the quiet, plain-faced Dorothée. The door into my new-found home, my new life, here in Ireland stood wide open and through it I thought I saw a cloudless sky. And yet, and yet ... when I tried to look through the door there was still always a nameless shadow that flitted across the rippling water of the lough that I could only catch out of the corner of my eye.

It was Teagan's minister, the good Mr Smale that married us in the summer of the following year. My memory of the ceremony is hazy but the tiny church was packed. The bishop and his family were there, of course. Mr Clogie, Murtagh King, Richard Castledine the carpenter and his family were there as well as Teagan's family and relations from miles around. Many of these were Romanists, indeed a couple were priests.

Teagan, my beautiful princess, walked towards me with head held high and with the steady even tread of someone bred to courtly ceremony. She and Leah had made her a gown in the Irish fashion of deep rich red woollen cloth. The skirt was so full and heavy with its almost tubular gores, that a double thickness of wool was needed on the bodice to support its weight. The strange but graceful Irish fashion had been followed as to the sleeves which were each simply a strip of the deep red fabric running from shoulder to wrist where they were joined to the cuff. Out of the silk that had been the Signora Madeleine's last gift, the girls had made an undershift or léine with the traditional huge, wide sleeves that made this Irish garment so distinctive. Yard on snowy white yard of priceless silk floated down to the red gown cuff, set off by the narrow strip of red that formed the gown sleeve above. Enough silk had been left to make a dainty scarf which Teagan wore pinned over the front of the gown. Of course I can recount these details only with hindsight. At the time I was aware only of a blur of deep crimson, of swirling shimmering sleeves and of Teagan's gentle voice as she responded to Mr Smale's questions with quiet and firm dignity. I wondered just for a fleeting moment about my own parents. Did they exchange their vows in Irish? In Latin? Were they rich, poor, learned, ignorant, noble, lowly? I would never know!

***

My new life with Teagan overflowed with joy. At last I thought I could see everything God had planned for me falling into place. Teagan was the crowning glory of all my mercies. The ache of loneliness left me for ever. What need had I of mother or father now? All was contained, wrapped up, in Teagan. Capable in household and farm management, I leant on her judgement in domestic matters. Shy and unconfident in the wider world, she leant on me. Sometimes her shyness coupled with the bearing she derived from her ancient lineage made her appear aloof, cold even, to strangers but to me she was always the warm, happy girl I had first seen standing in the water of the lough, singing. We planted and built and the little farm prospered. As I led her forward with firm gentleness, she began to find confidence to look up in the world outside her immediate circle. Together we worked; together we prayed; together we rejoiced.

But if I had found tranquillity and happiness, Bishop Bedell's life was anything but tranquil and the shadow of bereavement hung over him. That winter he and Mrs Bedell were very ill with the Irish ague. The Bishop began to recover gradually but his wife remained poorly —"crazy" as the Bishop described both her and his own condition in the letters Conall carried to the bishop's English friends.

Then came the terrible news from Dublin. John Bedell, his middle son, whom he had sent to study at Trinity College, having taken the same Irish ague, had died. The Bishop seemed to stagger under this loss at first, weak and "crazy" as he was from the ague himself. He tried to comfort his poor wife with the assurance that John, like little Grace, who had died so many years ago in Horningsheath, was now with the Lord and Saviour he served but her sick state of mind could not take in much of what he said. Somehow consolation eluded her. Leah and Teagan nursed her by turns but although her strength returned gradually, at least to some extent, her mind seemed weakened, her concentration broken. Letters from her eldest son Nicholas Maw, now a doctor in practice in London were a solace but she seemed less and less aware of her surroundings in this world and more set on the life to come. To Teagan and Leah she spoke often of heaven, saying she had felt it so near during her illness.

"How I long to be there!" she sighed one morning, looking out of the house window at the rain-washed landscape beyond the Bishop's beloved garden, where he was digging away with something of his old energy making a space for his new little sycamore tree.

"Where Ma'am?" asked Teagan who was helping her wash and comb her hair, Leah being busy in the kitchen.

"Those pleasant lands," she answered absently, still looking out of the window, "on the edge of Canaan where I could just see my Shepherd and my dear little lamb Grace in his arms—and now John too—but now, even when I strain my eyes, I cannot descry them through the mist of the cruel slaughter and battle."

"What battle, Ma'am?" asked Teagan, puzzled, but Mrs Bedell did not answer.

***

"Samuele," the Bishop confided one morning as we worked together in the study, "I never expected to have to bury one of my sons here in Ireland so far away from everyone ... but who knows what he has been spared?"

"John was a promising scholar," I said, wondering however I could express my sympathy for my dear old friend and encourage him, "it is hard for us to see God's designs."

"We will see one day," he replied at once, "and for the present we must bow to His providence."

Despite ague and bereavement, the Bishop's vigorous and energetic reforms and his care for his Irish flock never ceased and as a result he was soon embroiled in a series of battles. If in *my* happy labours in my translation work or on my little farm I was sometimes aware of a vague fleeting shadow, dark and solid shadows were cast over *his* work—quite apart from illness and bereavement. Those shadows were cast by the figures of Laud (now Archbishop of

Canterbury) and Lord Wentworth the Lord Deputy of Ireland. Their policies were at odds with Bishop Bedell's plans in almost every respect. An Arminian high church man, Laud made moves to alter the Articles of the Irish Church that had been so wisely laid out by Archbishop Ussher. Ussher had been concerned to unite as many godly men as possible in the church, whether they were Presbyterians or were in favour of a church ruled by bishops. Laud was concerned only with forcing men to assent to the rule of the bishops and with rooting out puritanism. Wentworth, meanwhile, cared about the prosperity of Ireland only in as far as it could provide revenue for the King or soldiers. Soldiers, that is, which would give the King military power with which he could overawe his more and more vocal and more and more puritan parliament in England.

Again and again Bishop Bedell was called to Dublin to defend himself in court. He hated going so much that he began to refer to legal matters as his "purgatory" and his trips to the courts in Dublin as "trips to purgatory"! Yet, as before, he remained unmolested by the courts: a figure of such rectitude, such disinterested legal expertise, such theological learning and such judgement and justice that his accusers were shown up as the petty, selfish and ignorant men they were. The constant journeying took up much time and with the addition of his circuits of his own diocese (which he made to ensure justice was done in local ecclesiastical courts) he spent many hours in the saddle. He deeply begrudged the time this took up and complained that his scholarly work had almost come to a stop as a result. There was one useful side effect, however. The exercise was very beneficial to him. He had noticed before that vigorous digging in the garden relieved certain pains he suffered from. Now he discovered that horse riding was just as effective and his health greatly improved as a result.

***

I sat in the Bishop's study copying carefully the latest sheets of the Irish Old Testament. The Bishop was working too, writing letters in his immaculate Latin. He looked up from his work, pushing back his chair.

"Conall will take these, I hope," he said, "he should be back from Dublin any day now."

"Are they for Dr Despotine?" I asked, knowing that the doctor was a frequent correspondent.

"Some of them are," he replied and a thoughtful, far-away look came into his eyes, "dear Despotine, he is always so concerned for me and my affairs! How I wish sometimes that I could sit by the fire with him and enjoy his wise company again."

I thought of the tranquil and comfortable home at Horningsheath that the bishop had exchanged for the turmoil and privations of life in Ireland and I was not surprised to see a distant expression in his eyes.

"The latest news from England is depressing, Samuele. Do you remember Dr Diodati's brother-in-law, Philip Burlamachi?"

"I do indeed," I said, "wasn't Dr Diodati worried about his financial dealings with the king when we were in London?"

"Yes he was," said the bishop, "and not without reason. He has been borrowing for years in order to lend to the royal treasury. He has recently been to France on behalf of the King with the object of bringing back the remainder of the Queen's dowry that was still unpaid. He was promised that he would be paid back out of this money. In the event he was not able to bring back very much cash, only assignments. Because of this, Burlamachi has not been paid after all and he cannot meet his obligations to his own creditors as a result. It does not take long for news of this sort of thing to spread all over Europe. He is a broken man, only protected from his angry creditors by the King who dare not surrender him to them since it is on his behalf that the debts have been incurred. Burlamachi has been acting in collaboration with his wife's brother (one of the Calandrini family I believe) who is very heavily involved and he has no royal protection, of course. The whole thing is a terrible mess, even the crown jewels are involved: Calandrini is holding some of them in Holland and refusing to return them until at least that part of the debt which is due to him personally is paid."

"Poor Burlamachi," I said and as I spoke my mind went back to the happy Lucchese family in Geneva with their extensive family relations with the Burlamachis and Calandrinis, "Dr Diodati told me that he is quite unlike many money-lenders. They can sometimes be sharp, hard people but the Signora Madeleine's brother is far from being a character like that."

The bishop sighed, "I have never met him myself," he said, "but I understand that he is a kind man, generous to the poor, willing to lend money and never harsh in his dealings."

"The Signora Madeleine was like a mother to me when I was in Geneva," I said, "She was the most kind and gracious lady, so gentle and so thoughtful. It sounds as if her brother is like her. News of his predicament must have greatly distressed her if she knew of it before her death."

"From Despotine's letter it seems that it was such news that hastened her end," he replied, "although she was already very ill by then."

I digested this sad circumstance in silence and the Bishop worked on without speaking for a while then:

"You know, if Teagan would spare you, you could take these letters for me and see the good old Doctor and be back again in a few weeks," he mused, returning to the matter in hand.

"Now there is an idea!" I said, "The farm would be quite safe in her hands and I would love to see Dr Despotine again. I could even take Conall with me; he's itching to travel further afield!"

***

Teagan was busy in the kitchen when I returned, cooking an Irish dish which I had come to love as much as *risi e pisi*. Called *colcannon*, it was a deliciously savoury mixture of potato and kale, with small pieces of fried bacon stirred through it and the whole dish topped with a pat of Teagan's good butter.

"Your favourite supper!" she cried as I entered, "and see how many eggs the hens have laid today! It was a good idea of yours, Samuele to get Conall to bring some more from Dublin, although I'm sure I don't know how they stood up to the journey on horseback so well!"

"Teagan," I said as I sat down at the little table and prepared to tuck into the steaming colcannon, "Would you be happy for me to go on a visit to England, to see my old friend Dr Despotine and take him some letters from Mr Bedell?"

Teagan put down the pan she held beside the fire and stood up straight.

"I will not go at all if you do not wish it, Teagan," I said, "but Mr Bedell has letters that need to go now. I was thinking of going when Conall returns and taking him with me."

Teagan stood silent and the colcannon grew cold on the table. I waited. Then she said quietly, "go and God bless you both, Samuele. I can keep the farm going here until you return."

***

Leah promised to keep Teagan company while I was away and offered to move into our house with her until my return if she wished. The two of them had become friends right from the time of Leah's arrival in Kilmore with her mother and step-father. How the two girls communicated was a mystery to me, since Leah never mastered Irish and Teagan had only the sketchiest notion of English, but their common interests in needlework and all that pertains to running a family kitchen surmounted every difficulty of language. Somehow Leah managed through gallamaulfrey (as the Irish called the mixed Irish and English which some spoke), kindness and the knowledge of the New Testament which the girls shared, to communicate well with Teagan.

By the time Conall returned from Dublin Teagan had prepared some gifts of preserves for me to take to Mrs Susan Despotine and the girls, Catherine, Isabell, and Anne, with her greetings. I hated being parted from her and it was as though the shadow had flitted again across our landscape making me uneasy during the whole trip until I was safely home again.

***

In the years that followed Conall and I made regular trips to St. Edmund's Bury loaded with letters in each direction and also with culinary gifts from Teagan and Susan Despotine to each other. I was also able to keep my financial affairs in better order as my Venetian money kept arriving via Dr Diodati and I was able to leave a good part of it with Dr Despotine for safe-keeping.

Once Mr Bedell had been made a Bishop, there were several attempts to have him appointed to an English bishopric and thus brought back to England. "It would be so good to have him home again," said Dr Despotine, as I sat with him beside his comfortable fire during one of my visits, "and think what good a man of such scholarship could do here in England where we are so much in need of good reformed teaching to combat the Arminianism that is in high places."

"I fear it is that Arminianism that will prevent him ever being called back," commented Susan Despotine, looking up from her needlework, "the times have changed since the death of our good Archbishop Abbot: anyone with puritan ideas will not get a bishopric these days."

"He will not want to come," I said, "he is doing such a great work in Ireland that he will not leave it, even to come home to England again."

My instinct proved correct. When the Bishop read Dr Despotine's letter suggesting that he should try to return and asking whether he should speak to Sir Thomas Jermyn about an English bishopric, he was adamant that his place was in Ireland.

"If I am fit for anything, it is to serve God here, not in England," he said, "don't mistake me, Samuele, I love my country and my old home but here I can do so much more. The behaviour of those who oppose me here is so extreme, and so obviously wrong in the eyes of all reasonable men that I am easily seen to be in the right. In England the opposition would be much more subtle. I would soon draw the hatred of all the powerful men upon me and be unable to do any good."

So Bishop Bedell's position in Ireland was confirmed; in his own mind and in the minds of his friends in England who would have loved to see him return. John had been buried in the churchyard at Kilmore and the Bishop had given instructions that when the time came he was to be buried beside his son: there would be no going back.

In the summer of 1637 Teagan's friend, Leah Maw married Bishop Bedell's chaplain, the hard working Mr Clogie. Teagan and I were delighted and Bishop Bedell was pleased that his step-daughter was married to such a good man. I had worked with Mr Clogie on the translation project and had come to like this energetic little Scotsman with his clear thinking and his love of anecdotes and stories. Teagan was pleased for her friend and just as Leah had helped make her own wedding gown, Teagan helped Leah make her own simple outfit.

|Alas for us all! Within a month of the wedding Leah was dead! The Irish ague had claimed another victim. Mr Clogie was devastated and poor Mrs Bedell, still weak and grieving for John, hardly bore up under the blow. Her own health began to go slowly but steadily further downhill from this time and she could no longer run the Bishop's household now she was without Leah to help her. Teagan did what she could but Mrs Bedell languished and the Bishop's household affairs became chaotic.

***

Every trip I made to England increased Teagan's confidence and made her less fearful of my going. I always anticipated my home-coming from these travels with much joy. Teagan would have had news that I was on my way and the table would be set for a dish of my favourite colcannon; my chair set by a cosy fire. She would always have seen me from quite some distance, even in the dark, and would be running down the path to meet me and draw me into the house. Here I would have to recount every possible detail of my travels from the moment I had left and she was especially keen to hear about Mrs Despotine and the girls. In spite of the distance, and the fact that they had never met each other, the Despotines had taken Teagan to their heart and they became genuine friends.

One trip that Conall and I made was in the height of summer. We had boarded the ship that was to carry us across to England and stowed our baggage in the tiny space assigned to us by the captain. By this time I had overcome my sea sickness completely and was as good a sailor as I had imagined I would be on my first sea voyage on the *Dolphijn* with captain Doomer. Conall and I were leaning over the side, idly chatting and enjoying the sunshine when a tall, lean figure walked up the gang plank.

Conall nudged me, "Look who is coming aboard," he whispered and I looked more closely at our new fellow passenger as he embarked. Dressed in black and carrying a very small bag by way of luggage the newcomer strode purposefully on board without any hesitation.

"Mr James Glendinning!" I exclaimed. There could only be one person with such a steady, piercing gaze, "I wonder where he is going and why!"

"One way to find out," smiled Conall, walking across the deck to greet him, "Mr Glendinning, Sir, welcome aboard! Where would you be going to this fine morning?"

Mr Glendinning fixed his eyes on us and there was something so wild in them, something so strange, that I shivered. "I am fleeing," he said softly, "fleeing from Armageddon, the great battle of evil against evil. The vial of the seventh angel is poured out even now! His wings are even now hovering over this island. The wrath of God is falling; it will not be long; flee, flee flee!" his voice rose in a crescendo.

"But where to, Sir?" I asked, "where are you bound?"

He became calm, sounding rational and reasoned as he explained his itinerary. "I am bound for Constantinople: I shall sail from London to the Netherlands. I am going to travel on to Constantinople and then carry on my journey and my search from there."

"But why, Sir?" what are you searching for in such a place?"

A look that was almost crafty, came into his wild eyes, "I am going to find the seven churches of Asia," he whispered, "the churches of the Book of Revelation. They will have the answer! The Great Answer!"

I was bewildered: the poor man was obviously insane but Conall persisted in trying to make sense of his wild talk. "What answer?" he asked.

But he received no reply that made any sense. Instead Mr Glendenning became very agitated, "Armageddon!" he whispered, "It is coming, coming, coming. I have seen it stalking towards us over the water of the lough. Armageddon!"

"Poor, dear man," said Conall as we walked away, "his mind has given way. We must pray for him."

I felt suddenly cold, in spite of the sunshine. The shadow had flitted across the water again and I shuddered.

Chapter 28: (1637-40) Shadows

Young Mr Wadsworth stayed at Kilmore for some time before continuing his travels back to England. During that time I learned to cordially dislike him. He rode around the diocese on his fine horse, taking every opportunity of sneering at the Irish and making many friends among the associates of the lay chancellor in charge of the church courts, the man whose one aim it was to return to the happy state of affairs he enjoyed before Bishop Bedell's arrival at Kilmore. The bishop seemed not to notice his loathsome behaviour and was prepared to excuse him for almost anything because he was the son of his old friend but I was thoroughly glad when he left in the early spring.

Not long after Wadsworth's departure Mr Johnson came riding in from his distant parish to give the Bishop news of his work on the Universal Character and to consult him on various difficulties he had come across in the project. The book was to be called *Wit-Spell* and, due to the nature of the characters Mr Johnson had used, it was to be engraved on copper rather than printed from moveable type and he and the bishop had a happy time together discussing their pet project.

Teagan and I invited Mr Johnson to our house for a meal and he was delighted with the comfortable home we had made of the house he had built.

"This is grand," he said cheerfully, as he pushed away his chair from the table at the end of the meal, "you live like a king here, Samuele, better than Lord Wentworth will ever do in the grand house I've designed for him at Naas, I'll be bound!"

"You designed a house for the Lord Deputy!" I exclaimed in surprise, "That is a step up from our humble farm and no mistake. I'm surprised you are not too busy for such a venture!"

"I am really it's true," said Mr Johnson, "but I have a wife and eight children to keep and my parish is very small. Work has been going on on the house at Naas for years now and I have been paid some instalments. The place is huge and built all of brick not stone— most unusual here in Ireland. The Lord Deputy has a Dutch brick maker on the site and, apart from a few decorative special bricks which he imports from the Netherlands, the bricks are made on the spot."

"Well what a disappointment," I smiled, "I was going to ask your advice about some land drainage, but you are obviously far too grand an architect and engineer to be bothered with my little farm now!"

Mr Johnson laughed and for answer got up from the table and fetched his hat, "Let's have a look at it," he said.

***

Mrs Bedell was now so ill that she remained in bed. Teagan nursed her tenderly, watching over her by day while the Bishop was engaged in his duties. At the end of March she became more disordered in her mind and spoke often of joining John and Grace. "Can you not see them through the window?" she would ask pointing at a view of the churchyard in the rain outside the window, "sometimes ... often ... the battle and terror obscures but not today ... look! See, the Shepherd stands with his lambs in those beautiful green meadows—and Nicholas is with them too."

"Nicholas is in London, my dear," said the Bishop gently, trying to remind her of her eldest son's work as a physician in that great city. But she did not seem to understand.

***

Mrs Bedell slipped away to join John and Grace with the saints round the throne in heaven later that month. The next day news arrived from London that Nicholas Maw had died of an illness contracted from one of his patients.

"I am glad I did not have to break that news to her also," said the Bishop, "and yet I think she already knew."

Now the bishop was bereft of his spouse who had been his unwavering support since the far off days in Horningsheath. Again I tried to find words of comfort and again, although I had no words, the Bishop obviously drew his strength and comfort from a better source. He buried her beside their son John in the Kilmore churchyard, preaching her funeral sermon himself to a congregation who wept to hear him. Blow after blow had fallen now on the long-suffering Bishop. With each blow he seemed to stoop a little more and his deafness seemed to increase. William, Ambrose and Mr Clogie were a great comfort to him and tried to bring some order in his household but it was the unseen, heavenly source of comfort on which he drew that enabled him to continue his work with an unswerving devotion.

He rode round his diocese with the same energy as ever, redressing wrongs, supporting the poor and preaching the gospel to every creature. Where the gospel was not preached by those whose duty it was to do so he admonished those responsible. Where possible he replaced them. As ever, he would engage in Latin debate with any Roman priest or titular bishop who would listen.

***

I followed Mr Johnson's suggestions, adding a ditch here and an embankment there on the farm and as time went on there was almost no unusable land left. Mr Bedell, whose own garden was still a source of pleasure and recreation to him in spite of his sorrows and troubles, constantly urged the trial of more fruit trees and provided slips and cuttings. He lavished much care on his own little sycamore tree which was growing sturdy and strong not far from the grave of Mrs Bedell and her son. A few of the fruit trees he urged on me survived well despite the Irish weather and so I had the beginnings of an orchard beside the house. The farm became far too big for us to work on our own and as a consequence we employed labour, thus spreading our prosperity in turn to others in the neighbourhood. The summers passed and we still had no child of our own, no little one to train up to carry on the work. Teagan felt this more keenly as the years went by but we encouraged each other to accept God's providence quietly. Since my own lonely boyhood I had longed for a family to belong to. For me Teagan still fulfilled that need almost completely. Only now and then did I remember with something like longing the happy Diodati children playing in Carlo's garden.

Teagan's brothers and sisters were growing up and some of them married and settled nearby. One of the brothers, Lorcan, however, was quite different to the rest. He gave Teagan and Conall great cause for concern. From a small boy he had been quiet, as Teagan herself was inclined to be, but rather than being thoughtful as his sister was, Lorcan was inclined to be sullen. As he grew older, this ripened into rebellion.

When Teagan's father died the whole family mourned. They missed the old man's wise council and Teagan's mother was particularly concerned for the young ones. It had been Teagan's father who had guided them in the truth of the gospel. Now that he was no longer there would they stray back into the old ways? But the family stayed firm, there was no going back: except for Lorcan.

Lorcan had always found it difficult to find work. The little family farm could not support him now that he was grown up. Teagan and I tried to employ him on our farm but he was resentful of our prosperity and sullen.

"Why should I work for you?" he asked, "when the land belongs to me in the first place? All this land was ours once to grant to whom we would. Now you expect us to starve on a tiny corner of it or work for you for money!"

"Lorcan," I replied, stung that we were being blamed for a situation not of our making, "this is not our doing. I am not even English and Teagan is your own sister."

"Then do not serve the English!" he spat, "Your English Bishop, English parsons! What do they know of us? All they care about is bleeding the Irish of money. Pay the tithes or die in prison! You with your Venetian money! Draining the margins of your land till it measures more than anyone else's! No wonder you do not suffer hunger! No wonder you can employ others to work for you. Learning our language to spy out our councils and report them to your masters!"

***

A few days after we had received this rebuff from Lorcan I arrived home from my work with the Bible translators in the Bishop's residence to find Teagan in a very anxious state.

"Lorcan has vanished!" she explained, "Mother and the others cannot find him anywhere!"

Before I could answer or ask for any further details there was a knock on the door and Conall presented himself.

"Not good news, I'm afraid!" he said, in response to my questions, "I'm pretty sure where Lorcan is and it's not a good place. There is a small band of robbers and ruffians that gain a living preying on travellers and other honest folk and they hide away somewhere in the boggy woods by Loughsheen. I have ways of finding out about their movements—I have to so that I can keep out of their way when I'm travelling in that area—and I've had news that he is with them."

***

"I wonder if Sir Henry Wotton could help us," mused Bishop Bedell as we worked away one afternoon in his study.

He had been pondering the best way of getting support for the publication of the Irish Old Testament and had so far drawn a blank.

He had himself sent to Holland at his own expense to have the type required for the project cast. Mr King who had been the mainstay of the translation team was now very old and to the Bishop's horror the Archbishop of Canterbury, Laud, and the Deputy Lieutenant Wentworth began to take steps to have the translation suppressed, claiming that Mr King (poor old man!) was ignorant and barbarous and could not therefore have made anything but a worthless translation.

"It grieves them," the Bishop lamented, "that someone has been careful of the welfare of this poor captive people! They are like Sanballat and Tobiah when the Jews were building the walls of Jerusalem under Nehemiah: they cannot bear to see the work going forward!"

"I am happy to go and see Sir Henry if you think it would help," I replied, "although I understand from Dr Despotine that he has very little influence at court these days."

Before we could make any definite plans however news arrived that Mr King was to be thrown out of his parish because of his involvement with the translation. The Bishop at once set off for Dublin where he defended Mr King in the church courts with his usual learned and unanswerable logic. This was not enough to protect Mr King, however, who was arrested and thrown into prison in Dublin where he became so sick that he was unable to answer in his own defence. Bishop Bedell wrote to Lord Wentworth petitioning him for Mr King's release and we waited eagerly for news.

Before any news of Mr King reached us, however, another and most unexpected visitor arrived at Kilmore.

***

When I received a message asking me to go up to the Bishop's residence to meet a visitor who had arrived I wondered whether at last there was some news of Mr King's release. "Who is it?" I asked Conall who had come up to the house with the message.

"You will never guess—so he tells me!" said Conall enigmatically, "but he assures me you will be pleased to see him."

This was very mysterious and I hurried off with him at once. I paused outside the Bishop's study door before knocking. I could hear voices speaking in Italian which made me more curious than ever.

"Come in!" called the Bishop and, opening the door, I saw a man of about my own age sitting with the Bishop at his study table. He rose as I entered and I could see that he was dark and weather-beaten and dressed in worn travelling clothes.

"Samuele!" he exclaimed holding out both arms to me, then in Italian, "don't you recognise me after all these years?"

I stared at the figure in puzzlement. Who was it? No one I could remember.

"Come, Samuele," encouraged the Bishop, "Do you not remember your dear friend from Venice?"

Venice! I hardly remembered where it was these days let alone anyone who came from the city!

"I will help you," said the stranger, "Fresh fruit! All fresh! Get your apples here! Fresh Fruit!"

"Luigi!" I cried, "No! Not here in Ireland! Not after all this time!"

"It is indeed," said Luigi grasping both my arms in a strong grip, "and praise the Lord I have found you safe and sound."

"Luigi! I never dreamed I would see you again!" I said, "how on earth do you come to be gallivanting here? What about your wife and family—and your business?"

Luigi's sunny face clouded over, "we had an outbreak of plague again in Geneva. My wife and my three sons ... ... all buried outside the city."

"I'm so sorry!" I exclaimed, "My poor dear friend ... what can I say? Oh I am so sorry, so sorry ..." my words trailed away and I gripped the hand of my old friend in sympathetic silence.

"Others suffered too—Carlo was very ill," said Luigi after a moment, "but he got the family away first to the mountains where there was no plague and they were all safe up there in the fresh air. Dr Diodati is safe and well also but Elizabeth was struck down and did not recover. Geneva is a sad place for me just now so ..." and here he smiled once more and his face suddenly looked familiar and boyish again, "I decided to travel—and who better to visit than my old friend? My business is safe enough in the hands of my nephew, the son of my dear wife's sister, at least for the time being."

"I am very touched, Luigi," I began but he interrupted.

"There is more to my visit than that, of course, Samuele," he said, "but it is a very long story."

"Come home with me and meet my wife then," I said, for I could see that the Bishop (impatient nowadays of any interruption however pleasant) was keen to get on with his work, "I have told her many times about you and she will be amazed to actually meet you."

＊

Teagan was indeed thrilled to meet my old friend and eager to make him at home. She soon had us sitting round the table ready to tuck in to some good hot colcannon, which Luigi declared delicious as soon as he had tasted it.

"It would not be hard to sell this stuff on the streets of Geneva," he mused, "Come and get your hot colcannon, steaming hot, all hot!"

I laughed, "Good old Luigi! You'd have a job selling it here in Kilmore though—there aren't any streets! But you promised to tell us your story and why you came. Surely not to find something new to sell to hungry Genevans!"

"No," he said, "I came because I have something for you."

"For me?" I asked "what is it?"

"Let me explain," said Luigi, "I don't know if you will remember John Milton; he tells me you only met him once."

"John Milton, Milton," I mused, "Oh yes, I remember, he was the friend of Thedore Diodati's son Charles wasn't he? He and Charles took me round St. Paul's when I was in London years ago with Dr Diodati from Geneva. How on earth do you know him?"

"He travelled to Italy last year," said Luigi, "he is beginning a literary career and wanted to see all the classical sights. Among other places he visited Venice. He was planning to go on to Greece but after getting news of the political situation in England, he decided to cut his tour short and go home via Geneva."

"Yes," I replied, "things are not good in England. I know Bishop Bedell and Dr Despotine are very concerned. Ever since the King tried to force the English Prayerbook on Scotland the situation has become very tense. The failure of the King's military expedition against the Scots means he will have to agree to all their demands— he has no choice—so he has not gained his objective. He has no love for the Presbyterians or the Puritans in the Church of England and for us in Ireland the repercussions have been awful."

"What repercussions?" asked Luigi, "I imagined that on balance things are improving, the King will be forced to call a parliament at last in England—the Scots have seen to that. Since he can raise the money they are demanding as compensation in no other way—

parliament will surely er … *advise* the King well and he will treat the Puritans and Presbyterians better."

"His treatment of them here in Ireland does not bear out your hopes," I said, "His Lord Deputy has just imposed an oath on all the Scots settlers in the North East of the country. They must swear not to sign the Scottish Covenant and swear that they will obey the King without question *whatever* he commands them to do. Of course, loyal though they are, they cannot swear to obey any command whether good or bad. The Lord Deputy is rounding them up, putting the oath (the Black Oath they call it from the evil it causes) to them, young and old, men and women alike. He imposes impossible fines on them which they cannot hope to pay when they refuse the oath and then hauls them off to prison."

Luigi shook his head, "No wonder Milton turned back then," he said, "he said he thought it would be base of him to be travelling abroad for amusement while his fellow citizens were struggling for liberty at home."

"'Struggling for liberty!' That is strong language—dangerous language in fact!" I said, "Where did you meet Milton then?"

"He stayed with the Diodatis in Geneva on his way back," replied Luigi, "but the important thing is that while he was in Venice he visited Brother Micanzio. Micanzio asked him if he would be able to take you some papers relating to you which he had found when clearing out Brother Paul's cell some years back. They include very valuable bonds apparently—to do with land—and he had been unwilling to trust them to his usual messengers. Milton said he would be glad to pass them on and would take advice from Dr Diodati in Geneva as to the best person to contact in England when he arrived home. Dr Diodati said the papers should go to England and then on to Dublin for you and I volunteered to accompany Mr Milton and act as courier if needed. I had been feeling low in spirits in Geneva and I thought I could do worse than travel for a little while."

"Brother Paul had mentioned, in a letter just before his death, that he had some odd papers of my father's that he had wished to send me," I said, "but I never received them and I assumed that they had been lost when he died. When Brother Micanzio wrote to me of Brother Paul's death he also mentioned sending on papers when they were found. Again I never received them, so my assumption that they were lost was confirmed. Fancy them turning up again after all this time!"

That the papers could have any financial value, especially after such a long time, I doubted strongly. However, Brother Micanzio was a very astute person and would not have held on to the papers waiting for a reliable courier such as Mr Milton unless he had good reason. Luigi reached into his jerkin and brought out a small paper bundle tied with tape, "Here it is," he said passing it over.

"I hope it's worth all the trouble," I said, turning it over in my hand, "If it's the documents Brother Paul mentioned to me just before he died they are just indecipherable scraps of paper of no value except as the only relic I have of my father."

Luigi shrugged, "Open it and see," he said, "I was glad to have an excuse to come and bringing it was no trouble to Mr Milton in any case."

I untied the tape carefully and spread the papers on the table, pushing aside the empty Colcannon dishes and spoons to make space. The papers were rather old and brittle and at first the outer papers did not seem to relate to me at all, being as far as I could make out, lists of amounts of money interspersed with scraps of Latin and an old map or plan. I turned to the innermost page which was written in a different hand altogether. What I saw made me gasp. Suddenly a key to my whole past life was in my hands!

Chapter 29: (1640) The Papers

"This is in Irish!" I cried, as the familiar Irish characters met my eyes.

"In Irish!" exclaimed Luigi, "What does it say?"

Teagan came up to the table and together we tried to read the paper. I translated what I could into Italian for Luigi:

"I Rory Mclure, head of the clan Mclure in all its septs and branches ... leave to my infant son, Samuele Rory Mclure, all the clan lands Mclure. All my other goods I leave as scheduled on the paper to the Servite brothers of Venice ..." I can't read what comes here: the paper is too worn where it has been folded over, "... in the true Gospel of ... and saints ... Amen."

I sat down heavily. *Both* my parents were Irish! My name was Mclure! That the lands spoken of in the document, wherever they were, had long since been sold away or taken and parcelled out to settlers I was sure (although Brother Micanzio could not have been aware of that) but that did not matter. I had a name! "Who are the Mclures?" I asked Teagan, "Have you heard of them?"

"And indeed I have," she answered at once, "as old a family as my own father's. The last of the Mclures disappeared years ago, in the time of King James I think it would be, and I'm sure their lands are all settled by now but they were a powerful family in their day."

I looked at the paper again, "No wonder Brother Paul could not understand any of this," I said, "it would have seemed like rubbish to him—or some barbarian tongue. He never knew where my father came from. Teagan, you've been married to an Irishman—with an Irish name—these past five years after all!"

"I have been married to a good man," said Teagan, "what does his name matter?"

***

It took me a long time to adjust to Luigi's strange news. The documents, which Brother Micanzio had thought were so valuable, were worthless as far as I could tell. Irish land titles such as these seemed to be could never be made to stick in a law court in these very changed times. Nevertheless, the news made me view the world differently.

"I should be able to be more help to you now," I said to Bishop Bedell, "the son of Rory Mclure must command the respect of the Irish even if he has no lands."

The bishop looked at me sadly, "Don't you remember the parable of the rich man and Lazarus," he said, "though one came back from the dead they will not believe if they do not believe the Word of God. I fear that it will not make much difference who tells them—even the son of Rory Mclure back, so to speak from the dead—if it is the message they do not like."

"Yes," I replied, quoting from Luke's Gospel, "they have Moses and the prophets, let them hear them ..." But the Irish don't have the law and the prophets! Something must be done, Bishop, to get the Old Testament in Irish published! Perhaps now is the time I should go to England and see Sir Henry Wotton. Maybe a new Parliament could advise the King that the Deputy's policy is all wrong ... the people must have the Scriptures. Sir Henry would know who to contact or your patron Sir Thomas Jermyn might help."

"Go then, Samuele," said the Bishop, "and the Lord go with you and help you."

***

As I walked home to the house I began to mull over my plans. Perhaps Teagan could come with me to England. Perhaps she would enjoy meeting her friends Mrs Despotine and the girls in person at last. Perhaps—now here was a thought—I could journey back to Geneva with Luigi! I began to formulate a plan. If the English would not print the Irish Bible perhaps Dr Diodati could have it done in Geneva. We could smuggle copies back into Ireland gradually. At first I dismissed this idea reluctantly. The Bishop would never approve such a course of action unless ... my meditation was broken off by a strange figure who approaching me in the opposite direction, hailed me in Latin,

"Is the learned Bishop at home? A poor scholar and a humble with news fair and foul ... God bless the Bishop and health to his studies ..."

I recognised the man as a travelling Romanist beggar who was entertained kindly at the Bishop's residence and at other places in the parish because, although a learned man, he was completely insane in his wits. Some said that too much learning had driven him mad, others that the loss of his wife and family from the Irish ague had left him witless.

"I think so, Sir," I replied as kindly as I could while concentrating on other matters, "but he is busy now preparing to ride round the diocese. Your best plan for entertainment is to visit Mr Smale. I am going that way. You may walk along with me if you wish."

The poor old man lifted his battered hat in acknowledgement of my suggestion and began to walk along beside me. I was very surprised to find a downcast expression on his face. He was usually insanely cheerful, chirping away in Latin like a distracted sparrow and always in quest of pieces of paper. These he squirrelled away until someone would lend him a pen whereupon he would write away industriously, covering the paper all over with complete nonsense in Latin written in a small neat hand. But I was too full of my own ideas to take much notice of the mad old scholar and I left him at Mr Smale's gate and hurried on to tell Teagan my ideas.

***

Teagan was on her knees by the beehives in the herb garden planting some wild thyme roots. She received my suggestions for travel with enthusiasm although she still plainly did not want to leave Ireland herself.

"I am not afraid, Samuele," she said, "and I will come with you, perhaps next time you go, but … there is so much to be done on the farm at this time of year I think I should stay behind and take care of it."

"Perhaps that would be best," I agreed recognising that I would feel easier in my mind about the farm if she were there to keep things going, "what would you say if I considered going on with Luigi to Geneva?" and I explained my vague plans for the Irish Old Testament to her.

"The Bishop would be hard to persuade to such a course of action," she said, shaking her head, "not because of the danger but because he would hate to be disloyal to his King. He would prefer to persuade the King to have the Irish Old Testament published legally."

"No hope of that all the while Wentworth is in control here," I said bitterly, thinking of what was going on in the pleasant farm lands of Antrim where the Black Oath was being administered.

"If you go to Geneva with such an idea you could discuss it with Dr Diodati, informally," said Teagan, "You could take your own copy of the Irish Old Testament manuscript and leave it there with him if he agreed. You could never risk writing to him on such a matter. You would put the Bishop in danger if the letter was intercepted. The Bishop need not know of your idea if you go—in fact it would be safer if he did not."

"Would you be happy for me to go so far on such an errand?" I asked.

"God has always protected you," she answered at once, "how can I object when you will be going in such a cause?" she stood up straight, my dear wife, and looking beyond me like a princess in a legend addressing her loyal troops she said, "Go! I send you! Go with my blessing and God reward and prosper you!"

***

Luigi had taken up residence in our little house and I put my proposals to him that evening.

"Milton might be able to help too," he said when I explained my ideas, "he has some influential friends and we could certainly ask Sir Thomas Jermyn for help. I talked to Milton about our old friend Sir Henry Wotton (he knows him quite well) and he tells me he is old and somewhat feeble now, I don't think he will be much help."

"What about my idea of travelling with you and taking a copy back to Geneva to Dr Diodati?"

"Yes, that's a good plan," said Luigi, "You could explain the situation to him and maybe the Diodatis could help—or the university … Does Irish require a special fount of type to be cast? It certainly looks as if it does from what I've seen of it."

And so we made our plans. Conall was to come with us as far as Dr Despotine's and then return with replies to the letters he would take with him. Luigi and I would then proceed to London. Here we would possibly visit Milton to ask for his support for the project before embarking for the continent and making our way to Geneva.

I had spent some time now trying to decipher the papers that had come from Brother Micanzio. I discovered that my father had travelled to Rome on pilgrimage taking my mother with him. I could not make out whether I had been born in Ireland before they set out or in Italy or even somewhere along the way. However, from my name, Samuele, (which was definitely Italian and not Irish) I concluded I was probably born in Italy. Bishop Bedell and I poured over the strange documents together for hours.

"Poor Mr King would be the man to decipher this Irish," I said, "he's not still in prison is he?"

"No," said Mr Bedell, "but his health has suffered so much that he relies on his daughter to look after him now and he cannot travel. Denis Sheridan could look it over for you if you had no objections."

"I'd be only too grateful," I said.

"Mr Smale tells me the mad wandering scholar is back in the area."

"Yes, I met him the other day. He was trying to pay you a visit but I told him you were off on your travels."

"No doubt he be here now that I'm back," said Mr Bedell, "poor fellow."

"He did not seem his usual cheerful self when I met him," I said, "he was quite down cast and he is usually so merry and chirps like a cricket."

"Mr Smale said the same thing," the Bishop replied, "apparently he was walking up and down in Mr Smale's house saying 'Where is King Charles now? Where is King Charles now?' and when he got hold of some paper—an out of date almanac I think someone gave him—he wrote all over it (you know how he does) 'we doubt not of France and Spain in this action.'"

"It's not like him to speak or write any sense," I said, "You are not implying there might be any meaning in it are you?"

"Well I do wonder what he may have heard in some of the popish houses he stays in, some rumour of a plot perhaps—but, as you say, it's not likely his ravings come from anywhere except his own distracted brain," said the Bishop.

I had told the bishop of my projected journey to Geneva via London—although not all of my reasons. He seemed to think it a good idea and was happy for me to go. "A good opportunity to accompany Luigi," he said, "and to visit Milton may be a good idea too. I will write to Dr Despotine and to Dr Diodati in Geneva and you can take the letters."

He took his latest letter from Dr Despotine out of his desk, "young Wadsworth has turned up again. Despotine takes a dim view of his activities."

"What activities?"

"Well apparently there is still money to be got for disclosing the whereabouts of Romanist priests and Jesuits," he explained, "although why, when they can be easily found in the Queen's own chapel, I do not know! Wadsworth comes from Spain and is the son of a prominent English Romanist so it is easy for him to worm his way into the confidence of English Romanists. Despotine tells me that he has been doing this and then, when he has got as much marketable information as he can, he runs off to the authorities and sells it."

I groaned, "That is no way to win them for Christ! I thought he looked a nasty piece of work."

"He has had a terrible life," said the bishop, "and I fear it has warped his mind. He suffered dreadfully himself at the hands of Mohammedan pirates: did you know he had been captured at sea when he was younger? He suffered slavery and torture for years until he escaped."

"Who told you all that?" I asked suspiciously, "himself? I'm not sure how much of it I'd believe from what you say!"

Conall, Luigi and I set off later in the spring. Teagan provided me with all sorts of gifts for the Despotines from her kitchen, until I was almost embarrassed by the number of little baskets and packets I had to look after.

It was not easy for me to leave Teagan. Somehow over the last few weeks, days even, she seemed to grow more beautiful than ever. Quiet, gentle strength seemed more than ever to radiate from her, almost as if she was glowing with new inner beauty.

On my last evening at home we wandered down the path to the lough side together. The wind was chilly and the surface of the water was ruffled with waves but already the sallows were green yellow with leaves against the sky and the black birch trees' twigs were edged with stubby catkins. The rich creamy song of a robin sounded from somewhere nearby among the brambles and sparrows squabbled, settling down for the night as the sun lowered herself into the water of the lough.

"Do you remember the day I first saw you just here?" I asked.

"How could I forget!" she laughed, "up to my knees in the washing. I must have looked a sight!"

But I was serious. "A sight I will never forget. In Venice I grew up where there were beautiful things—beautiful pictures, buildings, statues such as you have never seen—but there was nothing there in all that splendour which compared to the sight of you standing in the lough-water splashing drops that sparkled in the sun and singing."

"Dear Samuele," she replied, "I can never understand it! Please hurry back from Geneva!"

"One day I'll take you to see it all," I said, "Geneva, the lake, the mountains ... Venice even! How you would love the canals, the bridges and the sunlight! You have never seen sunlight like it! As much water as here but all tidied up into canals, with buildings, bridges, gondolas ..." I stopped seeing her smiling at my efforts to describe my childhood home.

"One day perhaps," she answered, "but now ..." she seemed to hesitate, "I think there is ... work for me here."

"Are you sure you are happy for me to go?" I asked, "I could still come back from Dr Despotine's just as I usually do if you wish."

"It is vital that you go," she replied seriously, "no one in England can really help us with the Irish Bible. At the very least we need advice from Dr Diodati. I will be safe and sound here. Conall will be back with his letters before very long ..." she stopped as though looking for words, "but I will be ... I will be always looking for your return."

"I will not linger a moment more than I have to," I replied, *"Trasna na dtonnta, dul siar, dul siar* ... the words will always be in my heart."

***

The fire in the comfortable parlour of Dr Despotine's house in St Edmund's Bury crackled with logs for, despite the spring's return, the evening air was still cold. Mrs Despotine and the girls had settled down to their spinning and were eager to hear as much news as we could tell of their old friend Bishop Bedell. If the Despotines were pleased to see me they were absolutely delighted to see Luigi and made such a fuss over him that he was quite embarrassed. To Mrs Despotine and the girls he was like a legend come to life but to Dr Despotine he was almost like someone come back from the dead. When they had all finished exclaiming over him they listened to all our news and were astonished beyond measure at my discovery of my parentage.

"Irish on both sides then!" cried Mrs Despotine, "One would never imagine it to look at you!"

"My dear," laughed Dr Despotine, "did you expect him to have shamrocks growing in his hair?"

"You should hear him speak the language!" said Luigi, "You would certainly know he was Irish then!"

"That's nothing to do with my parentage, I'm afraid," I said, "it is a difficult language and without Conall's patience I don't think I would have made much progress."

"Bishop Bedell has compiled a grammar though," said Dr Despotine, "in his letters to me he wrote of it."

"Yes," I replied, "that is always his method for learning new languages, and I must say it is a good one. His main objective is the translation and publishing of the Old Testament as you know and that is now completed. In fact, I have my own private copy here with me and I want to ask your advice."

I got out the carefully wrapped bundle of loose papers, untied them carefully and placed them on a small table. The ladies stopped their work and gathered around full of interest.

"And you can read this stuff?" asked Dr Despotine, almost incredulous, after looking at the manuscript for a few moments.

"Oh yes," I replied, turning over the loose sheets with care, "It is actually a most beautiful and poetic language. I wish I could give you an impression of Mr Nangle's version of the Psalms; they are truly elegant in Irish. Did the bishop tell you? He was converted from Romanism while he was actually making the translation! The only problem now is getting it published. I wondered if you might have any suggestions as to how we can proceed. Archbishop Laud and Lord Wentworth are dead set against it; in fact they have had the principal translator, Mr King, imprisoned!"

Dr Despotine was horrified, "In Venice one risked imprisonment for translating the Bible perhaps," he said, "but not here, surely not here!"

"I'm afraid so," I said, sadly, "but Teagan and I have had an idea about how the publication could be managed."

The ladies returned to their distaffs and I was requested to read a selection of their favourite verses and passages in the strange tongue as they worked.

"Here is a verse that is very precious to me," I said, "*Labhair, a Thighearna; oir do chluin do sheirbhiseach*, Speak Lord, for thy servant heareth", I'll never forget the day that Brother Paul told me to pray the same prayer as my namesake."

The warmth and the firelight, the conversation, the ladies industriously spinning, everything was so comfortable, so homely and settled. I was shocked to find therefore, when the conversation turned to affairs in England, that Dr Despotine was quite concerned that the relationship between the King and his parliament might degenerate further with consequences as grave as fierce persecution of all puritan sympathizers—if not actual civil war and fighting.

"Oh surely not! Not here in peaceful England!" I exclaimed, quite unable to imagine quiet St. Edmund's Bury as the scene of battle.

"The King has already marched against his Scottish subjects," said Dr Despotine, "and they have, in effect, forced him to yield. What would happen if a Black Oath were to be imposed here in England? Already over *six thousand people* have left their homes here in Suffolk to sail to Virginia so that they can be free of Laud's policies in the church. And as for the King, well, he has assessed the whole county for £8000 in "ship money" but only £200 of it has been paid! Sir Nathaniel Barnardiston and other puritans like him in this area say the tax is not legal and refuse to pay. The corporation of St Edmund's Bury itself has become alarmed that the King will simply seize all their assets since they are known to be sympathetic to the demands the parliament is making. They have taken steps therefore to place all the corporation's assets beyond his reach. Every day the gap seems to widen between the King and his subjects. I fear the outcome, Samuele, I fear it."

"The whole question is very difficult," I mused, "the Bible plainly teaches that kings and all in authority are placed there by God and must be obeyed. I know Bishop Bedell would rather die than behave in any way disloyally to his King. And yet ... the Bible also teaches that we must obey God rather than men."

"We have to face the fact that there can be times when the King's command must be withstood, then," said Dr Despotine very quietly almost as if he was afraid someone might be listening, "the question is: when does one reach that point?"

We were silent, thinking out the implications not just in abstract terms but—and this was chilling—with regard to what might happen, perhaps very soon. It was the very question already forced on the Scots settlers in Armagh when they were faced with the Black Oath.

"If the King's command is directly contrary to God's Word ..." I began slowly but Dr Despotine interrupted.

"The King would say that, since he is appointed by Divine Right that is a situation that cannot occur."

We were silent. The darkness was falling now and the light of the burning logs was taking over from the low sunlight that had streamed through the window. The ladies still spun as the comfortable furniture and the low table with my Irish Old Testament open on it fell into deeper shadow.

"I had thought of taking these sheets to Geneva and asking Dr Diodati's advice," I said.

"What does Bishop Bedell think of that idea?" asked Dr Despotine.

"He does not know," I replied. Even by the firelight I could see his eyebrows shoot up.

"It might prove dangerous for him to know," I said quietly, "if Dr Diodati's advice is to publish it in Geneva."

Dr Despotine sighed and was silent.

"My own people," I said, "do not have God's Word in their own language. I must do whatever I can."

***

Luigi and I travelled to London after staying with the Despotines to visit John Milton before we left England in part because Luigi was going to take letters back to Geneva for Milton.

We found him settled, after his continental wanderings, in quiet Aldersgate Street. This was a straight street of houses, headed by a grand new gateway commemorating the entry of the late James I into London when he arrived from Scotland after his succession to the throne. We paused to read the inscriptions. A bas-relief showed James in his royal robes and I translated the words from Jeremiah carved on the side to Luigi:

"Then shall enter into the gates of this city kings and princes, sitting upon the throne of David, riding in chariots and on horses, they and their princes, the men of Judah, and the inhabitants of Jerusalem; and this city shall remain for ever."

"He had a high opinion of himself, didn't he?" murmured Luigi but I put my finger to my lips and shook my head warningly.

The street itself was spacious and well laid out: quite unlike the area round St. Paul's where I had first met Milton. Each house stood in its own trim gardens and grounds and could almost have been in Noventa rather than in London. In one of these gracious houses, not far from the grand arched gateway, Milton was running a small boarding school.

"I began with just my nephews," he explained when he had welcomed us into his sunny parlour, "my sister is a widow and I was responsible for looking after the family, but I found I was soon in demand as a teacher with other parents as well."

Milton obviously had very high standards. The boys studied Latin, Greek, Hebrew, logic, arithmetic, geometry, history, French and Italian he told us and his description of their studies reminded me of my own childhood in the Servite monastery. Amazingly Milton still had time to write and plan epic poetry and he was also keeping a very close eye on the political situation. I was glad to be able to thank him in person for troubling to carry papers from Brother Micanzio for me.

"It was no trouble," he said, "I hope they were useful. Micanzio seemed to think they might be of great value."

"No value financially," I said, "but of incalculable value personally since they enabled me to discover who my father was, something I never knew before."

"And who was he?" asked Milton, "were you pleased with what you discovered?"

"Very pleased," I replied, "he was the last of the Mclures, a noble Irishman, who had been travelling in Italy on pilgrimage when he died. I had already discovered by accident that my mother was Irish. Now I know exactly who I am, I am more eager than ever to carry forward the project I have been involved in with Bishop Bedell." And I launched into an explanation of the Irish Old Testament translation. When I finished Milton was eager to see my Irish Old Testament manuscript. I fetched the packet of pages and untied them carefully, laying them out on his parlour table. He turned them over with a scholar's eye, pleased with my neat script and fascinated by the language.

"Remarkable," he kept saying as he browsed through, "remarkable!"

"The translation is of a very high quality, Sir, I can vouch for that but powerful interests are such that the principal translator, Mr King, a venerable scholar, has been imprisoned. Permission to publish has been refused because it is judged that Mr King, being Irish and therefore ignorant, cannot have made a good translation."

This made Milton very angry, "How can they know whether or not the translation is a good one?" he exploded, "from what I hear Bishop Bedell would be highly competent to judge that. I know who these 'powerful interests' that you speak of are, Samuele, and they would be motivated by considerations far other than the quality of the translation. They cannot read it and so they cannot tell its worth. They are interested only in keeping the truth from being known."

"Sir," I began, wondering if I could trust him with my plan without endangering Bishop Bedell, "I beg you to be discrete. I have taken this copy with me without specifically telling the Bishop. I must do what I can to enable my own people to read God's word. I wondered whether going to Sir Henry Wotton would help; I knew him slightly when I was still in Venice and …"

"Impossible. Did you not hear of Sir Henry's death last year? Diodati's your man," he interrupted even before I could decide whether or not to tell him what I had planned to do, "take it to him and get him to publish it in Geneva. Then it can be smuggled back into Ireland. That's what happened in England after all! Tyndale who first translated the New Testament into English back in Henry the Eighth's day would never have been allowed to publish it here. He published it abroad instead and it was smuggled in. People read it eagerly even though it was a deadly crime to have a copy. If your Bishop waits until he has permission he will wait forever. We English still use and love our Geneva Bibles: why should the Irish not have a Geneva Bible too?"

It was with Milton's words ringing in our ears that Luigi and I set off on our journey to Geneva.

***

Alas, our journey did not go smoothly. We had bargained on reaching the city sometime in the early summer but in fact it was October before we arrived. I will not weary you with the tale of our upsets, difficulties and frustrations except to say that we were immensely grateful when we crossed the border into Switzerland and made our way to the Diodatis' home. Imagine our disappointment, therefore, when we discovered that, although Dorothée (in charge of the household since her mother's death) and the rest of the family welcomed us joyfully, Dr Giovanni was away in the Netherlands on his travels and not expected home until after the winter.

All through our difficult journey I had sent letters back whenever any opportunity offered to Bishop Bedell and through him to Teagan but of course I had no way of receiving replies while on the move. Now as we settled down to wait in Geneva I could at least hope for some letters to make their way to me. I wrote, explaining that we were at last safely in Geneva but that Dr Diodati was away and we would await his return. The letters went off via the couriers used by the Signora Madeleine's brother in London directed via Dr Despotine in Bury where they could be collected by Conall on one of his regular trips.

The Diodatis' house was as full as ever with students, and the younger girls, none of them married as yet, helped their sister to run the household in a very capable way. Of the boys, only Philippe was still at home and studying at the university. But the bustling household somehow did not suit me. Hearing that Carlo's old shed-cum-cottage in the garden would be available to me if I wished to use it, it was not long before I made my excuses to Dorothée and took myself off to the peaceful garden, persuading Luigi to come with me. Although Carlo now owned gardens, orchards and plots all round the city and employed men to tend them, he had kept the original garden and it still functioned as a comfortable retreat for him as well as a playground for the younger children of his growing family.

And through it all, the terrible journey, the waiting, the waking of happy memories and the renewing of old acquaintances, I was numbly sick at heart with longing for Teagan. The weeks passed. There was no letter from her, from Bishop Bedell or Dr Despotine. Winter turned into spring and there was still no news from home. From time to time snippets of news reached us of affairs in England. The parliament that had been called had made the expected demands on the King and he dismissed it in rage after a few weeks. He had been unable to carry on without Parliament, however. Desperate for money to pay the Scots what they demanded as the price for evacuating Northumberland and Durham—counties which they were holding hostage as it were—he called another parliament. The mood of the members was such that they moved to impeach Wentworth and Laud. We judged from what we heard that they were now the two most unpopular men in the country. All this we put together from second-hand scraps of information carried by Frenchmen or Dutch merchants. Nowhere could we get any concrete news of Ireland.

"No news is good news," said Luigi cheerfully but I was full of foreboding.

Then, as April arrived and Lake Geneva began to reflect a clear blue spring sky, Dr Diodati arrived home. I was sitting in Carlo's garden house just finishing yet another batch of letters to Teagan, Dr Despotine and Bishop Bedell to go with some Dutch merchants, when Luigi appeared with the news.

"He's home at last!" he said, "but very tired after so much travelling especially so early in the year."

"I cannot disturb him yet," I said, "Dorothée and the others must have a chance to talk to him properly first."

In my mind's eye I saw Teagan as I spoke and pictured *her* greeting *me* as I made my own longed-for return to our lough-side home so far away. Try as I might the picture in my mind seemed dark and shadowy. I sighed as I thought how far apart we were and how long it would take me to reach her. But at least now Dr Diodati had returned, my own trip home seemed happily nearer.

"I'll go and pay my respects tomorrow then," I said, "and take the Old Testament manuscript with me. By then he will have rested and, if I know Dr Diodati, be ready for a good scholarly task like perusing the manuscript of a Bible in an outlandish tongue!"

***

"Samuele! This is wonderful!" exclaimed Dr Diodati as I was shown into his study next day, "Dorothée told me you were here waiting to see me. How good of you stay all this while!"

My friend definitely looked older. A life of travel and study had left its mark and his face, though keen as ever, seemed now almost haggard. But he was clearly still as energetic as he had always been and I eagerly unfolded my news.

"I am indeed very glad to see you, I replied, "and I have waited, I am afraid, partly from selfish motives. I have something here to show you," and I took out the precious manuscript sheets and laid the bundle on his study table, "this is a translation of the Old Testament," I explained, "not by me, although I have had a very small hand in its making."

Dr Diodati bent over the sheets as I untied the bundle and turned the pages, "a translation of the Old Testament?" he asked, looking puzzled, "into what language?"

"Can you not guess?" I asked.

He scrutinized the sheets for a moment and then looked up with a smile, "yes, of course I can, Samuele. You have been in Ireland—in fact Dorothée tells me you have discovered that you are Irish—it must be Irish. Don't tell me it is by our old friend Bedell!"

"No, not by him exactly," I answered, "although it is certain it would not exist without him. It is more the work of a committee he organised and of which I was part, as a scribe more or less, and a committee of which the principal translator has been in prison because of his work on this very thing."

"In prison!" exclaimed Dr Diodati in horror, "have things come to that pass in England—that is to say Ireland—now? But why has Mr Bedell sent you to me with the manuscript?"

"He has not sent me," I explained, " in fact, he does not know that I have this manuscript with me. It is my private copy that I made as I worked. The authorities in England—and hence in Ireland also—are blocking publication. The Irish, my own people, need this translation. I have come to ask for your advice."

"My advice! But I have no influence in England these days. I could not …" and his voice trailed away as he realised what I must be hinting at. After a long silence he said, "But it would have to be kept secret: that would be difficult. Would you see it through the press? It would need an Irish speaker to do that job. Whatever happens we must shield Bedell from danger. You must let me think, Samuele."

Chapter 31: (1641-2) Fever

When I left Dr Diodati I was in quite a confident mood. He obviously understood what I was implying and I was certain that if he could do anything to help he would do it. I left my precious manuscript in his study and returned to the garden where Luigi was preparing dinner in the cottage.

"How did it go?" he asked, "Will he do it?"

"He understood at once what I wanted," I replied, "but he needs time to think about the idea—about possible ways of doing it. There are practical problems and he is concerned about endangering Bishop Bedell."

Luigi nodded, "Hard to see how that can be avoided in the long term," he said, "but if anyone can do it, Dr Diodati can."

I sat down to my meal but all at once I did not feel hungry. There were too many ideas going round in my head. I thought suddenly about something that Dr Diodati had said. Who would see the book through the press if it were to be published in Geneva? I was the only person who could do so. But it could take many months! Was I prepared to stay that long? In my mind I had been planning to return as soon as I had seen Dr Diodati and to leave the manuscript with him. In fact, Luigi and I had begun to talk already of plans for a return journey. This now seemed very naïve. My food grew cold on my plate. I stared out of the window at the view of Carlo's flourishing garden—without seeing it.

"What's the matter, Samuele?" asked Luigi, "Something wrong with my cooking?"

"No, no, Luigi," I replied, shaking myself, "no ... I am just thinking about what Dr Diodati said ... and I have a bit of a headache."

***

That night my head began to ache in earnest. I tossed and turned on my bed and try as I would there seemed to be no soft place in the pillow which had become strangely lumpy, hot and damp. My mind kept filling with worries and concerns. I could hear Teagan's voice singing, *Trasna na dtonnta, dul siar, dul siar* ... How could I stay and leave her any longer? How could I go and leave the whole point of my mission unfinished? How could I go? How could I stay? How could I stay? How could I go? I tossed about, feeling hot and cold by turns. I needed air. The room was stifling. I threw off the bed clothes and stood up. My knees buckled under me and I fell in a dizzy heap on the bed. I tried to call to Luigi but my voice did not work and in any case it was Teagan that I needed; she always cared for me when I was weary or ill. Why did she not come when I called her? Time stood still. There was nothing but burning cold. A huge twisted face, long nosed yet feminine in its strangeness, loomed over me speaking to me but I could hear no sound except a strange snake-like hissing. My teeth rattled with cold and I was burning hot. "Teagan," I gasped, "put out the fire, it is burning all the pages I have written, put it out, I say!"

Voices came and went, " ... cordial, mother used to make it for fever ..." " ... I can watch him for you ..." " ... fresh air ..." "can you make him drink this? ..." " ... Elizabeth would still be alive if I had had some of this when ..." " ... no letters from his wife ..." " ... keep the windows shuttered to save his eyes ..." " ... needs more fresh air ..." " ... doctor ..." " ... just a sip at a time ..."

My brain was burning ice. Where was Teagan? I called for her again and again. The strange face came and went, issuing instructions, "..try to sleep ..." " ... drink this ..." " ... lie down ..."

***

I woke from a strange nightmare in which Teagan and Bishop Bedell had been trying to burn pages of the manuscript on the fire of the garden cottage and I was trying to find Luigi to put it out. A wave of relief swept over me as I realised that I had been dreaming. The cottage window was open and I noticed it must be late: the sun was high in the sky and the birds had stopped singing for their midday siesta. Then I noticed Luigi sitting on a nearby chair industriously mixing something up in a bowl.

"Goodness!" I exclaimed, "Luigi, it must be late! I must get up!" I tried to throw off the bedclothes and jump out of bed but my arms and legs would not properly obey the summons.

"Samuele!" he cried in delight, "Samuele! Dorothée was right! After all this time, you are getting better."

***

It took many weeks for me to recover from the effects of the fever. All the time Luigi was my capable nurse. At first I was hardly aware of what had happened to me. I lay in bed, glad to be feeling better; drinking medicine, gruel, soup, whatever the faithful Luigi offered me without asking questions. How long I had been ill, who had nursed me, what had happened to the Irish manuscript, all these were things it did not occur to me to ask. Gradually I began to leave my bed and totter to a chair each day, helped by Luigi at first, then on my own. I managed to sit outside in the warm sunshine, then take a few steps on the gravel walks of the garden but all the time my mind was strangely blank and I rested content in the present moment never contemplating the past or the future. And Luigi, loyal and patient, never probed, never tried to tell me. Instead he fed me, nursed me, cared for me, quietly waiting for the day when my mind would click back into the correct channel and I would want to know the answers to a thousand questions.

I was finishing some soup, spooning up the last tasty drops, when the garden gate clicked.

"You have a visitor I think," said Luigi rising to open the cottage door, "do you feel like company?"

It was Dorothée, with her plain, capable face and large Diodati nose, who stood there. When I saw her, it was as though the last of the fever dropped from my brain.

"Dorothée!" I exclaimed, "so it was you who I kept seeing when I was so ill!"

"Yes, Samuele," she smiled, her homely face lighting up at seeing her patient so much better, "but Luigi did all the hard work; I just supplied the medicines and cordials from my dear mother's recipes."

"I've been crazy!" I exclaimed, remembering Bishop Bedell's term for the effects of the Irish ague. Then as all the memories flooded back into my brain, "but what's the time, I mean what month is it? How long? Has there been a letter from Teagan or Bishop Bedell or Dr Despotine? What about Dr Diodati—the manuscript ..."

"Steady, steady," said Luigi, although his face was beaming with joy at my recovery, "one thing at a time!"

***

I had been ill altogether for nearly five months! The sunshine that streamed through the cottage window was already tinged with autumn chill. In all that time there had been no direct news from Ireland. Dr Diodati, very busy with his own concerns and with the Geneva Academy, had set the Irish Bible question on one side. My health made steady progress. I wrote to Teagan (thinking that even if no letters were reaching me that did not have to mean my letters were not reaching her) but I was careful to breathe no word about the Irish Old Testament. I became well enough to visit Dr Diodati and discuss our plans. He arranged for me to talk to an experienced printer but alas! before I could meet up with M. Jean de Tournes, a bout of fever returned, gripping me and prostrating me on the bed in the cottage under Luigi's vigilant care again. This time the fever was less intense and I was up and about by Christmas, although feeling very weak. Luigi kept the cottage snug, with warm fires and good hot food and in a few weeks I was able to totter around the garden on fine days, gradually building up my strength while the ever capable Dorothée brought medicines and cordials to speed my recovery.

***

"Still no news from Ireland, Luigi?" I asked one morning as I returned from a brisk lakeside walk. Luigi hesitated. Then he said, "no letters from Ireland, no. But I had a message from Dr Diodati. He has some news for you and wants to see you today."

I hurried off at once to the Diodati's residence, thinking Luigi meant news about the Irish Bible. When I arrived Dr Diodati was in and I was shown at once up to his study. He greeted me gravely and motioned me to a chair beside his desk.

"Samuele," he began, "I have at last some concrete news from England. A letter arrived from Dr Despotine today. I think you will want to go back as soon as possible. The situation in Ireland is very grave." He passed a letter over to me and as I took it a knot tightened in my stomach. The letter was dated November 30th 1641 and in Dr Despotine's flowing Italian handwriting I read:

My Dear Signor Dr Diodati,

I write with grave news from Ireland of our beloved mutual friend Bishop Bedell. It is with the greatest anxiety that I have to tell you that a fearful rebellion has broken out in Ireland and the Irish are savagely doing to death the English and Scottish, burning their homes and looting their property. At the outset they left the good Bishop alone, not wishing, even in their fierce madness to kill one who had always protected them and treated them with courtesy. He was therefore only made a prisoner by the rebels in his own home. I have had news that following this imprisonment English people, beaten and cruelly abused, fled to his house from their burnt and ransacked farms and dwellings. I am told that Bishop Bedell housed, fed and clothed them as best as he could until all his barns, outhouses and sheds were overflowing with rich and poor alike who were grateful to feed on boiled wheat and sleep in straw. This infuriated the rebels and they ordered him to throw out all those that had come to him for help. He, however, said that he could not deny his fellow creatures shelter. My latest intelligence is that for this reason, therefore, he has been removed by the rebels, together with his sons and step-son-in-law, to a prison tower standing in the water of a lake called (as far as I can fathom the Irish name) Clock Water Castle in Lock Slaughter.

Please pass on these grave tidings to Signor Samuele Paul. Tell him I can get no news of his wife or her family, my usual messenger no longer arriving; I know not whether because he has joined the rebels or because he has died at their hands. Tell him, if he is returning, to be sure to do so via my home, where he will not only be (as always) most welcome but also be able to have the best news and help, I having established a channel by which I can communicate with certain in Ireland despite the perils. Pray that the Lord will be gracious to his people in that unhappy country and that we all, looking upwards, may press towards that better, that is, that heavenly country.

Your friend in Christ and humble servant,
Jaspar Despotine
St. Edmund's Bury this 30th day of November 1641

The shock of this news made me reel. The shadow that seemed to hang over my homeland had become a solid and terrifying reality: the Armageddon of Mr Glendinning's ravings, the battle that blotted out the dying Mrs Bedell's vision of heaven and the gibberish prophecy of the mad old Irish scholar. "Dr Diodati! Oh my poor dear Bishop Bedell!" I exclaimed, "I must go back! What may have happened to Teagan?" I began to shake and the cruel fingers of fever started to take hold of me again.

***

Once more I burned with cold. Once more strange unfamiliar figures bent over me, their words unintelligible, their faces twisted. Rabbi Leo glided out of the past in his yellow turban but the Hebrew words he uttered were distorted and I could not catch them. Mr James Glendinning, the hair-raising preacher, his weird eyes glowing, was calling down Armageddon and beside him the old mad Irish scholar croaked, "Where is King Charles now? Where is King Charles now?" I cried out for Teagan and there was no answer except from a robin that twittered, *"Trasna na dtonnta, dul siar, dul siar"* from the rail of the bed.

***

But this time the bout and its aftermath lasted not months or weeks but days. In the meantime Luigi had been making plans. Even while he nursed me he made enquiries by sending out messengers to seek out couriers and get advice about how early in the year we could travel. When my fever left me and my strength returned, therefore, instead of worry and uncertainty I found a plan of action all ready for me down to the last detail and including supplies of Dorothée's medicines and cordials lest I fall ill on the way.

"Not that you will need them: you're winning the battle, Samuele," he said, "each bout of fever is shorter. But you needn't think you are going off without me, I'm coming all the way."

"I don't know how to thank you, Luigi," I replied, "what a friend you are! But you are surely not proposing to come all the way back with me again!"

"What stay here and miss the chance of visiting Dr Despotine and enjoying one of Mrs Susan's roast beef suppers!" he laughed, "beside, Samuele, who is going to look after you when you are raving about Armageddon, King Charles and Irish-speaking robins?"

The first signs of spring were beginning to return. My heath seemed restored and I had no more fever bouts. "Of course you must go back," said Dr Diodati, "and in God's good providence, when you have rejoined your wife, return here with her and finish the work. The manuscript will be safe here with me."

"Yes, please do, Samuele," added Dorothée.

"I am trusting God for her," I said simply, "but if Dr Despotine could get no news ..."

"I will pray for her every day ... for both of you," she said.

***

Despite the weather and the difficulties we made good time returning to England and I suffered only one quite short bout of fever on the way. But if the journey went smoothly, my inner life was anything but untroubled. The horror of the situation continued to break over me in waves of agony worse than anything I had suffered with my illness. Bishop Bedell in prison! Imprisoned, not by Wentworth's cronies but by the Irish he had defended and evangelised! I knew of the grim prison tower of Castle Cloughoughter which stood in the waters of Lough Oughter and even in my anxiety I smiled at Dr Despotine's rendering of this as "Clock Water Castle in Lock Slaughter." Why the rebels had put a mild and helpless old man in such a place I could not imagine. Yet if my concern for the Bishop was gripping, my fears for Teagan almost paralysed me.

"If only I knew what had happened to her," I said to Luigi a hundred times a day.

"Take heart," he always replied, "there is One who knows."

Before this time I had always prayed often and, as I thought, in earnest. Now I prayed as I had never prayed before, even perhaps on that momentous day long ago on De La Guerra Bridge in Venice, and I searched the Scriptures for every crumb of comfort, every hope I could grasp. My only prayer was that I would find Teagan alive. It was Luigi who constantly reassured me that God would not leave me without help and that he had a purpose in all that had happened.

"I can't think that your discovery that you are actually a descendant of an Irish noble family is just a coincidence," he would say, "remember what Manoah's wife said to Sampson's father when he feared they would be killed, God has a plan and purpose: take heart!"

I had no idea what we could do when we returned to Ireland and I revolved a thousand different hopeless schemes in my mind. All this was to no purpose since I had only the sketchiest idea of what was happening there.

"Samuele," encouraged Luigi, "Doesn't the Psalmist say, 'For thou hast delivered my soul from death: wilt not thou deliver my feet from falling, that I may walk before God in the light of the living'? God delivered you from the fever and I can tell you it looked very unlikely, at least to me. I am sure God has not delivered you from one peril only to allow you to sink under another."

By March we were aboard an English merchant vessel on her way to London. It was becoming clear that to obtain shipping to Ireland would be difficult and that the best we could hope for would be to reach Dublin where we would have to make our own way (who knows how perilous) to Kilmore for news of either Teagan or the imprisoned Bishop. We hoped that Dr Despotine would have some plan, some idea of what we could do.

***

I sat on deck on a coil of rope trying to read my Diodati Bible but finding it hard to concentrate. Luigi had gone off on some kitchen errand of his own, bent as he was on building up my strength with the best food he could find at all times.

"Excuse me, Sir," said a voice. I looked up to see one of the crew, a short man, brown as a nut from his life at sea, with a wrinkled face in which were set a pair of kind blue eyes, "do you speak English, Sir?"

"I do," I replied.

"That's good! I've seen you reading from that book you have there all the time and I think I can have a guess at what it is. It is a Bible in your own tongue, would that be right? I love to read that book!"

"Yes," I said, pleased to have found a fellow Christian, "it is my Bible and my great comfort!"

"Ah indeed," said the sailor, "God's Word—the best comfort we can have! It tells how we can be saved from our sins. Have you heard about that in your own land, Sir?"

***

Richard Lovelady, for that was the sailor's name, was a true friend in need. Luigi took to him immediately, although I had to act as translator because Luigi's English was still very rudimentary. Richard was able to tell us more about the situation in England although he knew little of Ireland. When I mentioned Bishop Bedell's name and that we were making, initially, for St. Edmund's Bury he became very excited.

"Your Bishop Bedell, now," he said, "he wasn't once a parson round Bury way by any chance was he?"

"Yes he was," I said, "why do you ask?"

"Because I've met him then!" was the surprising reply.

"Met him!" I exclaimed, "however did that happen?"

"In the year sixteen hundred and twenty seven," he began, "I was shipwrecked. You must know I was brought up to fishing and my father and I had a little boat. Where we lived is marsh country by where the Ribble flows into the sea. A grand place, with wide skies, broad and open with a great stretch of fresh water, the Mere, behind it full of wild fowl! My father brought me up to read God's word, poor though we were, but I would have none of it, not I! I took off fishing with a pack of wild characters from the marshes. We took our catches to sell at any port we could make. In the year I mentioned a storm drove us right down to St. Ives where we were wrecked. I don't know to this day how it happened, but although my companions were all drowned, I was picked up by a vessel all the way from Felixstowe that was trying to shelter in St. Ives Bay. When the storm ended they carried me with them back to Felixstowe and I then had to find my way home across land. There was nothing for it but to walk and beg my bread as I went. After three days of this I had reached a place called Horningsheath not far from Bury and pretty hungry I was too, folks not having been too generous ..."

"But I have met you!" I cried, "I remember you! You came to the door ... you had a pass ... you slept in the barn ..."

"You were never the young man who came with the parson to the door!" exclaimed Sailor Lovelady, "to think I've met you again and on board ship!" and he shook my hand with such vigour that I thought it would be wrung off.

"But carry on with your yarn," I urged, "what happened then?"

"I not only slept in that barn but I ate a good meal there too!" continued our friend, "and when I'd finished it *the parson himself* came and sat down in the barn to talk with me—think of that! He asked me about my soul. He told me how grateful I should be that my life had been spared and warned me that God would not spare me from the pains of hell if I did not repent. He pressed on me the very things my father had told me (and which the parson of our parish at home never mentioned) yet all kindly and like a father himself. Well, I thought on what he'd said as I trudged on homeward and I could not forget it. God had spared me this time but sooner or later the end would come. By the time I reached my father's house I had cried to God to forgive my sins for Jesus' sake and I know that he heard me."

At the end of this remarkable story Luigi (who had rejoined me carrying a bowl of soup) and I were almost in tears. I imagined Bishop Bedell going out to the barn to speak to the seafarer that night some fifteen years ago while I and the rest of the family were sleeping peacefully. How like him not to let anyone lodge under his roof without hearing the gospel! Then I thought of all the people who had been sheltering in his barns and outbuildings in Kilmore. What had become of them? It struck me that whatever had overtaken them in the end they would have heard of the love of the Saviour from the Bishop who had gone to prison rather than give up his fellow creatures to the cruel treatment of the rebels.

"Richard," I said, "Bishop Bedell is now a prisoner of the Irish rebels. Luigi and I are going to his friend in Bury, Dr Despotine for help and advice and then on to Ireland to try to help him. My wife is there also and I have no idea of what has happened to her."

"A prisoner!" exclaimed Sailor Lovelady, "how could anyone put such a man in prison. Can't I help you? How do you propose to get to Ireland? All the normal shipping is awry."

"We are going to make our way to St. Edmund's Bury first," I explained, "even though it is in the wrong direction. Bishop Bedell's old friend Dr Despotine has told us to go straight to him. Apparently he has some way of getting news from Ireland and he is insistent that we see him before we try to cross to Ireland ourselves."

"I can get you across easy enough you know," said the sailor, "my home, North Meols is the name of it, is hard by where the Ribble flows into the sea as I was telling you, opposite the Irish coast. Many's the time when I was a lad I've crossed over and back with my father. We can slip across quiet-like if that's what you need. I know plenty of little places on the Irish coast where we could set down where it's lonely."

I was deeply touched by this kindness but felt concerned. I did not want to drag this kind sailor into my dangers and problems.

"Richard, that is a most kind offer," I said, "but I do not know what dangers will be involved."

"Danger!" he exclaimed, "this is God's providence my meeting you again. I'd go through any danger to help that good man even if he is a bishop nowadays!"

***

And so it fell out that the three of us travelled to Dr Despotine's house in Bury together. Richard turned out to be a Presbyterian at heart, and greatly indignant at the King's treatment of his parliament. However, he had a rich sense of humour and could laugh at himself for setting off with us on a mad adventure to rescue—a bishop.

Chapter 32: (May-June 1642) Bury and Ireland

At the Despotines' there was a terrible shock awaiting us. We found the household in mourning. My dear friend and guide Bishop Bedell was now beyond any aid we could offer him.

***

That he had not died at the hands of the rebels or in prison in the castle was at least some comfort.

"The rebels exchanged him for some prisoners of their own," Dr Despotine explained, "and he and William, Ambrose, and Mr Clogie who had been in the castle were released."

"Was there anyone else with him in prison?" I asked, hoping at least for some clue that would lead me to Teagan, "Conall perhaps?"

"There was a carpenter, at least a man who had once been a carpenter," replied Dr Despotine, "but who had grown rich and given up his trade. The rebels knew him to be rich and imprisoned him to get his money and goods."

"That must be Mr Castledine!" I exclaimed, "was he released too?"

"No, not as far as I know," said Dr Despotine, "he was a great help to Bishop Bedell though, and the others, for he had some tools with him and managed to patch up the draughty windows and rotting floors of the castle tower and make it safer."

The mention of Mr Castledine brought a host of people flooding into my mind, Murtagh King, Mr Johnson, Conall and the rest of Teagan's family, but Dr Despotine had no news of any of them.

"The Bishop's own house had been taken over by the Popish bishop so he could not return there after his release. An Irish protestant minister, a Mr Denis Sheridan, took him in."

"I know him," I said, "he helped with the translation. He is very well connected to a powerful Irish family although he himself, being an orphan, was brought up by Protestants, the Hill family, related to Ambrose Bedell's wife, Mary."

"There were crowds of people in this Mr Sheridan's house seeking protection," Dr Despotine went on, "and so when the Irish ague broke out it spread very quickly, especially as most of the people were already weakened by their sufferings. Edward Maw caught it. Bishop Bedell nursed him devotedly, weak as he was from his sufferings in the castle tower, but he died and the Bishop then caught the ague himself."

Here Dr Despotine stopped with tears flowing down his face. I too felt overwhelmed with grief. I had not been with Brother Paul when he died and now my other "father in Christ" had gone to his reward and again I was not there.

"What do you advise me to do?" I asked, feeling helpless, "I must go and try to find Teagan and get her to safety. Are you sure she is not with Mr Sheridan?"

"I have enquired diligently," replied the old doctor sadly, "but it seems she was never there. However, my valuable source of information and news is here with me now. Susan, my dear, would you kindly send for him? He will give you up-to-date advice, Samuele, he only arrived back here yesterday."

In response to Mrs Despotine's summons a young man appeared whose face was strangely familiar. Looking at it was like looking at Conall's face or even Teagan's but distorted into something sly and not quite trustworthy. "Lorcan!" I said quietly, recognising Teagan's runaway brother, "how ever do you come to be here in England?"

The hard eyes seemed to soften a little at the sight of me, "I did not like what my people were doing, Samuele," he said in Irish, "It is one thing to get your revenge: it is another to force women and babies onto thin ice to drown at musket point or throw old men and children off bridges or burn people in their houses and fire at them when they try to run away ... so I thought it best to change sides."

"For the present!" I thought as I tried to weigh him up, but I kept my thought to myself. Luigi, I could see, did not like the look of my old acquaintance and Richard's eyebrows shot up in surprise at this new development.

"Since Conall has disappeared I have taken on his job," continued Lorcan, "and I have contacts which make me able to bring over news that is useful to others besides the doctor here."

I translated all this for the benefit of the others.

"*Voltagabbana*—doublecrosser," murmured Luigi.

"He is to be trusted," said Dr Despotine quickly in Italian, "he has seen things—horrible things—which convinced him he could not continue with them."

"What is this? Do you understand this Tower of Babel, Samuele?" asked Richard perplexed by the sudden changes of language, "and who is this character?"

"My brother-in-law," I replied, "and probably the only means I have of finding out if my wife is still living. Do you know where she is Lorcan?"

"I have no idea. My best guess is that she is with Conall somewhere if she is still alive," said Lorcan, "but this winter I have seen so much death, horrible death ..." to my amazement he stopped as though unable to keep his composure. A different, anguished face seemed to peer out from behind the hard-bitten guard. But it was only for a moment and he mastered himself and continued in a harsh tone, "she may well be dead."

"I don't intend to give up the search until I find her," I replied.

***

It was with some difficulty that I persuaded Luigi and Richard that my travelling to Ireland with Lorcan as a guide would be safe. Not that I thought it would be wise of either of them to cross over and travel about Ireland with me. Luigi could speak no Irish and little English and Richard would be in danger as an Englishman. In any case there was nothing now that Richard could do to help Bishop Bedell. But Richard was not a man to be put off.

"I've said I'll help and help I will. The good bishop (now I realize that there is such a thing!) has gone to his rest: he needs no help from me. But you need to find your wife and I think I can help you do it."

How he could get us across without endangering himself puzzled me but he seemed confident on that point.

"I've done it many a time," he affirmed, "on that coast it is wild and uninhabited for miles. I can hide away or even stand out to sea if need be. But we must have a reliable go between and I don't like the look of your brother-in-law—begging your pardon."

***

It was only later that I found out that Lorcan was not alone in changing sides in the rebellion. There were others who had been told, to start with, that they were commissioned by the King to disarm all the settlers by force. This was to be done so that he could, with the aid of the Irish who would then be in possession of the settlers' arms, "bring into subjection the puritan faction of the parliament of England." When it became obvious that (however much he might have wished to do this) the king had not in fact issued such a commission, they drew back from murdering their neighbours.

In the end the four of us Lorcan, Luigi, Richard and I set off together for North Meols but it was an uncomfortable journey linguistically and in terms of mutual trust. Luigi spoke only Italian, French and a little English. Richard spoke only English, although like all sailors he had a smattering of other words from all over the place. Lorcan spoke Irish and more English than he admitted. I therefore had to translate for all of them all the time. Luigi distrusted Lorcan but trusted my judgement. Richard plainly thought Lorcan only refrained from stabbing and robbing us there and then because we were three to his one and in any case he could sell us for a good price when he got us to Ireland. All three of us trusted God, however, and each other. Lorcan trusted no one, certainly not God, perhaps not even himself. He watched our daily prayer and Bible-reading with ill-disguised contempt.

***

North Meols was a dreary expanse of flat, sea-washed land where the fishermen's cottages cowered behind dykes and sea walls. Richard plainly loved it as a man who travels loves his home but I found the rain, cloud, wind and damp depressing. He knew every tidal ditch, every channel like the back of his hand but when I saw the little boat in which we were to cross to Ireland I wondered how on earth we could venture out in such a cockle-shell. He stowed it also with fishing tackle and gear so that I thought he was carrying the disguise (if that was what was intended) too far.

"Nay," he laughed, "no one would take you for a fisherman, Samuele! But this adventure—we don't know how long it will last now do we? How can we eat if we don't catch fish?"

If I disliked North Meols, however, Luigi, strangely, took an instant liking to the place. Despite being an Italian, brought up in the Venetian sunshine, Luigi felt at home in this watery landscape. That Richard's cottage was so tiny that, even when Lorcan insisted he would be more comfortable in the outhouse, there was barely room for us to all sit down let alone sleep did not matter to him. He and Richard's ancient father found an instant rapport despite all differences of language, background and experience. They could only converse on mundane topics with my assistance. By using their Bibles they could share deep Christian experience. Luigi used the Diodati translation, of course. Old Mr Lovelady still used the Geneva Bible despite the growing popularity of the new English translation of 1611. It was a joy to watch them seated together pouring over the books on their laps, comparing Scripture with Scripture and communicating without any language barrier in the things that really mattered.

We all had our concerns about what we should do next. I was worried about Luigi's vulnerability in Ireland and wanted him to stay in North Meols until we returned. Luigi was worried about Lorcan—or rather about leaving me with only Lorcan for protection in Ireland. "I wouldn't trust him not to just sell you for the best price he can get," he complained, "that is a man who would sell his grandmother—never mind his brother-in-law!" Richard's worry was waste of time, "We have to get under way as soon as the wind is right," he said, "things are deteriorating here in England, never mind in Ireland, and we don't want you out of the frying pan into the fire. We have to get you and Teagan and Luigi back here and then pack you off back to Geneva as soon as possible. At the moment I have contacts further down the coast who can get you onto a merchant vessel and away. Who knows how that might change if things get worse here in England?"

This was a sentiment which I shared. Things in England were becoming more and more unsettled. Civil war looked more likely as the King and his Parliament hardened their attitudes to each other. There would be no Irish Bible in Geneva unless I returned and I could think of nothing better than finding my dear Teagan and taking her there.

"I think the best plan would be for you to stay with Richard's father until we return," I ventured to Luigi, knowing that this would be an unpopular idea with him.

Richard joined in quickly, "That's by far the best plan, Luigi, and you know it," he said.

"But if you stay with the boat, that means Samuele is left at the mercy of that brigand Lorcan!" said Luigi, "I do not trust that cut-throat."

"You'll *have* to trust him," I said, "there is no other way. In any case the two of us will be able to get around more effectively on our own in the chaos over there. The more people there are involved the harder it will be to keep under cover if we have to. Besides, Luigi,

Richard would feel happier, I know, if you were looking after his father while he is away with the times so unsettled."

And with that my faithful friend had to be content.

***

And so we set off. Lorcan was dressed now in the saffron yellow léine, trews and shaggy mantle of an Irish kern. This he had carefully carried with him in England where he had discarded it for the plain dress of a servant to avoid notice. My own clothes were also of Irish make and so would not excite suspicion.

When Richard judged that we had a fair wind we set off in the little crowded cockle-shell. When he saw how we were packed in, Luigi's last doubts about staying were resolved.

"No room for me in that little saucer," he smiled, "I'm glad I trust you to know what you are doing, Richard, or I'd be worried."

Richard smiled in return, his father led us all in prayer on the damp and chilly beach and then he and Lorcan pushed the vessel into the water and we waded out and jumped in.

It was an uncomfortable and cold journey and Richard, usually chatty and cheerful, seemed strained and preoccupied as he dealt with the sail. After two days of damp, cramped and tense sailing we finally landed in a wild spot that Richard deemed safe. When we had pulled the little boat up onto the shore in the lee of sand dunes and rocks he said, "Well my friends, the Lord has blessed us! I own I was worried, being so very overloaded. The boat would have done badly in a storm or any rough weather. As it is we have sailed over a mill-pond with gentle winds all the way!"

I was somewhat unnerved by this piece of news but there was nothing I could do about it now. However, I was worried about the return trip.

"What about coming back?" I asked, "How will we manage?"

"Same as we've done this time," was the laconic answer.

***

The rough plan we had resolved upon while at the Despotines had been that Lorcan and I would set off to Mr Sheridan's house, attracting as little notice as possible, while Richard waited by the boat. After that if there was no news we were to act as we thought fit, trying to send messages back to Richard if we could. If he had to stand out to sea he would try to keep our landing place under observation and again we would have to trust to the kind Providence that had so far taken care of us after that. There was no way any of us could hazard a guess at what might happen. At least Richard was the proud owner of a perspective glass of the type I had been introduced to by Brother Paul when I was a child in Venice. With that we felt confident that he could keep the shore under his eye if he needed to move out to sea.

***

As Lorcan and I journeyed I tried to find out if he knew what had happened to various people I knew in Ireland. To my surprise I found that although he had no idea where Teagan was, his contacts were extensive and he knew about almost everyone.

"You don't know a man called Johnson, do you?" I asked, "he was a friend of Bishop Bedell's and a minister some way from Kilmore. He had a large family and ..."

"I knew him," said Lorcan interrupting, "He is dead, Samuele, and his eldest son. They were holding out on an island in a lough somewhere, he and his family. The wife and other children escaped and are on their way to Dublin."

"Dead," I said sadly, "poor, poor man. And his son too! Do you know what happened, Lorcan?"

"Not in detail," said Lorcan, "although someone told me they were very pleased to find a huge stack of copper sheets in his house. The tinkers got to work and used them all for mending pots. Copper has been in short supply."

"Copper sheets?"

"Something to do with printing," said Lorcan with careless indifference.

I remembered *Wit-Spell*, nearly finished and ready for the press when I left Ireland. All the special characters used would have had to be engraved on copper plates for the printer.

"Another one of Bishop Bedell's projects destroyed," I sighed but Lorcan did not understand.

Travelling with Lorcan through the bogs and moors of Ireland was an eerie experience. He was forever setting me on the right path, telling me to wait for him at some landmark or other, and then diving off the path on some errand of his own before rejoining me at the appointed place. After this had happened a couple of times I thought I should insist he tell me where he was off to.

"Samuele," he said, "I know you don't trust me much and I don't merit your trust I'm sure, nevertheless if you are going to find Teagan or find out what has happened to her you *have* to trust me completely. I have my sources of information. I know where there are people whom I can ask. If you know where and who they are there are circumstances in which you could willingly or unwillingly give them away. You must see that. I am not the only person who has a foot in more than one camp, and I'll give you just one example. You can take it from me I am not in touch with him or I would not mention his name to you but do you remember Phillip Mac Mulmore Reilly of Lismore?"

The Reillys or O'Reillys were such a numerous clan in the Kilmore area that it took me a moment to remember which of them was which and while I hesitated Lorcan continued, "he was with the rebels at first but as soon as he found out that they were not acting for the King he began protecting the English as much as he could." Then as I remained silent he added, "I am Teagan's brother, you know."

"Yes, you are," I replied relenting, "go and do whatever you can for her. I will not ask questions."

***

Lorcan took himself off on one of his expeditions before I presented myself at Mr Sheridan's. That good man was both shocked and delighted to see me.

"The danger! Think of the danger, Samuele!" he exclaimed, "I know you are really Irish and speak the language but the rebels are none too nice in the distinctions they make. They would kill you for the shirt on your back and ask who you were afterwards."

"How could I stay away?" I asked simply, "with Teagan unaccounted for?"

"Poor Samuele," said Mr Sheridan, "I wrote to Dr Despotine that I had not seen her and she was not with me but I suppose the message did not get to him. The fellow that took it was a rascal and I dare say never made the journey."

"I had the message," I replied, "but I am determined not to take no for an answer. But what about Mr Clogie and William and Ambrose? I thought they were with you."

"You have missed them by a few days!" said Mr Sheridan, "Let me explain how they come to be gone. Sir Frederick Hamilton had been besieged in his castle Keilach by the rebels as had Sir James Craig at his castle Tecrohen. The two castles were in touch with one another."

I remembered these two Scottish gentlemen well. Their castles were only a mile apart and very near Castle Cloughoughter where Bishop Bedell had been imprisoned.

"They did well at first,"went on Mr Sheridan, "and the rebels thought them much stronger than they were. One night they all crept out of both castles together armed with scythes fixed on long poles and made such havoc among the rebels that those that were not killed in the attack or taken prisoner ran away. It was for prisoners taken in this attack that Bishop Bedell and his sons were exchanged and allowed to come here not long before he died. Things went less well in the two castles after that, although the enemy did not realise how bad it had become. Eventually the besieged knew they would have to come to terms with the rebels."

"No doubt they ran out of food in the end," I said.

"Yes it was getting desperately low," said Mr Sheridan, "and fever was taking its toll. To their amazement they were able to negotiate, the rebels wishing to have the siege over with as it was taking up so much of their resources in this area."

"They never let them go!"

"Indeed they did! And not only did they negotiate their own safe conduct from the castles to Dublin but the Bishop's family and some others such as Mr Castledine were included in the terms of the surrender. They all left in a large party protected by Sir Francis Hamilton and his men from the castle and Sir Arthur Forbes from Keilach Castle with about 300 cavalry. Major Bailey from Belturbut was also there with the Belturbut trained band and its arms. They had escaped to the two castles by night at the beginning of the rebellion."

"When did they leave here?" I asked wondering if there was still a chance that Teagan was with them.

"On the 15th of June," he replied, "they were making for the port of Drogheda which is in safe hands. They aimed to continue to Dublin from there or (those that wished) take ship to England."

"Were there any women among them?" I persisted.

"Very many," he replied, "and children. All very hungry and ragged."

This roused my hopes. Teagan could have been in one or other of the castles during the siege and Mr Sheridan would not necessarily know about it. Lorcan would be able to track their route I was sure or we could make enquiries at Drogheda. Feeling more cheerful than I had done for some time I asked Mr Sheridan about Bishop Bedell's death. I was anxious too about his wonderful library, especially the great Hebrew Bible.

"He died as he lived, a servant of God," said Mr Sheridan, in answer to my questions, "he could not speak much towards the end but his last words to his sons were clear, 'Be of good cheer, be of good cheer; whether we live or die we are the Lord's.' As to his library, why it would break your heart, Samuele, so it would, to see how it was treated. The Popish bishop Swiney took over all his books yet the dear Bishop said he was glad his library would be in the hands of a scholar!"

"Swiney!" I exclaimed full of anxiety for the fate of the great Hebrew Bible and all the other wonderful books, "he is no scholar!" I could never imagine the greedy, drunken man Mr Clogie had once described as "Swiney by name and swiney by nature" reading Perkins on *Prayer* or any other of the Bishop's choice volumes.

"I did what I could," said Mr Sheridan, "being able to claim acquaintance with Swiney through his brother, a convert of Bishop Bedell's—you remember him don't you, Samuele? I was able to visit him in Bishop Bedell's old house and bring away some of the books Bishop Bedell particularly wanted."

"What about the Hebrew Bible?" I asked.

"The manuscript in three volumes? Yes, that is on its way with William to Cambridge as the Bishop wished. You know he left it to Emmanuel, his old college?"

"I hope it finds its way there safely," I said, "it is a great treasure to be making such a dangerous journey."

"But have your heard about the Bishop's burial?" asked Mr Sheridan, "that is the strangest part of the whole story."

"His burial? I assumed he would be buried with his wife in the churchyard on the other side of the wall to his beloved little sycamore tree," I began, and then thinking things out, "but of course, the church would be in rebel hands so that would not be possible."

"Ah, but it *was* possible," said Mr Sheridan, "Swiney would not have allowed it but Phillip Mac Mullmore O' Reilly, who opposed the rebels (though a Romanist himself) overruled him and insisted he be buried as he had wished in the corner of the churchyard beside his wife and son. Many others of the rebels wished to show their respect to one who had been so good to them, and they accompanied the funeral procession to the churchyard with drums and muskets. When they arrived at the grave they fired a volley over it as they do at the burial of their great soldiers. Then they gave a shout, "*Resquiescat in pace ultimus Anglorum,*" and left us saying that we could bury him with whatever service or form of words we chose. Mr Clogie, however, was afraid to go through the Church of Ireland burial service with so many of these armed rebels lingering about, lest it should provoke them to attack, and so the bishop was buried quickly with no service at all."

I shuddered at the meaning of that Irish shout: "rest in peace, O *last* of the English."

"There was a priest with them, Edmund Farilly, did you know him?" Mr Sheridan asked and I shook my head, "well, I heard him murmur as the bishop was buried, *'O sit anima mea cum Bedello—O that my soul were with Bedell'.*"

***

I was later able to confer with Lorcan, although he refused to come into the Sheridans' house. When I told him, with some excitement of the parties that had set off for Drogheda hoping to go from there to England or Dublin he at once scotched my enthusiasm.

"She's not with them," he said briefly, "I've known about them and where they are since not long after we landed. They have gone from here to Cavan, then Lara, then Corinary, then across country. I've had news of them at every step and she's not with them."

My hopes had been raised by talking to Mr Sheridan and in my mind's eye I had already been seeing Teagan trudging along with William, Ambrose and Mr Clogie towards Drogheda. I had imagined even in this short space of time a hundred different joyful meetings with her among this band of refugees and my heart sank at Lorcan's words. A black despair came over me.

Lorcan was watching me closely. There was a suggestion of a sneer in his voice as he said, "No doubt she is safe enough. No doubt your Protestant God will look after her."

I felt rebuked. "Yes, Lorcan," I said, "The God of all the earth will look after his children."

"My suggestion is that we go to your house and look for any clues there which might tell us which direction she took."

I shrank from this. The idea of returning to the happy home which we had shared, and of what I might find there, chilled me but I could see the sense in it. I hesitated.

"Come on, man," said Lorcan, "you must see that we can probably tell how long ago she left at the very least and maybe more."

***

I dreaded what we would find at the little house in Ballymulling. Lorcan too seemed nervous about going there. Apparently our route, though very short, lay across territory where he was less sure of his welcome and he insisted we travel by night.

Not long after setting off from Mr Sheridan's house he suddenly pulled me to the side of the track and into the trees, motioning me to be silent. I was surprised, having heard nothing except the soughing of the wind in the branches. Hardly daring to breathe I waited. Gradually the sound of horses clopping wearily and harness jangling reached my ears from the direction in which we had been travelling. The night was not dark, a full moon shone above a thin layer of cloud, giving a soft diffused light, grey and eerie, but allowing quite a good view of the path nearby. As the horses came into view I could see that the leading rider was an Irish kern, wrapped in the shaggy mantle that was their uniform. He sat silent on his animal, almost slumped in the saddle. He passed us, and behind him followed a line of fellow kerns, all silent and dog-tired looking. One or two seemed wounded with bandages on heads or arms, most rode bare-backed although some, like their leader, were seated on pack-saddles without stirrups. Some led horses behind them laden with bundles: the whole procession had an air of defeat about it. As we watched them winding past, three horses came into view in the soft pool of moonlight on the path. The first was ridden by a dejected-looking kern and the other two were roped behind him as pack animals. The kern passed us and as he did so the first of the pack animals stopped dead, let out a loud whinny and began to pull on the rope as if to break away towards us.

The kern came to life and began tugging and cursing loudly but he was not able to move the stubborn animal and soon the whole column was halted, those behind unable to carry on, those in front concerned about the disturbance. Lorcan and I were scarcely concealed among the trees and I was terrified. It was clear to me that the horse knew of our presence and, if allowed to escape from the pack line, would undoubtedly give us away. Commotion spread among the animals as the kerns tried to control the struggling horse and reform their line of travel along the path. Lorcan seized the opportunity and pulled me back further into the trees under cover of the noise and disturbance. Once in the trees the soft moonlight vanished leaving a thick tangle of darkness. My heart was in my mouth and I hung onto Lorcan as I tried to keep up with him. He seemed to be able to glide through the wood silently and easily even without the benefit of the moonlight. I began to think we must be far enough into the trees not to be spotted and I let go of Lorcan. The kerns were still struggling with the pack horses and I began to breathe more freely. I took a few paces towards where I thought Lorcan must be, tripped up on a root and came down with a crash that could be heard a mile away.

"You're on your own," whispered Lorcan as the shouting kerns began to investigate, "I'm off. Keep your mouth shut when they find you but make a noise now to cover me and I'll get you out of it later," and with that he made off through the trees. The only noise I could think of making was to shout and the only thing I could think of shouting was "help!"

**

By dawn the kerns had reached their camp. They had been involved in a disastrous attempt to raid a nearby castle and were now short of food and ammunition. One of them recognised me as soon as they had unroped me from the horse where they had bundled me after my capture.

"This is the old Protestant bishop's Italian spy!" he sneered, "Speaks Irish and reports back to the English. Well, now we've got you, Mr Paul, no more snooping round and asking questions for you! We can ask *you* a few questions before we finish you off," he drew his finger across his throat, "and if you're wise you'll tell us the answers or we'll find a more interesting way of bringing you to your end."

I staggered to my feet. "I'm as Irish as you," I began, "my name is …"

"Yes, yes, we've heard all about that. Anyone can produce a bit of paper and say he's the son of the Mclure—when the Mclure is dead and gone and not here to prove it false."

"I'm under the protection of Mr Sheridan," I said desperately, hoping that this name would have some influence.

"Not here, you're not," came the answer and I was pushed roughly into an area near the fire where some kerns were gathered, one of whom was obviously some sort of leader. Dressed in a jerkin and trews with his mantle thrown over the top he was engaged in eating a lump of meat which he held in one hand.

My captor described who I was. He gleefully finished up with a reiteration of the gruesome information he had previously outlined to me which amounted to a promise to exchange information for a less violent and protracted death. To my surprise the leader shook his head.

"No, no, Reilly," he said, "we must look after this one! If what you say is true he will be worth a good ransom. There are some notable prisoners we might exchange for this young man. But what I want to know, Samuele Paul or Mclure of Mclure or whatever you call yourself these days, is: what are you doing wandering round County Cavan on your own—if you are on your own?"

"I can tell you the answer to that," I replied, "I'm trying to find my wife Teagan Mclure. Do you have any information of her whereabouts?"

"Well, well, Teagan Mclure," he sneered, rolling the name slowly round his mouth as if savouring it in a way that made me shudder, "and how much would information about her be worth then?"

**

That night I lay bound hand and foot near the edge of the bawn or walled enclosure belonging to the ruined house the rebels had commandeered for their camp. I turned over desperately in my mind whether I had been wise in mentioning Teagan or foolish. Suppose I had put her in more danger by telling the rebels I was looking for her? If they knew where she was would they capture her and hold her to ransom? How on earth Lorcan would get me out of captivity also exercised my mind and I confess I was doubtful if he would even try.

Beyond the house the horses were tethered, scraggy old things for the most part, uncared for and under fed. I tried to see the one that had caused the trouble and I reflected on the misfortune of being given away by, of all things, a horse. One old mare, a little less unkempt and skinny than the others, seemed restless and instead of trying to get as much of the grass as could be reached, kept lifting her head and snuffing at the wind in my direction. "It must have been that one," I thought, "Why on earth would she ..." and then I looked again. I knew that horse! "Sneachta!" I exclaimed softly and the mare at once snickered joyfully and pulled at the picket line. The kern that was guarding me looked up at the sky. "No chance of snow at this time of year," he snarled, "and it will take more than a change in the weather for you to escape." He grasped his improvised pike more firmly. I sighed. Lorcan and I had been betrayed by the love and long memory of a horse.

***

As darkness descended again a small band of Kerns rode into the camp. They had been more successful than their associates and carried what appeared to be provisions, mostly of strong drink, no doubt raided from somewhere or other. Even had he wished the rebel leader could not have restrained his men under these circumstances and a grand drinking and gambling party began. The kern detailed to guard me was anxious to join in. He sneaked off to the fireside and came back with a bottle which kept him quiet for some time. "If only Lorcan would come," I thought, "We'd have a chance now!" On my own, even if I could somehow get away, I would have little idea of where to go.

The sun sank lower and the rebels grew more drunken. My guard seemed to have disappeared altogether now. I became aware of just how hungry and thirsty I was. I rolled nearer the bawn wall with some idea of trying to get away I suppose, and was startled to see a a wallet or saddlebag drop gently over the wall and into a bed of nettles a few yards from where I was.

Chapter 33: (June-July 1642) Ballymulling, Slieve na Calliagh

I froze, hardly daring to hope, and prayed that the wallet would be followed by Lorcan. The next moment, so quickly that you would doubt you had seen it happen, a shadowy figure slipped over the wall into the nettle bed and lay there immobile and silent quite unnoticed by the revelling rebels. I waited. The figure uncurled, keeping low despite the nettles. It crept towards me. In the gathering darkness I distinguished Lorcan's weasel face. He whipped out a knife and cut the ropes that bound me and at once fell to massaging the life back into my limbs. He began to give me whispered directions, "Pick up that bag. It's got oatcakes in it and a bottle. Go to Slieve na Calliagh, I'll meet you there. I have word that Conall was hiding there some time back. Start from Ballymulling … you could do with a horse: I'll try and steal one for you …"

"There is one here that will follow me anywhere," I whispered, "all you have to do is cut the picket rope."

Lorcan hoisted me over the wall. Unlike him I was not impervious to nettle stings and I repressed gasps of pain as I landed in more nettles on the other side.

"Stay here," he whispered, "I'll try for the horse, was it the one that gave us away?"

"Yes," I whispered, "she's called Sneachta."

"Excellent! Are you sure she'll make for you if I cut the line?"

"She's been trying to reach me all day."

"Good, I'll just let her go and disappear."

He gave further directions about where I was to wait near Slieve na Calliagh and then left me. I kept low under the wall listening anxiously to the sounds of drunken revelry. The rebels were singing now but I felt so elated by news of Conall (where Conall was surely Teagan would be!) that I did not even feel afraid. Their song rose and fell in tuneless drunken phrases. I remembered a line from the Psalms, "For by thee I have run through a troop; and by my God have I leaped over a wall." Although there had definitely been no leaping on my part I was over the wall and I raised a prayer of gratitude.

A few minutes later Sneachta's soft joyful whinny of greeting alerted me to Lorcan's success. "Steady girl," I whispered. Even in the dark I could tell that the mare was in poor condition, scarcely resembling the high spirited young animal I had ridden all those years before when I first met Teagan. Even so she was by far the best of the rebels' stolen horses perhaps because she had not been long in their hands.

I struggled onto Sneachta's back and we headed towards the path. As we set off towards Ballymulling I became aware that the rebels' song was breaking up in confusion. Had they discovered the loss of their horse? Their prisoner? With beating heart I urged Sneachta forward towards Ballymulling.

***

The sun was coming up again before I reached Ballymulling. Sneachta was tired and I was exhausted but at least I was sure now that no one from the rebel band followed us. As I rode down the path to the lough, a thousand memories bitter-sweet crowded into my mind. From a distance the little house looked strangely unfamiliar and with a sickening wrench I realised that it no longer had a roof. I felt like the swallow who having flown home after a journey of hundreds of miles finds the comfortable nest, of which he has been dreaming all through the long flight, broken from the eaves and smashed on the ground. The dykes that we had toiled to make had been deliberately and senselessly breached leaving the new fields flooded and useless. When I reached the farmyard the house looked so miserable, its door hanging off, its beautiful glass window broken and the timbers scorched, that I could not bring myself to go inside. Instead I made for the shed some distance from the house and was surprised to find, as I stumbled wearily through the low doorway that it was untouched. The rebels had concentrated on the house and left it alone.

I worked my way round to the end of the building and I found the little store by the end wall where Teagan and I kept sacks of oats and store potatoes behind the hay and straw. It was all unmolested! "Sneachta, old girl, you're in luck," I said, very pleased with such a find.

I found a curry comb and other gear that we used for our own horses, and despite being weary to the bone, I set to work to look after the animal that had betrayed me and to give her a good feed of oats. I bagged up some more oats, thinking to carry them with us so that she could have more good food on our journey to Slieve na Calliagh. I thought I would try to sleep for a few hours and rest Sneachta before setting off. I tied her to the rail where we had once stabled our own horses and made myself a hay bed near her. I could not bring myself to consider sleeping in the ruins of what had once been my happy home. However, I knew I must force myself to go and look while it was daylight. I dare not overlook any clue to Teagan's whereabouts. Feeling alone and helpless I knelt down to pray in the straw.

"Oh help me now, dear Father, help me to find Teagan, keep us both safe in Thy care. Keep my mind on things above as I go into the ruins of our poor house and help me to remember that I have no abiding home on earth—only in Thy heavenly mansions."

Sneachta nuzzled me softly as if to remind me that even here in the ruins of my farm I was not entirely without an earthly friend.

***

A scene of desolation met my eyes as I walked through what had once been our front door. Our little bits of furniture were overturned and broken and piles of rubbish lay about the place. It seemed as if a band of rebels such as the one that had captured me—perhaps the same one—had been using it as a headquarters or shelter. Not only were our own belongings lying about in broken heaps but the rebels seemed to have brought their own rubbish with them and left it behind them. Broken bottles littered the place and in one corner was a battered cradle—looted I supposed from some nearby family that had been driven from their home. It was a sturdy piece of work with some pretty carving on the sides in a style I recognised at once as Castledine's: loops of flowers and little leaves. The rebels had stored kindling in it, having camped in our roofless kitchen and made use of our fireplace. But somehow it was the sight of Teagan's linen-press, once full of linen layered with woodruff and now smashed and empty that saddened me most of all. Its wanton destruction seemed so pointless.

If I had hoped to find a message from Teagan or any clue as to her whereabouts or state I was disappointed and, as it turned out, the one clue that would have told me at least something about her I had completely misinterpreted. Depressed and disappointed I returned to the stable and tumbled onto the hay bed. I slept instantly a deep sleep of exhaustion and misery.

***

It was growing dark when I woke. I wondered whether to risk lighting a fire and making myself some sort of meal. In the end I decided I would have to, since neither oats or potatoes are very edible raw. The ruined house walls would shelter the fire from view and the growing darkness would make the smoke less visible. I set to, stumbling about in the growing gloom of the the roofless kitchen. Cooking always takes longer than you think but I eventually roasted some potatoes, skins and all, enough to eat now and to carry with me.

By the time I was ready to set out it was nearly midnight but there was a bright full moon and the sky had cleared so that conditions for travelling were good.

"May as well make a start," I told Sneachta, "you are not in good fettle; those scoundrels did not look after you. Even with some good feeds of oats you are not going to get to Slieve na Calliagh in one night. We will have to take it gently."

***

Compared to my recent adventures my journey was uneventful. I keenly missed Lorcan. I had become confident in his ability and had trusted him to look after me. Alone I was not cut out for travelling about a country ravaged by rebellion and strife. I was unarmed and in any case had no skill in weaponry of any kind. I had no skill as a woodsman or in tracking either and my sole contribution to our travels so far had been to get myself captured. Without Lorcan I would still have been in rebel hands now and I was afraid that I would soon make some further blunder from which he would be unable to rescue me. There was nothing for it, however, except to carry on following his directions although I constantly heard—or rather imagined I heard—the sound of rebel horsemen following me. At every moment I expected kerns in their shaggy mantles to jump out on me from behind the trees.

As the sun began to come up I arrived at a little house in a clearing in sight of Slieve na Calliagh. It was the kind of house that the Irish are proud of being able to build in one day, of leaves, branches and reeds all supported on a tent-like structure of poles. This humble dwelling was surrounded by a well cultivated patch of land, peat stacked ready for use, a potato patch, and two cows tethered nearby. Lorcan had told me that this house belonged to some squatters who, having no land of their own had taken advantage of the confused conditions created by the rebellion to settle on a plot of land. He had recommended that I stop there and was sure I would get a meal and somewhere to rest when I explained my errand. "They are on the spot too," he had added, "they may have news of Teagan."

Inside the little house I found a substantial family was already stirring ready for the day's work. Mother, father and six little ones slept inside the tiny shelter lying on rushes and wrapped in their mantles. They made me very kindly welcome to an outdoor breakfast as soon as I mentioned Lorcan's name, spreading out the best of their store for me: cold potatoes, buttermilk and eggs.

"No one else was using this land," explained the father, whose name was Brady, "and so we will use it until someone drives us off— and who knows when that will be, if ever. Meanwhile we can live, which is more than we could do before."

I looked round at the hens, the cows, the potatoes and a little patch of oats, "You certainly seem to have worked hard," I commented, "everything seems to be thriving."

Oh, yes," replied Brady, "everything here prospers because of the witch on the hill," his voice sank to a reverent whisper, "her curse was on all the land hereabouts and nothing would grow; mildew, rain, storms, cold wind, but we give her an offering of food everyday. We leave it on her great stone chair on the side of her hill—just a little but the best of everything and she keeps the weather smiling and the grass growing."

Before I had time to register my surprise at such superstitious behaviour or offer any advice regarding the true source of all prosperity there was a shout from the woodland path and Lorcan appeared on horseback.

"Hello, Samuele," he called as he dismounted, "glad I've found you. Brady, I'm famished! What's for breakfast?"

The hospitable Bradys scurried round finding food for Lorcan and he sat down on a log beside me by the cabin door.

"News, Samuele, news," he said, "Conall is in Dublin or on his way there. That's definite. My earlier information was off track: he's never been at Slieve na Calliagh, I'm afraid. He joined the party from Drogheda who were making their way there a few days ago. Mr Clogie sailed for England from Drogheda, young Mr William Bedell and Mr Ambrose Bedell are going to Dublin. Teagan was not with Conall. I am more and more confident from what I hear that, if she is still alive, she must be in this area; there is nowhere else left to look."

This was encouraging in some ways, although I still longed for something definite, "What did you do after I made off on Sneatcha?" I asked, knowing that something had happened to stop the rebels following me.

"I didn't just let *her* loose," he explained, "I let them *all* loose. There was chaos for a while with horses milling about everywhere and the men too drunk to know what to do. I slipped off quite unnoticed with this horse here although they were so drunk I think I could have marched out playing a pipe and drum and they'd not have stopped me."

Brady appeared now with more cold potatoes and a bowl of butter milk, "I was just telling the gentleman about the witch," he said conversationally, "You've heard about her have you not, Mr Lorcan?"

"What witch would that be?" asked Lorcan.

"The one on the hill yonder who looks after the farm here," he waved his hand towards his borrowed property, "I was just explaining how we leave her food offerings. The gentleman looked very shocked but you must understand that there are many witches in Ireland and it doesn't do to get on the wrong side of them now does it?"

I was about to try to explain the evil of worshipping witches and the like but Lorcan held up his hand.

"Samuele, Samuele wait before you speak, things are not always what they seem. She lives on the hill does she Brady?"

"Indeed, Sir."

"And have you seen her?"

"Seen her. O indeed, no, Sir, but I've heard tell of those who have seen her."

"And what does she look like?"

"Well, some say one thing and some another, Sir. There's some that say she has two heads, Sir, one black curls and one fair but I'd say that's less than likely. Most say she's an old, old hag, Sir, old as the hill itself."

"And you leave the food on the great chair?"

"Oh yes, Sir, and she always eats it."

"Or perhaps there are greedy rats in those holes in the hill!" said Lorcan with a laugh.

"Strange rats they'd be, Sir, that would take the dishes and wash them and leave the upside down."

"Sounds strange behaviour for a witch too! Samuele, if I were you I'd go and see this witch or hag and ask her advice."

I was about to roundly renounce such a superstitious course of action when Brady broke in in a voice full of anxiety, "Oh no, Sir, no! Don't do such a terrible thing, Sir. It's said she hates to be disturbed by daylight. Sure she'd turn you into a bat or an owl. Never go there, Sir. Oh, it is an evil, evil place."

"I need no advice from such an evil creature," I said.

"Well, Samuele," said Lorcan, "you must do as you think fit. I shall be making for Dublin myself. I think it would be best if I can rejoin Conall."

"You're not leaving me?" I asked, aghast at this suggestion.

"Not exactly," said Lorcan, "I will know where you are, never fear and I'm going to double back and see Richard first—tell him you are on your way and make sure he's got a supply of oatcakes and maybe some cheese if I can find some, and a skin bottle of good fresh water. He was very lucky with the voyage across you know and it could be totally different going back. If it takes days and days you will find yourselves living on raw fish if I don't get him well provisioned! But I say this strongly, Samuele: investigate this witch. Overcome your prejudice and go. If she can tell you nothing, I think you must assume the worst. Either way you must make for Richard and his little boat very soon now with or without Teagan and I can give you exact directions from here. You cannot expect Richard to wait much longer than two weeks and by the time you reach him it could be all of that since we left him camped there and living on fish!"

Again that cold feeling in my heart. How could I go back without Teagan?

"I'll go back," I said, "it is not fair to make Richard wait any longer for me. But I will tell him to go home to North Meols on his own if Teagan is not with me. I must find her or make my own grave here in Ireland also. My dearest friend is buried here and if my wife is buried here also I have no desire to be anywhere else. As for consulting a witch ..."

"I've told you: things are not always what they seem, friend," said Lorcan, "What is a witch? Only an old woman after all. In any case is not your Protestant God stronger than a witch?" Then after a pause he said with quiet emphasis, "I used to have an old auntie that lived hereabouts."

"I remember her well," I replied, "I once stayed at her house. Surely you are not suggesting that she is a witch? A simple soul perhaps but a witch! No!"

"What is a witch?" reiterated Lorcan, "just an old woman. An old woman who has found a good way of making a living in troubled times perhaps—who knows? But enough! We need to make serious arrangements before we part. I confess I wish you were handy with a weapon or knew a little woodcraft, Samuele. Letting a helpless scholar like you roam about the countryside in the present conditions is like letting a baby into a bullring."

"I'm very grateful, Lorcan, for your care of me," I replied, "as for using weapons and the like I only wish I could but I'm afraid I was never brought up to such things. One does not learn much about muskets or woodcraft in a monastery. I must trust God to take care of me by whatever means he sees fit."

"Talking of monasteries," said Lorcan, a wry smile on his face, "I came across one of the brothers from the monastery that used to be near Kilmore the other day. In fact, it was he that had news of Conall."

I steeled myself for the worst. These were the friars that had been converted to the Protestant faith when Bishop Bedell engaged in a written debate with them. Some he had even appointed as ministers in the Kilmore diocese. I waited for Lorcan to tell me with exultation that they had gone back to their old ways now that the rebellion was in full swing and they had nothing to gain from Protestantism any more. Lorcan was watching my face, "One of them has joined the rebel band that captured you."

"Only one?" I asked in a sad tone, "what happened to all the others?"

"Only one," he replied, "the others have stuck with their new faith. Some of them have died for it."

***

I was grateful for my good memory, so well trained by Brother Paul in my childhood, when Lorcan had finished giving me detailed directions to the little beach where we had left Richard. A turning here, a tall tree there, watch out for trouble here, don't go on this path in daylight—the instructions seemed to go on and on. When he had finished and I had gone over what he said to make doubly sure, he set off on his travels again with a cheerful wave of the hand and a final admonition to be sure to visit the witch.

"But don't go today, Samuele," he said, "Get a full night's sleep and rest the horse. Then set out very early tomorrow. Whatever you find or find out you will need food, rest and sleep before you set off to find Richard and this is your last chance of getting it."

So I was on my own again and, as far as I could tell, no nearer my goal. As I watched Lorcan disappear around a bend in the track it seemed cold comfort that Teagan could not be found anywhere else in Ireland.

Chapter 34: (July 1642) The Witch

At the first glimmer of dawn I set off on a well-rested Sneachta. The Bradys kindly gave me a supply of cold potatoes but were obviously worried and not just on my account. They were convinced that any upset to the witch might result in a dramatic reversal of their fortunes and nothing I could say would persuade them otherwise. As I rode off I felt that I had requited their kind hospitality with an injury —at least in their eyes. There was no other course open to me, however, and I gritted my teeth and went on with my journey.

I patted Sneachta's mane as we began to ascend the path to the hill, "You are looking fitter every day, Sneachta," I told her, "You did the right thing after all when you fastened on your old friend!"

The day was already warm as we began to climb the hill itself but a gentle breeze began to make itself felt as we climbed. What would we find? Just a splendid view from the top? A two headed monster? A gibbering old hag? Lorcan's auntie?

***

Not far from the foot of the hill was a wizened hawthorn tree which offered some shade from the sun. Here I tethered Sneachta, arranged some oats for her to eat and continued up the hill on foot. The huge pile of stones on the top, glittered cold as diamonds in the bright sunshine and to my anxious eyes it was somehow a sinister sparkle. I toiled upwards occasionally stopping and shading my eyes from the sun to look up at the hilltop but the dazzling white of the stones befuddled my eyes and prevented a clear view. The Bradys had spoken of a "great chair" where they left food at the end of each day before sunset. My own inclination would have been to go with them and then linger to accost the witch, or whoever she was, when she came to collect the food. Lorcan had counselled against this plan strongly advising an early start and so here I was. I could remember the chair-like stone now from my visit to the hill with Conall when I first came to Ireland and as I climbed I began to distinguish it from the white stones in the great pile. Massive, like a backless throne in shape, with great arms on either side of a huge, flat seat, it dominated the area where it stood. I remembered that its front surface had been scratched with strange marks and designs; spots, circles and zig-zag lightening flashes; hard to see because the weather had worn them faint and indistinct yet still clear enough to the eye to be puzzling and sinister as the whole glittering hill itself. As I continued up the hill I could see something moving by this chair, something small and dark —an animal perhaps. As I got nearer I realized to my surprise that it was a tiny child playing in the grass by the chair. Puzzled, I quickened my steps: this was not on my list of possible candidates for the role of hungry witch!

The child noticed me as I got near enough to see that he (or was it she? I had not had much to do with infants since the far-off days when I had played with the young Diodatis in Carlo's garden) had a head of tight black curls and had been busily engaged in picking long grasses. A tattered looking bunch of wilted stems was clutched tightly in his fat fist. He looked up at me without fear as I approached, "Get flowers Mamaí," he explained cheerfully, "Mamaí like flowers."

Before I could reply to my new friend a voice called from somewhere out of sight behind the hill beyond the chair, "Paul, Paul, where are you? Come here at once!"

A slightly guilty look crossed the child's face, "get flowers Mamaí," he reiterated by way of answer to the summons.

"You must go," I told him seriously, for somehow the rebellion, the lawlessness, the cruelty and suffering all around in Ireland seemed to make it all the more important that the first principles of normal life should still be observed when it was possible, "when Mamaí calls you must always go at once."

He turned obediently and, toddling towards the voice as fast as he could on the narrow path, he rounded the side of the hill and disappeared from my view. I leaned against the chair for a moment to ponder this unexpected new development. But the chair with its ancient riddling symbols provided no answer to my questions. Voices reached my ears. Footsteps were approaching round the side of the great pile of stones.

"Naughty Paul! Where have you been?"

"Get flowers Mamaí, talk gentleman."

"What gentleman? Where? You are a naughty boy to run off while my back was turned."

" Get flowers Mamaí. Mamaí give piggy back, Paul tired now."

There was a pause and then the figure rounded the corner, a woman with the child on her back, his black curly head peeping over her shoulder. The woman stopped when she saw me but only for a second. Then she gave a great cry and ran towards me. A whirl of amazement, joy, relief, flooded over me as all the little things fitted into place: the vanishing food, the two headed monster, the cradle …

"Paul, Paul," she sobbed as I folded her—both of them—my family—in my arms, "Daidí, Athair, he's come home just as I said he would! He's come! He's come!"

***

I lifted her tenderly onto Sneatcha's back, handed my little Paul up to her and we started away to Richard, *Trasna na dtonnta* to Luigi, to Geneva, to a new life, to safety and to freedom.

Chapter 35: (1685) Postscript by Paul Mclure

And so ends the story: the story which I, Paul Mclure, have known in higgledy-piggledy patchwork fashion since I was a child. It only remains for me to tell the sequel: the other actors in the drama have all gone to their reward. Dr Diodati, died in 1649, a venerable old man, worn out with travels and travails in his Master's service. He had been unable to publish the Irish Bible in Geneva. Dr Despotine, died in the following year, by which time, having gone through the upheavals of civil war in England, he was a respected elder of the Presbyterian church in St. Edmund's Bury. Old Brother Micanzio died in Venice a few years later after finishing his biography of Brother Paul. Kind "Uncle" Luigi has been gone many years as has gentle "Auntie" Dorothée. "Uncle" Carlo too has left us, although his beautiful garden, the childhood playground I shared with my younger brothers and sisters, still remains. My beloved mother went to glory the year before I set out to England with my precious paper burden. Alas! She never held a printed Irish Bible in her hands. My father saw it before he too departed to join her in that better country. The Honourable Robert Boyle, that great Christian man of philosophy and science, had it printed in London at his expense and he was helped by Provost Narcissus Marsh of Trinity College, Dublin who had received one of the original manuscripts from Mr Sheridan. My late father was one of the first to receive a copy. Bishop Bedell's great Hebrew Bible I have now seen for myself, safe and sound after all its travels and adventures, in the library of Emmanuel College in Cambridge.

And now I am about to leave England to make my journey at last to my native land, for I made a promise to myself that I would not go to Ireland without the printed Irish Bible in my hand. I am going at last to visit the ruins of Ballymulling where I was born and the witching hill of Slieve na Calliagh where I was hidden away by my resourceful mother after our flight during my babyhood. Perhaps too I may find the lonely beach where my parents and I waited for "Uncle" Richard to spot us with his perspective glass from his little boat far out to sea and come to fetch us away from Ireland. Now at last the waves will bear me home:

Trasna na dtonnta, dul siar, dul siar,
Slán leis an uaigneas 'is slán leis an gcian;
Geal é mo chroí, agus geal í an ghrian,
Geal a bheith ag filleadh go hÉirinn!

Bibliography

Bullen, Frank, T., *With Christ at Sea* (London,1902) I am indebted to this fascinating book for my description of a calm sea at night in chapter 20.

Burnet, Gilbert, *The Life of William Bedell* (Dublin, 1758)

Curzon, Gerald, *Wotton And His Worlds: Spying, Science and Venetian Intrigues* (Indiana, 2004)
Dorian, Donald Clayton, *The English Diodatis* (New Brunswick, 1950)
Dunlevy, Mairead, *Dress in Ireland: A History* (Cork, 1999)
Grell, Ole Peter, *Brethren in Christ* (Cambridge, 2011)
Judges, A. V., "Philip Burlamachi: a Financier of the Thirty Years' War" *Economica* 1926 Part 18 pp.285-300.

Kainulainen, Jaska, *Paolo Sarpi: A Servant of God and State* (Leiden, 2014)

McCafferty, John, "Irish bishops, their biographers and the experience of revolution 1656-1686" in Braddick, Michael J. and Smith, David L. (eds.), *The Experience of Revolution in Stuart Britain and Ireland :Essay for John Morril* (Cambridge, 2011)
MacLysaght, Edward, *Irish Life in the Seventeenth Century: After Cromwell* (London, 1939)
O'Toole, Fintan, *A Traitor's kiss,* (London,1998)

Parkes, Joan, *Travel in England in the Seventeenth Century* (Oxford, 1925)
Salmon, Vivian, *Language and Society in Early Modern England* (Amsterdam, 1996)
Shuckburgh, Evelyn, *Two Biographies of William Bedell, Bishop of Kilmore: with a selection of his letters and an unpublished treatise* (Cambridge, 1902)
Vreugdenhil, John, *God's Care and Continuance of His Church*

(Iowa,1991)

Wootton, David, *Paulo Sarpi: Between Renaissance and Enlightenment* (Cambridge, 1983)

Yates, Frances A., "Paolo Sarpi's 'History of the Council of Trent'" Journal of the Warburg and Courtauld Institutes Vol. 7, (1944), pp. 123-143

The *Mothers' Companion*
Home Education Flashdrive
motherscompanion.net

This book is part of the *Mothers' Companion* resources for Christian Home education.

Visit the website: motherscompanion.net for details of a huge compendium of home education resources presented on a flashdrive for you to print out yourself. The resources form almost a complete curriculum up to at least age 12 and cover Bible topics, reading, writing, maths, English, history, geography music, Latin, art and craft and much more. There are hundreds of pages of books, worksheets and exercises to keep you going day after day at your own pace. All the resources are tried and tested and the package has a strong Christian World-view at its heart that informs the whole character of the curriculum and its objectives. The low cost and the print your own system make this an inexpensive option. Visit the website for full details and sample pages.